To Pat + Don

I hope you
enjoy this half as
much as I am yours

Norma Hoem

ROPING THE WIND

A WESTERN ROMANCE

NORMA HOEM

KITSAP PUBLISHING

KITSAP PUBLISHING

Roping the Wind
First edition, published 2015

By Norma Hoem
Cover design by Autumn Kegley

ISBN-13: 978-1-942661-15-3

Published by Kitsap Publishing
19124 Jensen Way NE
P.O. Box 1269
Poulsbo, WA 98370
www.KitsapPublishing.com

Printed in the United States of America

TD 20150810

50-10 9 8 7 6 5 4 3 2 1

DEDICATION

Dedicated to the love of my life, Clifford A. Hoem

ACKNOWLEDGMENTS

Without the help of these wonderful people, this book would have never been finished.

Many thanks to:

My family, who always encouraged me.

My nieces, Nancy and Barbara, who patiently helped me navigate that contrary contraption, the computer.

My granddaughter, Autumn Kegley, who designed the book cover.

The Silverdale Writers Roundtable Group. They tried to teach me the "craft", especially Bob, Laura, David, Mary, Kerry, Matt, and many more.

To Connie, of the Alder Trail Animal Hospital. She gave the book its title.

CHAPTER ONE

Anna stirred under the heavy quilts in which she had cocooned herself. Something had awakened her, a noise. She raised her head up and listened. The air was so cold, she could see her breath in the dim morning light. The fire in the small wood stove had gone out during the night and the cabin was freezing. As she listened, everything seemed still. The snow that had fallen during the last few days had a quieting effect. Anna didn't want to leave the warmth of the bed. The mattress was only filled with straw and hay, on a frame of ropes, but it was warm and comfy.

The sod house she and her husband Henry had moved into and fixed up was small. It had one tiny window and a dirt floor. There wasn't a whole lot of room to be had. All it contained was a table, some benches, a small wood stove with a wood box near, and a bed. They had repaired the sod roof, and Anna had covered most of the dirt floor with braided rag rugs. She had done her part to make the place homey and comfortable. Henry had fixed up what furnishings there were and made a few improvements. But after the first year, it was clear to Anna; Henry Pierson was not very good at building things, nor did he seem to like hard work.

He'd been gone for two weeks now. Henry had said he was going to ride into town for tobacco, but a day after he left, Anna found he hadn't needed tobacco at all.

Suddenly, Anna heard what had awakened her. It was Adam, their mule, braying for all he was worth. The day before, snow had caved in one end of the poorly built mule shelter. Eve, Adam's mate, had been so severely hurt that Anna had been forced to shoot her to put her out of her misery. Anna had learned to do many unpleasant things since she and Henry had moved into the abandoned cabin, in southwestern Kansas, a little over two years ago.

Anna dressed quickly, putting on Henry's old work coat. The coat was too big for her, but it was warmer than her own thinner jacket. Taking rifle in hand, she quietly opened the cabin door. She could see what Adam was so frantic about. Several wolves were fighting over

Eve's carcass. The area of the corral was littered with bloody pieces of the poor mule's body. Anna slowly stepped outside.

A few snowflakes were falling. The hungry wolves were so intent on eating, at first they didn't notice her. Then, one big dark male turned and stared at her, baring his teeth. He uttered a low menacing growl. Anna took careful aim and fired, hitting him square in the chest. He was dead before he hit the ground. She fired again, wounding another wolf before they ran to the safety of some nearby cottonwood trees.

For a brief while Anna considered trying to save some of the mule meat, then decided it would be too painful to eat her old friend. Anna was sure the wolves would return soon and possibly attack Adam. She put a lead on him, and doing the only thing she could think of to keep him safe, took him into the cabin. It wasn't a very pleasant solution but she didn't have much choice. Pushing the sparse furniture around, she made a spot for Adam in a corner of the room.

Damn Henry anyway she thought, first you leave me out here alone, the food's almost gone, I'm getting low on firewood, and now I'm living with a mule. Adam didn't seem to mind the situation. He looked around as if to say, *Hmmm, warm and safe.* Shaking himself off, he gave a contented grunt and lay down in his corner of the room.

Anna dressed, and got busy building the fire to warm things up and fix something to eat. "More pancakes," she said to the mule. "I'm really getting tired of pancakes. Oh well, at least there's coffee. That will hit the spot, after being out in the cold to save your worthless old hide."

Anna became aware of another noise outside. She heard a horse whinny, and Adam shambled up from his sleep. At last, she thought, Henry's back. She didn't know whether to be glad or mad. As she raced to the door, there was a heavy knock. Without thinking, she opened it. Anna found herself facing a tall, rough looking stranger. He was dressed in fur from head to toe. Somewhat like the trappers or mountain men that she and Henry had seen while they were traveling west. The man had long, brown hair, and a full beard. He would have frightened her, except he had kind looking hazel eyes, and a nice smile. That is, what she could see of him through fur, whiskers, and snow.

Removing his fur hat, he said in a deep voice, "I was passing by when I heard gunfire, so I thought I'd see what was happening. I can see by the wolf outside that you've had a mite of trouble."

As he spoke, his eyes scanned the small cabin. Stopping at the sight of the mule, he remarked, "Mighty good idea, for keeping him safe." Finally, noticing her quizzical expression, he blurted out, "Oh, I'm sorry ma'am, my name is Jed, Jed Hawkins."

Anna realized she'd been staring at the man, leaving him standing in the open doorway. She recovered her senses saying, "I'm Mrs. Pierson, Anna Pierson. Yes, I was trying to chase some wolves off, and I'm afraid they will be back soon. Please, come in and sit down. I was just making some coffee and something to eat. Would you care for a cup?"

"Well that sounds fine, I've been on the trail since early this morning. I was down the valley at my place. I figured the weather was in for a bad change, so I decided to head for town. Excuse me for being nosey ma'am, but are you out here alone?"

Anna knew telling a strange man she was by herself was not a wise thing to do, but for some reason she felt safe in speaking the truth. "Yes," she answered. "My husband went into town a few days ago and hasn't returned. I really don't know what to think. Of course, it did start snowing…" her voice trailed off. As she'd been speaking, Anna could see this man found it hard to believe that her husband could not have made it back home, short of some sort of trouble. Suddenly she realized she felt the same way.

Anna could smell that the coffee was ready, and went to one of the crude shelves for tin cups. She brought them along with the coffee pot to the table, where Jed had seated himself, and poured them each a cup.

Anna felt embarrassed that she had no more to offer, and also by the meager surroundings of the cabin. If Jed noticed, he didn't show it.

He seemed genuinely content and pleased as he sipped the hot brew, not waiting for it to cool. "Good coffee," he said. "Nothing beats a cup of good coffee."

Anna was growing hungry. With some hesitancy, she stated that she was just going to make some sourdough pancakes and asked Jed if he would like some. Secretly she hoped he wasn't a big eater, because she was really getting low on food.

"Why thank you ma'am," he answered. "I ate a fair size meal before I started out this morning but I guess one pancake would taste mighty good. I purely do love sourdough pancakes."

He got up from the table saying, "I'll bring in some more wood and tend to my animals. I can take your mule outside too. While I'm about it, I think I'll drag that dead wolf and mule off aways, so's not to have my animals get spooked. If the wolves come back, I'm sure my horses will raise a big fuss. Between the two of us, we can give 'em a big welcome."

"That sounds good to me," she replied with a smile. "I'm not used to having mules in the house."

Jed went on out, leading a somewhat reluctant Adam. After a short while he returned with an armload of wood for the stove. Glancing at what Anna was cooking as he put down the wood, Jed grinned widely. He walked back out the door. Shaking his hat and coat off, he then hung them on pegs inside and returned to the table. Anna refilled his cup, thanking him for getting the wood.

She became aware of Jed watching her as she cooked their food. She didn't feel fearful, but wondered how she must appear to him. The dress she had on was faded. The hem was tattered and soiled. Her hands were work worn and she had done nothing with her hair, only tying it back with an old piece of cloth. She wondered about this man. He looked fairly old to her. He had helped out without being asked and appeared downright polite.

Jed *had* been watching her and thought to himself, *that's not a bad lookin' gal. That old dress she wearin' don't hide the fact that she's pretty shapely. She looks to be a little over twenty. Yes sir, I bet she could be downright pretty. Her man must be crazy for leaving her out here like this.*

When Anna had a small stack of pancakes, she brought them to the table then got a couple of plates and a jar of honey.

Jed looked surprised. "Why, I haven't had honey in a 'coons age, where did you come by it?"

"Last fall I found a bee tree down by the creek," she stated shyly. "I even got some wax for candles." Anna was embarrassed at how hard she had to scrabble for existence in this unforgiving place. She'd done all the gardening and was able to store some of what she'd grown in a root cellar. She'd dug it by herself. Henry had proved to be a good hunter, but game seemed to be getting scarce. It was probably the same for the hungry wolves she thought. Anna had felt it was her duty, as a good wife, to work hard. But, as time went by, she'd come to see that Henry wasn't really doing his share.

Henry was able bodied, and he'd wanted to go west to start a cattle ranch. However, after they had completed the really necessary improvements on the place, he'd lost interest. He only did what had to be done. He would get wood or sometimes carry water from the creek, but mostly he spent his days practicing with his hand guns. Then a few months ago, he started spending more and more time in town.

Anna knew that he liked to play cards and gamble. Sometimes, he would return from town all excited about winning money. One time, he'd even brought her some fabric to make a new dress. He knew she liked to sew. Anna figured it was his way of keeping peace, even though she'd never complained about his trips to town.

Jed and Anna finished eating and sat with another cup of coffee, talking of the weather and such. They'd sat for quite some time. Anna felt oddly comfortable with this stranger. Finally, Anna started to get up from the table saying, "Well, I'd better clean up."

As she began to clear the table Jed said, "You know, I've been thinking, if you don't know when your man might get back, maybe you should go into Meade with me. If we was to meet him on the way, you could come back with him. You might get news of him in town. I noticed you're low on wood and the weather is for sure gonna get worse. I'd hate to think of you out here all alone, what with the wolves and all."

Anna stood there, plates in hand, her mouth hanging open. "Oh, I don't think so," she finally said. She was touched that this stranger seemed more concerned about her welfare than her own husband. Then she scolded herself for thinking ill of Henry. Surely, she thought, he had a good reason for not getting home, but she wasn't entirely certain. "Why," Anna went on, "I wouldn't have a place to stay in town."

Jed looked at her, "I'm well acquainted with the folks that run a hotel, I'm sure you could stay there."

"Well, I wouldn't have any idea how long I might have to stay, and frankly, I don't have that kind of money. Besides, what would I do about Adam? I couldn't just leave him here for the wolves."

"No, you couldn't. Anyways, I noticed he's almost out of food." Anna was again surprised at how much Jed had observed. He looked thoughtful, saying, "You know, I could use a good mule. How about I buy him from you and that would give you some money to start. I'm sure if you have to stay very long, you could get work. My friends,

Mary and Mickey, own the hotel and restaurant, they would be glad to help you out." Jed didn't mention that besides being the best place to eat in town, some of the hotel's upstairs rooms were for Mary's soiled doves to entertain men in need of a woman's companionship, so to speak.

Anna was beginning to see the logic in Jed's plan. Besides, she thought, it would be wonderful to see people again and it sure would be better than waiting for Henry to show up. But she had never seen this man before and wondered if leaving with him would be such a wise idea. Then she thought, *why I could freeze or starve before Henry comes home.* The more she considered it, the more she could see leaving with this stranger might be a better choice.

Jed sensed her doubt. "Ma'am, I know you don't know me, but I couldn't leave you out here alone and not worry about it."

"Alright I'll do it, but how about you stop calling me ma'am? I'll call you Jed and you can call me Anna, if that's alright with you?"

Jed smiled and stated, "That would be just fine with me, ma'... I mean Anna."

CHAPTER TWO

Jed stood up from the table saying, "Good, I'll take my stuff and put it on my new mule. You can ride my saddle horse and I'll take the pack horse. By the way, how much do you want for your mule?" he asked, while putting his coat on.

Anna, was taken aback, "Why I have no idea."

"Then, how about I pay for the hotel room for as long as you need or until you decide it's enough?"

"Alright," Anna replied. "That sounds fine to me."

"Be sure to dress warm," he said. "You might not like it but I think if you have an extra pair of your husband's trousers handy, it might be better if you wore them instead of a dress." Then he went out to take care of the animals and get ready to leave.

Anna hurriedly straightened the cabin, and then made a small bundle of clothing. She found a pair of Henry's work pants and put them on. She couldn't figure what to do with the skirt of her dress. It wouldn't tuck in, and she couldn't wear it outside. In the end she took the dress off and put on one of Henry's shirts. She wrote a note for Henry in case they somehow missed one another, telling where she had gone and why. Looking around the room, she decided to hide the rifle. She didn't want to take it, but thought someone might steal it if it was left out. She'd long ago made a hiding place under the bed. Anna decided to also hide her china cups. She'd kept a small bag, with a little money, in the hiding place. It also held a cameo brooch her mother had given her on her wedding day.

As she reached to retrieve the small bag containing the bit of money and her brooch, she found it missing, along with its contents. She couldn't believe Henry had done such a thing. She didn't even know he'd found her hiding place. Of course, from time to time, she'd gotten money out and given it to Henry, but thought that she'd been careful not to reveal its location. *Henry must have been watching at some time, and discovered my secret. It had to have been Henry that took it,* she thought angrily, *No one else has been here. Now, he has left me destitute too.*

Jed returned to the cabin, lightly knocking on the door before coming in. As he entered, a broad smile crossed his face. "Well, he said, you can't say you're not dressed for the trip. You'll do just fine. Where are the things that you want to take? I'll pack them up."

Anna handed him her small bundle, wrapped tightly in a square of canvas. Chuckling as he started outside, he declared, "I do admire a woman that travels light."

Anna glanced around the cabin a final time. Putting Henry's old work coat on and a knit hat, she stepped out into the snowy morning. She felt excitement at the thought of going to town. It was going to be a cold trip, but she felt ready.

Jed and Anna had been on the trail for almost three hours. Jed led the way on his pack horse with Adam trailing behind him on a lead. Anna followed on Jed's saddle horse, a smooth-gaited sorrel mare.

The traveling had been a little slow because of the snowfall. The animals trudged steadily along. Adam seemed almost eager to be going someplace besides the small confines of his old shelter. Maybe, Anna thought, it had been distressing for him being around poor Eve's remains. Anna was warm enough, but she noticed that the snowfall was getting heavier. She really couldn't recall how long it had taken her and Henry to get to town. She'd gone only one time before and that was in the summertime. She thought it had taken about four hours then.

Jed stopped his horse, and getting down, he walked back to Anna. "It's getting pretty bad, we don't want to tire the animals. We left your place a little before noon, and I figure it's getting on towards two or so. With this weather, I'm afraid it's gonna get dark fairly early. There's a place a little ways from here where I sometimes stop and camp when I'm going to and from Meade. I think we'd better hunker down there for the night."

Alarmed, Anna asked, "You mean to camp out in this?" She was really beginning to worry about her decision to leave her home with this stranger.

"Oh, it won't be so bad. Why, you might even enjoy it," answered Jed, as he mounted up. Anna looked around, seeing nothing but woods and snow. She began to worry even more, as she wondered what sleeping arrangements Jed had in mind.

They traveled on for about another half hour, when Jed turned his horse off the wagon road and led them a short distance down a wide trail. They came to a clearing ringed by large boulders and some pine trees. Jed reined up and got off his horse. The snow was really coming down now and Anna couldn't see how they could possibly stay there.

Right away, Jed had Anna get off her horse, then led the animals off towards one side of the clearing, where the trees grew in a dense cluster. Anna could see that it would shelter them from most of the snowfall. He removed their packs and got out some canvas tarps. He then gathered some long poles that had been lying nearby, and shaking the snow off, he leaned them against the rocks and secured one of the canvas tarps over them. After clearing the ground of what snow he could, he placed the second tarp on the ground. When he'd finished they had a pretty good shelter from the snow. Jed scraped some more snow away, making a small clear spot in front of the shelter. Then he did something that really surprised Anna. She was beginning to see Jed had camped here many times before. He'd gone to a spot near the trees and come back with an armload of dry firewood. The wood had been stashed under a small rock overhang to keep it dry for use in the future. In no time at all there was a good fire going.

He went back to the animals, parceling out grain and water among them. After tending to the horses and mule, he got out some coffee, a pot and some jerky.

"I guess we should have brought along some of those pancakes," he said. "I'm afraid this isn't going to be much of a meal."

Anna's opinion of Jed was improving. She liked the way that he took care of the animals. Her father had once told her you could trust a man that cared for his stock. She'd been impressed at how efficiently he had set up a camp for them. After the coffee was done, they chewed on the jerky and sipped the warm brew from one cup. Jed hadn't thought to have Anna bring another.

After a while, Jed placed a really big log on the fire and began fixing places for them to sleep. She was relieved to see there were two spots for their bed rolls. It was still early and Anna wasn't sleepy. She was tired but not ready to go to bed. Jed sat rolling a cigarette then taking a small stick from the fire he lit it, then leaned back against the now warm rock. They each sat there, staring into the fire.

Anna wondered if she dared to ask this man about his life. She'd noticed a lot of the people she and Henry had met in their travels liked to keep their affairs to themselves.

Before she could say anything, Jed spoke up. "Mind if I ask how you came to be living out here in the Crooked River Valley?"

Anna was amazed how at ease she felt with Jed. *Maybe,* she thought, *It's because I haven't had anyone to talk to for so long, or perhaps he reminds me of my father.* In any case, Anna told him how she and Henry had lived in St. Louis. They'd known each other since childhood. Their families had been friends. Her folks owned a tailor and dressmaking shop and Henry's folks had a grocery store. Henry didn't have any brothers or sisters, but she had a half-sister, a few years older. Anna went on to tell Jed how it was that she and Henry had ended up where they did. She told him that when she wasn't in school, she'd spend her days in her folk's shop. In the evenings, they returned to their farm just outside town. Henry hadn't wanted to work in his father's store, and when he was old enough, he got a job working in one of the banks.

Henry's mother died from pneumonia one winter and not long after that his father shot himself. It had been a terrible thing. Henry spent a lot of time at our place after that. When she turned eighteen, he asked her to marry him and head out west. She went on saying how she hated leaving her folks alone. Angel, her half-sister, had married and was living in Kansas City and was seldom seen. Anyway, they married and started west. Henry had this dream of starting a cattle ranch, but he soon tired of the hardships of the trail. Coming across that abandoned place, Henry just decided to settle there. Anna stopped talking and stared into the fire, recalling how exciting and romantic it had all seemed at the time.

"Yeah," Jed said. "When the war was going there was a big demand for beef. A lot of folks came out here thinking they would get rich raising cattle. After a while there was cattle glut. Then the ranchers were stuck with cattle and no one to buy them. A lot of the would-be cattlemen sold what they could and left their places to return to where they came from. So you've been here how long?" he asked.

"Oh, let's see, it's been a little over two years now. Henry sold the store and his folks place. We had our wedding and were ready to be on our way. My folks were very happy and sad at the same time."

Anna fell silent again. As she watched the dancing flames she thought to herself, Jed had been right, she *was* enjoying their campout. It was so peaceful with just the crackling of the fire and the occasional nickering of the animals. As she sat there she thought back, realizing in her youthful excitement over marriage and going west, she had missed signs that her life with Henry might not be so rosy.

After Henry had sold all his folk's property, he'd gone on a spending spree. He bought fancy boots and clothing. He also bought a showy, bay gelding, along with a very nice saddle, a pair of pearl handled pistols, and a new rifle. He'd stayed in one of the better hotels in town. Anna had heard that he was gambling and seemed to be losing a lot of money.

She hadn't given much thought about his situation, until it came time to prepare for their trip west. He'd said a pair of mules and a smaller wagon would be a better choice for their needs. Now, as she thought back, she knew his decision was because he'd spent most of his money. Having a smaller wagon had meant Anna couldn't pack much for their trip. She'd been able to bring a small sewing machine her folks had given her. Her mother also had given her a few pieces of china, some seeds for a garden, a few gold pieces, and her grandmother's cameo brooch. They'd decided to name the mules Adam and Eve, because this was going to be the beginning of their new life.

Jed had finished his cigarette and stood saying, "I'm going to check on the animals before turning in."

Anna figured he was also going to answer nature's call and decided to do the same, going off in another direction. She had quite a time with the trousers. She hurried because she wanted to get back to the shelter before Jed. It would have been embarrassing for her to have him aware of what she was doing, even if it was a natural need.

Anna did get back before Jed, but when he returned he saw the tracks in the snow where she'd left the area. He said, "I should've asked you about needing to go out into the woods. Next time tell me, so I know where you are."

"I'm not a child," replied Anna, somewhat snappish. Then she realized that he was only looking out for her. "I'm sorry," she said. "I'm just use to taking care of myself."

"That's okay. Maybe we better try and get some rest. Hard telling what the morning will bring."

CHAPTER THREE

Jed was up before Anna. By the time she woke, he'd tended to the animals and was building the fire up. It had stopped snowing during the night. It was chilly, but calm and clear. Anna got up feeling pretty rested. She started off for the woods again, then stopping; she turned, calling in a loud voice, "I'm going into the woods!" They both chuckled a little. When she returned, Anna offered to make the coffee while Jed packed things up.

The stream was nearby. Anna filled the pot with its icy water. Looking around, she noticed some large tracks in the snow. As she and Jed sat with their coffee and jerky, she mentioned seeing them.

"Well, I didn't want to say anything. I knew something was creeping around. Early this morning the animals were nervous and they woke me with their fuss. I got up to check on things, and that probably chased it off."

"No wonder you wanted to know where I was, thanks."

Jed smiled and replied, "Us campers have to look out for each other." They finished their coffee, and after packing the gear were on their way again.

"I figure another two hours or more we should be in town. The snow isn't that bad, but it'll slow us down some. I hope you don't get too hungry before we get there. The food at the hotel is pretty good. I'll buy you some ham and eggs."

"Oh, what a treat that would be," Anna exclaimed with some excitement. "Why, I can't remember the last time I had an egg, let alone ham. Mom and Dad had all that on our place back home." She wished they could travel faster. Thinking of such good food made her mouth water, and her stomach growled in protest.

After what seemed forever, the town of Meade came into view. Anna's excitement grew. She wondered what the owners of the hotel would think. She felt very disheveled and dirty. Sleeping on the ground in Henry's old clothes had been necessary, but now she wished she could clean up some. She couldn't imagine how she must appear.

As they neared the town, it was as she remembered. The ragged cluster of buildings was situated near the banks of the Crooked River. A few tiny farms were on the outskirts, along with a church, and a simple schoolhouse. The main street had a livery stable with a smithy, the stage station, a marshal's office and jail, and a large general store. She also noticed there were several saloons with tinny music coming from a couple. Along with other things, there was a barber shop offering baths, and small shops that catered to the needs of ranchers and cowboys. There also seemed to be two hotels. Everything she could see, seemed to have a permanent coating of dust.

Jed had explained that trail herds often went by Meade, and they stopped to get supplies. He'd gone on to say the town could get pretty wild, but all in all it was a pretty decent place. As they rode down the main street, a couple of men yelled hello to Jed and he waved a greeting back to them. Anna could see the questioning looks the men were giving them. She hoped they would think Jed had picked up some down and out young man and was glad when they tied up at one of the hotels.

It was quiet inside as they entered the lobby. It was furnished with heavy overstuffed furniture. There was a desk at the back, where a rather stuffy looking, middle aged man was giving them a disdainful look as he pretended to be busy shuffling papers.

"Hello Homer," Jed said. "Is Mary in her office?"

"Oh, Mr. Hawkins," the skinny clerk stammered, "I didn't recognize you. Why yes, I'm sure that's where you can find her."

"Thanks," Jed replied. Turning to Anna, he said, "I'll go see Mary, then I'll come fetch you to meet her."

When Jed left, Anna felt very alone and alarmed. She watched him walk into the saloon. He hadn't mentioned the hotel contained one, and where she came from proper ladies never would enter such a place.

She could hear the tinny sound of a piano being played and men shouting greetings to Jed. Anna saw him walk up to the bar and shake hands with the smiling bartender. She heard him saying, "Well, Jed, you old son of a gun. Hardly knew ya with all that hair you got on your face. We figured the weather would drive you back into town. How ya been anyway?"

"I'm just fine Mickey, is Mary in her office? I've a proposition for her."

"Yeah sure," Mickey answered. "Go on in, she'll be glad to see ya."

From where Anna was sitting she could see Jed go over and knock on the office door. When it opened, a red-headed woman stood there with a huge smile on her face. She looked to Anna to be about thirty-five or more. She had a lot of rouge on her face and lips. She wasn't really fat, but she wasn't tiny either. She was poured into a bright green, silk dress and the seams looked ready to burst. She literally pulled Jed into the office and shut the door.

Anna sat there looking around. She saw that the restaurant area was on the opposite side of the lobby. Glancing back into the saloon she noticed a couple of girls in fancy dresses and hairdos, they also wore a lot of rouge. She began to feel very shabby, and wished she was anyplace else.

After what seemed like an eternity, Jed and the plump red-headed woman came out of the office, heading straight to where Anna was waiting.

"Anna," Jed said. "This is Mary O'Shawnesy. Mary and Mickey own this establishment."

Mary reached out her freckled hand to Anna, and with a smile proceeded to say Jed had told her all about the dilemma she was in, saying, "Now let's get something for you two to eat and we can talk this over." Anna was warmed by Mary's seemingly caring interest.

They went into the large dining room and sat at a table by a dusty window. Mary went into the kitchen and soon came out with a small pot of coffee. Cups were already on the tables, and Mary filled three of them, saying Cookie was fixing them some ham and eggs. Anna's mouth was fairly watering as delicious smells came from somewhere in the kitchen.

"Now Anna," said Mary, "Jed told me you could probably be of some help around here while you have to stay in town. Can you cook?"

Anna looked surprised. "Well I can cook, but if you mean cooking in a restaurant, I don't know if I could do that."

"Oh, if you can cook at all and ain't afraid of work you'll do fine. Truth is, I'm in a real bind here. Cookie slipped off the back steps a couple days ago. He broke his left arm and bruised his foot pretty bad. I've been trying to help out, but it's been a chore. He's back there now, cussin' and struggling. We could sure use another pair of hands."

Anna gave a tentative smile saying, "I'm not sure how I'd do, but I'm willing to try."

"Great," said an enthusiastic Mary. "After you finish here, Jed can get your things and bring you over to my office. I'll take you to what will be your room, then you can take a bath and get out of that pile of clothes you have on. When you're ready, I'll take you in to meet Cookie. I gotta tell ya, he ain't very refined. He cooked for trail drives for years and sometimes he forgets himself around women folk. About two years ago, the herd he was with came through here and we got acquainted. He said he would like to light in one spot. So we offered him a job. When they came back through, on the way back to Texas, he stayed. I'd been doing the cooking up 'til then, but it got to be too much for me. We have a married Chinese couple that help out too, Susie and Lee Chang. You'll just have to be Cookie's left arm."

Standing, Mary said, "I gotta get back to the office. I'll see you in a little while." Turning to Jed, she said, "You bring her on over when you're done. Take your time." Then she bustled off.

CHAPTER FOUR

In a short while, a slim built man dressed in a black pants and a tunic-like top, came shuffling from the kitchen, carrying two large plates of food. Placing them before Anna and Jed, he bowed his head and backed from his task. Anna noticed he wore a black silk skull cap over his pulled-back hair.

Jed stood and shook the man's hand. "It's good to see you Lee, how have things been?" Lee seemed glad to see Jed, and replied that everything was fine. Jed introduced Anna and added that she would be helping out in the kitchen.

"That be good," replied Lee. "Mr. Cookie need help." When Lee left, Anna and Jed sat in silence as they both were so busy eating.

After a while, they slowed down and Anna said quietly, "I've never seen a real Chinese person before, he seems to be very polite."

"Lee's a pretty good guy," answered Jed. "He was a laborer for the railroad when it was being built to Kansas City. The Chinese workers were treated pretty bad by some people. One night a bunch of drunken workers jumped him and cut off his *queue*. After that, he and Susie decided to run away and take their chances someplace else. They showed up here one winter with nothing but the clothes on their backs and Mary took them in. They have their own little place now. They are good, honest, hard working people."

"Kinda like me," Anna mused. "Mary seems to help anyone who needs it."

"I told you she would help out," smiled Jed.

Hesitating, Anna asked, "What's a *queue*?" She was almost afraid of what part of a person's body the answer might be.

"Oh," said Jed, as he rolled a cigarette, "That's a braid that Chinese men wear. It has very special meaning to them. For someone to cut it off is very disgraceful. I'm not sure why."

Jed smoked his cigarette and sipped the last of his coffee. "Boy that was some meal wasn't it? Now that I see you're going to be fine, I'll bring your things in, then I'll be saying goodbye. I've got some things to take care of and then I need to catch the stage to Kansas City if the snow doesn't hold it up."

"Goodbye?" asked an alarmed Anna. "You mean you're not going to be in town?"

"Oh, I'll be back in a couple weeks or so. You'll be fine, Mary will see to that, anyway your husband might show up. If you want, I can send the marshal over to talk to you. He might know something about your Henry's whereabouts."

"Yes," she answered. "That might be helpful. Thank you for all the help you've given me. I don't know how I can ever repay you."

"Oh it was mighty nice having your company coming into town, and I'll see you from time to time. I hope things work out for you. Well, I guess I'd better go out and get your things. You can wait in the lobby. I'll be right back."

They walked back out to the lobby and Jed went outside to get Anna's things. When he returned, they started through the saloon. The men at the card tables were staring at Anna as if they didn't know what to make of her. Jed didn't seem to worry about her appearance at all. He stopped at the bar and introduced her to Mickey. Jed kept smiling as if she were dressed in some sort of finery, instead of ill fitting, men's work clothes.

"Nice to meet you Anna, any friend of Jed's is a friend of mine."

"Anna's going to help Cookie out," Jed told Mickey.

"Well I'll be," laughed Mickey. "I hope he don't burn your ears off little lady. He can get riled up pretty easy and now that he's hurting, that old coot is like a rattlesnake with a sunburned belly. Good luck to ya."

Anna couldn't help but worry as they continued toward Mary's office. As they were going past the piano, Jed stopped. "I'll introduce you to Fingers, he is pretty hard of hearing." Fingers was a tall skinny guy with a horse-like face. He had on an old stove pipe hat and an unlit stogie dangling from the corner of his mouth. Jed tapped him on the shoulder and Fingers looked up from the keyboard.

"Fingers," Jed said in a loud voice, "This here is Anna."

"Oh sure," Fingers answered in a booming voice. "I know that one." And he started playing a lively rendition of *Oh, Susannah*. Jed and Anna looked at each other, and smiling, continued on towards Mary's office.

Jed rapped on the door and Mary yelled at them to come in. She was sitting behind a cluttered desk. She started to stand, but Jed motioned for her to stay seated saying, "Don't get up, I'm just bringing your new help. I'll be leaving now. I need to tend to my animals and take care of some stuff, then I'm going to leave town for a few days."

Mary stood from her desk anyway and walked over to Jed, giving him a hug saying, "Don't you worry about this girl, I'll keep my eye on her for you and don't be a stranger. Why, when you get back, Anna will probably have Cookie behaving like his old ornery self."

Jed smiled at Anna replying, "That would be something to behold. I'll look forward to it." Handing Anna her small bundle, he touched the brim of his hat saying, "I'll see ya 'round," and left. Suddenly Anna felt very alone. She wasn't so sure she had done the right thing in coming to town.

CHAPTER FIVE

Mary got right down to the business at hand and said, "Come on girl, let's get you up to your room." Anna followed Mary up some stairs, leading from the bar to the second floor. For a fair sized woman, Mary moved quickly, and Anna found she had to hurry to keep up with her. At the top of the stairs, there was a railing where a person could overlook the saloon. But that open landing was only a brief expanse before they entered a narrow, dimly lit corridor.

As Mary started down the hallway, she waved her hand at the first six doors, stating that the first room was Mickey's and her's. She said that the next five belonged to her girls. Anna was beginning to wonder about Mary's girls. Mary stopped at a door that had a tin number nine on it. The nail meant to hold the top of the number in place was missing, so that it had fallen a little off kilter. Mary opened the door, saying to Anna that this was where she would take her bath. "Be sure and put a chair under the door handle. The lock got broke and I keep forgetting to tell Lee to fix it."

Mary moved on. "Altogether, we have fourteen rooms. Five are for hotel guests, and number nine is for them to bathe in and such. Of course, sometimes we have to use it to put guests in. There are two smaller rooms, one is for storage, and the other will be yours. It's small, but it's comfortable."

Towards the middle of the hall, Mary went on to say, "This second stairway goes down to the hotel lobby. See that door at the end of the hall? That takes you outside to the privy. That privy is for the hotel guests only. We can't have those cowboys using that one." Giving a lusty laugh, she said, "Their aim ain't too good after a few drinks."

Mary stopped at a room with the number eleven on it, and unlocking the door she handed the key to Anna. "You go on in and get settled, then go down to that room nine. Susie will have a tub ready for you. After you've cleaned up, come to my office, and we'll go meet Cookie." Turning on her heel, Mary left Anna on her own.

When Anna entered the room, she was thrilled at what she saw. True, it was small, but to Anna it was perfect. There was a window with a view of the farmland outside of town. The window was covered with real lace curtains. To Anna the bed looked heavenly, and she whirled around, flopping full out on it. Sitting up, she took a look at the rest of the tiny room. There was a wash stand with a water pitcher and bowl. On the bottom shelf sat a chamber pot. A small table stood beside the bed, holding an oil lamp. There was a tiny stove to heat the room, and a dresser with a mirror.

Anna was shocked when she saw her reflection. She hardly recognized the disheveled and haggard looking woman gazing back at her. She picked out some clean clothing from her parcel, and headed out the door for her bath.

As she walked down the hall towards room number nine, Anna was thinking about how long it had been since she'd had a real bath. Henry and she had used a small tub for bathing. It was the same tub she'd used to wash their clothes in. It was so small, they couldn't sit in it and had to stand, pouring bath water over themselves. In warmer weather, they had bathed outdoors in the creek.

Entering the room, Anna found the bathtub behind a wooden screen. It was filled with hot water, and was of fair size. She couldn't wait to get out of the things she had on and sink into the wonder of a nice relaxing bath. Putting the chair under the door knob, as Mary had instructed, Anna quickly undressed and eased herself into the heavenly water.

She could have stayed in the bath forever. Someone had placed good smelling soap and a soft wash cloth on a small stool beside the tub and there were towels stacked on another nearby stool. After what seemed like much too short of a time, Anna decided she had better not keep Mary waiting too long.

Suddenly, there was a loud knocking on the door. Anna started to open it, then decided she should ask who was there. A gruff voice answered, "I was told to go to room six and here I am."

In a loud, somewhat frightened voice, Anna answered "You have the wrong room. You have room nine, go away!" She could hear some grumbling as the intruder departed. When Anna opened the door to return to her room, she was careful to check the hallway. She didn't want to run into anyone from the saloon. Safely back in her room, she combed her hair into a neat bun at the nape of her neck and started down to Mary's office.

When she passed through the saloon, on her way to the office, she noticed there were a lot more men milling about and she saw two more girls. They were dressed in revealing gowns and had on the same heavy rouge she'd noticed on Mary and the other two girls she'd seen earlier. Remembering Mary had mentioned she had five girls, Anna wondered where the fifth one was. She also suddenly became aware of what the girls were there for, as she observed them brazenly flirt with the men. Feeling very out of place, Anna hurried on to knock at Mary's office door.

Knocking on the office door, Anna wondered what she might be getting into. Mary shouted for her to come in.

Mary looked up from some bookwork as Anna entered. There was a smile of approval on her face. She got up from the desk and walked to Anna. Looking her over, she said, "Well, well, you clean up pretty good. I hope none of those wild men out there gave you any trouble. My girls might not like that."

Anna had to ask - she was bursting with the question. "What do you mean when you say, *your* girls?"

"Why honey," Mary answered, "Half of the upstairs is what you might call a house of pleasure."

Anna was shocked. Of course she knew of such places, but she never thought that she might be living in one. Then with a sudden gasp, she asked, "Did Jed think that I…?"

Before Anna could finish, Mary put her somewhat heavy arm across Anna's shoulder saying, "Oh, no, no. You'll have nothing to do with that part of our business. No, don't you worry hon, all you have to do is survive Cookie. So let's go meet your new boss." Mary started to the door, heading for the kitchen, as usual, Anna was racing to keep up.

CHAPTER SIX

They could hear him before they reached the kitchen door. Cookie was yelling at Lee about something. Mary pushed through the swinging doors, telling Cookie to calm down or she would fire him and let Lee be the cook from now on. Cookie let out another bellow, stating how he needed more help now that he was so crippled up. His voice trailed off as he took in the frightened looking Anna.

"Who's this?" he asked, in a still grouchy voice. "How come you to bring a stranger into my kitchen?"

"This stranger," Mary said, taking hold of Anna's arm, "This is an angel from heaven and she is going to be the help that you were just asking for. Cookie, meet Anna."

He stepped forward, a scowl on his grizzled old face. He looked Anna over from head to toe. "There ain't much to her," he growled.

Anna found his statement somewhat amusing, seeing as how she was a few inches taller than the wizened old man.

Anna smiled sweetly and reached out her hand saying, "I'm glad to meet you Cookie, I can see that it must be hard working with just one arm. I'll do my best to help out."

Cookie's eyebrows were big as gray bushes and his dark eyes fairly shot out sparks. He glared at Anna and replied. "Well now, I guess meby we'll see how much help you can be. Are you ready to start working? It's about time to start getting things ready for that hungry dinner crowd, so we'll just see what ya got."

"I'm ready," Anna answered with more confidence in her voice than she felt. "Just tell me where to start."

With a big humph, Cookie snatched a dingy apron off a peg and handed it to Anna.

"See, I told ya," smiled Mary. "Why, I think you two will get along just fine, *won't you Cookie?*" she asked in a threatening tone. Then to Anna's dismay, Mary turned and scurried off in her usual speedy manner, and Anna was left alone with Cookie, who had a rather evil looking smile on his leathery old face.

"Well," he said. "You can start by peeling them spuds over there. These gents do love their spuds and gravy."

Anna thought that wouldn't be so bad, until she saw the huge pile of potatoes Cookie was pointing to. She was determined to prove herself to this crabby old man, so she dug into the task with all the energy she could muster.

Cookie busied himself setting out steaks, while Lee sliced bread and gathered other things that would be needed. Anna got a fair amount of potatoes peeled and put them on to cook. She went back to her peeling, until Cookie told her she had done enough of them.

Cookie had been ranting about the customers liking biscuits better than bread, but he couldn't help that. Biscuits and pies, would just have to wait until he had his arm back.

Anna waited for a lull in his tirade, then piped up saying, "I could make biscuits and pies for you, why that would be fun."

"Fun, fun!" shouted Cookie. "Why it's purley nothing but work."

"Oh but I'd like to try," replied Anna.

"Okay little lady, in the morning we'll just see how much fun you can have. I'll have Susie wake you early and you can try your hand at fun… making biscuits. These cowpokes love biscuits and gravy for their breakfast."

The rest of the afternoon and evening was a whirl to Anna. Lee and Susie waited on the customers, while she and Cookie got the food out. It was like a blur, but slowly Anna got into the rhythm of things. Finally, as quickly as the rush had started, it was over.

When the cooking was over, Anna was relieved to find that Susie and Lee were going to do the cleanup. Anna couldn't see how Susie could work so hard. She was like a tiny bird, so delicate appearing. Her hair was the blackest that Anna had ever seen. Sometimes when the light hit it just right, it had blue highlights. Susie's eyes were almond shaped. Her skin was flawless, and she always wore a small smile.

Cookie left the kitchen as soon as the cooking was over and Susie told Anna that she was done for the night. Anna said goodnight to her and Lee, then drug her weary self up to her room. She hardly had the strength to get undressed. She wasn't sure how long she would be able to keep up this pace, but she didn't give the matter too much thought, because as soon as her head hit the pillow she was asleep.

There was a light tapping on the door of Anna's room. She had a hard time waking from the sound sleep she had been in. She stumbled to the door, asking who was there, wanting to make sure it wasn't one of Mary's customers from down stairs. It was Susie telling her it was time to go to work. Anna told Susie she would be right down and hurriedly dressed and combed her hair. After a trip to the outside privy, she washed her face and hands in the cold water at the outside pump and then went on into the kitchen. To Anna's surprise, Cookie wasn't there. She asked Lee where he was.

Lee smiled, "Susie and me think it be good joke for you to beat him to work."

"Where do I start?" she asked.

"I have coffee on already, it be good to make biscuits, I show you where everything is." Soon Anna was elbow deep in flour. It did seem like fun to her. Everything she needed was close at hand.

She was humming a little tune when Cookie came stomping into the kitchen, loaded for bear. The wind was taken out of his sails when he eyed Anna and the pans of good looking biscuits she had ready for the oven.

"Well I hope those are edible," he grouched, not giving Anna any credit for all the work she had done. Anna hadn't missed the small look of pleasure on the old man's face.

There was the same frenzied activity getting breakfast out, but everything seemed to go pretty smoothly. After things quieted down, Cookie got a cup of coffee and left the kitchen. That seemed to be the cue for Lee, Susie, and Anna to stop and eat. Afterwards they worked together to clean things up.

After a while Cookie returned, saying to Anna, "We don't cook lunch around here. Most people eat a big morning meal, then come on in for dinner. So you can start having fun making those pies. I think ten oughta do it. There's dried apples and peaches in the storeroom. You seem to know where the other stuff is," and with that said, he left. Anna learned later that Cookie spent most of his spare time at the poker tables.

She stood there for a few seconds after he'd left, wondering what she'd gotten herself into. Ten pies didn't sound like a whole lot of fun after all. Around three and a half hours later, she had the ten pies ready for the ovens.

Anna felt pleased with the job that she had done. She stoked up the fire in the huge cooking stove, put the pies in to cook, and after cleaning things up, she sat down to have a cup of coffee.

She sat there thinking about the hotel and the work. She realized she hadn't even wondered about Henry's whereabouts at all. The work had kept her so busy. But then she thought it wasn't nearly as hard as life had been at the cabin. Between carrying wood, hauling water, cooking and trying to keep the place clean, she had found little time for herself. Anna recalled days when she hadn't even gotten her hair brushed. She looked down at her thin arms and work worn hands and thought that her hands already looked softer.

As she sat there, Mary came in through the swinging doors, in a rush as usual. Anna started to stand up, thinking she should look busy.

"Sit, sit," said Mary, "I just thought I'd come by and see how you're doing. Jed told me that I had to keep an eye on you and make sure things were okay. Anyway I wanted to tell you that a few customers commented that Cookie had never done such a good job on his biscuits. Of course he's taking all the credit. Some of the men said maybe they should keep his arm broken."

Anna smiled saying, "If it keeps him happy that's okay with me."

"Say," asked Mary, "Is that apple pie I smell?"

"Yes," answered Anna, "Cookie had me make ten pies. That sure seemed like a lot to me."

"Oh no," Mary replied. "Pie is a favorite around here. It's a real treat the cowboys don't always get on the trail. Why, ten might not be enough if your pies are as good as the biscuits!"

Anna secretly was a little worried about how Cookie would feel with the fact that she seemed to be doing so well.

Mary had gotten herself a cup of coffee and seated herself across the table from Anna. As Anna looked at her she thought she must have been a stunner when she was younger. She figured Mary was somewhere in her late thirties. She had a hard time guessing peoples age. She was only a little over twenty herself. Everyone seemed older to her.

Mary took a drink of her coffee, then setting the cup down and gazing at Anna, she said, "Ya know Jed said that you might be a diamond in the rough. He might be right, why you already look healthier than when you got here and it's only been what, a day and a half? Must be all this hard work."

Anna smiled, "It does seem longer. I've been so busy, I've hardly had time to breathe, I've enjoyed it. It's not as hard as the work I had at home."

"Oh, by the way," Mary said, "The marshal was by, I guess Jed told him about your husband. Anyway, he wants you to stop by his office. I couldn't give him the information that he needed, I didn't remember you or Jed mentioning your last name or your husband's name, for that matter, and I sure as heck didn't know what he looks like. Anyway, if your man was in town, Marshal Sam, that's his name, Sam will know about it. So what is your last name, anyway?"

Anna had gotten up from the table to check on the pies. Answering Mary's question, she said, "My husband's name is Henry, Henry Pierson." Anna's back was to Mary, and didn't see the frown on her face when she heard Anna's answer.

As she took the pies from the ovens, Anna described Henry to Mary. "He's sorta tall, a little over six foot. He has dark hair, it's a little curly. Actually he's not a bad looking fellow. He has sideburns too and a mustache."

"Well, I'm sure he'll turn up," said Mary with little enthusiasm and changed the subject. "Say, those pies smell tempting, let's have a piece."

"You're the boss," said Anna. She gingerly cut them each a piece of very hot pie. They sat in silence as they waited for the pie to cool enough to eat. Anna wondered why Mary had suddenly seemed so deep in thought.

CHAPTER SEVEN

After Mary left, Anna straightened the kitchen up. She took off her apron and brushed flour off her clothes. She had decided to go straight to the marshal's office. She went on up to her room to get a shawl and brush her hair.

While going through the lobby to the front door, she noticed the saloon sounded pretty lively. She glanced in as she passed by and saw the fifth girl that Mary had mentioned. The girl was tall with black hair and dark sultry eyes. Her full lips were painted a bright red and she had on a matching red silk dress. She was well endowed. Her waist was tiny and she had full hips. Most of the men seemed in awe as they stared at her with lustful eyes. But the girl seemed uninterested in any of them, as she stood watching Fingers play his piano. Anna turned away and went on out the hotel door towards the marshal's office.

The snow had stopped the day she and Jed had gotten to town. Now the street was a muddy mess. The sky was a leaden gray and everything looked dingy. Anna hiked up the skirt of her dress and made her way across the street to the marshal's office. She had managed to keep pretty clean of the slush and mud. She was stamping her shoes on the wooden sidewalk, to rid them of any mud, when the door to the marshal's office opened. A stocky built man with snow white hair and neatly trimmed short beard motioned her into the office. He had the clearest bright blue eyes that Anna could recall ever seeing before.

"I saw you dancing your way across the street. Come on in. It's not often I get lady visitors. I'm Marshal Jefferson and you must be Anna, Mary said she would send you over."

"Yes, I'm Anna, Anna Pierson," she answered.

"I guessed as much, maybe you better sit down, we need to talk." He guided her to a chair by his scarred old desk.

Anna looked around the room, as the marshal went to an old potbellied stove for a cup of strong smelling coffee. The room was small with a bench under a window that faced the street. One wall had a cabinet filled with guns of all sorts, with a chain running through the trigger guards. A small table held a water bucket with a dipper hanging from the handle. There was a door that she figured led to the jail cells in back. The marshal turned to her and asked if she would like a cup of coffee? Anna declined, thinking the coffee could probably skin the inside of her throat.

The marshal seemed a little uneasy. As he sat behind the desk, he kept shifting his weight in his chair. Anna had a sense that he wasn't eager to discuss her husband. "Well now!" he finally started, "Jed told me some of your story. He said that your man had left you alone at your place and that he had chanced along and felt it would be best if you came into town."

"That's right," Anna explained, "My husband had been gone for two weeks or so. I couldn't imagine why he hadn't come home. He'd been gone before, but not for so long. Anyway, Jed convinced me to come into Meade with him."

"Well," the Marshal said, "I think it was a very wise choice, what with the weather and all. You sure you don't want some coffee?"

Anna smiled a weak smile and said no again. She felt the marshal was trying to find a gentle way to tell her some bad news. Suddenly she thought Henry may have been hurt or even killed, and her stomach did a flip-flop.

"Marshal," she said quietly, "If you know of my husband's whereabouts please tell me."

The marshal took a sip of his coffee. Then steadily looking Anna in the eyes he said, "This ain't gonna be easy, Mrs. Pierson. I know who your husband is." Anna was relieved to hear the marshal speak as if Henry wasn't dead. "In fact," the marshal continued, "Your husband is known by quite a few people here in town. I'm afraid he's not very popular."

Anna was surprised, she had thought that the last few months, Henry had been a little full of himself but---

The marshal went on, "About a week or more ago, Mr. Pierson was gambling in one of the saloons. As I got the story, he and some others had been playing cards all day and he had been losing. Anyway, he accused one of the players of cheating. There was gunfire and your husband shot and killed a man."

Anna sat stunned. She knew Henry had done a lot of practicing with his hand guns, trying to see how fast he could draw, but she never dreamed he would kill someone. Her throat felt very dry. "Could I please have a drink of water?" she asked the marshal in a quiet voice.

The marshal went over to the table that held a bucket of water, and with the dipper, he poured her a cup. Taking it over to her, he went on, "I couldn't prove who drew first. Mr. Pierson had been hanging out with a couple toughs that had come into town about three weeks ago. The three of them had caused a bit of trouble here and there. The two hombres that your man had hooked up with swore that it had been a fair fight, and no one stepped forward to say any different. So I told Mr. Pierson and his buddies that it might be best if they moved on. They pulled out the next day. I'm not sure where they were headed, but they looked to be going north towards Dodge or Kansas City. Well," the marshal said, rising from his chair, "I'm afraid that's all I have to tell you. I'm sorry that I couldn't be of more help."

He came around to where Anna was seated and she realized that he meant that their meeting was over. She rose from the chair and extended her small hand out to the marshal. She hoped he didn't notice that it was shaking a bit. "Thank you, at least I know more than I did, even if I'm not sure what to do about it. It appears my husband is now a different man than the one I married."

The marshal patted her hand saying, "Well, if you don't mind some advice from an old man, I think you should stay where you are. Mary seems pleased to have your help, and Jed thinks you'll do just fine. You never know, your husband may figure he's headed for trouble and come on home with his tail between his legs."

Anna thanked him again. As she was going for the door, the marshal spoke up again, "If I hear anything more I'll let you know, and if there's anything else I can do for you just let me know. I've always had a soft spot for a helpless woman. But you don't strike me as one of those women folk that faint at the drop of the hat."

"No," Anna smiled back at him, "I guess none of us knows what they can handle until they're tested." She stepped out into the cold air, pulling her shawl tighter around her frail shoulders and crossed the muddy street to the hotel.

Taking the stairway in the lobby, Anna went straight to her room. There was some time before she was needed in the kitchen. She sat on the bed, and it suddenly sank in. She was now truly on her own, and tears began to spill down her cheeks.

CHAPTER EIGHT

After a while Anna pulled herself together and made the decision to follow the marshal's advice. She would stay in Meade, at least until spring. If Henry didn't return by then, she would have to find a way to earn money to return to her parent's home. Asking her folks for the money would be a last resort. Anna knew it would be a hardship for them. It surprised her that the thought of returning home to her parents and forgetting about Henry didn't seem like such a hard decision at all. Feeling a little better, she washed her tear stained face and went downstairs to go to work.

After the first few days of working in the kitchen, work began to fall into a routine. Get up early to get breakfast out; bake pies or whatever Cookie ordered; take a break; then start getting dinner ready. After helping to clean the kitchen, Anna spent the evenings in her room.

It had been a month since she had come to the hotel and Anna wasn't one to just sit around. She began to wonder if there was some other work that she could be doing in the evenings. Maybe, she thought, I could ask Mary if she could think of anything. Once again she went down to Mary's office.

As she went through the saloon area, she spent a little more time looking around. In the evenings the place was packed with loud cowboys. Mary's five girls were smiling and flirting with the jovial men. The fifth girl, the one Anna had seen the day she had gone to the marshal's office, was leading one smiling cowboy up the stairs to the second floor. Anna couldn't imagine how these women could do what they did for a living.

When she and Henry had married, she knew a wife was to give herself to her husband. The honeymoon had been an unpleasant experience for her. Before the wedding, her mother had told her that it was a wife's duty to be available for her husband whenever he wished and it was something that a wife must endure without complaint. She wondered why these women would willingly put themselves though that.

As she watched the girls, Anna noticed that the gowns they were wearing were somewhat shabby. An idea popped into her head. She would ask Mary if she could sew some new clothes for them. Excitement grew as she knocked on the office door.

Obeying the usual shouted order to come in, Anna entered. Mary looked up from her always present pile of papers and ledgers. "Well Anna, how are ya doing? I'm sure hearing a lot of good things about the food. How's it going with old Cookie?"

"Things are just fine," replied Anna. "Lee and Susie are such great help and Cookie seems to be content, at least for now."

"So what brings you here?" asked Mary.

"I guess you know I went to see the marshal awhile back. He told me that my husband had left town. Well, actually the marshal said that he told Henry and a couple of his friends to leave town."

"Yes, the day we had pie and you told me your last name, I knew what Sam had to tell you. Mickey knew those two men that your man left with and he says they're bad news."

"I know," Anna replied, "that's why I'm here. I need to earn some money. I've decided if Henry doesn't return by spring, I'll go back home to my parents. Anyway, in the evenings I have all this time on my hands and I was wondering if you had any other work I could do?" Not waiting for Mary's reply, Anna went on, "I noticed your girls could probably use some new dresses. I'm a pretty good seamstress. Do you think we could work something out?"

"Well aren't you a caution," Mary said. "Why, is there anything you *can't* do? It sounds like a grand idea to me. I've noticed that their outfits are a little worse for wear too. Maybe it's all that taking off and putting on that does it." Mary laughed lustily at her joke.

"You mean I can really do it?" cried an excited Anna, "I could meet with each girl and we could decide what they want. You could tell me how much you want to pay. I'll work cheap, as I'll be slow, what with sewing by hand and all. My sewing machine is still back at my cabin. Maybe when the weather gets better I can borrow a horse and wagon and go bring it into town. I would be able to work much faster then."

"Slow down girl," laughed Mary, "It seems like a good plan. Don't you worry, I'll talk to the girls and let you know how we can arrange things. We may have to ask Zeke, down at the general store, to special order material. I don't think he carries the sorta stuff my girl's wear. Why maybe you could even make something for me. I'll pay you good, and if your sewing is as good as your apple pie, we're in business."

Anna was so pleased, she could hardly believe it. Now she could save a little money, and sewing was one of her favorite things to do. She thanked Mary, then asked, "What are your girls' names, anyway?"

"Well," answered Mary, "There's Ellie, she's kinda tiny with blonde hair; then Julie, that's the redhead; Ruby has brown hair; Gracie, she has the same eyes and hair as you, in fact you two could be sisters, and last but not the least there's Madeline, she's the prettiest. Her hair is real black."

"I'll try to remember who's who," replied Anna.

"Oh don't worry about that. I'll have to figure when the girls can come to your room. They really aren't allowed on the hotel side. Some folks are real tight laces, when it comes to soiled doves. I'll let you know what I come up with."

Anna left Mary's office with a better feeling about her future. When she walked back through the saloon, she gave even more attention to the girls, trying to match them up with the descriptions that Mary had given her. The girl called Madeline, was nowhere to be seen.

To Anna's surprise, Mary appeared in the kitchen the following morning after the breakfast rush. "Well it's gonna work out fine," Mary announced as she got herself a cup of coffee. "The girls are all excited about new clothes. Well maybe not Madeline. She's pining away over her no-account cowboy. All these girls are sure some Prince Charming will come and take them away to a new life. It does happen sometimes, of course. I was one of their type. Then Mickey came along and we fell in love. Anyway, we came out here to Meade to start a new life, but Mickey is a rare breed. Most men respect women, no matter what they are. But they don't take a soiled dove home to meet their Mamma. Each girl will come to room nine when they have some time. Susie will let you know when, and which girl is there. Zeke gave me a sorta catalog of fancy materials. I told him to let you have anything you need and charge it to me. So you're all set. You'll find Zeke very helpful. The girls will decide who goes first. Well, I gotta get back to work. I sure hope you ain't biting off more than you can chew. It seems like a heap of work to me." Without waiting for Anna to answer, Mary set her cup down and raced out the kitchen door.

After doing her work, Anna walked to the general store for a tape measure, paper, and pencil.

When she went in, she introduced herself, telling Zeke that she was going to do some sewing for Mary.

"Yes, yes," he said. "Mary was here this morning. She's very excited over the new dresses, so let's get started."

"I really don't need much today. I'm not sure when I'll start the dresses, but I need a few things to begin with."

"That's okay," replied Zeke. "A body's gotta start someplace don't they? You just come in when you need anything. I'll make out a bill for you to sign and give it to Mary and that's all there will be to it. Mary is one of my favorite people and she's always been a good customer."

Anna was pleased as she left the store with her things. Zeke was a jolly fellow with a hearty laugh, which he burst into often. His wife, Hester, was equally jolly and they made the store a pleasant place to visit.

That night as Anna was relaxing, there was a knock at her door. When she opened it, there stood Susie, pretty and serene looking as usual. She always amazed Anna with her quiet calmness. "Missy Anna," she said almost in a whisper, "Missy Ellie say to tell you, she be in room nine in little while." You come with me now please."

Anna gathered the things she had gotten at the general store and the two women walked the short distance down the hallway to room nine. Anna noticed the number was more askew than before. They entered and Anna placed the paper, pencil and tape on a table. Susie had lit the lamps and there was a fire in the small stove.

"What is Ellie like?" Anna asked Susie.

"She good girl," answered Susie. "She maybe want marry someday and have baby."

"That's what Mary told me," replied Anna. "She told me that all her girls want to marry and leave this work."

Hmmm… Anna mused, *I'm married and things aren't so wonderful.*

CHAPTER NINE

After Susie left, Anna didn't have to wait long before there was a light tap on the door. "Come in." The door opened and a small slender blonde entered. She smiled shyly, behaving as if she was in the presence of someone above her station in life. Anna reached out and took the girl's small hand in hers. "You must be Ellie?"

"Yes," answered Ellie in a quiet voice.

"Well, I hope we can work together to fix you up with a new dress you'll like. Do you have any idea what you want?"

"Oh I don't know," Ellie said. "I guess something blue, I always liked blue."

"Yes," replied Anna, "It must be blue, because of those big blue eyes of yours." Anna was looking over the gown Ellie had on and could see how it could be improved upon. She took a piece of paper in hand and drew a simple sketch for Ellie.

Ellie watched with great interest. After a bit she remarked, "That's mighty pretty, can you really make that for me?"

"Oh sure, it won't be so hard but first I have to take some measurements. You can look at the samples of material that Zeke gave me and pick something out. I'll order it and after it arrives it won't take too long for me to finish sewing your dress."

As Anna began to take the measurements she needed, she noticed a lot of scarring on Ellie's arms. Without thinking she asked, "Ellie how did you get all these scars?"

Ellie folded her arms tightly about herself in a feeble attempt to cover the unsightly marks. "Oh, ah... once I lived with a couple, after my ma and pa died, anyways, the wife she always beat me with a belt that had a big buckle on it. So I put my arms out, and she beat me so bad that buckle cut right into my skin. She always thought I was after her husband, but t'was the other way around. He was always gittin' me in some place and having his way with me. Finally I just up and run away."

"That's awful!" exclaimed Anna. "How old were you? Where did you go?"

Ellie looked thoughtful for a few seconds, then said, "I think I were about fifteen year old. I just hid out in town for a couple days. Then one night, a man told me if I would be nice to him he would give me some money. So that's how I come to this life. Mary saw me one night when another man was making up to me. She said I might as well come to the hotel where I would at least be safe."

"That's a sad story," Anna replied, shaking her head.

"Oh it's not so bad," answered Ellie. "We have nice warm rooms and food. Mary never lets anybody treat us bad. Why, if'n some cow-poke does something bad, Spook takes care of him."

"Spook?" questioned Anna. "Who's that?"

"Oh, Spook is always around somewhere in the saloon," answered Ellie. "Mostly he hangs out behind the bar or in the storeroom. He helps Mickey. I guess you ain't never seen him yet. He's called Spook because his eyes are so pale blue, that they's almost white. It's down-right scary, anyways that's why he's called Spook. He kinda stays out of sight, but everybody knows better than to cross him. He's a real big, tough fella, but he's real nice to us girls."

While they had been talking, Anna had decided something. "You know what? You seemed embarrassed about those scars, and you're a real pretty girl. I'm going to put long sleeves on your dress, if that's alright with you?"

Ellie smiled from ear to ear. "Why I never thought of such a thing, that would be real nice. Thank you so much for being so kind to me, but if'n you're done, I better be gittin' back to work."

After Ellie left, Anna was determined to make a perfect dress for her. *She deserves it*, thought Anna. Thinking of all that the young girl had related to her, Anna couldn't help but wonder how Ellie could be satisfied with the life she was living. It seemed so unfair. This sweet girl's childhood had been stolen from her. She doesn't even realize she could do better.

CHAPTER TEN

The next morning after Anna finished working in the kitchen, she started for the general store. She wanted to order the material for Ellie's dress. Zeke told her that he would do the best he could to hurry the order along. On the way back to the hotel, she ran into Marshal Sam. They smiled at one another, then Sam's smile faded, "I was just on my way to see you," he said, with a serious tone in his voice.

"Oh, have you heard something?"

"Well, I'm not rightly sure it means anything," he answered. "I just got a wire about three men that robbed a bank in the town of Fowler. It's a little to the northeast of here. I'm afraid the description of the men is awful close to your husband and his friends. I'm real sorry to have to tell you this," he continued, "If it's what it seems, you need to be careful should your husband show up. They're wanted men now. A man was shot and killed. So they mightn't be too particular what they do next."

Anna felt shocked and a little sick. "I can't believe Henry would do such a thing. If he did, he has really changed from the man I married." In her heart, she knew that the marshal would not have bothered to tell her if he didn't think that Henry was involved.

The Marshal touched the brim of his hat saying, "You just be careful. If you need me for anything you know where I am."

Anna continued on to the hotel, her mind in turmoil. What if Henry did return, she wondered? Would she come right out and ask him? No, she would be able to tell the truth just by the way he behaved. She had a very uneasy feeling now. She wasn't even sure that she wanted him to come back.

Cookie's health was improving every day and Anna could see that he was eager to be the master of his kitchen again. She toyed with the idea of spending less time in the kitchen and more time sewing, and not just for the girls, maybe for others in town too.

About the time Ellie's dress material arrived, Cookie announced that he was going to start making the biscuits again, and that he never rightly cared for pie making. So Anna continued working in the kitchen on busy days. She still made the pies but there was less and less for her to do now that Cookie was so improved. She couldn't believe how fast his arm had healed. He was really a tough old bird she thought, smiling to herself.

At the end of the day, Anna was hot and tired. The evening meal time had been especially busy. Spring was on its way and the first trail drive of the season was passing by Meade on the way to Dodge. The herd had been bedded outside of town, while the cowboys took time off for supplies and fun in town. Anna decided she would like to have a relaxing bath. She had asked Susie to prepare one for her. Gathering up some clean clothes, she headed down the hallway.

As Anna reached the door to room nine, she saw that the number had fallen completely over, so that it now looked like a six. She shook her head and went on in.

Susie was busy preparing things and she looked up as Anna entered, "Missy Anna, when I go you put chair under door handle, it still not fixed."

"Thank you," said Anna, "I sure don't want any company while I bathe." Susie started to leave, and turning to Anna said, "Maybe I be back after a while. I will knock on door."

Anna had really come to enjoy this luxury. As she undressed she glanced at herself in the mirror on the commode. She saw a different person than when she had first come to the hotel. Her hair and skin looked much healthier and she had gained some weight. She lingered in the warm bath for quite some time then decided she should get out. She was drying herself off when she heard a light knock on the door. Thinking it was Susie, she wrapped a towel about herself, walked over and removed the chair that held the door closed.

Anna had turned away, as she heard the door open and then close. "Well now," said a man's deep voice. "What have we here? This is really fine."

Anna froze in her tracks. She turned, clutching the skimpy towel tightly about her with both hands. "What are you doing here?" She demanded.

"Why little lady you know what I'm doing here," he answered in a slightly slurred voice. "Only, I never expected to find such a treat. Why just look at you. You're prettier than a speckled pup under a red wagon."

Anna stood there, confused for a moment, then she said to the rugged, but good looking cowboy, "I'm afraid you've made a mistake."

"Naw, I don't think so," he answered, smiling widely as his eyes appraised the startled Anna. "I was told to go to room six and here I am. Nobody told me heaven was waitin' here."

"But this isn't room six," Anna started to say. She seemed to lose her power of speech as the cowboy reached out with one hand and brushed a tendril of wet hair from her face. Then he gently ran his finger down the side of her cheek. He continued downward stroking her neck with his somewhat rough thumb.

Suddenly, Anna became aware of a tingling sensation of pleasure from his touch. He put his other hand on her bare shoulder. Anna let go of the towel with one hand to fend him off. In doing so, the towel slipped down a little. The look of delight on the cowboy's face was frightening to her and yet she was drawn to him as his eyes held hers. With his free hand he gently removed the rest of her grip on the towel and it fell in a heap at her feet.

As Anna stood there, completely naked in front of this stranger, she couldn't understand what was happening. She had never felt so alive or drawn to anyone before. She knew that she should scream and Spook would come and throw this cowboy out, but she felt immobile. He touched her bare waist with his rough hands and then she knew she didn't want to be rescued from the pleasure that she was experiencing. He stepped closer and Anna was fascinated *and* frightened. He gently kissed her on the neck and moaned softly as he breathed in the cleanliness of her. Anna all but fell into his arms, weak as a kitten. She clung to him as he caressed her body. She knew it was wrong but couldn't bring herself to try and stop him.

Now she understood why the men sought out Mary's girls. They must be driven by the same need she felt with this stranger. She could feel the need with her whole body. The cowboy gently maneuvered her to the bed and laid her down. Anna was so eager, she could hardly wait for him to remove his clothing. She reached a hand toward him.

"Easy now girl," he said. "I don't have much time but I want to enjoy this as long as I can. I have to be back to the herd soon but I'm sure gonna be looking you up when we come back through town."

He lay down beside her, their naked bodies touching, his hands exploring her body. She couldn't control her desire as she eagerly pressed herself against him. Soon he was atop her. Anna had never felt such pleasure before. They rocked in mutual need and excitement.

Suddenly Anna heard a catch in his breath as he finished what he had come for. At the same instant her body reacted and she softly cried out. It left her amazed, she had never dreamed that being with a man could be like this. Then, as soon as it was over, the slightly drunken cowboy turned onto his back and was softly snoring.

Anna suddenly became aware of what had taken place. She was a married woman that had just been bedded by a total stranger. She carefully got up from the sleeping man. Putting the chair back, to hold the door closed, she quickly but quietly bathed in the now cold bath water. Then, after dressing, she cautiously peeked into the hallway. Seeing no one about, she hurried to her room. Closing the door behind her she leaned against it, almost in shock at what she had just done. Maybe no one will ever find out, she thought. She still couldn't believe how she had lost all control.

As she thought back she realized she couldn't have stopped herself, even if the building had been on fire. She still felt aroused just thinking about what had occurred. A feeling of deep shame came over her. Anna had been attending church on Sundays. Now she had broken one of the Commandments. She had committed adultery. These unhappy thoughts filled her mind as she got into bed and finally drifted off to a troubled and guilt ridden sleep.

CHAPTER ELEVEN

The next morning Anna felt much rested. She had never felt so female before. The spring morning seemed brighter and sweeter to her. But then she recalled the cowboy saying how he was going to look her up when they came back through Meade after selling the herd. She had to leave the hotel now. He would see her and everyone would know what had happened.

As she was leaving her room, she saw Lee working to fasten the number back in place for room nine. The door was partially open and she could see Susie cleaning. "I see, Mary finally remembered to tell you about that," she said to him.

Susie came to the doorway saying, "I come to clean tub after your bath and find cowboy asleep here. I have Spook throw him out. Man say he in room six and want to see girl again, to thank her."

Anna felt her face grow warm, "Oh," she lied. "I guess I didn't shut the door when I left. I wonder what he meant?"

"I no know," Susie answered, "Anyway, he said he had to leave."

"Well, I'd better get to work," said Anna, and she hurried away. *At least the cowboy's left town. I hope Susie didn't see through my story. Now I'm telling lies to everyone*, she thought bitterly. Anna knew the time to leave Meade had come. Spring had arrived, Henry had not shown up, and Cookie really didn't need her anymore. The time had come for her to return back to St. Lewis and her folks.

She decided that after the breakfast rush, she would tell Mary that she planned on wiring her folks for money to help pay her way home. She would tell her that she was sorry to be leaving but the time had come to go back home, and try to forget about her husband. Of course, she would finish Ellie's dress before leaving. Having made the decision, she felt a little better.

After the morning rush and clean-up, Anna made the pies. She then left the kitchen, taking a small plate of food and a cup of coffee out to the nearly empty dining area. As she was sitting there deep in thought someone spoke.

"Well, look at you, you look like a different girl." Anna looked up to see Jed. She was glad to see him, but had the uneasy feeling that everyone could see her guilt.

"Anna," Jed said. "How about I sit with you?"

"Of course," Anna replied. "You look different too, all duded up in your town clothes."

Jed smiled at her saying, "I was just sitting here dawdling over my coffee. I just got back to Meade a few days ago. I spent some time in Kansas City, with my sister. While there I ordered some windows and other things to take out to the cabin I'm building and they finally arrived here. So I'm on my way back out to my place on the Crooked River. I was hoping I'd run into you. I've been wondering how things were going for you."

He sat down across the table from her, and she realized once again how comfortable she always felt in his company. Smiling at him she answered his question, "Things are fine, well maybe not so good. Cookie is healed enough that he really doesn't need me, and my husband hasn't shown up. I don't want to do it, but I've decided to wire my folks for some money to help pay for my trip back home. I can't stay here in the hotel if I can't earn my keep."

Jed's heart sank. He'd deliberately hung around in town because he wanted to see her again. "I'm sorry to hear that things are going so bad."

"Yes," Anna continued, "I was just getting to like it here. I still bake the pies and was going to do some dress making but…" Anna's voice trailed off as she stared at her plate of food. She sat there thinking that she really was going to miss the people she had come to know in Meade. *If only I hadn't done such a stupid thing last night,* she thought, *I wouldn't have to leave.*

"You know…" Jed said, interrupting Anna's thoughts, "I know a place you could stay at here in town. Well, at least near town. You wouldn't have to pay anything, and maybe with your pie making and sewing you could save enough money to buy the ticket yourself and it would give your husband more time to show up."

"I'm not sure I want him to show up anymore," she said quietly. "Marshal Sam thinks that he may have helped rob a bank and a man was killed."

"Hmmm, maybe it's all a mistake, anyway if you want to stay a little longer, it can be done."

"But how?" asked Anna?"

"Well, this place is empty. Susie and Lee look after it and when I'm in town I have a room in the barn. I'm leaving today to get back to my place in the valley, but if you want to look at it, I'll tell Susie and Lee. You can have Susie walk you there to see it, if you want."

"Oh, I don't know," replied Anna.

"Well, you think about it. I think you'd like the place and it would relieve Susie from having to dust it." Rising from his chair, he took Anna's hand and urged her to at least go have a look at the place, telling her that she would need nothing and Lee would keep her in wood or whatever else she might need. "Why if you decide to stay there, you could go out to your place and get anything that you would like to bring back to town. We left in quite a rush, you know?"

"You make it all sound so easy," said Anna, "But then your advice to come into town last winter turned out okay. Maybe I *will* ask Susie to take me there."

"Good," replied Jed. "You won't be sorry and if you want to go out to your place for anything, just go down to the livery and tell Gabby that you need a horse and wagon. I'll tell him to keep a look-out for you."

"How can I ever thank you for all that you do for me?" Anna asked.

"Aw," Jed answered, almost shyly. "It's just that you remind me of someone." He hoped she wouldn't guess at his real reason for wanting her to stay in town.

They said goodbye. Watching as Jed left, she thought, *Maybe he lost a daughter and that's what he meant about her reminding him of someone.* Anna still thought of Jed as a much older man. He still had the beard and long hair, although it was a little neater.

CHAPTER TWELVE

She finished her meal then went off to find Susie. She wanted to see what Susie thought of Jed's offer.

Anna found Susie putting some towels away in a storeroom. As she passed room nine, the happenings of the night before came to her mind, giving her pleasure and guilt at the same time. She shoved the thoughts from her mind. "You sure do work hard," she said to Susie.

"It not so hard," answered Susie. "I work much more at railroad camp and the men were mean."

Anna told Susie about Jed's idea. Susie smiled, "I think it good idea, I think you like house. It would help me too."

"Well then," said Anna "When would you be able to show the house to me?"

Susie frowned, "I no can do today. I give you key, you find it easy."

"Are you sure that's all right?" asked Anna.

"Sure," Susie answered. "House be empty long time, it be good thing to have you there."

Hearing Susie's approval, Anna made up her mind to at least go look at the place, so she took the key from Susie. It was really nice to be out in the spring weather thought Anna, as she started up the street. Susie had told her which way to head out of town. She told her that it wasn't too far a walk and what the house looked like. Anna walked along enjoying the fresh air. The trees and grasses were starting to green up and birds were flitting about singing. She'd almost forgotten how much she enjoyed the out of doors in the springtime.

She needed to walk about a half mile along the tree lined road. When she reached the edge of town, she noticed a kind of mid-sized, black and white, shaggy dog, with ever alert ears following her. At first she was alarmed. The dog followed closer and closer. Anna stopped and spoke to it. The dog stopped too, wagging its tail. Anna figured she had attracted him because she probably smelled like the food from the hotel kitchen. She walked over and patted the dog on his scraggly head. He waged his tail wildly. "So you want to be my friend?" Anna said to him. As she continued on, the dog walked happily beside her. Soon she saw the picket fence and the house that Susie had described to her.

The fence was in need of repair and surrounded an overgrown front yard. Anna could see that it had been cared for at one time. There was a big maple tree shading the front porch that ran across the front of the house. The place had a homey look about it, even though it was empty and a little neglected. Anna went through the gate. The dog sat on the outside of the fence, with its head cocked to one side. "Oh all right," she said. "You might as well come along too." When she held the gate open for the dog, he pranced in like he was on top of the world. He was sniffing here and there, at a half run with his tail held high and wagging.

As Anna started up the steps, the dog jumped in front of her, preventing her from moving forward. At first she was annoyed, but then the dog leapt forward to a sunny spot on the porch. To her amazement, he grabbed up a large snake in his mouth. He shook it violently, then tossed the limp body into the air and out into the yard. Anna didn't know if the snake had been a poisonous one or not, she hadn't seen it, and was glad that the dog had. Then and there, she decided if the dog belonged to no one and she was going to stay at the house, the dog was moving in with her. "You're a good dog," she cooed, as she patted his head. He looked at her with great brown eyes that just seemed to be filled with love and devotion. "How would you like to be my dog?" The dog answered with a happy bark. "Let's go see what the place looks like," she said, as she unlocked the glass paneled front door.

"You wait here boy," she told the dog and he lay down on the porch. Anna walked into the cool interior of a large front parlor. There were draped windows on each side of the front door. She opened them to admit more light. The room was completely furnished. There appeared to be an overstuffed sofa, some side chairs, and tables. Everything was covered with sheets. She noticed a fireplace and to Anna's delight, a piano. Her mother had taught her to play some simple tunes, when she was young; it seemed so long ago now.

Off to one side of the fireplace, was an archway to the dining room. Anna couldn't believe what she was seeing. It was as if whoever lived in the house had up and left without taking a thing with them. The mystery grew as she explored further. On the opposite side of the fireplace was a set of stairs leading to the second floor. Beside the stairway was a locked door that Susie had explained was not to be entered.

Anna went up the stairs to a landing that had doors to two comfortably furnished bedrooms. She found the same situation as in all the other rooms. Everything anyone would need was there. She could see that Susie had kept things neat and dusted. Anna could also see she could be very comfortable here. She even figured that one of the bedrooms would be great for sewing, as it had good light from two windows. She happily floated down the stairs as she went to explore the kitchen. She already knew that she was going to take the house, but she sure was going to ask Susie about what had happened to the owners.

In the kitchen she found a large sunny room. There was a big table with four chairs. The kitchen had a lot of cupboards and counter space and even contained a pump at the sink. There was a pantry that had some canned goods; a few staples; pots; pan; and all the utensils a person would ever need to run a household. On one side of the kitchen there was a door that opened into a small room that contained a bathtub. The room had a dressing table with a bench and shelves of clean linens and towels. She became more and more puzzled. Anna opened the door to the back porch. The dog came bounding around the corner of the house to greet her. There she found wash tubs sitting on a stand and a mop bucket. There was a scrub-board, mop and broom hanging on the wall.

Out in the back yard, she saw what had once been a garden. There was an outhouse, a woodshed, a water pump, and a barn. See could see a large amount of fenced pasture too. Anna spoke to the dog again, "I can't figure why this place is just sitting empty like this; but if it's okay with whoever owns it, I guess I'll move in. What do you say boy? Wanna move here with me?" Locking the doors behind her, Anna went back out into the street heading back to the hotel, the dog prancing along beside her.

As she neared the hotel, she became a little tense. Had the cowboy really left town? What if he saw her, would he recognize her? Well, she would just have to cross that bridge when and if she came to it.

CHAPTER THIRTEEN

Anna patted her new found friend on the head. They were at the back door of the hotel kitchen. "You wait here," she told him and went into the empty kitchen. Finding some scraps of food, she took them out to the dog. He was obediently waiting just where she had left him and was eager for the food.

Anna was feeding him when Cookie came out the door. "What are you doing feeding that mangy cure?" he shouted.

"He's a nice dog," replied Anna. "Do you know who owns him?"

"No," answered Cookie. "I seen him around. I think he stays down at the livery stable. I don't want no dog hanging around my kitchen, begging for food."

"I don't think you have to worry about that," Anna said. "I think he'll be moving soon." Anna went back into the kitchen to see if Susie had arrived for work. She found her peeling potatoes. Anna put on an apron and began to help.

"Susie," Anna asked, "Who owns that house? It's so nice but it's strange how everything's in place. It's as if they just suddenly up and left."

Susie looked at her in surprise. "Mr. Jed no tell you?"

"Tell me what?"

"It Mr. Jed's house," answered Susie.

"What?" asked a shocked Anna. "No, he never said a word about it being his house. If it's his house, why does he live in the barn?"

"Oh," Susie replied quietly. "Mr. Jed very unhappy long time after wife and baby die."

"Wife and baby?" repeated Anna.

"Yes," Susie answered. "When baby come they both die, Mr. Jed no want to live in house. It make his heart hurt."

"Oh my," Anna said. "I wonder why he didn't tell me."

Susie shrugged, saying, "Mr. Jed no like talk about it much to people. If he say you stay in house, it okay."

"Well, I don't know," Anna said. "It seems kinda strange, but I do need to move."

"I know," Susie said, giving Anna a sideways glance.

She knows what happened, thought a panicky Anna. No one realized that Susie always went quietly about her business seeing all that took place in the hotel. She was very good at judging people and she liked Anna. She would keep Anna's secret as she did all the other secrets, locked away in her memory.

Dinner was busy but not as bad as when a herd was being driven by. After clean up, Anna gathered up all her courage and went into the saloon to find Mary. She found her talking to the girl called Madeline. Mary seemed quite upset with her. As she neared them, Anna heard Mary telling the girl that she needed to stop pining for that no account cowboy and pay more attention to the customers. Madeline gave Mary an icy stare and stomped off, but not before Anna noticed a brooch pinned to her dress. *Her brooch*, the one Henry had taken. She suddenly knew the man Madeline was pining for, as Mary had put it, was Henry. Anna stood there staring after the beautiful girl. Mary spoke to her twice before Anna heard her.

"My, aren't we deep in thought?" asked Mary.

"I'm sorry," replied Anna. "I need to talk to you. Can we go into your office?"

"Sure little one, come on." And she hurried across the noisy, smoky room towards the office door. As usual Mary took a seat behind her cluttered desk. After she got settled she asked, "So what's on your mind? You seem so serious."

"Well," Anna started with hesitancy. *This isn't going to be easy*, she thought; Mary had been so kind to her.

"Out with it girl, I don't have all day," said the ever impatient Mary.

"Well," Anna repeated, "I think I'm ready to move on." Once she started, the words poured out. "Cookie is pretty healed up and I think he would really like to have things back the way they were before he got hurt but I can keep on making the pies 'cause he don't like to. I have a place to stay and I would have more time to sew. Of course I'd expect to be paid something, not much you understand but--"

"Whoa, girl!" Mary said holding her hands up in the air. "I've been expecting this; you don't belong working in the kitchen, you're too much of a lady. I figured as soon as Cookie was healed you would be moving on. You've been a great help and I'll surely miss you of course.

Don't you worry about payment for any sewing you do. I consider myself a fair person. So where are you going to stay?"

"Oh, Jed offered me his house. I didn't know it was his until a little while ago. Susie told me. I don't know why he didn't tell me that he owned the place. He just said he knew of a house I could stay in. Susie said he didn't like to talk about it."

"Sure and that's the truth," said Mary. "It was a tragic thing that happened. It hit Jed hard. He worshiped the ground that Louise walked on and he really looked forward to that baby being born. Anyways, Louise died having the poor little thing and then it died too. Jed moved out of the house and took to the hills. Mostly he just comes to town in the winter. But I'll tell you what," Mary continued, "He seems to have come out of his shell a little and I'm thinking you have something to do with it."

"Me?" declared Anna. "Why, I've hardly passed the time of day with him. I've only seen him a couple times."

"Yes, I know," Mary answered with a knowing smile, "But it seems every time he sees you he wants to look out for you."

"Well, I guess it does seem that way, but he's just a real gentleman that would come to any girl's rescue," replied a surprised Anna.

"That may be true," said Mary, "But I'm thinking he would like to be a lot more than just friends with you, if you weren't married, that is."

Anna gave Mary a look of disbelief. "I don't think that's true, why, he's been nothing but a perfect gentleman. I don't know where you got such an idea."

Mary chuckled, "I get my ideas from watching people. The way he looks at you it don't take a genius to figure things out. By the way, what are you gonna do about that husband of yours?"

"I really don't know," Anna answered. "Before Jed offered me his house, I was ready to wire my folks for some money to help pay for my way back home. I guess you know, the marshal thinks Henry and the other two that he's with robbed a bank, and killed a man."

"Yes." Mary said, "It seems you picked a rotten apple."

Anna smiled a weak smile. "Jed said I should wait a little longer and so did the marshal, but I have a feeling he had no doubt that Henry took part in the robbery."

Anna almost felt like crying, especially when Mary got up from her desk and came around to put an arm about her shoulders to comfort her. "Well," Mary said, "Maybe it would be best to wait a little while longer."

At that point, Anna got up the courage to ask Mary about Madeline and the cowboy she was mooning over.

Mary gave her a sympathetic smile, and confirmed her suspicions. She went on to say how Henry had always favored Madeline. Madeline believed that he loved her and that he was going to marry her one day. "I'm sure she has no idea that he is already married, or that you're his wife," she stated.

Anna was a little surprised at how she accepted news. Instead of feeling hurt or upset, she almost felt glad to hear the truth. She suddenly realized that she had stopped caring for Henry and now she wasn't sure that she ever had.

Mary, being the wise old gal she was, patted her on the back saying, "It don't seem like you're losing a whole lot to me. Why any man that would choose Madeline over you is a big fool."

"Thanks," Anna said. "I think I figured that out myself. You have been such a good friend." She gave Mary a big hug, well, as big as she could, considering her girth.

"Okay, go on with ya now," said Mary. "You just let me know when you're leaving and we'll work out the sewing stuff."

"I think I'll leave when I finish working in the morning," Anna replied.

"Okay then, I'll tell Cookie you're leaving and we will make arrangements for the pie making too. You go along now."

CHAPTER FOURTEEN

Anna left the office feeling better about things. She would move the next day, after making the pies for Cookie. As she went out through the bar, Mickey yelled hello to her and Fingers struck up *"Oh Susanna."* She smiled at them, thinking, *I'm really going to miss this place.* Just then she saw Madeline. *You two deserve each other,* she said to herself. *But somehow I've got to get my brooch back.* The next morning Cookie was actually in a good mood. Anna didn't know if it was because she was leaving or he had appreciated her help when he needed it. It made the morning more pleasant, not having him do his usual cussing and stomping about.

Susie told her how they would miss having her about adding that Lee would be doing chores at Jed's place and promised she would visit her when she could.

The morning went by quickly. When her work was finished, Anna packed her meager belongings and was on her way. After saying her goodbyes, she left the hotel for her new home.

She started up the street, with a feeling of joy over her newfound freedom. To her surprise the dog fell in beside her, as if he belonged there. "I guess you're ready to move too," she said to him. "Tomorrow we'll have to go to the livery stable and find out if you belong to anybody." They reached the house in short order. As Anna started up the steps, she noticed how the dog had gone protectively ahead of her. She liked that.

She entered the house, and putting her things down, went around the parlor; opening the drapes and windows. Anna liked the house even more than when she had first seen it. She went in the kitchen to see what she might need to buy for food. She knew she would have to be careful, as she didn't have a whole lot of money.

Finally, she took her things up to the bedroom she had chosen to sleep in. She flopped full out on the bed, finding it very comfortable. She lay there a few minutes, then jumping up, ran down the stairs and out the back door to explore the place a little more. When she opened the door, she found the dog lying on the back porch. He jumped up to greet her. Deciding to make a bed for him, they walked together out to the barn, to look for some feed sacks.

While in the barn, she couldn't resist the urge to peek at the room Jed had said he stayed in. She was surprised at how nice it was. It had everything he would need to be comfortable. She also noted how Jed kept the place neat and tidy. Feeling like an intruder, she closed the door to the room, and taking some feed sacks, went back outside.

After fixing the dog his bed, they walked around the house and yard together. Noting the warm early spring weather, Anna commented to the dog that she might start a garden. Working in the garden was about all she missed about her and Henry's place.

Anna and the dog spent quite a lot of time out in the warm spring air. On a whim, she decided they would walk to the livery stable. She wanted to keep the dog but needed to find if he had an owner before she got too attached to him.

Locking things up, she and the dog started back to town. When they reached the livery no one seemed to be about. Anna walked through the huge barn, where a couple of horses were contentedly munching on hay. The place smelled wonderful to her. The sweet smell of hay and horses reminded her of her father's barn. She felt a tinge of homesickness and vowed to write her folks soon. That was something that she had neglected to do for some time.

The sound of voices coming from the other end of the barn broke into her thoughts. She walked on until she reached a big outer doorway. Two men were there. One was a huge black man that was shoeing a horse. He had bulging muscles and glistened with sweat. The other was a skinny, bald man wearing overalls. He looked about forty years old. He was talking a blue streak. Jed had described them to Anna. She knew the one shoeing the horse was Buck and the other was Gabby.

As she approached the two, the black man stopped working and stared in her direction. Gabby stopped talking as he followed the black man's gaze. "Ma'am," questioned Gabby, "What can I do for you?"

"Hello. I'm Anna Pierson. I'm staying at Jed Hawkins place."

"Oh ya," Gabby said. "Jed told me about you. Said I was to let you have a horse and wagon, should ya need 'em."

"That was nice of him but that's not why I'm here."

"Oh!" exclaimed Gabby with a suspicious tone in his voice. It was clear that he didn't have a lot of trust in women folk. Jed had mentioned this to Anna.

"No," Anna replied, "I came to see if you know who owns this dog." The dog had stood quietly at her side, keeping a wary eye on Gabby.

"Who owns that dog?" Gabby half shouted. "Why nobody, but he thinks I do 'cause when a herd went through here last year, somehow he got a hurt leg and took to hanging around the barn. Ol' Buck here, he ups and starts feeding him," Gabby continued on. "Now ma'am, mind you, I like animals but this here dog thinks he should go out in the pasture and herd my customer's horses whenever he feels like having some fun and I can't have that. I'm always running him off but he just shows up again."

When Gabby stopped to catch his breath, Anna said, "Then it would be alright if he stayed with me?"

"Alright?" answered Gabby. "Hells fire girl, I'd consider it a downright favor, if you'll excuse the language, ma'am?"

Anna smiled, and reaching out, shook Gabby's hand, "Thank you," she gushed.

"Jumpin-gee-hoseafat girl! You'd think I gave you a gold piece or something."

The big black man put down his tools and walked over to where Anna stood with the dog. Bending down to one knee, he ruffled the neck of the now tail wagging dog, saying, "He's good boy ma'am. I'll be happy knowin' he has a good loving home."

"I know he's a good dog," Anna declared. "Why, he already saved me from a snake and I really like him."

Gabby made a *humph* sound and spit a string of brown tobacco juice into the forge embers, "I say good riddance."

Buck and Anna smiled at each other and the dog wagged its tail as if he knew what was going on. Anna thanked the men, then left. She felt like skipping out of the barn. When they reached the street, she stopped and bent over the dog. "We'll have to give you a name." With a serious look, she studied him. He stared lovingly at her with his great brown eyes. "Let's see," she said, "I think I'll call you Tag, that suits you fine. Come along, Tag." They headed up the dusty street.

Anna stopped at the general store, telling Tag to stay. As she went in, Zeke looked past her at the waiting dog, saying, "Looks like you got yourself a new friend. Old Gabby's been complaining about him for months."

"Well, he's my dog now. I think he's going to be a great friend."

"That's fine," said Zeke. "At least I won't have to listen to Gabby complain about him anymore, but knowing him, he'll find some other burr under his skin. So what can I do for you today, little lady?"

"Well," Anna answered, "I need a couple cans of beans, some sugar, flour, and coffee."

"I hear you're staying at Jed's place," Zeke said, as he began to gather up the things Anna wanted. "That's good, it's a shame to see the place sit empty."

"How did you know about my staying there?" asked Anna.

"Oh, not much goes on in this town that everybody doesn't know about," he replied.

Anna frowned, saying, "It must have been a bad time for Jed."

"Yes, yes," said Zeke, shaking his old head. "It really hit Jed hard. I never seen a man so broken up. But he seems to be coming out of it some."

"It makes me feel a little strange, staying there, but Mary and Susie think it's okay. Maybe after a little time I'll feel better about it. I couldn't stay at the hotel forever, especially since Cookie's healed up and doesn't need my help anymore."

"I'm sure you'll do just fine out there." Zeke said, handing her a package. "Here's the things you wanted."

"Oh, I hope so," she replied. "I really like the place."

Anna went on out the door and Tag jumped up, ready to follow along. They stopped at the hotel to see if there were any scraps of food for Tag. Susie had promised to try and save some for him. She had kept her word, having a big pile of steak bones and other goodies for the dog. The walk back to the house was pleasant. Tag kept sniffing the wonderful smells coming from the kitchen scraps. Anna hurried along, now she could give her new dog his dinner in his new home. Finding some bowls in the pantry, she filled them with food and water, taking them out to the porch to a jubilant Tag. Anna went into the kitchen to make herself something to eat. Taking a bowl of beans out to the back porch, she sat there eating with Tag. Watching the scruffy dog eating, she decided in the morning she would find something to brush out his tangled hair. Anna knew he would be just beautiful.

CHAPTER FIFTEEN

Things were working out fine. Mary had sent a boy, named High-pockets, with supplies for the pies Anna was to make. There was a note, saying that unless she heard otherwise she needed only to make six pies every other day. If she needed anything, she was to send a note back with the boy when he came to pick the pies up. The note also said that Susie would bring the next girl to have a dress made. Anna had finished Ellie's dress and it looked great on her. The other girls were all eager to have their own new dresses.

Anna had sent a note back to Mary, saying that Susie could bring the girls anytime. So the days went pleasantly by. She and Tag worked in the yard in the mornings, after she'd finished any baking that needed done. She had found some work gloves to wear. She didn't want her hands to get rough while she was working with the delicate fabrics for the dresses. Tag stayed by her side as she worked to clean the yard and start a small vegetable garden. Much to her delight, Tag kept rabbits and other small critters out of the yard.

One morning, as Anna was working in the yard, a woman in a small cart stopped at the front gate. "Hello!" she shouted, "I heard Jed had somebody staying here." The woman got down from the cart and walked around to where Anna was working. Her arms were loaded with parcels. She kept a steady stream of chatter going. She intro-duced herself as Sarah Covington. She told Anna that she and her husband had a small farm outside town and they sold butter, milk, and eggs to people in town. Sarah went on to say that they had a passel of young'ns - eight in all. "Oh, I heard your name is Anna. Is that right? I see ya got Gabby's dog." Before Anna could answer, Sarah was talking again, saying how nice it was to see someone caring for the place again. "It always looked nice when Jed was here."

"Yes," Anna replied. "I could tell that."

"Well," continued Sarah, "I thought maybe I'd give you a welcome with some eggs, butter, and milk."

"That sounds wonderful!" exclaimed Anna, "But I must pay you something."

Handing the things to Anna, Sarah exclaimed, "Oh no, not this time. If you want to buy something in the future, just flag me down. I go to town every other morning."

"Would you like to come in for a cup of coffee and pie?" Anna asked.

"Why that would be something," said Sarah. "I guess I could spare a few minutes."

As they went to the kitchen, Anna noticed how shabby Sarah's clothes were. She looked like a hard working woman.

She had her graying hair in a bun. Her faded dress hung on her wiry frame. The muslin apron she had on was badly stained. As they sat with their pie and coffee, Sarah jabbered on about her family, saying that the boy that did the deliveries for the hotel was her oldest son. As Anna listened, she could see the resemblance, same wiry build and hazel eyes. Sarah went on to say that they had named him High-pockets, because he was all legs. After a while she slowed down in her constant chatter to eat her pie. Then she said, "I heard you were making the pies for the hotel and you sew for people."

"Yes," Anna answered. "I've been thinking, that if you wanted, I could sew something for you, in exchange for your eggs and things."

"Why tarnation!" said a somewhat excited Sarah. "Wouldn't that be great? I can't sew a lick, anyways with all the work, I ain't got time."

"Well then," Anna replied, "The next time you have a little time, you stop and we'll figure a fair deal."

"You betcha," answered Sarah, giving Anna a broad, somewhat toothless smile. Then she got up to be on her way. "Thanks for the pie, you do a mighty fine job. I'll see you in a day or so." Anna walked out with her and waved goodbye. Tag had lain quietly in the yard, before Sarah's arrival and while she was leaving. Anna wondered if he was going to be a very good watch dog, after all. In time, she would find that Tag knew which people were good and who were a threat.

A couple of weeks had gone by since Anna had moved into the house. She was having a bit of trouble keeping up with the sewing. Sarah and Anna had worked out their deal and Susie had brought the ample bosomed Julie to be measured for the gown that she wanted.

One evening, as Anna and Tag sat on the back porch, she said to the dog, "You know boy, I think I need to go out to my old place and get my sewing machine and maybe a few other things." The thought of going after her things made her a little excited. She seldom even thought of Henry and had pushed the night with the amorous, but somewhat drunken, cowboy from her mind.

In the morning, she packed some buttered bread and hard boiled eggs and walked to the livery with the ever present Tag beside her. She found the two men in the barn. Gabby was shouting at Buck again. *Evidently*, she thought, *Gabby has found a new problem to devil him.*

"Dag nabbit, Buck," he was yelling. "Ya know I don't want ya feeding those barn cats. Them there cats need to be hungry for mice and such." Just then he spied Anna and Tag. "Oh no," he cried, "You ain't bringing that dang dog back are ya?"

"No," Anna replied. "He's a great dog. I'm here to see about that horse and wagon.

"Well, I'm glad to hear you and the mutt are hitting off so good. Sure, we can fix you up. I've got a smaller buckboard you can take and a nice calm, gentle mare for ya. Jed said to give ya whatever ya needed."

"Well, I should pay you something." Anna said.

"Oh no," replied Gabby. "Why girl, don't ya know Jed owns this here livery stable?"

"No," said Anna. "I didn't know that."

"Well, he does. He's my boss so I just do what he says."

"In that case, I'll take what you offer. I expect to be gone overnight."

"That could be a problem," said Gabby. "Jed said somebody should go with you."

"Oh, I don't think that's necessary," Anna protested.

"Hells fire, girl!" Gabby half shouted. "You can't be goin' off overnight by yourself. Somebody needs to go with you."

"It will be fine," said Anna, "Besides I've got Tag, "

"Humph! Why that's a big relief," Gabby grouched. "You just be careful, I don't want Jed gittin' upset with me over some darn fool girl's hard head."

Buck and Gabby hooked the wagon up, making sure Anna knew how to harness and unharness the horse. Gabby put some grain in the wagon for the horse.

As Anna stood scratching the somewhat swayback, gray horse's forelock, Gabby said, "She's some long in the tooth, but you'll find her a mighty fine old horse."

"Thanks," Anna said, as she put her food under the wagon seat and climbed aboard. With Bucks help they had gotten Tag to jump up into the back of the wagon and were on their way.

CHAPTER SIXTEEN

Jed sat inside the cabin that he'd been building for the last two years. When his wife and baby had died, he just wanted to be by himself. He had come across this piece of land one time when he had been out hunting. After looking over the fertile little valley, he had decided to buy it. There was a fair size pond on it and the Crooked River ran through it. So it was that when he had left town to be alone, he had come to his valley and started a cabin.

Now the cabin was nearly finished, and to his surprise he missed the company of people. But more than anything he missed Anna. He had spent endless hours thinking of her. Remembering that she was a married woman upset him. His sensible side felt hopeless, but his heart felt different. He had known from the first time he saw Anna, that there was something that drew him to her. As time went by he knew he had fallen in love with her, and wanted to have her for his own.

The facts seemed insurmountable, but he dreamed about the possibility of again having a woman to love. Finally, he decided he would go back into town and at least keep track of Anna's situation. So Jed closed the cabin up and loaded the mule and pack horse up for the trip. He had killed a deer and packed a good deal of meat to take into town with him.

Henry and his friends had been hiding out at Henry's place. They had indeed robbed a bank. Jack, the trigger happy lowlife, had shot one of the tellers when he had failed to move quickly enough for him.

Henry had been upset about it, but he didn't say anything. He'd grown a little afraid of Jack. Jack had cruel dark eyes, long black hair and a handlebar mustache. He wore a pair of pistols tied at his thighs. He was fast on the draw and short on temper.

The three didn't get much money for their efforts because Dan, the third member of the group, had argued that they needed to hurry. He was afraid that the gunshot would bring the law down on them. At first Jack started to disagree with Dan but he soon saw things Dan's way and they rode out of town.

Henry couldn't figure how Dan got away with telling Jack what to do but he always seemed to be able to talk some sense into Jack's somewhat blood thirsty brain. Dan was short, with scraggly looking, dirty blonde hair. He had a whiney voice that got on Henry's nerves. In fact, everything about his new companions was beginning to get on Henry's nerves. He was having thoughts about alienating himself from them. They had been holed up in the now messy cabin that Anna had somehow managed to have kept so clean.

Jack was always out shooting at something and Dan was always complaining about anything and everything. They had been living on venison and coffee for weeks and all three of them were ready to move on.

They were sitting outside and had decided to rob another bank in a town to the south. This time they vowed to do a better job of things. Having made the decision, their mood picked up and they were celebrating with a couple bottles of whiskey. Each going on at great lengths about what they were going to do with their share of the money they would get.

Henry had read Anna's note when they had first arrived at the cabin. The other two men thought he should go into town and drag her back where she belonged. They further stated that no wife is allowed to just up and leave her husband. Henry had a hard time convincing them it wouldn't be a very good idea, especially since they were now wanted men and the marshal knew them all by sight.

The half-drunk men sat outside talking of the upcoming bank robbery and how they could then sneak into Meade and bring Anna back to cook for them while they stayed in what they now considered their hideout. One of the horses in the pole corral lifted its head and whinnied. The other two stared off toward the road to the cabin. Henry, following their gaze, said in an urgent tone, "I think we got company coming. Let's get inside." The three men scurried inside, and crowded at the window.

Just before the turn-off to the cabin, Tag ran to the front of the wagon bed. He put his front paws on the back of the seat, letting out a low, menacing growl. Anna stopped the wagon and Tag immediately jumped down. He walked forward, his hackles up. Anna had come to put a great deal of trust in the dog's senses, so she got down too. Tying the horse to a bush, she walked forward with caution. Getting behind some trees she looked across the valley towards the cabin, catching sight of the three men hurrying to get inside. Anna could make out Henry's horse. "Well Tag, it's too late to turn around and head back to town. Besides they know someone is coming. If I don't go down there, they might come after us. I've got to face him one day, this might as well be the day." Anna was pretty sure that Henry wouldn't let any harm come to her.

Not wanting to take the wagon down to the cabin for fear they might decide to steal it, she decided to hide it and the horse. That way it would give her a way to get away if she had to. Leading the old horse some ways off into the woods where it couldn't be seen, she unhitched her, tethering her near a small trickle of water. Giving the horse some grain, Anna went back to the road. With a small branch from a bush, she brushed away what signs of the wagon that she could.

Anna had no idea what Henry would expect of her. Would he want her to stay at the cabin or go on a trail of crime with him? Recalling what the marshal had said about being careful, she wasn't sure if she should continue on. *Of course*, she thought, *they know someone is coming so they might come looking.* Tag at her side, they continued on to the cabin. Anna hoped that they would believe she had walked all the way from town.

CHAPTER SEVENTEEN

Anna didn't need to act tired - she was tired. As the men stood looking out the small window, Henry exclaimed, "Well I'll be, it's Anna!"

"That's your wife?" asked Jack. "She's not bad looking."

Dan asked, "Do you think she walked all the way from town? That's a fair piece."

"Well, I don't doubt she did," Henry replied, "She's a strong willed gal. I wonder where she got the dog?" They all watched with interest as Anna and Tag slowly approached. She was in no hurry to rejoin her long gone husband.

Thinking things over, Anna decided she would go on the defensive. She had seen that most men were not comfortable with a woman's wrath. When she reached the cabin she sat down on a block of wood as if to rest. The three men came out the cabin door. Henry led the way, Jack and Dan sauntering behind him. Jack was busy giving Anna the once over. Dan, on the other hand, seemed a little shy.

Because the two men had been telling how he should put his wife in her place, Henry stood with his legs apart, hands on hips. "Where have you been?" he demanded sharply. "I get home and all I find is a note. A woman should stay home and be there for her husband."

The very idea that he had the nerve to speak to her in that way after leaving her in such a fix, let alone that he had been carrying on with Madeline, Anna felt a rage she didn't know she was capable of. She thought, *If I had a gun I could cheerfully shoot him.* "How dare you talk to me like that? You left without food for me or the mules. The snow killed Eve and the wolves ate her. You stole what money I had, along with the brooch my mother gave me. A storm was coming so Adam and I lit out for town. I had to sell him so I'd have something to live on. I got a job as a cook, not that it's any concern of yours. And I know you and your so called friends have been breaking the law and are wanted for bank robbery."

"Now you just hold on!" shouted Jack. "You don't know anything about us."

"Oh yes I do." Anna said with a glare, raising her voice another notch.

"Hey Henry," snapped Jack, "You're the boss; you'd better shut this woman up and make her behave like a good little wife should."

"Now Anna," Henry said, "You just calm down. We'll talk about this later." Tag had been standing beside Anna, ears back, the hair on his hackles raised. When Henry stepped towards Anna, he let out a low growl, from deep within his throat.

Jack spoke up again, "You better keep a handle on that unfriendly mutt or he might end up pushing up daisies." Then he let out an unnerving laugh, which sent chills up Anna's spine.

She stood her ground. Glaring at the cruel Jack, she said with pure hatred, "You better not touch him or you'll be sorry."

Jack laughed at her. Dan could see it was time to calm the half-drunk killer. "Never mind," he said to Jack, "We got bigger fish to fry. Let these two talk over their problems. Let's go have another drink."

Anna was relieved to see the two leave. She was thinking she should've turned the wagon back to town when she first saw the three men at the cabin. In fact, she was feeling a little weak in the knees. Henry stood, a look of confusion on his face.

"Anna, I'm not sure I want to be around these two, but I'm not going to live like we did anymore. In the morning we're going to get some money. Then I'll come back for you and we can leave here for a new start."

Anna stared at him, "You don't need to worry about me. I no longer care if you come back, I know about you and Madeline too." Henry's mouth fell open as Anna continued, "I can take care of myself now." It was clear that he was taken aback by her new found independence and the fact she knew about Madeline.

He recovered, saying, in a gruff tone, "You're still my wife, and you'll do as I say. When we get back, I'm parting with these two and you'll go where I go. Now get on inside."

It was clear to Anna that Henry's pride was wounded. He didn't really want her but he didn't want Anna to be the one to end things.

Tag was still showing signs of protecting her. Anna didn't want him to get hurt so she patted him on the head telling him to go lay down. She followed Henry into the cabin. The messy condition of the cabin and the foul air from whiskey, cigarette smoke, and unclean men almost sickened her. She looked around at the dirty dishes with remnants of fried venison and the unmade sleeping mats on the floor.

Jack saw Anna's look of disgust and said, "Maybe this woman of yours could clean this dump up?"

Anna glared at him, "It looks like pigs live here."

Jack started to rise from the table where he and Dan had been drinking, "Sit down," Dan firmly ordered. "Have another drink. Henry will see that she takes care of things."

"Sure, why not?" Jack answered. "We got to take it easy and rest up for tomorrow." Jack was getting very drunk by now.

Anna was grateful to have an excuse to keep busy. She worked straightening things up, hoping to stall long enough for the men to drink themselves into a stupor. She worried about Tag and the old horse. Anna built a fire to heat some water and was pleased to see that the warmth in the tiny room was causing the men to grow drowsy. Jack was even resting his head on the table. Dan succeeded in getting him over to his sleeping mat and then lay down also.

Only Henry was still awake, his eyes following her every move. Finally he said, "Anna I think it's time we went to bed too."

Anna felt panicky, she didn't want to go to bed with him but there was no way to avoid it. "I suppose," she said, walking reluctantly to the bed. Making no attempt to undress, she lay down, pulling the old quilt about herself.

"What's this?" hissed an angry Henry.

"I'm not undressing with those two animals in here," replied Anna. "If you had any honor left at all, you wouldn't ask me to." She knew that she had touched a nerve. Henry had always considered himself a gentleman.

"Well," he replied. "I'm not so sure that's your reason or if maybe you're planning on running out on me again. I just think I'll see that you don't go wandering off." With that statement, he found a piece of rawhide and bound their wrists together. Actually, Henry was relieved Anna had remained clothed. He didn't know what he would do if Jack thought there was a partially undressed woman so near. One of the things Jack talked about constantly was women. Unlike himself, he knew Jack had not a shred of honor or morals.

CHAPTER EIGHTEEN

Anna had gotten little sleep. Once or twice, when Henry was snoring, she thought of trying to escape but knew hooking the wagon up in the dark would be near impossible. There was no moon and that would make it hard to even find the wagon before Henry discovered her missing. Anna had finally drifted off, when she was awakened by Dan going outside. Henry woke up too and untied the rawhide that had bound him to her. The bindings had left Anna's wrist red and tender. When Dan came back inside, Anna was making coffee and Henry was putting his boots on. Henry started outside, and she went with him. When they returned, Dan was waking Jack. There was a lot of grumbling but after they had cigarettes and coffee, their mood became a little better.

Anna found enough makings for biscuits and gravy to go with their venison. The three ate heartily and talked about how they should get started. To Anna, time was standing still. She began to think they would never leave. After cleaning things up, she started to take some food scraps out to Tag.

As she reached the door, Jack asked loudly of Henry, "Where's she think she's going?"

"I'm going to feed my dog," Anna answered for Henry.

"Oh yeah?" snarled Jack. "Maybe you just want to walk back to town and set the marshal on us?"

"That's not a bad idea," she replied, giving him a dirty look. "But then I'd have a husband in prison, I don't think I want that." She went on out the door looking for Tag. He was sitting under a scrubby bush at the edge of the clearing that surrounded the cabin. His tail wagged wildly when he saw her. "Good boy," she said, placing the food in front of him. Tag was hungry. She wished there was more for him. "We're in a lot of trouble boy," she said to the dog as she stroked his head. "You just stay out of sight, and when those lowlifes leave we'll hightail it for town and the Marshal's office." Anna hoped he understood, but knew better. With a heavy heart Anna started back to the cabin. Stopping inside the doorway, she saw the three men were still sitting at the table. Her heart sank. They seemed in no hurry to leave.

Suddenly feeling she was going to be sick to her stomach, she stood a little unsteadily just inside the doorway.

Jack spoke up. "We told Henry we better take you along just in case you decided to take off for the marshal."

"I already told you--" she started to say. The bile was rapidly rising within her throat. Anna half stumbled out the door just making the corner of the cabin before everything came up in a violent rush. She was standing there with one hand on the cabin wall and the other holding her skirt aside, when the three men came rushing out of the door.

"Well, we thought you were trying to make a run for it but I guess that's not your trouble," said Jack.

"What's wrong?" asked a concerned Henry.

"I don't know," answered Anna, after she had recovered herself. "Maybe it's something I ate or I'm coming down with something."

"I ain't traveling with no sick person!" declared a nervous looking Dan. "God knows what she might give us."

While her stomach had calmed down, she still felt weak and clammy. Thinking these three weren't too bright, she glared at them. "You don't even have a horse for me."

"That's right." Jack replied. "She can't ride with me and what if we have to make a run for it?"

"Don't you worry," replied Anna, as she took Henry's arm in hers. "I'm not going anywhere, besides Henry and I have plans." Jack and Dan looked at each other, it was clear they didn't like the sound of that. It was decided Anna would stay at the cabin.

After what seemed forever, the three men rode off. Anna stood in the doorway watching until they were out of sight wanting to make sure that they were really gone. It was getting close to noon as she gathered the things she wanted, stacking them outside the cabin. Tag came running to her side. "I'm glad you stayed away while those men were here, now let's go get the wagon." They walked up the road to where she'd left the old horse and wagon. Anna was afraid of what she might find, but the old mare looked as if she hadn't moved all night.

Quickly harnessing the horse to the wagon, she drove down to load the things chosen to take to town. While loading them she managed to feed and water the horse. She decided to take the sewing machine, her china, a few odds and ends, and some clothing left behind when she had left with Jed. Anna also took the rifle. She was glad Henry hadn't thought to look in her hiding place. Taking a few moments, she wiped off the oil she'd put on it to keep it from rusting in the damp cabin. In the back of her mind was the thought, *If Henry and his friends decide to come after me I'll put up a fight.* She knew it would be foolish but worth a try. Finally everything was ready. This time she left no note. Closing the door behind her, she drove the wagon from the yard. There was a great relief and a sense of joy to be leaving this place of disappointment.

CHAPTER NINETEEN

After driving about an hour or so the high spirits she had started out with were giving way to fatigue. *I must be so tired from no sleep and being around those men.* Looking about, Anna realized she was near the place where Jed had made a camp, when she had gone into Meade with him. Thinking it would be good to rest, she guided the horse and wagon off the road and into the clearing. It appeared much different, without the snow covering everything. It was quite large, making it easy for her to maneuver the horse and wagon. New grass covered the area and Anna tied the horse with a long rope, allowing her to graze to her content. Tag sat with her as she leaned back against one of the big boulders that partially ringed the clearing.

Jed had been on the trail for about an hour, when he noticed his horse turn its ears forward, detecting something ahead. Not knowing what he might run into, he led the packhorse and his mount off the road for a small distance. He became aware of the sound of hoof beats. Taking pistol in hand, Jed edged closer to the road, staying concealed behind some trees. Three riders approached. Jed studied them as they rode on by. He didn't know any of them but they looked to be pretty hard cases to him. Remaining concealed until they had passed, he mounted up and continued towards town.

Anna had no idea how long she'd slept, when Tag woke her with eager whining. Grabbing the rifle in one hand and Tag's collar in the other, she scurried behind one of the huge boulders. Tag lunged towards the clearing, causing Anna to lose her grip on him.

Jed appeared, gun in hand. When he saw Tag he bent down to pet him saying, "What are you doing way out here boy, did Gabby chase you off?" Looking about he saw the buckboard and the old horse. "Come on out with your hands up," he shouted. "This is my wagon and my mare."

When she heard Jed's voice, Anna was beside herself with relief. "Do I really have to come out with my hands up?" she shouted.

"You bet," he answered when he recognized her voice. "I'm real hard on horse thieves."

When Anna came from behind the rocks the relief she felt at seeing him overcame her and she rushed forward, putting her arms around his waist. Jed had instantly put his free arm about her, and holstering the pistol, he encircled her with the other, pulling her tightly to him. With surprise, Anna realized his embrace was more than casual. Feeling she'd overreacted to seeing him, she released her hold on him. She looked up at him, feeling embarrassed and suddenly shy.

Jed was gazing back, with an undeniable look of something more than friendship. Anna knew Mary had been correct in guessing he was smitten with her. Both of them sensed something had happened between them. Each knew that their relationship had changed to something more than just friends. They became a little distant with one another. Neither was sure of what to say.

Finally Jed asked, "What are you doing out here by yourself?"

"Why, I came out to my old place to get a few of my things," she replied. Not mentioning anything that had taken place while she was there.

Jed shook his head saying, "I told Gabby he wasn't to let you come out here alone."

"Oh, he told me that, but I told him I'd be fine with Tag."

"Tag?" Jed questioned.

"Yup," she smiled. "He's my dog now."

"Well I'll be," said Jed. "So here we are again. We might as well have something to eat. I'll put the animals up and hang this deer meat someplace. Are you hungry?"

"I sure am, but I'm afraid I don't have any food."

"Well, I'll build a fire and we can make some coffee and roast some of this venison."

After they'd eaten they sat with their coffee. This time Anna had gotten out one of her china cups.

"That's a mighty pretty cup you have there."

"Yes," Anna replied. "My Mother gave me some china when I left home."

"So, you decided to get some of your things and stay in town?"

"Yes," she answered. "Why didn't you tell me that the house was yours?"

"Oh, I don't know. I guess I thought you might feel beholdin' to me and wouldn't want to stay there. You needed a place, and it's not good to leave a house empty for so long."

"I did almost change my mind when Susie told me, but I really like it there. I've been sewing for different people and I'm still making pies for the hotel. Anyway, that's why I came out here. I needed my sewing machine."

"You have a machine that sews?" asked Jed.

"Yes, when my folks got a newer machine for their shop, they gave me the old one but it works fine. I'll show you sometime if you want."

"I'd like to see something like that in action." Jed was so happy to be with Anna again it seemed he couldn't stop smiling. "How come you have that ol' stray dog?" he asked, as he scratched Tag behind his ears.

"Oh, Tag?" she answered, "We just became friends one day. He's a great dog. I asked Gabby if I could have him and he seemed real glad to be rid of him."

"Where did he get the name Tag?"

"Oh, I named him Tag because he just tagged along wherever I went."

Jed spoke to the dog. "I don't blame you for tagging along with such a pretty gal. It seems to me that you are a mighty smart dog." Anna quickly looked away as she felt her face blush with pleasure. No one had called her pretty for a long time. "Say Tag," Jed said, "What ya say to spending the night?" Tag cocked his head as if he understood and ran to Anna, wagging his tail. "What do you say?" he asked Anna. "Are you ready to camp out again?" Jed didn't want this time with her to end.

Thinking it was late in the day and how tired she had felt, she said, "Why not, it's a beautiful night, not like the last time with the snow and all."

Jed set about making a place for them to sleep. He had gotten his bed roll and Anna got the quilts she'd wrapped some of her things in.

They sat by the fire talking. He looked at her saying, "You know Anna, it wasn't a very good idea for you to come out here alone. While I was on the road coming here, I saw three pretty rough looking fellows."

"Oh," questioned Anna, "What'd they look like?"

"Well, one sorta looked like a dude. He was on a bay horse. The others looked like real hard cases, especially one of them. He had long, dark hair, and a handlebar mustache. I'd hate to think of what would have happened if they ran into you all alone."

After sitting in silence for a bit, she said in a quiet voice, "I did see them."

"What?" asked a startled Jed. "What do you mean? Why if I'd known that---"

Anna spoke up before he could go on. "Jed, the one you said looked like a dude was my husband, Henry."

"What happened?" Jed started to ask, then saying, "I guess it's really none of my business but--"

"That's okay," Anna interrupted him again. "Everyone in town knows about Henry. He and those other two robbed a bank in a town called Fowler. The one with dark hair shot and killed a teller. When I got to the cabin, they were there. They'd been hiding out there and now are on their way to rob another bank. Henry told me I had to stay there and wait for them to come back then he and I would go back east."

For a second Jed worried that Anna was going to high-tail it with Henry, then he said, "But you didn't stay there."

"No," she answered. "I'm not going to stay with a bank robber. I'm going to go straight to the marshal and tell him about them."

Jed's heart soared, he tried to look concerned. He was concerned for her safety but he realized that now there might be hope for him to court Anna.

Some time passed, and they decided it was time to turn in for the night. Anna was very tired and sleepy. Just having Jed there made her feel safe and relaxed.

Jed was far from sleepy. He hadn't been so happy for a long time. He remembered how it had felt when holding Anna close, even if it was only for a moment. He lay awake watching her sleep, wishing he was in Tag's place, snuggled up beside her.

Anna was thinking of the embrace too. The way Jed had pulled her to him left no doubt in her mind. He had wanted to continue holding her until... *Oh my, what should I do? I like Jed but... Now I'm living in his house. I don't want to hurt his feelings. He's such a nice old man. I wish we could just be friends. He makes me feel so safe and has helped me so much. When he looked at me in that way, I felt a little frightened. Why hadn't I felt like that with the cowboy? Why, had I been so drawn to him? Why can't I forget that night? I'm married. I must get these thoughts from my mind.* Anna drifted off with these troubling thoughts swirling about in her head.

Tag's growling and the sound of horses stomping and whinnying woke Jed. Picking up his rifle, he quietly walked towards the ruckus. Hearing the snarling of a cat, Jed knew at once what the trouble was.

A cougar was after the deer meat he'd hung in a tree. As he drew closer, he could just make Tag out in the early dawn light. The dog was in a standoff with one of the biggest cats Jed had ever seen. The reflection from the embers of the fire gleamed in its watchful eyes. Jed raised the rifle to shoot. With that movement the cat turned its attention to Jed. It was about to spring towards him when Tag leapt in to attack it. The dog was on the cougar before Jed could fire. The cat took a swipe with its huge deadly paw, sending a yelping Tag through the air. Blood streamed from one of his front shoulders. The big cat quickly turned its attention back to Jed. Switching its tail and growling, it was ready to spring upon him.

Tag's yelps woke Anna. She was terrified. The horses were making an awful fuss. There was another sound that sent chills up her spine, the snarling of the cat. Seeing Jed was not in his bed, she grabbed her rifle and headed towards the frightening sounds.

Jed had turned to glance at Tag, and catching his foot on something, he fell off balance, causing him to drop his rifle. Anna stopped in her tracks at the sight of the huge animal getting ready to spring upon Jed. Without thinking, she raised her rifle and shot. She only wounded the cat. The pain of the wound drew its attention away from Jed, giving him time to recover his rifle and take aim.

The cat became enraged, leaping towards Jed, just as he pulled the trigger. His shot hit the cougar in its massive chest. It fell upon Jed, knocking the wind from his lungs. It tore at his shoulder, taking his head in its mouth before it succumbed to the wounds. A bloody and hurt Tag lay whimpering off to one side.

Anna was shaking, but with strength, she didn't know she possessed, she managed to pull the heavy dead weight of the cat off the now quiet man. She couldn't tell where Jed had been hurt, as both he and the cat were covered with blood and dirt. Tears were streaming down her face. She was sure he was dead. When she said his name, he moaned softly.

"Oh Jed," she cried, "You're alive, can you get up?"

Jed moaned again, saying softly, "I think so."

"You just lay still, I'll get something to stop the bleeding. We'll get you into the wagon and head for town." She ran to the wagon. Taking some of her underskirts from the clothing she had packed, she bound up his wounds, trying to stop the bleeding. "You're losing a lot of blood, I'm going to bring the wagon over. We've got to get you to the doctor."

With shaking hands, Anna hooked the old mare up to the wagon. She knew one of the younger horses might be faster, but wasn't sure if they'd pulled a wagon before. She decided to turn the packhorse and Adam loose and hoped they would follow the wagon into town. Getting the wagon as close to Jed as possible, she urged him to try and stand. It was a struggle, but with Anna's help, he was able to get into the bed of the wagon. He was getting weaker by the minute. Anna had put some of their bedding down and then she covered the now unconscious Jed. Going to where Tag lay, she gently carried him to the wagon, placing him beside the now pale looking Jed.

She loosely tied Jed's saddle horse to the rear of the wagon in case she would need it. Everything else was left behind.

Anna urged the horse out to the roadway. The old mare was a little slow, or maybe it just seemed that way to Anna. The mare seemed to pick up on the urgency in Anna's voice and trotted faster than she had in a long time. The miles were being left behind, so was Adam and the packhorse but she couldn't worry about that. What mattered now was getting Jed to town. After what seemed like forever the outskirts of town were in sight. Anna urged the mare even more as they got closer. The wagon entered town in a cloud of dust. Stopping at the livery stable, Anna yelled for help.

Apparently the sound of panic in her voice was not lost to Gabby and Buck as they came running out to the wagon. It didn't take any time for them to see what the trouble was. Buck untied Jed's horse as Gabby jumped up, taking the reins from Anna, and headed for Doc's house.

Reaching the house, Gabby jumped down and raced inside. Several men had appeared around the buckboard. Doc came out and immediately ordered some of them to carry Jed inside.

"Mind you," he cautioned, "Be careful as you can."

Anna was relieved to hear Jed moan, as the men carried him into the doctor's office. Going to the back of the wagon where Tag lay, she sat shaking, too weak to move. After a few seconds she took a look at the blood covered dog. His shoulder had stopped bleeding and he lifted his head to lick Anna's hand.

A gray haired, middle aged woman in a clean white apron approached the wagon. "Anna," she said, "I'm Doc Stones wife, Nora. Doc would like you to come in and tell him what happened."

"Oh, of course." Anna replied. She patted Tag on his head, telling him to lay quiet.

Seeing the wounded dog, Nora said, "Don't worry, I'm sure Doc will take care of him too." When the two women started for the door the quiet crowd that had gathered parted to let them by.

CHAPTER TWENTY

Anna was comforted by the cool, clean interior of the doctor's office. Nora sat her down on a bench in the waiting room and went through a door to the doctor. She'd left the door ajar and Anna could see Jed on a table with a sheet over him. Bloody rags were strewn about the floor. Nora spoke to the doctor and he looked out at Anna, saying something back to her.

Nora came out to the waiting room, closing the door behind her. She told Anna, Doc would be busy for some time and wanted Anna to tell the details to her, then she could relay it to him as he worked on Jed. As she spoke, tears began to fall.

Taking Anna's hand, Nora asked, "Are you alright? Are you hurt?"

"No, no, I'm fine. I'm just so scared for Jed."

"Don't you worry so," Nora reassured her. "Jed is a strong young man. I'm sure he will be fine. Now, I must get back to help Doc. You just sit here while I help him then we'll see to you and your dog." Anna found herself wondering, *Why is she calling Jed a young man?*

Gabby came in the door, hat in hand, a worried look on his old face. He sat down beside Anna. "What happened?" he asked. Anna was touched by his obvious concern. She repeated the story again, telling how brave Tag had been.

"Well, I guess he's not such a bad dog after all," he said. They waited in silence for a long time. Gabby paced the floor while Anna kept repeating silent prayers.

After some time, the doctor came out of the room, drying his hands on a towel. "Hello, Gabby, and I guess you're Anna?"

"Yes," she answered. "How's Jed? Will he be all right?"

"I think he'll be just fine. He lost a lot of blood and I had to stitch up a lot of wounds. It all looked a lot worse than it was. Head wounds tend to bleed a lot. He's going to be real sore and weak for quite a while. The one thing we need to worry about is infection." Anna and Gabby both let out sighs of relief. Doc went on, "My wife tells me that there is another patient out in the wagon."

"Oh yes," said a grateful Anna, "It's my dog, Tag."

"Well, let's go have a look," Doc said, as he headed for the door.

When he opened the door, he was peppered with questions from the small crowd. He held his hands up to quiet them saying, "Jed's gonna be just fine, now I have a dog to look at."

The crowd kept asking questions. As Anna and Doc climbed into the wagon bed, Gabby held his hands up to silence them. With great authority and some embellishment, he told the story to all within ear-shot. Anna and Doc smiled at each other. Gabby was clearly enjoying his new found importance.

When Tag saw Anna, he gave a weak wag of his tail. "Well now," Doc said to him, "You look pretty good." Doc gently examined Tag's wounds saying, "He's not too bad off. Dogs are pretty tough animals. I'll have Gabby and someone take you home and get him settled. I'll come up later to clean his wounds and put something on them. He should be fine in a few days. I understand you're staying at Jed's house?"

"Yes," Anna answered. "Tag and I've been living there."

"Well, I think Jed should stay here tonight. In the morning I'd like to have him moved to his place, if he's up to it. He's gonna need some care for a while, do you think you could do that?"

"Of course," replied Anna.

"Well then," he said, turning to Gabby, "Could you and a couple of men take this girl home and help get things settled?"

"Why, sure Doc." Gabby answered, even prouder of his new found importance. He set about ordering a couple men into the wagon and they started for Jed's place. On the way Anna told Gabby about the things she had left behind at the campsite and that she was worried about Adam.

"Don't you worry about a thing," replied Gabby. "I'll take some men and take care of everything. I'll bring that cat back too."

When they got to the house the men carried Tag to his bed on the back porch and unloaded the things Anna had brought from the cab-in. Gabby took the wagon and old mare back to the livery.

Doc showed up shortly after with his little black bag. He gently cleaned Tag's wounds with disinfectant. Tag lay there patiently not making a sound. He seemed to know it was for his own good. "He's a pretty good fella," Doc said, "Just keep an eye on him for infection."

After Doc left, Anna still sat by Tag. She looked down at the blood and dirt covered clothing she had on. "Well boy, looks like I need to clean up some. I'll do it in a little while but first I think I'll lay down for a bit. You just rest here."

The morning sun shone on Anna's face. She opened her eyes and couldn't believe she'd slept all night. As she got up she felt a little nauseated again. She started downstairs to check on Tag. As she reached the bottom, she could smell fresh coffee. At once the nausea she had experienced the morning before returned. Anna couldn't believe it, nor could she stop it. Stumbling out the kitchen door she leaned against the house as the bile came up, leaving her weak. Just then, Nora drove Doc's buggy into the yard. Anna was mortified. Not only was she a dirty, bloody mess, she had thrown up in front of Nora.

"Doc sent me up to see how things were going with you," Nora said. "I saw you out here as I drove up the road. How are you two doing?"

"Oh, we're both fine. I'm a little sick to the stomach. I was just going to lie down for a few minutes yesterday and I slept all night in these messy clothes."

Nora stood there with a knowing smile on her plump face.

"I'm so embarrassed," said Anna. "It must be all that's been going on. I'll be fine once I get cleaned up."

"Oh you'll be fine," replied a still smiling Nora, "But I'm afraid it will be some time before you get over this."

"What do you mean?" questioned a puzzled Anna.

"Well dear, morning sickness lasts different amounts of time for different women, but it eventually goes away."

"Morning sickness?" cried a horrified Anna.

"Why, yes dear, I've seen enough expectant mothers to know morning sickness when I see it."

"But that can't be, why I...." Anna's voice trailed off. She sat down on the back steps with a thud, as what Nora had just said sunk in.

"Well, dear," Nora said, "If there's anything I can do you just let me know. Doc is coming by later to bring Jed home. I'll send some ginger tea with him. That and dry toast a'___s helped me."

Anna's head was spinning - she hadn't even heard what Nora was saying until she caught her last remark. With a sly smile and shaking her head, she was saying, "That Jed, he's a caution but he's a good man Anna."

"No wait," Anna started to say. She realized Nora thought Jed was the father. Anna was so confused she didn't know what to reply. Finally she asked, "How is Jed?"

"Oh, he is going to be just fine but it's going to take some time. I'm sure with good care he will be up and around in no time. Yesterday I asked Susie to open up Jed's bedroom. I hope she did it."

"Well," said Nora, patting Anna on the shoulder, "I've got to be getting back."

When Nora was gone, Anna sat there too stunned to move. Tag was wagging his tail and she looked over to see someone had brought him a plate of food. "Somebody thinks you're a brave dog." Patting him on the head, Anna said, "I'm sure in a real mess, Tag."

Anna went inside, closing the kitchen door behind her. Leaning against it because she felt a little weak in the knees, she lamented aloud to no one, "What in the world am I going to do? How could I have been so stupid? God must be punishing me for my sinful ways." She knew without a doubt, the night she had spent with the cowboy was when she became pregnant.

CHAPTER TWENTY ONE

Susie had prepared Jed's room. Seeing Nora leave, she walked the short distance to Anna's kitchen door. As Anna opened the door for her, she took in Anna's state and commented, "You not look so good Missy Anna. Mrs. Doc ask me to fix room for Mr. Jed. I made coffee for you too. If you want, I make a bath."

"Oh Susie, that would be wonderful. I'm *not* feeling very good."

"Missy Anna, you go get some clean clothes. I fix bath. When done put dirty things in water to soak. I take care when I get done at hotel."

After a bath that she only half remembered, Anna put the bloodied clothing into the bath water to soak. She no sooner got dressed when there was a knock at the front door. Thinking it was Doc with Jed she went towards it with dread. Anna knew she had to tell Jed about the baby and that Nora thought he was responsible for her condition.

Her stomach did a flip flop as she grew closer to the door. Much to her surprise it was Sarah Covington.

"Good morning Anna," she said in a cheerful voice. "My man and Highpockets went with Gabby to bring in the stuff you had to leave behind. They're gonna skin that cougar and bring the hide in too. They left real early this morning. My boy Highpockets was sure excited. That was quite a story Gabby told. Why you must be plum tuckered considering your condition."

"My condition?" Anna repeated.

"Why sure honey, I saw Nora a few minutes ago and she told me the news."

This is terrible, thought Anna. *Everyone in town will soon believe that I'm having Jed's baby. Why are they all so happy for me? How am I ever going to break the news to him, especially now when he is hurt?* Anna had been standing with the door open. Sarah had her arms full and didn't wait to be invited in as she bustled on by Anna. Sarah was still talking a mile a minute.

"I brung ya some fresh bread, eggs and butter. I figure since Jed is going to be laid up for a while he'd need some good vittles." Anna followed Sarah into the kitchen, her mind in a fog. "Do you have any coffee?" Sarah asked. "I brung us some cinnamon rolls too."

"There's some coffee. Susie made it but I haven't had any yet. It didn't set right with me this morning."

"Good." Sarah said, "I can't stay long. With Aaron, that's my husband, and Highpockets gone I have extra chores to do. There hasn't been this much excitement in town for some time." The two women sat down to eat the rolls Sarah had brought. They tasted wonderful to Anna. She was quite hungry but she hoped the food would stay down.

"So when is the little one due?" Sarah asked, between bites of roll.

Anna gave Sarah a blank stare. She thought, *This is too much. Don't these people have anything more to do than meddle?* Then she felt ashamed, Sarah had become a good friend. In fact everyone in Meade had treated her kindly. "I'm not sure." Anna said, as she thought back, trying to count the time that passed since Henry had left her. She thought it had been around the first of February; Jed had brought her into town a little after that. As she sat there figuring the weeks in her head, she noticed Sarah looking at her waiting for an answer. "Ah, I think sometime in December," she replied.

"Why, won't that be a grand Christmas present?" said an enthusiastic Sarah. "What do you want, a boy or a girl?" Sarah went on, as usual not waiting for an answer. She rattled on about what she liked about each.

Anna wasn't listening, her mind was in a whirl. People would be thinking Jed was the father. She knew Jed would know better and he would also know it wasn't Henry's child. Anna decided that her original plan to go back to her folks was all she could do. She would tell her folks that she didn't know where Henry was.

The thought of leaving made her sad. She had been so happy lately and what was she to do with Tag? Anna became aware of Sarah getting up to leave. "Oh!" she said. "I'm afraid I haven't been listening. I guess I'm just tired."

"Why sure you are," Sarah replied. "Nobody listens to me anyways." The two women stood. Sarah patted Anna on the stomach. "Say goodbye to that pretty figure. Junior here is going to take care of that. But they're worth it. Well, I gotta run. You just sit. I'll let myself out." Anna did just sit, staring off into space.

❧———❧

Around noon, Doc and Jed started out for Jed's place. Jed could walk but he was sore and weak. Doc held onto his good arm as they made their way out to Doc's waiting buggy. Jed was a different look-ing man. In order to clean and stitch all of the wounds, Doc needed to shave off Jed's beard and cut off a lot of his hair. Lee had gone to the general store and gotten some new clothing for him too. The two made it to the buggy and were on their way.

"How do you feel about staying in your house again?" Doc asked.

"Well," Jed answered, "I said that I never wanted to go back there. But you know Doc, when you think your life might be over you see things a little clearer. Why I'm just happy to be alive. I think if it hadn't been for Tag and Anna, I might not be here at all."

They were approaching the house. Jed hadn't seen it since Anna had moved in. "The place looks pretty good doesn't it Doc?"

"Yes, I've heard Anna keeps the yard up some and she even has a little garden going. She's quite a gal," Doc continued, "I think she'll make a good mother."

"What do you mean?" asked a stunned Jed.

"Oh, oh, I guess I let the cat out of the bag. Nora tells me Anna's in a family way." Jed couldn't speak. The buggy stopped and Doc helped the dazed man down.

Anna heard the buggy and looked out the parlor window. At first she didn't recognize Jed. He looked so different. She thought, *Why he's not as old as I thought.* Her heart was racing at the thought of having to tell him about the baby and what people were thinking. He'd been so kind to her and now--- Doc's knocking interrupted her thoughts.

As she walked toward the door her feet felt like lead. "Hello," said a smiling Doc when she opened the door. "I brought you your patient."

"Yes, I see," she said quietly. "He doesn't look the same."

"No," replied the Doctor. "I had to play barber to patch him up but it's Jed alright."

"Hello Anna," Jed said. "How are you?"

"Fine," she answered. They both felt a little awkward.

Doc looked rather confused at their somewhat formal greeting. "Well, let's get this man to bed."

"Oh yes," Anna replied. She and Jed had been standing, staring at one another. They crossed the parlor to the room Anna had never been in.

Doc said, "We had Susie come up last night and get things ready. I guess you were sound asleep."

"Yes, I was very tired."

"Well that's no wonder, you went through a lot." Turning to leave, he said, "I have to be going. See that Jed rests a lot. Oh, by the way how is the dog?"

"He's doing pretty good. He was walking around in the yard this morning and he doesn't seem to be hurting too much."

"Dogs are pretty tough alright," Doc said. He was still watching the couple with curiosity. They both seemed to be in deep thought as they stole furtive glances at one another then quickly looked away. *Well, who knows what goes on in the heads of these young people?* he thought to himself. "Oh by the way," he continued, reaching into his pocket. "Here's that ginger tea Nora promised you. I hope it helps, she knows a lot about that sorta thing."

"Thanks," Anna said, as she quickly took the package from him and shoved it in her apron pocket. She didn't know Jed already knew her condition.

"Well, I'll be saying goodbye. I'll be by in the morning to change the bandages. I'll see you two later." Anna walked Doc to the front door.

When she returned to Jed's room she found him lying on the bed. He had all his clothing on except for his boots. Doc had supplied him with some moccasin-like slippers which were on the floor. Anna couldn't believe how different he looked. She had always thought of him as being much older than herself. Now he looked to be only a couple years older. He even seemed kinda handsome.

She was very nervous, knowing she had to tell Jed about her condition. Stalling for time, she asked, "Can I get you anything? Would you like some water or something to eat?"

Jed opened his eyes and looked at her saying, "No, I can't believe how tired I am."

"Of course, you just rest." As she started to leave he called out Anna's name. "Yes?" she said, with a question in her voice.

"Oh never mind, maybe we could have a talk after I rest?"

"Of course," she said, eager to leave the room, glad to have a little more time before she had to tell him about the baby.

CHAPTER TWENTY TWO

Anna went to the kitchen for a cup of tea. Then she began to wash the clothing that had been left soaking in the tub. All of the blood stains wouldn't come out. After doing what she could, she took them out to hang on the line to dry. While she was working to clean the bedding that had covered Jed and Tag, Susie came into the back yard carrying a big cooking pot.

"Hello, Missy Anna," she said. "You should leave clothes for me. The men that go for Mr. Jed's things bring back deer meat too. Mr. Gabby take it to Cookie. He send this for you to eat."

"How nice," Anna replied. "It really smells good."

"Cookie say you not worry about pies he make them now."

"Oh I forgot about the pies." Anna said.

"It no matter, everybody so excited about cat. Mr. Gabby nail skin to livery wall. He say it biggest cat he ever saw. He say you hit it in ear and Mr. Jed hit in the middle."

"It's a wonder I hit it at all," Anna replied. "I was so scared."

"Missy Anna," Susie hesitated, "People say you and Mr. Jed make baby."

"I guess I'm going to have a baby, but it's not Mr. Jed's."

"I know," replied Susie. "Your husband gone and Mr. Jed too. I see you with cowboy one night."

Anna paled, asking, "You mean you saw us?"

"Yes," said Susie. "I come to clean room. I just leave, you no see me. I no tell."

"Susie," Anna said in desperation, "I don't know what came over me. I didn't even know that cowboy. He came in the room when I was taking my bath and somehow it just happened. I can't even explain it to myself. Now I'm going to have a baby. I'm so ashamed I just don't know what I'm going to do."

Susie gave Anna an understanding smile, saying, "Sometime we just need love, that's all."

Anna sat down on the porch steps and asked Susie to sit with her. It was such a relief to be able to talk to someone who knew the truth. "You seem so wise," she said. "I'm so upset and now I have to tell Jed that I'm having a baby and everyone thinks it's his. I guess I'll be leaving and going home to my folks."

"That good idea," Susie said. "You will love baby and your mother and father will too. But I not like to see you go."

"I don't see any other way." Anna replied, "It wouldn't be long before everyone figured out that the baby isn't Henry's or Jed's and that wouldn't be a good thing."

"No," answered Susie. "I sorry for your trouble but try not to worry so much. It be okay someday."

"Thanks for being such a good friend." Anna said, getting up and giving Susie a hug before she left.

Anna carried the still warm pot of food into the kitchen and was shocked to see Jed slowly walking into the room. "Should you be up?" she asked.

"Sure," Jed smiled. "I need to try and get my strength back and lay'in around in bed won't do it. What smells so good?"

"Oh, Susie just brought some of your deer meat. The men brought it back from where we were camped. Gabby gave it to Cookie to cook for you. I guess they skinned the cat and have it hanging on the livery stable wall. Susie said people think it was a pretty big cougar."

"Well it looked big to me," Jed replied. "But then I was pretty scared."

"Me too. Susie said that I hit it in the ear and you hit it in the middle."

Jed gave her a grateful look saying, "When you shot it that gave me a chance to recover my balance and get my shot off. I feel you saved my life and I want to thank you."

There was an awkward silence. Then Anna said, "I'm not so sure of that but you're welcome. Are you hungry yet?"

"I sure am. Let's see if that meat is as good as it smells." Anna busied herself getting some bread and butter on the table and coffee to go with the food. They ate in silence except when Jed commented on how good everything tasted.

After they had eaten, Anna started to rise to clear the table. As she reached for his plate Jed took hold of her hand. She was surprised at the pleasure his touch gave her. In a serious tone he asked her to sit back down. She sat again, afraid of what he might have on his mind. "Anna," he started, "Doc tells me that you are going to have a baby."

"Oh no!" she exclaimed. "I meant to tell you before you heard about it. I'm so ashamed." She felt tears starting. "The awful part is that everyone in town already knows and…." she hesitated, lowering her eyes. She found it difficult to look at him as she said, "They think you're the father."

Jed looked crestfallen as he let out a weak, "Oh, then it's true?"

"Yes," she replied, fighting to hold back the tears.

Still holding her small hand in his, he looked into Anna's eyes, asking, "Anna, have you met someone?"

She was surprised at the question but then it made more sense for him to think she had fallen in love with someone than to think that she had been immoral. She was quiet for a second thinking it would be easier just to lie and tell him yes, but she couldn't lie to Jed, he had been so kind to her. She answered, "No, there's no one. I can't explain to you now, but it just happened. It's not Henry's child either. I don't care if I ever see him again. I've decided that I'm going home to my folks as soon as I can."

Jed was both shocked and relieved. Here he was with a woman that he felt he could love and now she was having a child by someone other than her husband and was planning on going out of his life. They sat for a while in silence then he rose from the table saying, "I think I need to lay down for a spell."

Anna sat staring after him as he left the room. To Anna's thinking, Jed was angry and disappointed with her. Jed laid on his bed, his mind in turmoil. He couldn't let her leave. He was upset, wondering about the baby's father. Finally he drifted off into a fitful sleep.

Anna took some food out to Tag and sat on the back steps for a while. The pleasant spring evening felt good, but did nothing to cheer her. She felt very confused and unhappy. After a while she went on up to her room but there was little sleep for her.

In the morning, Jed had gotten up before Anna. He had somehow managed to get a fire going and had coffee on. When Anna awoke, she smelled the coffee and was at once on her knees over the chamber pot; the morning sickness taking its toll. When her stomach settled, she washed up and went down to the kitchen. "I'm sorry I'm late," she said, as she put an apron on.

"I guess morning sickness isn't much fun. I could hear you."

"No," she replied. "I don't see how I can travel home until it stops." Looking at Jed drinking his coffee, she asked, "How are you feeling this morning?"

"Pretty good today. I've been thinking maybe I should be staying in my room out in the barn."

"Oh no," Anna said. "You can't do that. I've already caused you enough trouble. I'll not have you leaving your own house. Doc said I needed to take care of you. I'm sure he wouldn't want you to be out there by yourself either." There was a knock at the front door and Anna hurried to open it.

It was Doc, "Good morning," he said. "How's our patient?"

"He's having some coffee. But I'm afraid you'll have to settle a problem we're having."

"Oh, what's that?"

"Jed thinks he should move into his room in the barn."

"What on earth for?" asked a puzzled Doc. He couldn't understand these two. "I'll have a talk with him." They went on into the kitchen where Jed sat drinking his coffee. "What's this I hear about you wanting to move out into the barn?" Doc went on. "That's not a good idea, at least not for a while. You need to be very careful of infection and get a lot of rest." Jed looked at Anna as if she had been a school yard tattle tale.

"Whatever you say," Jed answered in a resigned tone.

"Good, now let's go change those bandages and see how things look." Turning to Anna, he asked her to bring some warm water into Jed's room. After Doc was finished he said,

"Well it looks like things are healing up pretty good. You're one lucky fellow Jed. Sometimes these wounds from wild animals can be pretty bad. Oh, by the way, later I'm going down to the livery to see the cat that did all this damage. It's the talk of the town. When you're up to it, you outa' go see for yourself." Putting his jacket on he said, "Well I have other patients to care for, you take good care of him Anna. I'll drop by sometime tomorrow."

Jed had already returned to the kitchen when Anna returned from walking Doc to the door. "I'll make you some breakfast," she said.

Jed watched her as she moved about. He was thinking about the first time she had fixed him something to eat. The day he stopped at her place. He remembered how he had felt and he noticed how much prettier she now seemed. The feelings he'd felt the first time he had seen her returned even stronger than before. *I can't lose this woman,* Jed thought.

CHAPTER TWENTY THREE

Anna had made some scrambled eggs and again they ate in silence. After a bit Anna looked up from her plate to see Jed staring at her. She also thought she detected something in his eyes that gave her a little flush of pleasure. She lowered her eyes and Jed spoke her name. She looked up at him again wondering what he wanted to say. What he said to her next, was truly unexpected.

"Anna, you probably think that I've helped you because I'm some sort of gentleman."

"Well, yes," she replied.

"The truth is," he went on, "I think I've been falling in love with you from the first time I saw you." Anna couldn't believe her ears yet she had always felt close to this sweet man. How could she not have known when Mary had even seen it?

"But Jed," she stammered. "I'm married and now there's going to be a baby."

"I know, but I can't stop the way I feel about you. I've given it some thought. When I'm with you I'm happier than I've been my whole life. I want you to marry me and we will raise the baby just as if it was ours together." Sensing Anna's confusion, he begged, "Oh please, Anna say you will think about it. I know we could be happy."

"But what about my husband?" she asked.

"I've been thinking about that too. I've a friend in Kansas City. He's a judge. If you promise to think about it, I'll go there and see what can be done. After all, your husband did leave you and now he's a wanted man."

"Oh, I don't know," she replied. Then she remembered the times Jed had found solutions for her problems. She also thought how relaxed and safe she always felt around him. Could she learn to love him?

Jed spoke again, "Please, Anna, I'd take good care of you and the baby, and even Tag. I would never leave you."

Anna looked at him in wonder and felt her heart soften. "Well, maybe we can think about it," she said, smiling at him. She stood up to clear the table. She needed to be busy and think. As she worked she felt joy in her heart and couldn't stop smiling. Was it because Jed was again solving her problems or did she feel the same as he and hadn't realized it.

Jed got up from the table, saying. "I'm getting cabin fever. I'm going to go out and sit with Tag."

"I'll be out shortly," she told him.

Anna finished up and went out to the back porch. Tag was wagging his tail as Jed spoke softly to him, saying, "How would you like to be a family boy?"

As Anna went out to water her small garden she thought, *It would be nice to be a family.* Soon they heard the sound of hoof beats. Looking up, they saw Highpockets bringing Jed's two horses and also Adam into the yard. "Howdy," he said. "Gabby wanted me to bring your animals up here. It's getting a little crowded at the livery." Anna ran to Adam, stroking his old head and scratching him behind his ears, as he brayed a happy greeting. Tag ran in circles around everyone. After unsaddling Jed's horse, Highpockets took the three animals through the pasture gate.

"Thanks," Jed told Highpockets. "They'll give me something to do while I'm on the mend."

"You sure look like that cat tore you up good," said Highpockets.

"It looks a lot worse than it is. It could have been real bad."

"That's what Gabby says," replied the boy. "Why to hear him talk, you'd think your whole head was almost ripped off."

Jed chuckled, "Well at the time it felt like it!"

"Gabby wants to know if you want me to bring a buggy up so you can come on down and see the size of the cat?"

"That sounds like a fine idea. Maybe tomorrow. I'm still a little weak but I'd sure like to see it. You go ahead and bring a buggy up before lunch tomorrow."

"See ya then," and Highpockets started walking back to town.

"I'm feeling a little tired," Jed said to Anna. "I guess I'll go get some of that rest that Doc talked about. This being so weak, sure gets old."

"You'll be well before you know it," she said. "I plan on taking good care of you." They smiled at one another and Anna thought, *I think I care more for this man than I realized.*

CHAPTER TWENTY FOUR

It didn't take long after Anna got out of bed before the morning sickness struck. She sure didn't much like it but at least she was prepared for it. After cleaning up and dressing, she went downstairs.

She found Jed had gotten up early and made his coffee. He also had tea water and toast ready for her. Anna appreciated his thoughtfulness and thanked him.

They sat at the table, Anna sipping the tea and taking occasional bites of toast. It did seem to calm her stomach. "I'll fix you something to eat pretty quick," she said. "This morning sickness seems to leave me a little worn out."

"That's alright," Jed replied. "I'm in no hurry. I have to feed the animals anyway."

When Jed returned from outside, Anna had breakfast for him. He finished eating, then rolled a cigarette. Looking up at Anna, Jed asked her if she felt like riding into town with him to see the cougar hide.

"I do need to go see the marshal," she answered. "I also thought it would be good to tell Mary that I might be leaving."

Jed looked at her with pleading eyes, "Anna, please don't leave."

"Don't worry Jed," she said. "The way I feel in the mornings, I'm in no hurry to travel. I haven't forgotten what you asked me to think about either."

"Good," replied Jed. "We'll go into town together then."

Anna looked at him, asking, "Don't you worry about how everybody thinks that you and I are having a baby?"

"Why, nobody better say anything about you." He smiled, "I'd have to fight 'em with only one arm."

"Well then mister tough guy, I'll get ready for town."

Highpockets showed up right after lunch and rode back to town with Jed and Anna. Highpockets had been telling about the people that had gone to the livery to see the cat hide. He said some of the drovers that brought the herd through awhile back were in town on their way back to Texas. He went on to say they had raised quite a ruckus last night.

Anna felt a sudden rush of fear. Would the cowboy be in town? If he saw her would he recognize her? She was terrified.

Jed had noticed the change in her demeanor. She had gone from cheerfulness to sudden quiet. "Are you ok?" he asked.

Not wanting him to guess the real reason she replied, "All the sudden I feel a little tired. I think I'll wait for you in the marshal's office."

"That's fine if it's what you want, but what about Mary?"

"Oh, that can wait," Anna muttered.

Jed was secretly pleased. Anything that delayed Anna's plans for leaving was fine with him. They stopped at the marshal's office and Anna rushed in. She didn't want to take any chances on running into the cowboy. As Jed drove off he was a little puzzled at the way Anna had hurried into the marshal's office, when she had just said she was feeling so tired.

The marshal's office was empty. Anna sat down to wait for his return. After quite some time, she heard voices and heavy footsteps on the wooden sidewalk. The door opened and in walked Jed, the Marshal, and to Anna's shock and dismay the cowboy. She had a time to keep from fainting. Her heart was racing and she knew that she had paled.

"Hello Anna," the marshal said. "Jed said you wanted to see me. He told me you were a little tired. You do look a little pale."

"I'm really fine." she answered, with her head slightly bowed, not wanting to be noticed by the cowboy.

"Well," Marshal Sam said, "I just have to take care of a little business. This here trail boss came to get one of his men out of jail. We won't be long."

The cowboy had been staring at Anna. He spoke up saying, "Excuse me ma'am but don't I know you?"

"No, I don't believe so," Anna lied in the steadiest voice she could summon.

"Huh?" he said, taking a hard look at her. "I swear you look just like somebody I met a while back." Tipping his hat, he said, "My name is Luke Evans, you sure do look familiar. Well Marshal," he finally said, turning away from the relieved Anna, "Let's go get that trouble maker out of the pokey."

The two men left the room and Anna let out an audible sigh.

Jed studied her, asking, "Are you sure you don't know that cowboy?"

"I may have seen him someplace, but no, I don't know him." She told herself that it wasn't a lie because she didn't really know him at all.

The three men returned from the cell portion of the office. The prisoner was sporting a beautiful black eye and swollen lips. It was clear that he had been jailed for fighting. As the two men headed for the outer door, the cowboy again tipped his hat to Anna, saying, "Bye ma'am, you sure do look familiar." Much to her relief he went on out the door with his hangdog friend in tow.

"Okay now," the marshal asked. "What can I help you with Anna?"

Anna told him about the plans Henry and his pals had to rob another bank, telling him how she had to spend the night at her and Henry's place and that they were planning on returning there. "I was on my way to tell you when Jed found me and then we had the trouble with the cougar."

"I already know about the bank," the marshal told her. "I got a wire a while back. The banker was killed. One of the men was wounded before they made their escape. The descriptions left no doubt that it was your husband and the other two. From what was said in the wire, it didn't sound like it was your husband that was wounded. I was going to come out and tell you today but I ran into Jed and he told me you were waiting here. I must tell you again, Anna these are wanted men. Please be careful."

"I'll watch out for her," Jed said.

"Well, you're kinda handicapped right now but keep your eyes open."

Anna had recovered some of her composure but the thought of running into the father of the baby caused her to feel she did need to leave this town. As Jed and Anna left the marshal's office she turned to him saying, "It's not right that I'm bringing you all my troubles. I think I'd like to go see Mary after all."

Jed's heart sank as he looked at her, "Alright we can go over to the hotel. I can visit with Mickey, but don't you be thinking you're causing me any trouble. You're worth it to me." As they crossed the street to the hotel they could see that Luke and the drovers were riding out of town. Anna could not help but to feel relieved.

As they entered the hotel and started through the saloon they were greeted like some kind of town heroes. Men were crowding about Jed asking all sorts of questions. Anna slipped away to knock on Mary's office door.

"Come in!" Mary shouted, as Anna entered room. Mary jumped up from her desk coming at her with open arms. "Well if it isn't the cat killer. How are ya? Why, I heard you're expecting too! You are a mystery for sure."

Anna didn't comment on the baby, she just plunged right in. "Well, that's why I'm here. I'm going home to my parents soon and I wanted to let you know."

"Oh," Mary said with a frown, "I thought you were doing good?"

"I have been but with my husband in such trouble I decided it best to leave. Anyway I wanted to tell you I might not be able to finish making dresses for the rest of the girls."

"Well, there's only two left. Gracie left to go to Dodge. So that just leaves Ruby and Madeline. Ruby has a pile of pretty dresses so I guess that just leaves Madeline."

Anna wasn't looking forward to having anything to do with Madeline but then she wondered if it would give her the chance to get her brooch back. "Sure," Anna said. "When could she come to my place?"

"Things will be a little slow around here for a while. If it's alright, she could make it tomorrow after supper. She won't be missed, anyway. She's still mooning around over your husband. She has no idea that he is married, let alone that you are his wife. So you don't have to worry about that unless it would bother you?"

"No," Anna replied. "Nothing Henry could do bothers me anymore. The marshal just told me that Henry and his friends robbed another bank. This time they killed a banker."

"No wonder you want to leave," said a sympathetic Mary. "Seems like a lot of people are leaving town. I hated to see Gracie go. She was a sweet girl. She reminded me a lot of you. Come to think of it you two looked a lot alike. Why just last night some cowboy was in here asking for her. When I asked him what the girl's name was he said he didn't know her name but he sorta described Gracie. According to him she was in room six and the sweetest girl in the world. That was one disappointed cowboy." Mary chuckled saying, "These men are all alike. Give them a little love and a girl could have one eye in the middle of her forehead and they wouldn't notice."

Anna felt a little flushed. She had to get out of there before Mary put two and two together. "I'd better be going," she said. "Jed's waiting and he might be getting a little tired. He's not out of the woods yet."

"Why, I'd better go out and see that man. I heard he's finally staying at his house."

"Yes," Anna said. "He needs some care. Doc wants him to rest and be careful of infection."

They went on out into the saloon. Mary looked at Jed saying, "Why you look like your old self with all that hair gone. You're down right handsome, you devil." Jed and Anna knew Mary had heard the rumors but the subject never came up. They said their goodbyes and headed for home.

When they arrived, Jed put the buggy away and the horse in the pasture. He was keeping them at the house for further use. They were both tired and went to their rooms to rest. Anna was emotionally drained and Jed was worn out. In the evening Anna prepared their dinner. Jed had been watching her every move with longing eyes. It didn't go unnoticed by Anna and it was making her a little nervous. To break the silence she told him about Madeline coming to be measured for a dress the next evening. Jed scowled saying, "I don't think I want to be here while two women are busy with that. I think I'll go down to the livery. I've been neglecting some of the things that need to be taken care of down there."

Anna looked concerned asking, "Are you sure you won't get too tired?"

"No," he replied. "With all these good meals and care, I feel stronger by the hour."

CHAPTER TWENTY FIVE

Henry, Dan, and Jack had reached the town where they had planned their next robbery. They'd hung around town for a couple of days checking out the law and lay of the place. Finalizing a plan, they were ready. Dan would hold the horses in back of the bank while Jack and Henry went in to rob it. They figured early morning would be best because it appeared the sheriff lived out of town a ways. It didn't seem he was in any hurry to come in to work early. That left only one deputy to watch things. The three had been staying on the outskirts of the town. On the day they were going to carry out their plan they rose early. Jack was in his usual foul mood, complaining because there hadn't been enough money for a decent room or a good meal.

"Well," Dan said, "When this job is done we should be sittin' pretty."

After some coffee and jerky they mounted up and headed for town. The place was fairly deserted as they rode down the dusty street. The three loitered about a water trough across the street from the bank. Finally they saw a well-dressed man walking up the street, towards the bank. Pretending to be talking to one another, they slyly watched as the man headed for the bank door. Seeing the banker was making ready to unlock it, they mounted up. They rode across the street into the alley leading to the bank's back door. Henry and Jack dismounted and Dan took their horses.

While the banker was getting ready to unlock the door, he had noticed the three scruffy men. Seeing three of them had gone into the alley and only two came out walking towards the bank, he quickly went inside and relocked the door. The banker was no dummy and he was taking no chances.

Jack and Henry reached the bank door just as the banker stepped to one side, out of their sight.

Jack tried the door. Finding it locked he swore, "I know that old man's in there, he better open up this damn door." Jack began to pound on the heavy door, growing more angry and louder by the second. Henry chided him, but to no avail. The gunman was losing his temper.

Then to Henry's shock, Jack took his pistol out and shot the lock of the door. He kicked it open and stomped in. Seeing the old banker, Jack demanded money. The banker raised his hands above his head, telling Jack, he hadn't opened the safe yet.

"Well, you better get it open or I'll have to shoot you." Jack snarled, waving his gun at the now frightened banker. Henry had stood aside worried that Jack's gunshot would bring someone to investigate.

"Okay," the nervous banker replied walking to the safe. "Just don't shoot mister." He started working on the combination lock but his hands were shaking so much he failed on the first and second tries.

"You better not be stalling old man!" shouted the increasingly impatient Jack.

"No, no," stammered the banker. "Just give me a minute."

Hearing voices outside, Henry told Jack, "People are coming we gotta get out of here."

"You old fool!" Jack shouted. "I'll teach you to mess around like this." Without hesitation he shot the banker.

"Come on!" yelled a stunned Henry, as he ran toward the back door. They just got the back door unlocked as men came in through the front of the bank, guns drawn.

Henry and Jack leapt to the horses Dan had been holding at the ready. The three raced off. Someone came out the back door shouting at others to mount up and give chase. The man at the bank's back door shot several times at the fleeing trio but they had reached the cover of some trees.

Keeping their horses at a full gallop as bullets whizzed by, they soon were up in the hills. They stopped once to check their back trail. Seeing no one in pursuit they rode on. Feeling they had a good head start they continued climbing, needing to find some ground that wouldn't leave a trail for the town folk to follow. Finally coming to some shale, they picked their way across and found some hard rocky surface to travel on.

A good half mile was covered on such ground before they came to more timber. Stopping to give the horses a rest, Jack got off his mount saying, "Well damn, that didn't go so good." Not even admitting blame for the foul up.

Henry looked at Dan, who had remained on his mount. He saw that the front of Dan's shirt had a blossoming circle of blood just under his left shoulder.

Jack noticed the look on Henry's face and followed his gaze saying, "Damn boy, looks like they got ya."

"I'm afraid so," Dan answered in a strained voice. "I'm shot up pretty good. Can we rest a while?" His face was chalk white and was dripping with beads of sweat.

Jack looked at Dan replying, "If we stop now we'll all get shot up. We have to go a little further to make sure we lose 'em. Just hang in there as best you can."

The three rode on for another hour then stopped. Dan slid off from his horse to the ground with a quiet moan. "I ain't gonna make it," he whispered to the other two. "Just go on without me."

"We can't do that," said an upset Henry. "Maybe after you rest some you'll feel better."

Jack sat on his mount, rolling a cigarette and looking at Henry as if he were crazy. Finally, he said to Henry, "Look, Dan knows he's done for. I'm not staying here to get shot up too. You can stay if you want but if he isn't ready to ride when I finish this smoke, I'm riding out."

Henry knew he wouldn't stay and felt ashamed at what a coward he had become. Also he was worried. Dan had always been able to keep Jack somewhat under control, now they would be going on without him. Henry decided then and there that when they got back to his place, he was somehow going to get Anna and head back east.

When Jack finished his cigarette he spoke to Dan, "Are you ready to ride boy?" Dan never answered, he was gone. He still sat, his back against a tree, unseeing eyes staring straight ahead, his mouth agape.

"What do we do now?" asked Henry.

"Why nothing," answered an uncaring Jack as he dismounted. "Grab his legs; we'll toss him over this bank so they won't find him."

Henry was amazed that anyone could be so cold about a person that had been a friend. It sickened him to do the deed. It seemed to him Dan's unseeing eyes were accusing him for such a thoughtless deed. Once it was done the two mounted up, and leading Dan's horse they rode on.

That night they slept under the cover of some trees. Jack slept but Henry couldn't. He wanted no more to do with Jack. He wondered why he had been so drawn to this killer in the first place. Late morning of the next day the two rode into the yard of Henry's place.

"I sure hope that woman of yours has something for us to eat," Jack grumbled.

It didn't take long to see the place was deserted. This time there was no note. Henry was both glad and disappointed to find Anna was gone. He wasn't sure what he would have done had Jack made trouble for her.

"Well how's that for ya?" Jack snarled. "Your sweet little wife lit out on you again. She's probably at the marshal's office right now. You need to teach that little lady a lesson. We sure can't stay here now, thanks to her. A posse might show up anytime."

"Where can we go?" a worried Henry asked. He didn't want to go anywhere with Jack but knew he was probably right about the posse.

"Oh," Jack replied. "I know a couple guys hiding out not far from here. We'll just have to ride on." They traveled through the hills back of Henry's place. Henry had never explored that far and was surprised when they came upon a rundown cabin that was well hidden.

"Hello the house!" Jack shouted out. "It's me, Jack Black." Looking at Henry he chuckled, "I just made that last name up. Pretty good huh?"

"Yeah," answered an exhausted Henry. "Pretty good." He thought to himself, *Black suits you just fine.*

"Come on in!" someone shouted back from inside the cabin.

"Let's go. Maybe they'll have a drink or two. I could sure use one."

The cabin was small with a couple bunks, a stove, a table, and a few handmade benches. The place was dark and smelly. There were two men, one was huge and rough looking the other was a slim looking dandy.

"Hello Jack," said the large man extending his ham like hand. "Who's the pilgrim?"

"Oh, he's a friend of mine. His name's Henry."

Turning to Henry, Jack said, "This here's Bear. I guess you can see why." Indeed Henry could see why, not only was the man huge, he had wild unruly hair and a big tangled beard. Then turning to the other man, Jack told Henry, "This here's Slick. You don't want to get into a card game with him, not unless you're ready to lose your shirt."

"Howdy," Henry said with a nod. He noted Slick really looked the part of a card shark. He had the pale pallor of a person who saw little daylight. His hands were smooth with long slender fingers. He was dressed in clean clothes, unlike Bear. He had a thin dark mustache and eyes that showed no expression as he looked Henry and Jack over.

"You old horse's got anything to eat or drink?" asked Jack.

"Why sure," Bear answered. "There's some stew on the stove there and I'll break out a jug." Henry and Jack were starved. Henry hoped the whiskey would calm his nerves. "It's been some time since I saw ya. What ya been up to?" Bear asked. "Where's that other fellow you used to hang out with?"

"Why, he up and got shot," Jack answered between bites of stew. Then he raised his cup of whiskey saying, "Here's to Dan, may he rest in peace."

Bear sat his cup down saying, "I heard you were wanted for killing a bank teller."

"Yeah," Jack replied. "He wouldn't do what he was told."

Bear laughed, "Well, that's what happens."

"How did you come to know about it?" Henry asked.

Slick looked at Henry through narrowed eyes. "Why, I spend some time in Meade playing cards. I hear everything that goes on in this country. I was there right after you and Jack had a shootout over some card game. I hear your woman's living there too."

"Well good for her," smirked Jack. "Henry here needs to teach that one how a wife's supposed to behave. Don't 'cha Henry?"

Henry ignored Jack's comments, asking Slick, "Do you know where she is in Meade?"

Slick blew out a stream of smoke from the long thin cigarillo that he had between his thin lips saying, "Sure, I can tell you exactly how to find her, it's easy."

Henry figured this was his chance to break free of Jack. He would sneak into town, get Anna, and somehow they would head east. *She surely would have some money*, he thought, *Anna always was a thrifty sort.*

The four men sat about the rest of the day. Henry sat listening to the tales of their times together. As the day drifted into early evening, Henry told them he thought he'd call it a night. Getting his bedroll, he put it down in a corner. He slept fitfully dreaming of men chasing him and Jack shooting everyone in sight. Once in a while the drinking men would wake him with their laughter. Then he would lay awake wondering how he ever got in such a mess. *Well, in the morning he would figure a way to get Anna and leave this all behind.*

After Henry woke, he had decided on a plan. He would tell Jack he needed to take Dan's horse to bring Anna back. The three men showed no sign of waking up. It was getting late and Henry was eager to leave. Finally he walked to where Slick slept and gently shook his shoulder. Slick woke enough for Henry to get the information he needed to find Anna. He told Slick he was going to take Dan's horse to bring her back.

Slick looked at Henry with bloodshot eyes saying, "I don't think Jack's going to like that."

"It's okay," Henry reassured him. "Jack won't care. I'll be back as soon as I can. Tell him not to worry. I'll make sure nobody sees me." Henry started to the door. Slick had rolled over and resumed his snoring. The longer they slept, the better, thought Henry.

CHAPTER TWENTY SIX

After Jed left, Anna put on her best dress and fixed her hair. She didn't want to admit it but she was a little jealous of Madeline's beauty. There was a knock at the front door and it sent Anna's heart racing. When she opened the door, Madeline appeared as nervous as Anna felt.

She really is a beauty, Anna thought, *No wonder Henry carried on with her. He always did like flashy.* "Please come in," she said rather formally, "I thought we could have some coffee while you tell me what you have in mind for your dress. Also I have to take some measurements."

"Sure," said the hesitant Madeline.

Anna didn't realize how out of place Madeline felt. Madeline couldn't remember the last time a woman from the town had treated her like a lady and not someone to be looked down on.

As they sat in the lamp lit kitchen, Anna saw that Madeline was wearing the brooch Henry had taken. "That's a pretty pin," she said casually.

"Yes," Madeline replied. She lifted a hand to where it was pinned. "It's very special to me."

They started talking about color and style for the dress when suddenly, there was a low growl from Tag. Anna looked startled saying, "Tag never growls unless something is wrong. I think I'll lock the door. It's probably just a coyote or some other critter after his food. I wish Jed were here. I'm not as brave as I use to be, ever since the cougar thing." Anna walked over to lock the door. Tag let out another growl, then a yelp. "Oh my!" exclaimed a now frightened Anna. "I have to see what's the matter." As she reached the door, it swung open on its own and there stood a smiling Henry.

"Hello Anna!"

Anna was speechless, then she heard a commotion behind her. She turned to see a half laughing, half crying, Madeline running towards Henry, arms held out to embrace him.

Madeline cried out, "Oh Henry I've missed you so! I knew you would come for me."

As she wrapped her arms around a stunned Henry, he thought, *My God what do I do now?* Anna stood there with an amused grin on her face. The look on Henry's face was payment enough for all the grief he'd caused her.

"Madeline," he almost whispered. "What are you doing here?"

"I was going to have a dress made but I won't need it now. I know you can't stay," she gushed on. "Oh, I'm so happy to see you. Why, I can leave town with you this minute. I really don't need much from the hotel."

As Madeline rattled on, Henry had just stood there, his arms hanging down. He seemed unable to move. He was staring, almost pitifully at Anna.

Madeline became aware of how unresponsive Henry was. She looked up to see him frantically looking at Anna, who still had the smile on her face. Then Anna's smile faded as she remembered Tag's cry of pain.

Pushing her way past the two, she asked sharply, "What did you do to Tag?"

"Oh come on now, Anna," he replied. "I just gave him a little kick, he was growling at me."

Anna went out to where Tag sat, licking his leg. Kneeling beside him, she could see one of his wounds had opened and was bleeding a little. "Why you're lucky he's hurt or he might have given you what you deserve."

Henry had disengaged himself from Madeline and went out to where a distraught Anna was kneeling beside Tag. "Now, Anna," he said, "It's just a dog. He's got no business growling at me."

"I don't know why not," Anna retorted. "He knows who needs to be growled at and who doesn't."

Madeline had been taking in the exchange between the two and it began to dawn on her that Henry and Anna knew one another. She stepped out to where the two now stood, asking Henry in a questioning voice, "Do you know her?" Henry turned to her with his mouth open but nothing came out.

"Why don't you answer her?" Anna asked, her voice deliberately dripping with honey.

"Why is she talking so sweet to you?" demanded Madeline. She was growing angry.

"I don't----" he started to say, when Anna stepped to him.

Taking his arm in hers, and smiling up at Henry Anna said, "Tell Madeline how we know each other dear." There was a bit of delight in her tone.

"I want to know what's going on," demanded a glaring Madeline, hands on her hips. "Have you been seeing this woman behind my back?" she asked, with increasing anger.

Henry felt as if he were falling deeper and deeper into a pit. "Well," he stammered, "Anna's my wife."

"Wife!" shouted a now furious Madeline. "Why you low down snake in the grass! To think I've been wasting my time waiting for you, dreaming of the day you would come for me. Why this is probably a piece of trash, just like you!" Madeline undid Anna's brooch, throwing it at Henry's feet.

Anna picked it up saying, "This isn't a piece of junk to me, it was my grandmother's."

Anna was clearly enjoying Henry's discomfort. However, she had not given any thought to what the outcome might be.

In the dim lighting, neither Henry nor Anna saw the small derringer that Madeline had taken from somewhere within the folds of her skirt.

Without warning, she pointed it straight at Henry and with hatred in her voice she hissed, "I'll show you."

Before she could fire, Henry batted at her hand, just as the gun went off. Tag jumped up biting Henry's leg. His leg burned with pain, as he shook Tag loose.

Anna let out a small cry and fell to the floor of the porch, a pool of blood spreading from her head.

In disbelief, Henry shouted, "Oh my God you've killed her."

Tag charged at Henry again. This time Henry kicked him in the head, sending him flying into the yard. The dog landed on his already painful wounds and lay there.

Madeline, realizing what she'd done began to tremble. "What shall we do?" she cried.

"I don't know about you," Henry replied. "I'm getting out of here."

"You can't just leave me here," wailed Madeline. "What do they do with women that kill people?"

"I don't know," Henry said in an agitated tone. "I ain't stickin' around to find out."

Henry turned to leave. Madeline grabbed onto him. "Let go of me," he snarled. "I gotta go before somebody sees me. I'm a wanted man."

"Well," Madeline said, "I'm going with you. This is all your fault." As Henry headed for the waiting horses, Madeline stumbled along behind him.

This was a far different outcome than the one Henry had envisioned. He was again running from the law and now he was saddled with Madeline.

They quickly left the area. Henry had no idea where to go as they rode off into the warm spring night.

CHAPTER TWENTY SEVEN

Anna lay still on the porch, then moaned as she tried to open her eyes. Everything seemed out of focus and dark. There was horrific pain in her head. For a bit, she wondered where she was and what had happened. Then, feeling something in her hand, she realized it was her brooch. She started to recall what had happened. Reaching up and feeling about, she came to the sticky blood, flowing down the side of her head. Anna was having trouble staying awake.

Hearing Tag's whimpering through the roaring in her ears, she tried to call him. Tag drug himself up the steps and lay down beside Anna, as she drifted off into blackness.

Sometime later, Jed drove through the back gate. He noticed the kitchen door open with the lamp light spilling out onto the porch. His heart skipped a beat. He was warmed by the thought that Anna was waiting for him. Then he took a better look.

As he drew closer, he saw what looked like a pile of something lying on the porch. With shock, he saw that it was a person. Jed drew the buggy to a quick stop and jumping down he ran to the still figures. He couldn't believe his eyes.

Anna laid motionless, blood still streaming from the side of her head. Tag lay whimpering beside her. Jed fell to his knees, so shaken he could hardly speak. "Anna! Anna!" he cried, as he felt her face and took her hand in his. Anna moaned softly. "You're alive," Jed said in a rushing breath he hadn't realized he had been holding. "What happened?"

Anna tried to open her eyes again, the throbbing pain was too much to bear. She knew Jed was there but couldn't gather her thoughts to speak. She allowed herself to drift back into blissful darkness.. .

Jed wasn't sure what he should do. He knew she needed the doctor but should he go get Doc or try to take her to town? He decided to take her to town. He ran into the house gathering a couple of blankets, putting one over Anna and the other on Tag. Running to the buggy, he drove it as close to the porch as he could. Wrapping the blanket about the still unconscious Anna he carried her to the buggy, half dragging her because of his injured arm. It was a hard task to get her limp body into the seat. Getting in beside her, Jed leaned her against him, holding her as best he could with his injured arm.

Racing to town, Jed pulled up in front of Doc's. The speeding buggy had drawn some attention. Jed shouted out to anyone to come and help him get Anna into the doctor. Three men raced up; one took hold of the horses, while another helped Jed with Anna. The third ran to knock on Doc's door shouting out, "Come quick, Doc, Anna's been hurt!"

Doc and Nora had been getting ready for bed, when they heard the loud pounding on the door. Doc hurried downstairs, his shirt half on. On opening the door he started to ask what all the fuss was about but taking one look at the now blood covered Anna, he directed the men to take her into his examining room. As Jed and his helper lay Anna on the exam table, Doc asked, "What in the world happened?"

A shaking and pale Jed answered, "I don't rightly know Doc. I was in town and when I got home this is how I found her. Her and Tag were both lying on the back porch, hurt."

Doc had been busy examining Anna, as he listened to Jed. Looking up he said, "Anna's been shot."

"Shot?" exclaimed a confused Jed. "Will she be okay? Will this hurt the baby?"

Doc turned to the man that had helped Jed bring Anna in, "Tim can you go fetch Sam?"

"Sure thing Doc," Tim replied, rushing towards the door.

Turning back to Jed, Doc said, "It looks like the bullet grazed her head just above her temple. All I can do for her is to clean the wound and wait for her to come to. Anna's a pretty healthy young woman. I think the baby will be fine. We can only wait and see."

"When will that be?" asked a frantic Jed.

"Well, that's hard to say. You say Tag was hurt too?"

"Yes it looked like his wounds were bleeding again. I covered him up with a blanket."

"Good," Doc said, as he prepared to work on Anna. Doc's wife had come into the room. "I'm going to have Nora help me here. Why don't you go on out to the waiting room and tell Sam what happened when he gets here. Tell him it looks like a small caliber gun. Good thing too, it could have been a lot worse. Go on now, we need to get busy here."

Jed took a look at the pale, quiet, Anna. Suddenly he was more frightened than he had ever been in his whole life. He knew how quickly a life could be taken.

Just as Jed entered the waiting room, Marshal Sam came through the office door.

"What happened, Jed? Tim said you brought Anna in and that she didn't look too good."

"I don't know what happened, Anna was home waiting for one of Mary's girls to show up to see about a dress. I was down at the livery. When I got home, I found her and Tag on the back porch, bleeding something awful," Jed went on, fighting to control his emotions. "Anna wouldn't wake up. Doc says she's been shot with a small caliber gun."

"Shot? Where?" asked the marshal.

"Doc says the bullet grazed the side of her head and that she has a concussion. Marshal, I don't know who would want to do such a thing, she's the sweetest thing ever."

The marshal gave Jed a wry smile. "I think I know who would. I'm going over to the hotel to tell Mary that I need to talk to the girl that was at your place. Maybe she can shed some light on this."

Jed was a bundle of nerves, he would sit, then pace the floor, he couldn't sit still.

After what seemed a lifetime, Doc came out rolling his sleeves down and looking tired. He reached into his trouser pocket and drew out the brooch. He handed it to Jed saying, "She was clutching this in one hand. It's a nice piece, I can't believe she didn't drop it. She sure had a grip on it."

"How is she Doc?" asked a worried Jed.

"Well, I think she'll be just fine. She lost a lot of blood but the wound isn't that serious. She just needs to rest. Yes, I'm sure she'll be fine but I'm keeping her here until she wakes up. So you just go on home. Nothing more can be done and you need your rest too. Boy you two sure keep me busy." Doc patted Jed on the back and guided him towards the door. "When you get home check on that dog of hers to see how he's doing. Make sure he has water and keep him warm."

"Sure but after I check on Tag, I'm coming right back to town. I'm gonna stay at the hotel. I want to be close by."

"Okay if that's what you want to do, but be sure and get the rest you need."

As he told Doc he would do, Jed drove on home to check on Tag. He found him happy to see him. He was resting and his wounds were no longer bleeding. After putting out the lamps and locking up, Jed headed back to town. Marshal Sam and Mary were sitting in the hotel lobby when Jed walked in. Mary rose to greet him and the marshal followed.

"How is she?" asked a worried looking Mary.

"Doc says she'll be fine but I'm going to stay here in the hotel tonight if you have a room."

"Sure we do, come on over to the desk and I'll get a key for ya."

Jed followed her over to the desk. Reaching into his pocket, intending to get money, his hand seized the brooch. He laid it on the counter.

"Where did you get that?" exclaimed a surprised Mary.

"Doc gave it to me. He said Anna had it in her hand."

"See, Sam," Mary said turning to the marshal. "It's like I told you, Madeline never came back to the hotel. This here's the brooch she always wore. Anna's husband gave it to her and Madeline never took it off. It surely looks like she's involved, somehow."

The marshal turned to leave, saying, "They can't be far. Jed I'm going out to your place and have a look around. I'll stop by the office and have my deputy round up a couple men."

Jed wanted to go with Sam but he worried about leaving Anna. In the end he decided to go with him. There was nothing he could do waiting around town. "Wait!" he hollered after the marshal, I'm going with you. Maybe we can find some tracks that will tell us something."

When the marshal and Jed got to Jed's place, they got a couple of lanterns from the barn and began to search the area for any signs that might help solve what had taken place. They found where two horses had been tied just outside Jed's fence line. They could make out the boot prints of a man and the tiny shoe print of a woman.

"It looks like they're headed north to Dodge."

"Yes," answered Sam. "If it's Henry, I'm sure he won't head back to his place. He'd figure that's the first place we'd look. It looks like they left in a hurry." Jed put the buggy up, grabbed his rifle and saddled his horse. The deputy showed up with three men.

"I can't see why they had to shoot Anna," said Sam.

"Me neither," replied Jed. "But whoever did, is gonna pay. Let's get riding, maybe we can catch them by morning, before they reach Dodge."

"Now hold on there Jed," cautioned Sam. "We can't trail 'em in the dark. We better wait 'til morning."

"While we wait they'll be getting further away," protested Jed. "We can go real slow and check the road careful like. There's plenty of us to look around with lanterns. There's a lot of this road that nobody's gonna leave even in the daylight. I'm going, even if I have to go alone."

"Well if you're that set on it, I guess we can give it a try," said a somewhat doubtful Sam.

CHAPTER TWENTY EIGHT

It was coming onto morning when Anna moaned and started to come to. Nora had slept in the room to keep an eye on her. "Are you awake, dear?"

"What?" Anna replied in a weak voice. "Nora is that you? Where am I? What happened?" Then moaning again, she said, "Oh my head hurts."

"Just lie still, you're at the doctor's office. Jed brought you in. You were hit on the side of your head by a bullet."

"Oh but I…." Anna started to say groggily. "Yes I remember now. Madeline was going to shoot Henry, but then he put his hand out… that's all I remember."

"Well that explains a lot," Nora said. Doc came hurrying into the room.

"I heard voices."

"Yes she's awake," and she repeated what Anna had told her.

"Madeline you say? She always did strike me as one mixed up gal. So now I guess her and Henry are on the run."

Anna drifted back to sleep and Doc and Nora left. Later Nora took Anna some tea and toast, remembering her morning sickness.

With Nora's help, Anna was able to get a little tea and toast down, and surprisingly it stayed down. Nora smiled at her and said, "Jed will be glad you're okay. I never seen a man so upset."

Anna looked up from her toast and asked, "What about when his wife and baby died?"

"Yes." Nora answered, "That was a sad thing."

"Why did she die?"

"Well, no one really knows for sure," replied Nora, "But I have my own opinion about why. I don't think she wanted to live."

"What do you mean?" Anna asked.

Nora sat for a few seconds, then she answered, "Like I said, this is just my way of thinking but I think Doc feels the same. You see, Louise was somewhat pampered. Her Dad, Mr. Brown, came here to start a bank. Her mother, Emma, didn't really care for their life here. Emma had always lived in the city. They came from St. Louis. Louise's folks always had help; you know a cook, housekeeper, and such. Her Dad had that house you're living in, built before Louise and Emma came out here. That room in the barn that Jed was living in was for servants' quarters. Louise was a very pretty girl. When she set her cap for Jed, he didn't stand a chance. Why he didn't know if he was coming or going. Anyway, before he knew what happened, he was taking part as the groom, in the biggest wedding this town will ever see again. A lot of people came from back east for the doings. Seeing all her old friends just made Mrs. Brown want to return to St. Louis more than ever. Eventually, she wore Mr. Brown down. They gave the house to Jed and Louise, as a wedding gift. Mr. Brown sold the bank and returned east."

"After her folks left, Louise became depressed. Jed didn't think they needed the help Louise had been accustomed to. He did everything he could to help out, trying to make her happy but she just became more disagreeable. When she found out she was going to have a baby, she really became difficult. She hardly ever left her bed, even though she was pretty healthy. Doc tried to tell her it wasn't good for the baby or her. He told her that she needed to get out now and then. She told him that she didn't want to be seen in her condition."

"Jed had ridden to Dodge to take care of some business for the livery stable. Louise was alone when the baby started to come; it was about a month early. Jed got home in the late afternoon to find her half crazy with pain. He hurried to get Doc. When Doc got there, he found the baby was breach, a son, and it was not alive. Louise had fainted away and was bleeding bad. In the end there was no saving either of them. Jed left right after the funeral. Well, that is the baby's funeral. Mrs. Brown had Louise's body taken home to St. Louise for burial. Anyway, Jed went off to some place where he has some land. In the winters, or other times when he came to town, he stayed in that room in the barn."

"What a sad story. No wonder he didn't want to stay in a house that has so many bad memories."

Nora stood, saying, "That's enough talking, you need to get your rest. I'll bring you some soup later. Don't forget, you have a little one to care for too. Jed is probably worried something could happen to you too. But I can tell that you're a pretty healthy girl, I don't think you'll have much trouble."

"Nora," Anna started to say something about the baby not being Jed's. Then she thought better of it.

"I know," Nora said with a sympathetic smile. "You're married to someone else. I don't think anyone with a lick of sense would hold you to your vows the way your husband has turned out." Patting Anna's hand she continued, "You're not the first woman in the world to have this happen and you won't be the last. Mark my words, if Jed can find a way to make you his wife and take care of his child, he will. I really must go now to give Doc a hand, he has other patients you know."

"When do you think I can go home?" asked Anna.

"Well, I can't say. Doc will decide that later. Anyway I heard that Jed went with the marshal to look for your husband and Madeline."

"Oh no, I hope no one gets hurt."

"Don't you worry about that. Marshal Sam knows what he's doing. You stay still now. I'll see you a little later."

Anna didn't need coaxing as she drifted off, the room was quiet and the shades were drawn.

CHAPTER TWENTY NINE

Henry had kept the horses at a brisk trot. His head was in a whirl. They couldn't go back to the cabin where Bear and Jack were, even if he could find the place in the dark. Besides Madeline would give away what had happened and they wouldn't want the trouble that might bring. Deciding to stick to the well-traveled road, they rode on.

Madeline was in a state; she hadn't ridden a horse for some time, and was hanging on to the saddle horn with all her might. Her teeth felt as if they were being jarred loose and she had many sore spots as well. She couldn't believe what had happened or how she had fallen for this weak, two-timing coward. Now she was forced to follow him to God knows where. Madeline lifted her hand to her breast, something she had always done for comfort. With sudden shock, she recalled removing the brooch and throwing it at Henry. "Oh my God! They will know I was there when Anna was shot."

"What?" asked Henry.

"Oh, ah, nothing," she stammered. "Can we please stop to rest? I'm ready to collapse."

Henry hadn't forgotten the bullet had been meant for him. He wished he could rid himself of this woman. He thought, I'll just leave her in my dust. But he was not a man to face problems alone. Slowing his mount to allow Madeline to come alongside him, he said, "Maybe we can go a little slower but we don't know how much time we have before they find Anna."

As he spoke, it hit him how bad the situation was. It was one thing to kill a man over a card game, but to kill a woman? They rode on, Madeline fuming. Henry was growing more worried every minute.

Dawn had begun as the weary couple came to a hilly area. "This looks like we could take off here without leaving much trace."

Madeline glared at him. "Are we going to rest? Do you have anything to eat?"

"As soon as I find a place that looks safe," he replied, losing his patience. "We can't have the horses too close to the road, they might give us away if they hear other horses. No, I don't have anything to eat. I didn't expect to be in this mess, no thanks to you."

"Now you just wait a minute, you low life!" Madeline snarled. "It's not my fault you lied to me, telling how you were going to take me away to a better life. Ha! What a laugh."

"This isn't getting us anyplace. We need to find a place to rest us and the horses. I know this road goes to Dodge. We'll just have to try and stay out of sight until we get there."

"Then what?" demanded an angry Madeline. "Do you have any money? Look at me, my clothes are dirty, my hair's a mess."

"Shut up, Madeline!" Henry shouted at her. "No, I have no money to speak of, just enough for a meal. Maybe you could find a lucky cowboy to pay for food."

"What??" shouted a now furious Madeline. "You want me to make money for the likes of you? I'll take care of myself thank you. I've done it before and I can do it again and when we reach Dodge, you're on your own."

"That suits me fine." But he wondered how he was going to manage once they reached Dodge. Well, he'd worry about that later.

After they left the road, they traveled up the rocky hillside, trying to avoid any grassy areas that would leave sign of their passing. Crossing a slide area of shale and coming to a small stream, they and the horses drank, then continued on into some trees. Soon they came to a small clearing. Henry tied the horses by a small patch of grass, and lay down to rest. He hadn't even bothered to help Madeline from her horse. If he was going to be on his own, he thought, so was she. He wondered what he had ever seen in this bitter, complaining female.

Madeline glared at him as she stomped past him to a small patch of morning sun and lay down. Soon the quarreling ex-lovers were fast asleep, each with their own angry thoughts.

CHAPTER THIRTY

Sometime around midnight, Sam pulled his horse to a stop. "I think this is a good place to rest." It had been very slow going for the marshal and his posse. In the dark it had been difficult to find any sign of tracks. Carefully checking to make sure the two hadn't left the road, the Marshal felt that they had done a thorough job. He was tired and so were his men.

He got no argument as the men dismounted and led their horses to drink in the river that ran near the road. Then the men bedded down. Even Jed was ready to rest.

But as tired as he'd been, Jed was the first one up. He washed his face in the cold river water. By the time the others were up he was chomping at the bit.

"Calm down, Jed," the marshal chided. "I'm sure those two aren't going to be hard to find. We'll just mosey on down the road, until we find some sign." Sam had been a tracker and guide for the army before becoming a marshal.

The group was able to travel much faster with better light and before long Sam held a hand up. He had seen some turned over stones where a horse shoe had scraped a rock. "It looks like they left the road here. I think we'll split up. Some of you take Tink's and my horses."

"Wait a minute," Jed interrupted, "I want to go with you."

"Well, alright," Sam said, "But you have to follow my orders if we spot 'em."

"Sure," Jed answered.

"Okay then," Sam continued, "Bob and Jeff you wait here with the horses. Tink, you and Bill go on down the road looking for any other sign. Jed and I will check this out. If this is where they left the road and we spot 'em there's likely to be some shooting. I'm not sure how this is gonna go. I know Henry's armed but he's got a woman with him. Hard tellin' what he might do. Bill and Tink, don't go to fast, if this don't pan out we'll catch up with you. If we get 'em, I'll send Bob and Jeff after you."

Jed and Sam dismounted, and taking their rifles left the road. Staying several feet apart, they started up the hillside both searching for any sign horses had passed. Following Henry's trail wasn't difficult for Sam. As he and Jed approached an area of loose rocks they jumped a big buck that had been lying in the morning sun. It scampered off, making quite a bit of noise. "Damn!" whispered Sam. "They crossed this slide for sure. They might've heard that."

Unlike the exhausted Madeline, Henry had slept fitfully and the sound of clattering rocks, brought him wide awake. He thought about waking Madeline but he knew if someone was coming, they would surely hear the commotion she would make. He decided to quietly lead his horse further into the trees and watch their back trail. If he saw anyone, he would keep going on the faint deer trail they'd been on. Whoever it was, they could have Madeline. As he led his horse off, Madeline never stirred.

Jed and Sam stood still for a few minutes. Thinking it over, Sam decided to go up higher. As they climbed the sparsely treed hillside, they kept behind brush. It was a hard climb. They had to be very quiet and the sun was getting a little warm. When they reached a pretty good height, Sam couldn't believe his eyes.

There was Madeline asleep and off to the side of a clearing, under some trees was Henry.

"Well I'll be," said a satisfied Sam. "Would ya lookie there?"

"What do we do now?" asked Jed.

Sam studied the layout, "Looks like Henry's got himself in a fix. See there," Sam said, pointing towards where Henry was, "He can't ride that way. If he thinks he can go off on that trail he's done. The hillside drops completely away. About the only way he can go is back the way they came. So you go back down to where they rode in there, and wait with your rifle. When you're set, wave your hand."

"Alright," said a slightly nervous Jed. He hadn't shot a man since some Indian fighting he'd done when he was a much younger man.

Jed carefully retraced his steps back down to where Henry and Madeline had ridden into the trees. It had taken him a lot less time than the climb up. When he reached a spot where he had cover, he waved at Sam.

Henry had been hiding for some time. He decided that the noise had been caused by an animal. After all he thought, we had been on a deer trail. He rode his horse out to the small clearing where Madeline still slept.

All the sudden, the hill side rang out with Sam's commanding voice. "Henry, this is Marshal Jefferson, from Meade. Unbuckle your guns and throw them and your rifle down to the ground. Get off your horse and start walking back down the trail you came in on. I've got the drop on you, so don't try anything foolish. There's armed men waiting for you, so don't think of running."

Madeline sat up with a start. At the sound of the Marshal's words, she knew it was over and jumped up from where she had been sleeping. She started screaming at the top of her lungs. "Marshal, help me, please! He took me at gun point. Please help me. He's a killer!"

"What are you saying?" snarled Henry in disbelief. Madeline ignored him, continuing to cry out for help. Henry realized she was blaming him for Anna's death. In a panic, he turned his horse and raced blindly back into the trees, down what he thought was a good trail.

Sam saw what Henry was doing and shouted down to him, "You can't go that way, its suicide!" Henry heard nothing. He only thought of escape, spurring his horse into a flat out run.

Sam couldn't see what happened, but the awful screams of horse and man, told the tale. Henry had been unable to stop. He flew off into space falling several hundred feet.

There was silence, then shaking his gray head, Sam shouted down to Jed, "I'm coming down, you go on in and get the woman. Then we'll see where the fool landed."

Madeline stood, pale and shaken, as Jed approached. "Oh," she cried. "I'm so glad to see you. I didn't know what was going to happen to me after he shot that poor girl."

Sam walked up and hearing Madeline he said, "You'll be fine now ma'am. We'll help you back to the road as soon as we see what happened to Henry."

Madeline gave them a weak smile. There was no doubt that Henry was dead and she felt certain she had pulled off her lie. Everyone would believe Henry had shot Anna. "Don't worry Marshal, I'll stay right here."

Sam and Jed walked through the trees to where the drop-off was. Looking down they saw Henry and his horse had fallen so far they ended up near the road below.

The men below, were already making their way toward the grue-some tangle of man and horse. Henry's horse was still alive, though barely. Mercifully, they put it out of its misery. There was nothing to be done for Henry. "Well that takes care of that," muttered Sam.

Sam led Madeline's horse as they retraced their climb down the hill-side. When they reached the road, one of the men had already left at a gallop to bring Tink and Bill back. When they returned, Sam had them gather Henry's saddle and belongings, saying it would pay for the undertaker.

Henry's body was tied to Madeline's horse. She averted her eyes, feeling nothing, except relief, thinking everything was going to be fine. Sam had her ride with him on his big roan.

Madeline was tired and sore but she decided not to complain. Sam had given her some jerky so her hunger was somewhat satisfied. Even though she was a mess, the men kept stealing envious glances at Sam and his passenger. They knew how she made her living, and any one of them would have welcomed a chance to have her on his horse.

They hadn't gone far, when Jed rode abreast of Sam. "Marshal," he said, "This slow pace is too much for me. If you don't mind, I'd like to ride on so I can see if Anna's come to yet."

Madeline had almost dozed off until she heard Jed's words. She felt the blood rush from her face and almost lost her grip around Sam's waist.

"Sure Jed, I know you're worried about her, go on ahead."

As Jed rode off, Madeline gathered herself enough to ask, "Anna's not dead?"

"No," Sam answered. "The bullet just grazed her head. Doc says she has a concussion, but that she will be fine."

"You mean that she's going to be okay?" Madeline asked, trying to control the trembling in her voice.

"Sure," Sam answered. "She hadn't come to when we left, but Doc says she'll wake up in time."

CHAPTER THIRTY ONE

Madeline couldn't believe she'd told the marshal Henry shot Anna. *What was I thinking? No one would blame me for trying to shoot Henry.* She wondered what would happen to her when Anna told how she got shot. Madeline had been so preoccupied with her thoughts, she didn't notice they had almost reached town.

Sam broke into her thoughts, "Well ma'am, we're almost back to the hotel." Then he turned to the men, directing Tink and Bill to take Henry's body and belongings to the undertaker's. Sam reigned up at the hotel and helped the worried Madeline down from his mount and into the hotel lobby.

Mary came running to them. "Some men said you were back." Looking at Madeline, she cried out, "My God girl, look at you! Well, you're home now. I'll have Susie fix you a nice hot bath. If you want anything else, just tell her. You look like you could use a drink or two, I'll have Ruby bring some to you." Madeline gave Mary a blank smile. "You go on now. You look plumb tuckered out."

In a daze Madeline, climbed the stairs to room nine. *Maybe I'll think of a way to get out of this,* she thought to herself.

Susie came into the room, to fix the bath for her saying, "You feel better, after bath and rest." Madeline said nothing as she undressed.

There was a light rap on the door and Ruby came in with a towel covered tray, setting it on a stool beside the tub. "Mary sent this up, she had Cookie fix a sandwich too. We're glad you're back." Madeline paid no attention to Ruby as she got into the tub and leaned back, closing her eyes. Susie and Ruby exchanged worried looks and left the room.

At the closing of the door, Madeline opened her eyes. Noticing the tray, she idly removed the towel. Ignoring the food, she picked up the oversize glass of whiskey, downing the liquid in a few large gulps. Madeline wasn't a drinker and after the first scalding swallow, her body became less tense. As she sat in the soothing water she thought, *I can't go back to this life. These men are just using me for their pleasure, they care nothing about me.*

Then, she recalled how she had come to this pitiful existence. Once she had been in love, and had felt loved. She was only eighteen and he was twenty-two. His name was Thomas. He was handsome and caring, and seemed deeply in love with Madeline. Thomas was a photographer and had saved his money so they could marry. After their marriage, Thomas planned to travel out west taking pictures of everything, the people, the country, and Indians. His excitement was contagious.

So the two of them set off on their adventure. They had a covered wagon and had joined a small wagon train, traveling west. Life was good. Thomas always taking pictures, Madeline doing wifely things, cooking and caring for the interior of their small wagon. They'd traveled all spring and into summer, when her happy world had come to an end.

The wagon train had spent a night outside an Army outpost, near the Cherokee Strip. The post commander had warned the group about some renegades that were on the prowl. The men of the wagon train felt they could handle a few Indians and outlaws, so the group left early the next morning.

Thomas was looking forward to seeing Indians. He believed they would be so fascinated at seeing their own picture, they would consider him magical. Madeline was not so confident in his belief, but Thomas assured her things would be fine.

Things weren't fine. Half a day out from the outpost, the renegades struck the wagon train. Thomas had been away from the train, taking pictures of some scenery they'd passed. Madeline had been driving their wagon.

As she lay in the tub of water at the hotel, she recalled the attack with a shudder. The men of the wagon train had put up a valiant fight, but were no match for the kill crazed men. Soon all Madeline could hear were the terrible screams of men, women, and children.

Then two men pulled her from the wagon seat. There was no question as to their intentions. Throwing her to the ground, they tore off her clothing, sometimes using their knives to cut away fabric. She tried to fight them but one hit her on the head and she drifted in and out of consciousness. She could still recall the awful smell of their sweat, and their grunts and groans, as they each took turns with her. She lost track of how many had abused her. It seemed to go on forever. She felt as if she could no longer endure the abuse, when she heard gunfire.

It turned out Thomas had been returning to the wagon train, when he heard the fight between the raiders and the men of the train. Seeing what was happening, he raced back to the fort for help. He returned on an Army mount, having almost run his horse to death. When Madeline realized the renegades had left, she opened her eyes. Thomas and an army sergeant were standing over her.

The sergeant had looked at her with pity. She would never forget the look of disgust and almost loathing on Thomas' face, as he stared at her bruised and naked body. He walked over to the sergeant's horse and getting a blanket from behind the saddle, he came back to where she still lay, now in a fetal curl. Thomas threw the blanket at her, telling her to cover herself. The sergeant glared at him and stepped over to Madeline, helping her up and into their wagon. She climbed into the bed and pulled the covers tightly about her, as if to block out the physical and mental pain.

Thomas decided they would return to Kansas City. She now recalled how painful the trip towards home had been. Thomas no longer wanted to be near her. He always seemed to have a look of distaste when he looked at her. As the days passed, she felt more and more isolated. It was as if he thought what had happened had been her fault. Once, he even implied she might have enjoyed the ordeal.

They reached Meade and camped just outside the town by the Crooked River. One morning, he gave her some money and told her to go into town and buy herself a new dress. She was surprised and encouraged by his new concern for her. It would be a real treat and she was excited as she walked towards town. At the general store, she hadn't been able to find any dress that appealed to her and ended up just buying some ribbon and a small bag of candy. She had taken her time, enjoying the spell away from the judgmental Thomas.

In the afternoon, she started the half mile hike back to their wagon. When she got there, that's all she found, the wagon. There was a note on the seat, held down by a rock. All it read was, "I'm sorry, Thomas." She looked in the wagon and found all of his camera equipment and personal belongings were gone, along with their two horses. She was crestfallen. He had left her alone.

For two days she'd stayed at the wagon camp, not knowing what else to do. She had hoped Thomas would have a change of heart and return for her. By the third day, she became quite bitter and decided to walk back to town and see if she could find some work to get her by until she had figured out what to do.

First she went to the hotel to get a cup of coffee. That's when her life changed, again. The woman, she would soon know as Mary, had come into the dining room. She was clearly angry and upset as she stomped to a table near Madeline, where a scantily clad blonde sat alone. Standing with her hands planted firmly on her broad hips, Mary accused the girl of stealing from a customer. She went on in no uncertain terms to tell the girl that she was to pack up and get out, she was fired.

The girl stood up, glaring at Mary. She didn't deny the theft, stating she hadn't liked the place anyway, and flounced from the room.

Mary had then gotten herself a cup of coffee and sat nearby.

Madeline had no idea what sort of work the girl had done but she thought, it's a job. She approached Mary, asking if she could sit down.

"Sure honey," the now friendly Mary had said, as she introduced herself. "Me and my husband own this here hotel."

Madeline introduced herself to Mary then said she couldn't help but overhear what had happened, and she was in need of work.

"Is that right?" Mary had said, with a laugh. "Are you sure you know what you're talking about?"

"Well no," Madeline had admitted. "But I'm sure I could do whatever she did."

Mary let out a ruckus laugh then lowering her voice some she said, "That blonde was one of my girls, you know, one of my working girls. They take care of men that come looking for a little fun." Looking Madeline over she stated, "You are a beauty. You'd have a room of your own, all the food you wanted, and 20 percent of what the men pay. I stand for no mistreatment of my girls and as you heard, I stand for no thievery."

It slowly dawned on Madeline what Mary was talking about. She thought, *It couldn't be worse than what I had endured when the wagon train was under attack. Anyway, if Thomas was any indication, no man would want me now. That is except the men who paid women for their services.* She made her mind up and told Mary, "If you want me, I'll take the job." She returned to the wagon for some personal things, then asked the man at the livery if he would sell the wagon and its contents for her and just left that part of her life behind.

As the days working for Mary had dragged by, she learned to endure the parade of men, always dreaming of the day when she would leave. Then she met Henry. He had treated her like a lady and after his second visit, he professed to be in love with her. He told her he wanted to take her away with him. *That dream is gone now*, she thought bitterly.

After the attack and Thomas' indifference, she'd thought of ending it all, and now that dark thought came to her again.

Her eyes rested upon a straight edge razor sitting on a shelf across the room. As if in a trance, she rose from the tub. Getting the razor, she returned to the tub and slowly slid down into the water. Holding the razor, she slashed first one wrist then the other. She dropped the blade onto the floor and laid her head against the back of the tub. There was a small smile on her lips as she thought, peace at last, while her life's blood flowed into the reddening water.

Susie rapped gently on the door of room nine before going in. At first, she thought Madeline was sleeping. As she drew closer, she saw the bloodied water and the razor on the floor. Taking a closer look, Susie saw that Madeline was dead. Leaving to tell Mary, Susie locked the door to room nine, where one life had ended and another had been conceived.

CHAPTER THIRTY TWO

Susie had hurried to Mary's office, knocking frantically on the door.

"Come in!" shouted an irritated Mary. One look at Susie's face and she knew something was wrong.

"Miss Mary, Missy Madeline dead."

"What?" exclaimed Mary. "What do you mean?"

"She look dead to me."

"Dead? How?" Mary asked, as she rose from her desk and started for the door.

"I not sure, the water all red and razor on floor. She not breathe." Susie was on the verge of tears.

Mary patted Susie on the shoulder telling her to sit while she found someone to go get Doc and the marshal. Leaving Susie in her office, Mary went out to the saloon, sending Spook after the marshal and another man after Doc. Then she went on up to room nine to see what had happened for herself.

❧——❧

Jed had gone to Doc's when he got back into town. Doc told him Anna was doing fine and Nora had taken her home and was staying with her until Jed got back. He also told Jed what Anna told about how she got shot.

Jed stared at him, "Why, Madeline let us believe Henry shot Anna." After relating the details of their search and Henry's death, Jed told Doc he was going to go check on Anna, then go see the marshal with the truth.

Anna and Nora were sitting at the kitchen table when Jed rode up. He was so happy to see Anna was fine, he couldn't stop smiling. Then he realized he had to tell Anna her husband was dead. "I'm glad to see you're okay but I'm afraid I have some bad news for you." Anna and Nora looked at him expectantly.

Jed stood shifting his feet, feeling uncomfortable. He wondered how Anna would take the news. After all, he thought, she had been married to the man.

Anna noticed his discomfort. "For heaven sakes sit down and tell us what happened."

Jed related everything, then studied Anna's face, looking for a clue as to how she felt about her husband's death.

She had sat there, looking off into space, while Jed had told the tale. She didn't really know how she felt. There'd been times when she wanted to be free of Henry but she never wished him dead. Noticing Nora and Jed watching her, she knew they were wondering how this news set with her. "Funny," she said softly, "I feel like I'm supposed to at least cry. I guess I've done enough of that these last couple months. Maybe I have no tears left. Henry and I started out with such hopes but somewhere along the way, he just went kinda crazy. Maybe he was always that way and I didn't see it." She stopped talking and sat staring into her cup of tea.

The silence grew and Nora stood. Walking over to Anna, she gently put her hands on her shoulders. "You should go lay down dear. You've had quite a lot to deal with."

At Nora's tenderness, emotions suddenly rose to the surface. Whether it was relief or sadness, Anna didn't know, but tears began to fall. Unable to speak, she nodded her head and rose from the table to leave. Nora started to go with her but Anna put her hand out to stop her and went up the stairs to her room.

"I guess she wants to be alone for a while," Nora said. "She's a strong girl. Things will work out fine, you'll see."

"Nora," Jed said, "I forgot, I need to go tell Sam how Anna really got shot. I know he'll want to talk to Madeline after the way she led us to believe it was Henry. It might not matter much, but I think he'd like to know the truth. Anyway, could you stay a little longer, until I get back?"

"Why sure, you go along and don't worry about a thing. I don't mind staying a while longer at all." Jed gave her a smile, and rushed out the door.

When Jed arrived in town, Sam was just leaving his office with Spook. Sam looked up at Jed, "I figured you'd be getting some rest."

"Well, I was until Doc told me how Anna really got shot."

"Anna came to?"

"Yes, she told Doc Madeline was going to shoot Henry. She was mad because he'd led her on and he didn't tell her he was married.

Anyway, she missed and the bullet hit Anna. I thought you'd like to know."

"Well I guess so," Sam declared. "I'm on the way over to the hotel now. Mary sent Spook after me, seems there's some kind of trouble there."

The three men started across the street towards the hotel. As they grew near, they saw a worried looking Mary at the door greeting Doc. Sam and Jed entered the lobby in time to see Mary and Doc, hurrying up the stairs.

"Mary!" Sam shouted. "What's going on?"

"Oh Sam, I'm glad you're here, come upstairs with us." Sam hurried to catch up with the two. Jed stayed where he was, thinking whatever was wrong, he should just wait.

As they reached room nine, Mary turned to Sam, "Madeline's dead. You might want to wait outside 'til Doc takes a look see."

"What?" exclaimed a stunned Sam. "Sure, I'll wait right here."

Doc and Mary entered the silent room. Doc drew in a sharp breath, "My God, she is dead, no doubt about that" stated a somber faced Doc. "See here, she cut her wrists. What a waste. Can you help me get her onto the bed? Nora would ordinarily be here but she's with Anna."

"Alright," said a somewhat hesitant Mary. "This is terrible, why would she do such a thing? She always was hard to figure out, but this…"

"None of us knows what goes on in people's minds," Doc replied.

Mary placed some towels on the bed and with some difficulty, they got Madeline from the tub and on to the bed. Mary covered her pale body with a sheet.

"We need to send somebody after the undertaker."

"I'll send someone," said a somber Mary. They went out to the hallway where Sam had been waiting.

After they told him what Madeline had done, he said, "I'm not surprised, she lied herself into a corner and probably thought she was in a lot of trouble." He told Mary how Madeline had tried to blame Henry for what she thought had been murder. Then when she found Anna hadn't died, and would tell the truth, well…

"Did you know that she thought Henry loved her?" Mary asked Sam.

"Not until a little bit ago, Jed just told me."

CHAPTER THIRTY THREE

Jed left town for home after learning of Madeline's death. It seemed a long and tiring time since he and the others had left to find Henry and Madeline. Now it was over. As he rode home in the warm spring air, his thoughts turned to Anna. He wondered how she really felt about her husband's death. Remembering her tears, he worried Henry had meant more to her than she had known. He had wanted so badly to take her in his arms and comfort her. But it somehow didn't seem the right thing to do. She knew how he felt about her and might have thought he was glad Henry was dead. In his heart, he knew he was. Nora's right, he told himself, I'll just bide my time.

When Jed reached home, he found Nora and Anna sitting on the back steps. Tag rose up, wagging his tail in a happy greeting. Stripping his horse and turning it out to pasture, he walked over to them. Patting Tag on the head he gazed at Anna, saying, "Well, everyone looks pretty good. How are you doing?"

"I'm okay," replied Anna.

"Then maybe you'd better get ready for another shock."

"Really? What's wrong?"

"Well, when I went in to talk to Sam he was on his way to the hotel. It seems Madeline killed herself."

"What a terrible thing!" exclaimed Anna, "She was such a beautiful girl. It's too bad she was taken in by Henry.

"Well," Jed replied, "Mary told us she'd always been a pretty unhappy person."

After Jed told them the details Nora said, "I guess I'd better be going home, this has been something. Doc's probably ready for a nice quiet dinner. Jed, if you don't mind, will you hook my buggy up for me?"

"Sure thing, thanks for staying so long."

Nora smiled at him, "It wasn't a problem. I had a chance to get to visit with this sweet girl." Patting Anna on the head, she went into the house to gather her things. Jed brought the wagon up to the back porch. Nora got in and drove off, waving to them as she left the yard.

Alone, thought Jed as he sat in silence beside Anna and Tag. They sat for a long time, just enjoying the sounds and smells of a now peaceful afternoon. After a while, Jed turned to Anna asking if she was hungry.

"Not really, Nora and I had lunch, how about you?"

"I'm a little hungry, I'll go fix myself something."

"I'll help you." Anna stood up too quickly and her head started to spin. She staggered forward and Jed jumped up, catching her in his arms.

He couldn't help himself. He'd wanted to hold her in his arms for so long and he tightened his hold on her as he whispered her name.

Much to her amazement, Anna felt a surge of warm contentment and love. She leaned against him as they stood together. In wonder, she realized, she did feel more for this man than friendship.

"Anna," he said again, his face pressed against her hair, "I know it's too soon but I can't stop how I feel. Please say you'll marry me. I know it's a terrible thing to ask, since you just lost your husband." Jed never got to finish what he was saying. Anna had turned a little in his arms and reaching up, she pressed her fingers against his lips.

"Jed, it seems shameful to me too, but Henry was gone from my life long before he died. I have strong feelings for you too but have you forgotten about the baby?"

"Anna, I told you before; we'll just raise him like he was ours."

Anna smiled up at him, "What makes you think it's a boy?"

Jed kissed her forehead, saying, "I don't care what it is. Why, if it's a girl, I'll have two of you to love. We can always try for a son later."

"You seem to have given this a lot of thought."

"Yes, you've been all I could think about ever since the first time I laid eyes on you. Please say we can be married."

"What will people think? Why, my husband just died."

"Never mind what people say. Let them think the baby's mine. What do we care? We can have a happy life, I just know it. We can have the preacher marry us and I'll take you to the cabin I built. Oh, Anna you'll love it there. When it's time for the baby, we'll come back and stay in town."

Anna was feeling very comfortable in Jed's arms and his plans for them seemed wonderful to her. She thought, *I have never heard such a long string of words from this dear man.*

She again placed her fingers on his mouth, to still him. Gazing deep into his eyes, neither had to say any more as they held one another close and kissed. Tag was circling the two, his tail wagging wildly. Anna felt him brush against her. Breaking away from Jed, she smiled at him and said, "I guess Tag says yes too."

They went into the kitchen to fix something to eat. Jed announced he was still going to stay in his room in the barn. Stating he didn't trust himself to be close to Anna. He would wait for their wedding night.

As she lay in bed that night, she wondered how Jed could be so different than the cowboy. It had seemed nothing would have stopped him from making love to her. Was Jed worried because of her condition?

CHAPTER THIRTY FOUR

Two weeks since her husband had died, running from the law. Two weeks since Jed had asked her to marry him, and now just two weeks until the wedding. Anna was in the upstairs bedroom. She had been finishing her dress for the upcoming wedding. Now she sat staring towards the window, the dress lay forgotten. The warm spring air coming in the open window was gently billowing the lace curtains. Anna didn't notice; she was deep in thought.

There was no longer any doubt in her heart and mind that she had strong feelings for Jed and that she could love him. But thoughts of how she felt when the cowboy looked at her would return and she wondered what it would be like if she were to be marrying him. She swept the thoughts away, after all he was a stranger to her. Then again, to marry so soon after Henry's death seemed wrong, even immoral. *f* She had voiced those concerns to Jed and he told her the only people that mattered were the ones that knew the truth. *They only think they know the truth*, Anna thought with a sour smile.

Then the constant shame crept back into her mind: how could she have allowed a half drunken cowboy to seduce her, a total stranger? She would never understand.

He wasn't a complete stranger anymore. His name was Luke Evans. The marshal had introduced him when Anna had gone to report Henry's plans. The cowboy's face lit up when he saw her. He'd asked if they hadn't met before. Anna was stunned at seeing him again. Of course she denied any knowledge of him. She was even more shocked at the way she felt when she had momentarily looked into those hypnotic brown eyes. Her body had reacted involuntarily at his presence. She felt goose bumps rising on her arms and a little weak in the knees. *What would he think, if he knew she was carrying his child?*

She sat there remembering Jed asking who the father of the baby was. She just couldn't bring herself to try and explain how it had happened. It was something that she couldn't explain, even to herself. Jed had said it wouldn't matter that it wasn't his child. He would raise it as his own, saying it was part of her and he would have all the more to love. Well, she thought, people say foolish things when they're in love.

Her thoughts were interrupted by Tag barking a greeting to someone. Leaving her sewing, Anna went to the open window. Pulling the curtain aside, she saw Sarah Covington had driven her cart up to the front gate. Anna called down to her to saying she would be right down and to come on in.

Sarah had an armload of eggs and milk. Anna raced to relieve her of the items before something tumbled to the floor. Sarah always seemed to be balancing her parcels like a juggler in action. On top of that, there was the constant chatter. Anna had come to enjoy Sarah's non-stop talking, even though a person couldn't get a word in edgewise.

"So," started Sarah, "I guess you've been up stairs workin' on your weddin' dress."

"Yes," Anna started to say but Sarah was off and running.

"Everybody's in a dither about the big day. I hear Mary's having a big dinner for Jed and you, after the deed's done. Why, ain't that something? Say you got any coffee? I got a little time to sit down and visit."

"Well yes, sit down." Anna turned to get cups and the coffee.

Sarah continued on, "I hear Mary's girls are going to help serve at the big doings. A lot of the women folk in town are a little shocked at that. Some are saying they don't want to be in the same room as those girls, but you just wait and see. They'll be there alright, 'cause they gotta know everything that goes on in this town. It don't make no never mind to me. A party's a party and we don't git too many of 'em."

Sarah had kept her chatter up, stopping now and then for a gulp of coffee. Finally she rose from the table saying, "Well, I better get about my deliveries. You just keep those eggs and milk as a gift." Anna started to protest but Sarah kept talking as she headed towards the front door. "I hear Mary's gonna go all out for this shindig. She thinks the world of you and Jed."

Anna smiled a weak smile as she bid the exuberant Sarah goodbye. She wished people weren't so excited about this wedding. She was having a hard time getting excited about it. Was she doing the right thing, by marrying Jed?

CHAPTER THIRTY FIVE

Mary had approached Anna with the request to have her girls help out with the dinner, telling Anna they wanted to show their appreciation for the dresses she'd made them. Mary assured Anna her girls would dress like proper ladies. Looking at Mary, dressed in another of her bright, tight fitting gowns, Anna wasn't sure Mary knew what proper dress was, but she told Mary it was sweet of the girls. After all, she thought, how could she say no to Mary when she'd done so much for her?

As she returned to her sewing, Anna thought how long ago it seemed since she had come to Meade with Jed. Had she really been that bedraggled girl, living in a remote cabin with a dirt floor, waiting for an unfaithful husband to return? So much had happened since Jed had brought her into Meade. She felt very at home and content here in town, except for the child growing within her.

Jed had arranged for the church and preacher a couple days after Henry's and Madeline's funerals. He now was at his Crooked River ranch. He wanted to finish the house before they were married.

Anna was thankful for Jed's help with what had to be taken care of for Henry's burial. Everything had been done as quickly and as simply as possible. Few people had attended the funeral: only the marshal, a deputy, Doc, and Nora. They were there for Anna.

Madeline's burial had been taken care of by Mickey and Mary. Anna hadn't attended, but Sarah told her some of the people from town were there, because Madeline's suicide had been the talk of the town.

After Sarah left, she no longer felt like working on the dress, there wasn't much left to do anyway. She went downstairs and out the back door. Tag came running to meet her. "What a good dog you turned out to be. I hope you'll like the new home we're going to." She walked out to the small garden thinking she'd do a little weeding or watering, but she seemed unable to settle to any task.

She missed Jed's company. Anna had grown to like living in Meade and worried about leaving the comfort and the people. Jed had promised they would return when winter came and it was close to time for the baby. They would go back to his ranch in the spring.

Jed hoped by then he would have a barn built for the horses, Anna's old mule Adam, and other stock. Anna had also asked if they could have a milk cow. She was becoming a little excited, even if she had some reservations about marrying so soon after Henry's death.

Hearing a noise, Anna looked up to see Susie driving one of the small livery wagons into the yard. Susie raised her small hand in greeting. Anna was surprised at how well the tiny Chinese woman handled the horse and fully loaded wagon.

Alighting from her seat, Susie greeted her, "Hello Missy Anna."

Noting the questioning look on Anna's face she went on, "Mr. Jed want Lee and me to live in his place in the barn. He think it be easier for us and a better home too. We can take care of things when you go to ranch."

"Oh yes, I remember now, he did mention that. How can I help you?"

"You no need to work, Missy Anna. What I have to do is not hard. You keep me company."

"Sure," Anna replied. They walked into the barn and to Jed's room. They were surprised to see Jed had removed all his personal things, and the place was spotless.

"That Mr. Jed," said Susie, "I think I would have to clean. This place more big than where we live. I guess I bring things in."

In spite of Susie's objections, Anna pitched in to help move the meager belongings into the room. Anna could tell the usually calm and serene Susie was thrilled with her new home. It made her ashamed when she thought how fortunate she was. They had the job done in no time, and Susie wanted to fix tea. She rummaged through the bundles and retrieved a carefully wrapped tea set. It looked ancient to Anna.

"That's very pretty, is it old?"

"Oh yes. I bring from my country, it was my Honorable Grand-mother's."

Anna was happy to sit with Susie, she was the only person that knew who the real father of her baby was. It was a great relief to be able to talk about how she felt. Susie seemed wise beyond her years and Anna valued her advice. Although Susie would never attempt to tell anyone what to do, she had a way of helping to see more clearly.

Anna told her of still having doubts about the marriage.

Susie listened, then placing one small hand on Anna's, said, "Mr. Jed love you, I can see. You will love him and make him happy. That make everything okay. You see. Maybe one day Mr. Jed ask about father again then you tell him. Every person make mistake sometime. When baby come Mr. Jed be happy. It break his heart when wife and baby die." Susie got up from the table saying, "I go back to work now, everybody miss you, I think even Cookie."

"I sorta miss working too and I even miss that old grouch." Anna thanked Susie for the tea and making her feel better.

Susie climbed up to the wagon seat, waving and smiling her knowing smile said, "Everything be okay, you see."

CHAPTER THIRTY SIX

It was afternoon when Anna returned to her kitchen. Feeling a little hungry, she scrambled up a couple of Sarah's eggs.

While eating, she gazed about the room and it hit her. She had no idea what to pack for the move to the ranch. Jed hadn't said anything about it, in fact, a lot of things were left unsaid. Where would they stay after they were married? It would be too late in the day to go to Jed's new home. Would he want to spend their wedding night in the town house, in the same room he'd shared with his first wife? Would she?

She wondered what the wedding night would be like. Jed cared for her, of that she was sure. Suddenly the passion she had felt with the cowboy came to mind. Shocked and upset by the memory, she wondered, *Is that what's making me feel so unsettled and at odds?*

She felt sure she loved Jed, but realized he hadn't shown the unbridled need she had seen in the cowboy that night. Was it because she was pregnant? Was Jed being considerate because of her condition? He seemed to be in complete control of his feelings and desire.

What was love, anyway? Was it the feeling of contentment and safety she had with Jed or was it the physical need she felt with the cowboy? These thoughts often whirled in Anna's head. To her, finding the answer was like roping the wind.

No, she knew she didn't love the cowboy, how could she? She knew nothing about him, other than he was a drifter, looking for a good time in town. She thought of Jed: honest, hardworking, and strong; but were those the things that made love strong? Recalling her mother and father, there had never been any great show of affection between them, but they had seemed happy. Of course, she thought, her father was a widower, twenty years older than her mother. Was he looking for a mother for his motherless child?

With shame, she asked herself, *Am I looking for a father for my child? No, that might be part of my decision, but I care a great deal for Jed and I know we could be happy.*

Thinking of her folks reminded Anna that she needed to write them and tell of Henry's death and her upcoming wedding. She composed a letter, leaving out how Henry had died, only saying his horse had fallen, killing him. She wrote of moving to Meade and making money sewing for some of the women in town. She didn't write the women were some of the local prostitutes. She went on to say that this might come as a surprise to them, she'd met a very nice man and they were to be married in two weeks. She wrote on after we're married we will move to his ranch outside Meade. I'm very happy and I have a dog that I named Tag. We will return to Meade in the winter, so you won't get another letter until then. Ending by writing she loved and missed them, she signed it: Your Loving Daughter, Anna. She certainly didn't mention she was going to have a baby.

Rereading her letter, she was satisfied that she'd been able to inform her folks without revealing Henry's death had been quite recent and the wedding was very sudden. She would write of the baby after it was born.

Evening shadows were beginning to fall as Anna went to sit on the back porch with Tag. Upon hearing her come out the door he bounded from his eternal "critter" watch to sit with her. It was something he seemed to enjoy as much as Anna. "Well boy, I guess after a couple weeks the rabbits and such can have a party in the garden. Maybe Susie will take care of it." Tag just wagged his tail and muzzled her hand asking for more pets. Anna soon went in to go to bed.

Tag lay down on his padding, his eyes closed, his ears and nose open, ready to chase any interlopers even thinking of invading his self-assigned territory.

Anna woke early the next morning to the sound of birds and the bright spring sunlight, streaming in the bedroom window. She realized, with great delight, her morning sickness seemed to be over. In fact she felt pretty good and was as hungry as a bear coming out of hibernation.

While dressing, it seemed the dress she put on was just a tad snug. She decided after breakfast, she'd better try her wedding dress on, to see if it still fit. It was strange to think of her body changing shape. She wondered what it was going to be like having a huge belly. She'd seen women that were large with child but had never given it much thought. Gently patting her stomach, she found herself talking to the child hidden within. Stopping suddenly, she realized she had accepted there was a person growing inside her. A small smile played on her face. Right then and there, Anna knew she would love this child no matter how he or she came to be.

Coffee even tasted good again. After breakfast she went out to water the garden and was surprised to find Lee cutting wood and Susie hanging some clothes on the line. Susie walked to Anna, a big smile on her face.

"Susie how can you be here so early? Don't you have to be at the hotel to help Cookie?"

Laughing, Susie replied, "Miss Mary tell us she do work this morning so we could stay in our new home. We worry it might be bad. She say, she take care of Cookie 'cause she the boss. So we say okay, here we are. You need anything for us to do?"

Anna hadn't ever heard such a long string of words from Susie. It delighted her to see her friend so happy. In answer to Susie's question she replied, "No I can't think of anything. I'm feeling pretty good today. It would be nice if you and Lee would take the garden over, I hate to see it go to waste."

Susie seemed overjoyed, actually clapping her small hands together, "We never had place to grow things before. Lee very good at making garden."

Anna finished her watering then returned to her sewing. She hadn't been at the sewing for very long, when at last the dress was finished. Removing the dress she had on, she said aloud, "Well here goes nothing," and slipped the wedding dress on. It wasn't tight on her...yet. She decided to go buy some hair ribbon and mail her letter. She headed into town.

Tag happily trotted along with Anna, sniffing here and there, for invisible scents that excited only him.

Nearing town, a man raced his horse past her. Anna thought nothing of it but there did seem to be a little more activity than usual on the main street. Ordinarily the sleepy little town had few people about so early. This morning, there were a couple big wagons at the store and quite a few horses tied outside the hotel and at other saloons. A tinge of worry crossed Anna's mind. *Could there be another herd going by Meade? Maybe I should go back home? What if the cowboy is back? No, that's silly. There are other herds that go through here, besides it's not been that long since he was last here.*

CHAPTER THIRTY SEVEN

Anna decided to stop and see how Mary was doing without Susie and Lee. Going into the hotel lobby, she could see the bar was packed with noisy cowboys. Not wanting to traipse through the bar to Mary's office, she glanced about for the cowboy. Seeing no sign of him, she turned towards the restaurant and was shocked to see a couple of Mary's girls clearing tables as Mary took orders.

Mary saw Anna and rushed towards her, a look of desperation on her flushed face. "Oh, Anna! Am I glad to see you? What a fix I'm in. I sent somebody to go get Susie and Lee. A cattle drive stopped outside town late last night. Now they're all here. We're just about going crazy trying to keep up. Why look at my girls? They're so confused, they don't know if they're selling food or loving. Then with one of her hardy laughs she said, "At least they can practice for you and Jed's party."

Anna wasn't sure what to think of that as she watched Julia and Ruby flirting with the men while they moved about the dining room.

Mary brought her back to the situation at hand, "Can you help out for a while?"

Taken back by the request Anna stuttered, "Of course, where do you want me to start?"

"Well, if you could just take care of things out here 'til Susie and Lee get here, I'll go help Cookie."

"Alright," mumbled Anna, noticing Mary was racing towards the kitchen, not waiting for her answer. She forced herself to calm down and looked about for the cowboy, then watched the girls for a minute or so. First off she could see that the girls needed a little directing, or advice, or something. She wasn't sure what. Catching their attention, she crooked a finger at each of the giggling girls and they came flouncing over to her, followed by many admiring glances.

Speaking quietly to them she said, "Girls you're mixing business with pleasure."

"What do you mean?" asked Julia, a sly smile on her pouty lips, "Pleasure is our business."

"Of course, but this here is different. Mary needs you to act a little more...ah, she didn't know how to put it, I guess more ladylike, not so...."

Julia broke in, "Ya mean act more like you?" as she gently patted Anna's belly.

Anna was mortified. "Well, I guess so," Anna answered, not knowing how they really felt about her. It seemed everyone in town knew she was pregnant. At least they thought the baby was Jed's.

"Sure," replied Julia, "we can do that. Why it will be just like play acting, won't it Ruby? Let's git back to work."

Anna was floored as she watched the two girls. An amazing transformation had taken place. They were moving among the tables with ladylike calmness. Their movements almost demure. Anna began to take orders and deliver meals. Spook had come in from the bar to take money from the patrons when they were ready. Finally Susie and Lee arrived and things got back to normal.

All at once there was a commotion at one end of the room. A couple of cowboys were squared off, fists doubled up. "You apologize to the lady or I'll knock your block off," shouted a tall good looking young man, eyes blazing. A frightened Ruby stood aside, a look of amazement on her face.

"Apologize? Are you nuts?" shouted a stocky, older man. "Why she's nothing but a---" He never got to finish. The younger cowboy's fist flew out, smashing the older man in the mouth, rocking him on his heels. Shouts broke out as he wiped the blood from his split lip, and prepared to finish the battle. They circled each other like a pair of wild animals. Anna was horrified.

Suddenly, a blur of movement materialized between the two men. It was Spook. He towered over the two, but they seemed more irritated than intimidated with his presence.

"Get out of the way!" shouted the older man. "I'm gonna teach this young whipper-snapper a lesson."

"I don't think so," Spook said. His deep voice quieted the rowdy crowd as they expectantly looked from the fighters to Spook. "Now what's this all about?" he demanded.

The young cowboy shouted, "This here galoot insulted the little lady."

The older man *humphed*. "That's no lady, everybody knows that, why just look at her."

Now Ruby was standing with her head down, like a child caught in wrong doing. Anna felt very sorry for her.

Spook reached with both his ham-like hands, grabbing the would be fighters by their shirt fronts, almost lifting them off their feet. "Now," he said in a firm tone to the older man, "You *will* tell Ruby you're sorry. Then you two take this outside, or I'll finish it right now." He left little doubt he couldn't do it.

"Well," snarled the man. "I guess she has a right to live the way she wants."

"That don't sound like no apology to me," said Spook, as he tightened his grip on the man. "Why don't you try again?"

The older cowboy's face was starting to get red, either from anger or Spook's tightening grip on the shirt. "Okay, okay, I'm sorry I insulted her." Spook glared at him. The cowboy looked at Ruby saying, "I mean, I'm sorry I insulted you."

"It's okay," she replied, shyly.

Spook released his vice like hold, giving the two a shove towards the way out. There was the sound of many chairs scraping the floor, as some of the men hurried after them, eager for more excitement.

Anna moved forward, putting her arm around Ruby's slender waist. Ruby looked up at her with wonder in her eyes. "You know, Miss Anna, that's the first time anybody called me a lady and they were going to fight about it. Imagine that. It made me proud. Do you think I could be a lady?" Ruby prattled on, "Why, if 'n I see that young cowboy again, I think I'll give him a big thank you." Then giving a coquettish smile she went on, "Maybe not in the usual way, since he thinks I'm such a lady." Ruby was standing near Spook, gazing up at him in obvious admiration. Taking hold of his massive arm, Ruby gushed to Anna, "Wasn't he wonderful? Why, he don't even carry a gun. I never in all my born day seen nobody so brave. Did you?" Anna noticed, with some surprise, that Spook seemed a little embarrassed and frustrated.

Mary came hurrying into the dining room, having gone to her office a little earlier. "There you girls are," she almost shouted. "You girls need to get back to work. The place is packed with lonely cowboys."

Anna noted the crest fallen looks on the girl's faces. It was as if they'd felt what it would be like to be regarded with some respect. Now they were being told to return to the only life they'd known and having realized it made them feel degraded. They mumbled goodbyes as they left with Mary.

Anna stood with Spook, "What you did **was** brave. I heard that you watched out for the girls. I guess it's true."

"It's what I get paid to do ma'am."

"Would you like to sit with me and have some pie and coffee?"

"I sure can't refuse that," answered the now gentle giant.

They chose a table, and Anna got the pie and coffee. As they sat there she asked, "How did you get into this sorta work?" As soon as the words came out, she thought, *There I go asking personal questions again.*

Spook didn't seem to mind, he looked thoughtful for a second, "Well, I don't much talk about it. I guess I feel at home here." He cast his pale eyes about, and seeing no one other than Anna was listening, he continued. "Ya see, when my ma was no more than sixteen, she fell in love with a no-account preacher. He got her in a family way. Of course he denied it and everybody believed him. So her shamed folks sent her off to San Francisco, to live with my grandma's sister. The family didn't know she was a madam. Anyway, turned out Phoebe was a great ole' gal. She took my mother in. My mother died having me, so Phoebe just kept me. I called her grandma and all her girl's helped raise me." After another bite of pie, he went on, "I'll tell you what ma'am, no youngin' was ever cared for and made over like I was. So you see I have a soft spot in my heart for Mary's girls. Anyhow, as you can see, I grew up to be big and healthy. It just came natural for me to look out for my family."

Anna smiled at him, "Well, you were still brave to get between those fighting men. Don't you worry that you don't carry a gun?"

"Na, most times when cowpokes start fussin', they're drunk and couldn't hit the broad side of a barn. Sometimes wearing a gun can cause trouble. I use to wear one when younger. I was pretty good with it too. Then one night a cowboy got out of line and when I told him he had to leave, he drew down on me. Well, killing that man didn't set right with me. After that I decided to see some country and here I am."

"Well I still think you were brave and I'm glad you are around for the girls. It kinda looks like Ruby has eyes for you."

Spook answered with a somewhat sad smile, "I kinda like her too but I'm only a tough that lives in a saloon. Well, would you just listen to me? I ain't never gone on so. Just forget all this blabber."

Anna patted his big hand, "You're a good man, Spook. I hope things work out for you someday."

Finished with the pie, he rose to leave, "Don't worry 'bout me ma'am, I just go along and see what comes about."

CHAPTER THIRTY EIGHT

Luke Evans had come in from the bar and sat watching Anna working in the dining room. Right off, he noticed she wasn't dressed or made up like Julia or Ruby. Now, he was positive she was the girl he'd spent time with that night, and he hadn't been able to forget her. It had seemed to him she didn't belong in that profession. She was different from the other girls. What was she doing in that room? He also felt there had been something more between them than a brief sexual encounter. Why had she denied knowing him, that day in the marshal's office?

The men in the saloon were still talking about how Henry and Madeline had died. He was sure the Henry Pierson they talked about had been her husband. What was she doing working at the hotel? Now that he knew her husband was dead, he wanted to talk to her. What he hadn't heard was Anna was soon to be married, or that she was going to have a baby. Men in bars were more interested in bloody stories than weddings and babies. He walked to where she was sitting.

Anna was tired but content. She enjoyed being back at the hotel. She sat staring into her coffee, thinking of all Spook had told her, when a shadow fell across the table. A deep voice broke into her thoughts.

"Mind if I sit down Mrs. Pierson?" She was speechless; she knew that voice and couldn't bring herself to look up.

"Mrs. Pierson?" he repeated.

She steeled herself and looked up into the brown eyes that always sent her heart racing. Thoughts rushed into her mind, *Why does he arouse me so? This cannot be happening.*

Removing his hat, he sat down without waiting for her answer. Anna tried not to look at his handsome face. She calmed herself as best she could, placing her hands in her lap to help hide the nervousness she felt. She was afraid to speak for fear she would betray how shaken she was.

"I'm going through with another herd. It seems we run into each other every time I'm passin' by, don't it?"

Anna gathered her courage and with a benign smile said, "Yes, but then Meade is a small town."

"I guess that's right, but it's always nice to run into old friends."

Anna worried about the meaning of his remark. He'd been drinking, that night. She'd hoped when she'd denied knowing him, he'd think he had the wrong person. Remaining as aloof as she could, she said, "We're hardly friends, I've only seen you once before."

"Well, maybe it just seems like I've known you for a while," he replied, gazing steadily at her.

She was drawn into those eyes, and struggled to break away from them. Turning her attention to the dishes on the table she muttered, "I really must go now. Can I have someone take an order for you?"

"No thanks, I just saw you and thought I'd say hello." Getting up from the table as Anna did, he put his hat on and touching the brim, said, "It was nice to see you again, Anna."

Hearing him say her name in such a familiar way caused her knees to go weak. She gave him a small smile and turned to go into the kitchen.

Luke hadn't missed how she had reacted to his presence and it gave him hope. Then he realized he'd be leaving in the morning. Thoughts of returning to Meade and settling down filled his mind. Yes, that's what he'd do, come back and pursue this woman. At least he had to try.

Susie and Lee were busy cleaning up. Cookie had already left the kitchen. Susie looked up from what she was doing when she saw Anna had come in. She got a puzzled look on her face and rushed to where Anna was leaning against the door jam.

"Miss Anna, you okay? You look pale."

"I'm fine, just a little tired," Anna replied, in a still unsteady voice.

"You sit," Susie almost demanded. "I bring you tea."

"Well, maybe a little." She really didn't want tea but thought if she waited some, the cowboy would be gone for sure.

Drinking the tea did help to calm Anna's nerves. She said goodbye to a worried looking Susie and went out to get the patiently waiting Tag to walk home.

Walking home in the warm spring afternoon should have been relaxing, but Anna was still shaken by the chance meeting with the cowboy. It was easier to think of him as the cowboy than to acknowledge she knew his name. She kept recalling how just the sound of his voice had affected her. She thought of those eyes that seemed to reach into her soul. No, she must not even think of the affect he had on her. Patting her stomach, she said out loud to the baby, "I know he's your father but we don't even know him. He's a drifter. He may be charming and handsome, but you'll only know Jed as your daddy. He'll take good care of us."

Anna didn't even remember the stroll home and was surprised when she reached the front gate. She busied herself in the garden, until it began to grow late. Still unable to forget the chance encounter, she decided to see if she remembered how to play the piano. It didn't take long to recall a few of her favorite songs and she played until her fingers grew tired.

Mounting the stairs to her room, Anna hoped she could clear her mind of the cowboy and get some sleep. She realized she hadn't mailed her letter to her folks or bought the ribbon. "Oh well," she sighed, "Maybe tomorrow when I'm sure that herd left town."

CHAPTER THIRTY NINE

Thoughts of the chance meeting with the cowboy had kept Anna tossing and turning most of the night. To her dismay, she woke several times to find she had been dreaming of Luke. After a small breakfast she thought, *Here it is another day closer to the wedding. I should be making some preparations for the move to Jed's ranch, but where to start? I just can't settle down to it today.* In the end, she decided to start making things for the baby. Sewing was very relaxing to her. She'd saved some money from her sewing and would walk to town for baby flannel; *I can also mail the letter to my folks and buy those ribbons I forgot about yesterday. I must stop thinking about that...Luke Evans. He upsets me so.*

Anna ran into Sarah at the general store and told of her plans to start on baby clothes. There was no keeping Sarah away. Almost before Anna had returned home, she showed up with armloads of baby things and lots of sewing advice. Anna was fascinated at how small the baby things were.

Sarah laughed, "Well, they do seem that way. Mercy, I recall fearin' I'd somehow break the first one. After they kept comin' it got easier. Now I miss having a little one around."

So it was that Sarah and Anna were hard at work, when they heard a commotion in the back yard. Tag was barking his greeting to someone. The two women went to the window. Jed had driven into the yard with a huge wagon, loaded to the top. They hurried downstairs and out the door. Jed was just getting down from the wagon as Anna raced towards him.

Jed wrapped his arms about her and kissed the top of her head as he spied Sarah.

"I missed you," he said in a husky voice.

"Oh me too," replied Anna, looking up at him. "It's been so lonesome here. I wanted to pack things, but I didn't know where to begin."

Jed held her at arm's length. "Why, Anna you don't need to pack anything but your clothes. I told you not to worry about that. I bought this wagon in Kansas City. It's filled with everything we need... I hope. I just have to take it out to the ranch."

"You mean you're leaving again?" asked a dismayed Anna.

"It's just for a few more days, then we'll be married." Hugging Anna tighter, he asked, "What do we have to eat around here? I'm starving."

"Why, ain't that just like a man?" laughed Sarah. "I guess that's the end of our sewing. Besides, it looks like you two need to be alone. I'll be going home. I gotta git some vittles for my tribe too." Then she turned to leave.

"Thanks for all the help," Anna called after her.

"What have you two been working on? Aren't you finished with your wedding dress yet?" Jed asked, as they walked arm in arm towards the kitchen.

"Oh yes, my dress is finished. We were making a few things for the baby."

"Oh," he replied.

Anna thought he sounded a little upset at being reminded of her condition. It bothered her. Was she making a mistake? Would Jed end up resenting the child? Her worry was soon forgotten as they entered the house.

"Do I smell fresh baked bread?" he asked.

"Yes, I baked some this morning but I'm afraid there's only a pot of beans to go with it."

"That sounds fine to me, I could eat a cow; hide and all."

After they had eaten, they went out to sit on the porch. Jed lit a cigarette. Then looking at Anna, he asked, "Are you getting excited about the wedding?"

"Oh my yes, but..."

"What?" Jed asked.

Anna found it difficult to answer. She was embarrassed, and looked down at her feet as she said, "I was wondering where we would spend our wedding night."

"Why, Anna, I do believe you are blushing."

"It's just ... I didn't think you would want to spend it here... you know because it's where you and Louise started out."

Taking her chin in his large hand, he gently kissed her cheek, "I gave that some thought too. It wouldn't bother me 'cause since I found you no nobody enters my mind. I figured you wouldn't take much to the idea of staying here, so I made arrangements for us to stay in that fancy Hotel Royal in town." He didn't mention he'd learned a few things about women. Louise had complained long and bitterly, because he hadn't planned a honeymoon trip instead of going down the street to their home.

"Oh, Jed, you are so wonderful. You don't know how I worried about that."

Rising up, Jed took her in his arms, "I don't want you worrying about a thing except being the prettiest bride this here town ever saw. Now I'm going into town for the night. I want to get an early start in the morning. I can't stay here with all this temptation. I want our wedding night to be special. Is there anything you need before I go?"

"No," answered a letdown Anna, "No, I'm fine. I just don't want you to leave again."

"Don't be tempting me." He held her closer.

Anna felt flushed with desire as she kissed him with passion.

"My lord, girl, you don't make leaving any easier but I'm sticking to my guns." He freed himself and headed for the wagon, shouting over his shoulder, "I'll see you at the church. Just pack your clothes."

Tag followed behind for a short distance, then turned back to stand by Anna as they watched the wagon trundle down the dusty road to town. Anna thought, *Maybe I am doing the right thing after all. Kissing Jed was almost as exciting as ... What am I thinking? Luke is out of my life.*

CHAPTER FORTY

The last few days before the wedding seemed to drag by. At last the big day arrived. The ceremony was to be at one in the afternoon. Anna donned the pink and white checked cotton dress with lace collar and cuffs. It fit like a glove. Anna's maid of honor would be Sarah who arrived with her family around noon. Everyone was in their Sunday best. The usually harried looking Sarah fairly shone. She had on the pretty pale blue dress Anna had made for her. She'd even washed her hair and fixed it in an attractive style. The ever present bun had been replaced with curls.

"Why just look at you!" exclaimed Anna.

"I know," a beaming Sarah replied. "Why even my man said if'n I wasn't taken he'd ask for my hand in marriage. Are you ready to git to the church? We made the kids squeeze up, so's to make lots of room for you. Are you nervous?" As usual, Sarah went on before Anna could answer. "Have you got everything? You sure look pretty. Your dress turned out real nice. So let's git this show on the road."

Anna got into the wagon. She was thankful for Sarah, she was feeling a little shaky, excited, and nervous.

⚬———⚬

They made their way into town, with Tag running along behind. Lots of people seemed to be driving towards the church and Anna could see many wagons were already there.

Sarah's husband drove into the church yard and helped the two women from their perch and they started for the church stairs. The doors were open. As Anna and Sarah headed for the small ante room to the side of the front doors, they glanced into the half-filled church.

"My goodness," Sarah said in a very loud whisper, "The preacher needs more weddings to fill this place up. Why look at all the people. It looks like everybody in town is here."

They waited and fidgeted with hair, ribbon, and dresses. Fifteen minutes or so passed when there was a light tapping on the door. It opened and a thin, pale lady, with drab brown hair, and faded brown eyes came into the room.

"Afternoon!" declared Sarah, in her usual loud voice. "Are we ready to get this deed done? Oh, Anna, this is the preacher's wife, Violet."

"Hello, it's nice to meet you Violet."

"Yes," the mousy woman replied. "I mean yes, it's nice to meet you and yes as soon as you hear the music start, you can come down the aisle." With that Violet left, leaving the door cracked open enough to admit the sound of the church organ.

"Poor Violet," said Sarah, in what she considered a whisper, "It's a pity she never had any little ones. Being a preacher's wife is a hard life."

When they heard the music, Anna's knees felt weak but Sarah had a firm grip on her arm as she led her to the aisle, then walked ahead of her towards the alter.

Anna wasn't sure if she could make her legs move. She saw smiling faces, but they all seemed a blur. She did take note of Mickey, Mary, and her girls.

She looked up to see Jed. His eyes seemed to glow with love and pride. He looked handsome in a black broadcloth suit, with a white shirt, and string tie.

Anna's heart swelled as she gazed at him. She had a feeling of such overwhelming love.

Jed reached out and took her hand. The rest seemed dream-like. The words were said and vows exchanged, then Jed placed a plain gold band on her finger. The preacher pronounced them husband and wife, telling Jed he could now kiss his bride. Then he turned to the crowded church, saying, "I would like to introduce Mr. and Mrs. Jed Hawkins.

Anna and Jed headed down the aisle amid much cheering and applause. They took Jed's buggy to Mickey and Mary's hotel, trailing a long line of guests behind them.

Arriving at the hotel dining room, Anna was amazed to see Mary and her girls had gotten ahead of them. She was even more surprised to see they really did look lady-like, including Mary, who had on a very sedate, high necked, light blue dress. She looked quite pretty without all the usual makeup; as did all the girls.

The dining room had been transformed. The scarred old tables were covered with white tablecloths. Each held a bouquet of spring wild flowers. There were two long tables aside from the others, one held food of all sorts and the other was covered with delicious looking homemade pies and cakes.

Mary had come to the couple, to tell them they needed to start eating, stating she didn't think she could hold back the hungry crowd much longer.

As Mary pointed out their special table, Anna asked where all the food had come from. "Why the women folk in town did it. Ain't it a wonder?"

"Yes, it is," replied Anna, "Thank you so much for all this."

"Oh don't thank me, the girls took care of everything. I'm really proud of them."

Jed and Anna did as Mary instructed. Jed heaped a plate saying, "I couldn't eat this morning. I guess I was too excited. Boy, this stuff looks good."

"Yes, I'm sorta hungry too," Anna said, as she filled her plate and they headed to their table.

Ellie was there, looking sweet in a plain pink gingham dress. "Would you like some coffee? We get to wait on all the people. It's gonna be fun."

Jed looked up at Ellie, saying, "You sure look nice, Ellie. Yes, I'll take some coffee, how about you Mrs. Hawkins?"

Ellie poured their coffee and moved on. Anna thought the girls looked like spring flowers as they moved about the room in their colorful dresses. She also noticed that some of the young men were watching with admiring eyes. *Maybe there is hope for these girls after all.*

Mary came to where they were seated, "My, don't you two look grand?"

"So do you," replied Anna. "You look very nice."

"Ain't it a caution? Why, Mickey even said I looked nice. He hasn't said that in years. But you know, I'm a little worried. The girls got together and picked out the dresses for all of us. It seems ever since they helped out in the dining room awhile back, they decided to be more lady- like. I'm not sure that's such a good idea. The next thing you know, some of these cowboys are gonna ask 'em to get hitched, then where will I be? Most of 'em fell into this life on account of things that happened to them. Of course, Julie's a different cup of tea, she likes workin' here. I hope it's a passing fancy. Guess I'll go say hello to a few of the people. It's wonderful to see you two so happy. Good luck to ya." With that, Mary bustled off in her usual speedy manner.

As Anna watched Mary leave, she thought, *I hope the girls do find another life for themselves.*

CHAPTER FORTY ONE

Jed looked at Anna with adoring eyes. "This is sure some shindig but I wish we were alone."

"Me too, but we can't up and leave after all the work they've done to help us celebrate."

"I know you're right, just the same..."

About then Mickey came to their table with two glasses and a bottle in his hands, "How are the new mister and missus?" He had on a new green embroidered vest. He put the glasses and bottle down announcing, "We got some champagne for this special occasion."

"Oh my," Anna declared. "I've never had champagne before."

"Well, I had some once, it's not to my liking, but this is surely a special occasion." He didn't mention it had been at his first wedding.

With nimble fingers and strong hands, Mickey popped the cork. Turning to the crowd and banging a knife on a glass to get everyone's attention, he announced in booming voice, "Ladies and gents you will notice that the servers have given you some wine for wishing the bride and groom a long and happy marriage. So now lift your glasses in a toast to the newly hitched bride and groom."

The crowd erupted into loud cheers and hooting. Anna drank her champagne, deciding it was something she could live without.

Again, Mickey raised his hands in the air to quiet the crowd, "Now we've a surprise for all of you. You might have noticed, Fingers has moved his piano in here and Ruby will sing a song for the bride and groom."

Anna and everyone else were surprised to see Ruby walk to Fingers and his piano. There was a great deal of whispering, however, it quickly died as Fingers began and Ruby started to sing, 'I Dream of Jeanie', replacing Jeanie with Anna's name. Her voice rang clear as a bell, and everyone seemed spellbound. It was very plain to see Fingers was struggling to keep from pounding the notes out in his usual manner. For a few seconds as the last strains died, there was total silence. Then gradually the crowd began to applaud. It was so long and loud, it fairly hurt one's ears. Ruby looked both surprised and pleased.

Together, Anna and Jed walked to the piano, giving Ruby a big hug and a thank you. Anna declared, "That was wonderful. How come no one heard you sing before?"

Ruby shrugged, murmuring, "I thought nobody would like it."

"Well, you're wrong there, that was beautiful," Jed remarked.

Anna noticed Spook off to one side, a look of awe and admiration on his pale face. She thought, *That man's definitely in love, I hope something can come of it.*

Mickey pounded on the table. Getting the crowd's attention again, he turned to Jed and Anna, and said, "Jed, you've always helped the people of Meade and now we want to return the favor." There was a smattering of applause. "In the morning, we are going to your ranch with you and your new bride. We know your barn isn't finished, so we're gonna finish it for you and bring a milk cow, a pair of hogs, and some laying hens, and a rooster to keep 'em happy." Someone shouted, "Maybe the hens won't be so happy but the rooster sure will." Raising his hands to still the laughter, he went on, "You two needn't worry about a thing. The town folk have this all planned, so be ready for us at dawn."

Clearly touched, Jed stood and in a faltering voice thanked them. "I can't believe all you've done already. Anna and I will be happy to have you as our first guests." Turning to Anna, he continued, "Mrs. Hawkins and I would be mighty proud to have you follow us in the morning but for now, I think we will say goodbye."

Anna smiled bravely, as she wondered how in the world they could entertain all these people. Amid much cheering and good wishes the couple left the happy crowd.

Mary's girls were among the well-wishers. Anna could see the longing in the girl's eyes; she felt guilty, having so much more in life than they did.

It took some time but the couple finally made it out to Jed's buggy, and he drove the short distance from Mickey and Mary's hotel to the Hotel Royal.

Anna began to feel nervous, this was it, the wedding night. She wasn't sure she was as eager as Jed. He kept looking at her with a huge smile on his face. There was no doubt he was looking forward to the evening.

They pulled up to the hotel and a young man came forward, saying he would take care of the buggy. Jed gave him a half dollar, then taking their small bags in one hand and Anna's arm in the other, they went in to the lobby.

Anna was surprised at how much fancier this hotel was. Everything looked much more expensive and luxurious than Mickey and Mary's place.

The well groomed desk clerk greeted them, "Good evening folks. I sure hated to miss the party, but someone had to stay here. Your room is ready, I'll take the bags and show you the way."

The room was on the second floor. When the clerk opened the door, he stood aside. Jed gave him a half dollar tip also. The clerk had a puzzled look on his face as they just walked into the room.

Looking back at him, Jed realized why. "I'm not going to carry my wife over the threshold Thomas, that can wait until we get to our new home. By the way, this is Anna."

"Oh, everyone knows who Anna is, but I'm glad to meet you Mrs. Hawkins. You'll find Mr. Sherman, the owner, brought a bottle of wine up for you and Mr. Hawkins, he thinks Jed is a fine man." With that Thomas left and they stood there alone.

Jed walked toward Anna and took her in his arms. Anna was surprised to find she suddenly felt shy. He held her very close and she could feel his need, as he began to kiss her.

He brushed his lips over her cheek, then her mouth, "Oh, Anna, you don't know how many times I thought about this. We will have a good life."

"Yes," she murmured, as she began to warm to his embrace.

Jed gently pushed her away and started to undo the tiny buttons on her dress. He was having great difficulty because they were so small and he was so eager.

Anna smiled, as she removed his fingers and said, "Jed, I think I'd like to take my shoes off first." She sat on the nearest chair and lifted her dress and began unlacing her high-top shoes.

Jed watched her for a bit. Seeing all the laces he knelt down, "Let me help, that looks like a heap of work to me." When he got Anna's shoes off he moved his hands up her legs to the garters that held her socks and slowly pulled everything down, all the while smiling up at her.

Anna let out a small gasp. His hands caressing her legs made her feel as eager as Jed.

Jed rose up asking, "Would you like a glass of wine?"

"Yes, that sounds nice. I'm a little nervous. I guess that seems silly to you."

"No, no, nothing you do seems silly to me. I just can't believe you are mine at last."

Jed moved to the small table that held the wine. Anna walked over to join him. Jed stopped what he was doing and took her into his arms. The wine was forgotten as they moved together towards the bed. The rest of their clothing seemed to fall off on its own. Jed gently guided Anna onto the soft bed and lay down beside her. Anna closed her eyes in pleasure as he gently caressed her. Soon he was atop her. As their bodies joined together, Anna experienced an overwhelming feeling of love for this man, and she clung to him as he reached his release. He gently kissed her forehead, telling her how much he loved her. Then as he lay, with one arm across her, he promptly fell into a deep sleep.

Anna lay looking at him in the dim light from the lamp. She was somewhat amazed at this new found feeling. True, she hadn't experienced the total abandon she had felt with the cowboy, but neither did she feel unsatisfied. It had seemed enough to be so loved by this kind and gentle man.

Sometime during the night, Anna struggled to wake up as Jed whispered, "Anna, Anna, are you all right? You were moaning in your sleep."

She slowly realized she'd been dreaming of her night with Luke, *This can't be happening. It must never happen again.* "I'm sorry I woke you. I'm fine. I must've had a bad dream. Go back to sleep." Anna wondered if she ever dared to sleep again.

CHAPTER FORTY TWO

Anna reached out for Jed only to find empty space. Her eyes popped open. Just as she started to get up from the bed, the door opened. Jed came in with a small coffee pot and a cup.

"Good morning, Mrs. Hawkins, would you like some coffee?"

Anna sat on the edge of the bed and stretched. "How long have you been up? Why, you're all dressed to go to work."

"You bet," Jed replied. I'm ready to hit the road to our place and you need to get ready too. We can get breakfast downstairs." With a somewhat wicked smile, he asked, "Did you sleep as great as I did?" He took a cup over to Anna, who was partially covered with a sheet. Jed sat beside her putting one arm around her waist. Handing her the coffee, he kissed her on the cheek. "I wish we could stay longer, but some people are already on the road."

Anna wished the same thing. She was warming up to Jed's amorous mood but knew they needed to get going. "Oh my, I guess I'd better get dressed, but first I'm drinking this wonderful smelling coffee." She hesitated to mention how good it was to be rid of her morning sickness. It wouldn't seem right to call attention to her condition, she figured that would be evident soon enough.

"A penny for your thoughts?" he asked.

"I was thinking how nice it is sitting here with you, but I guess I'd better get a move on."

Taking the cup from her, he placed it on a nearby table and gently pushed her back onto the bed. He kissed her about the neck and face. He moaned softly, then releasing her he rose up saying, "You're in for big trouble when we get into our own place, but you're right about getting underway."

Anna thought, *Yes, it will be nice when we aren't in a rush. We need to be alone.*

After a hearty breakfast, and taking sandwiches with them, they picked up one of Jed's larger wagons and drove to get Anna's things from the house, then they were on their way.

Jed tied his horse to the back of the wagon. Tag had been waiting for them and seemed to feel the excitement. Adam had been sold to a farmer and he too had a new mate. When they left the yard, Tag raced here and there exploring. The spring day was pleasant and warm. Plants were coming to life after the long winter months. The air was filled with a wonderful fragrance from the awakening trees and grasses.

Excitement seemed to be in the air too. As they drove out of town they encountered some of the families headed to Jed's ranch. They all waved happily to the newlyweds.

After about three hours on the trail they stopped at Jed's usual resting spot. He let the animals drink. Then Anna and he ate their lunch. Some others had already stopped; the children were running about letting off steam from the long ride. It was like a big picnic. After a while Jed lined his team up and they were on their way again.

As the day began to cool, Anna put a shawl on, and feeling a little tired she closed her eyes. She was awakened when Jed put a hand on hers, saying, "Just a little ways further and you'll be able to see your new home."

Then, rounding a gentle bend, there it was. Anna was in awe of what lay before them. It was a beautiful green valley. A fair sized stream ran down the middle and there was a sturdy looking bridge that crossed the water. Willows and cottonwoods were along the banks. The road ran across the valley, and on the opposite side were low hills. In a cleared area sat a good size log home. The hills that rimmed the valley had alternate patches of lingering snow and the dark green of trees. Anna thought it looked like a giant patchwork quilt.

"Oh, Jed, it's wonderful!"

"Well, I'm glad you like it," he said with some emotion in his voice. Anna could tell that the ranch meant a good deal to him.

"Looks like a few folks have already made themselves at home." Anna could see what he meant as she saw a few tents and lean-to's going up.

They crossed the fertile valley and Anna could detect the delicious odor of food being prepared.

There were happy shouts and greetings as the two drove into the encampment. There was so much for Anna to take in, her head reeled. As someone took care of the animals, Jed lifted her from the wagon seat. Amidst loud cheers he carried her up the two broad steps of their new home, and with a flourish he opened the door and carried her inside. With his arms still about her he set her down. Holding her close he kissed her long and with passion. As they broke away from one another, Anna gazed about the room. There was a huge fireplace at one end and windows that looked out over the valley. Jed had partially furnished it with a large table, some sturdy chairs, and there was even a sideboard that contained a few pretty dishes. He had built a bench by the door and there were pegs for hanging things. He took her towards the back of the room. There were two more rooms. One had an archway, the other had a door. Through the archway she could see a cook stove and lots of pots and pans. Several shelves contained all sorts of provisions. It was hard for Anna to believe all Jed had done.

He led her back out to the main room and to the closed door. Opening it, he said in a husky voice, "This is our bedroom."

Anna could see how he had worked to make a pleasant retreat. The bed was handmade of peeled poles. The bedding all looked new, with fat pillows and a very pretty quilt, covering a comfortable appearing mattress. Jed had purchased some furnishings: a couple of chairs, and a dressing table with a mirror.

Anna suddenly felt tears coming. Seeing a look of concern on his face, she whispered, "Oh Jed, you did so much. These are tears of happiness. I don't know how I could be so lucky to have married such a perfect man." She rose up on her toes and kissed him, and before she knew it, he was returning the kiss with unbridled passion.

After a few moments, Anna gently pushed him away, "Jed we have company in the front yard, I can hear them. Don't you think we should invite them in, or something?"

Jed released her with a groan and look of regret. He replied, "I guess you're right but I'd rather carry on with this. I guess we'll have plenty of time later."

Sarah and her family had arrived and she directed some men to set up a plank table. It was soon covered with all sorts of food, and she was calling, "Come and git it!" Everyone dug in, sitting about on the ground with their heaping plates.

After cleanup, someone got out a fiddle and started playing some lively tunes. There was a little dancing, but most were tired, and drifted off to the places they had prepared to sleep.

Jed and Anna said goodnight to their guests and headed for bed themselves. Someone shouted out for Jed not to get too tired, as they had a lot of work to do in the morning. There were chuckles among the men, and chiding from some of the women. Anna felt a little embarrassed at the remark but Jed seemed to take it in good humor, saying to her in a low voice, "I'll try not to get too tired but I can't guarantee it."

CHAPTER FORTY THREE

So here we are, thought Anna, starting our new life together. In the dim lamp light she watched Jed as he started to undress. Anna became aware of a feeling of desire and began taking her things off too. She noticed Jed never took his eyes from her.

The minute she climbed into the comfortable bed, Jed made his desire known. His love making was urgent and quick. Anna would have been disappointed, had she not been so tired. While Jed drifted off to sleep, Anna lay awake for a bit. *Well, we're both tired and we'll soon be alone then things will be different.*

As usual, Jed was up before Anna, with coffee made and was raring to go. Anna could hear a lot of activity outside the cabin. "I guess I'd better get busy," she called to Jed, as she climbed from the bed.

"Yup, there's gonna be a lot to do today." She dressed and came out to where he was sitting. "Good morning, Mrs. Hawkins." It still sounded strange to be addressed that way, but she liked the sound of it.

There was a knock on the door and Anna went to answer. There stood a smiling Sarah. "Well good morning!" she nearly shouted. "Hope I didn't wake ya. I ran out of salt. How about that? I get to be your first neighbor to borrow something." When Anna invited her in for coffee, she replied, "Lord no girl. Why I been up for hours. No, if you'll just give me some salt I'll git on fixin' breakfast. Why if you two want, come and join us. The men are all waitin' for Jed anyways, so they can get organized and to get to work.

"Sure," Jed answered for Anna. Anna realized she had no idea where the salt or anything else was, thinking *I've got some work ahead of me in here.* Jed walked to one of the shelves in the kitchen for the salt and they went outside to join the crowd. It seemed everyone was already busy. The men were tending to their animals and the women were getting breakfast out. Soon they were all eating a hardy meal of ham and eggs, with fried potatoes, and lots of coffee. The men were soon off to start the work and the women cleaned things up.

When they were finished, Sarah announced to Anna that the other ladies wouldn't mind a tour of the new home. Anna happily obliged them. Later they started lunch.

The men only stopped for lunch and dinner, working until dark. There was no party tonight, as everyone was very tired.

As Jed got ready for bed, he told Anna, "The barn is nearly finished and some of the men are working on a pig pen and chicken house. What a great bunch of people."

"Yes," she replied. This night Anna could hardly keep her eyes open and was asleep before Jed got in bed. The next day was a repeat of the first and at the end of the third day, everything was finished. The barn was done and all the animals were in their new homes.

Anna and Jed stood in the early morning sunlight, watching and waving, as their friends drove from the yard on the way back to town.

"Well, here we are alone," smiled Jed.

Anna looked around to where all the people had been camped. "Yes, but it seems a little lonely without them. Now that they're gone you can show me around your ranch."

"Why, Anna, it's your ranch too. You don't need to ride out to see all of it today. See that hill?" He asked, pointing to one end of the wide valley. "That's the north boundary. Our land is about five miles wide and ten long. One day soon, I'll take you around it all but right now you just get acquainted with your new home, while I do some cleanup and chores.

That night, their love making was much more to Anna's liking. She decided life with Jed was going to be as great as she had hoped for.

They settled into a routine of sorts. Anna knew how to milk the cow, so the chickens and cow became her job. Jed built fences and improved things. He also plowed a small area for Anna's garden. She and Tag explored some, but they didn't wander too far. Anna worried about what animals could be in the trees on the hills, and in the brush and trees by the stream.

A few days later, Jed announced he was going to ride out to check on the cattle that were roaming around on his land. "Will you be afraid to be alone?"

"No, have you forgotten how you found me?"

"You're right, I'll never forget the lucky day I found you." He drew her close, "I guess I don't need to worry. I might be gone overnight but you have Tag to watch things. I'd like to take you but I don't think that's a good idea."

Anna was disappointed, yet she thought it might be nice to alone and take it a little easy, and was eager to get to know where things were in her new home.

⌒——⌒

Jed had ridden for one full day, checking all the areas where his cattle might be gathered. He camped that night by a small stream. He lay awake for some time thinking of Anna. He worried maybe he expected too much of her. Now she had to feed the pigs, besides all her other duties. He'd seen more new calves than he'd expected. It had been another milder winter than usual and the cattle were thriving. *I'm going to be real busy this year,* he thought as he drifted off.

After breakfast he began his search again. He'd traveled for some time, then suddenly stopped. There, a ways ahead, was what looked like a teepee. Not sure if it was friend or foe, he approached with caution, hand on his rifle.

As he drew closer, he saw an Indian woman tending a small fire. She had a baby upon her back. "Hello the camp!" he shouted. The woman dropped her stick and ran into the teepee.

As fast as she'd disappeared, a short, bearded man emerged. He was stout but not fat. He looked to be about fifty or so, it was hard to tell. His tanned face and hands told of a life lived in the outdoors but he wasn't Indian. He held a huge buffalo gun down along side of his buckskin pants.

"Who be ye?" he called out. Jed raised both hands, indicating he meant no harm. "Well then, come on in and sit a spell. It gits somewhat lonely out here."

Jed rode on in. Dismounting, he kept his horse between him and the wicked looking buffalo gun. The man came forward, limping slightly. He had an engaging smile, except for a few missing teeth. Putting his hand out he said, "Name's Ezra, Ezra Tobias. Who might you be?"

"Name's Hawkins, Jed Hawkins. What are you doing out here?"

"Why any fool could tell what we're doing. My squaw and me thought this was a mighty fine place to light."

"Well, that may be but this here is my land. I guess that makes you some kinda squatter."

Ezra looked a little concerned at Jed's remark. He began to sputter an apology, saying he wouldn't mind movin' on. That was, as soon as they et their mornin' vittles.

He asked Jed to join them, so Jed dropped his reins and walked over to the small fire. "I ate, but that coffee smells good."

"Lilly," the man shouted, "It's okay. We just have to eat and move on. This here fella would like a cup of coffee."

Lilly came from the teepee. She sat the baby on a blanket and got Jed his coffee. Lilly and Ezra worked together to prepare their meal. She was making some sort of corn pancake. Jed found Lilly to be pretty, with a slight build, black hair and eyes. Her clear skin was a nice bronze color. Jed also saw, by the way he treated them, Ezra was very fond of Lilly and the baby. Lilly offered Jed one of the cakes and he decided to try it. He was pleasantly surprised at how good it was.

After they finished the meal, Jed offered Ezra a smoke. The men sat while Lilly put things away. After a bit Jed asked, "How come you and Lilly are in this area, anyway?"

"Well Sir," started Ezra, "It's a long tale. Ya see, I was a buffalo hunter. A couple years ago, while ridin' amongst a herd, I got a big bull. Then my horse stepped in a hole and fell. We each broke a leg. Course I had to put my horse down. I figgered I was a gonner for sure. I'd been huntin' alone, so nobody was around to give me a hand. I lay there for some time, then around evening, a couple Indian bucks came ridin' up. I've spent some time with those buggers, so I was able to palaver with 'em. I told them they could have the buffalo I'd shot if they'd help me. Course they was all for it. They wanted my horse too. Seems they're fond of horse meat. I was lucky, they could have just taken both and left me, but they turned out to be a good sort. Anyways, they took me to their camp and Lilly took care of me. Nature bein' the way it is, we naturally took to one another. It took some time for me to heal. By the time I was ready to walk, I wanted to leave that Indian village. I don't know if you ever spent time in one, it can be real hard on the nerves, what with kids, barkin' dogs, and yappin' women."

"I asked Lilly if she wanted to go with me, as by then she was carrin' our little one and she said yes. I got a horse from the Indians, gathered up my gear and here we are. We been livin' off the land. Once in a while I sell some hides for things we might need. We been gittin' along just fine, that is until today. But it's not a problem. I don't mind moving on. I think Lilly misses her people. Movin' on might take her mind off it. Twilly will be walkin' soon and that will help. She won't need to be carried then."

Looking puzzled, Jed asked, "Twilly, that's a different name, is it Indian?"

"No," chuckled Ezra, "When the baby came I told Lilly that we should name her Lilly too. Lilly laughed and said two Lilly, only when she said it, 'Twilly' is what came out."

"Well, she's a mighty fine lookin' little girl." Jed meant it. Twilly had her mother's fine features. Her hair was dark although not as black as Lilly's and it had a little of Ezra's natural curl. The most startling thing were the bright blue eyes. He thought, that's one pretty child.

"My wife is going to have a baby, come winter." Jed said.

"That's fine. Why there's nothin' like havin' a little child around to make things interesting, it's like a miracle the way they grow. "Course Lilly does most all the caring but I do enjoy both of them. Yes sir, there's nothin' like having a family."

"I'm sure you are right," answered Jed. While he'd been watching Lilly and listening to Ezra he thought, living like this has to be a lot of work. "You ever think of working on a ranch?" he asked Ezra.

"Why, no, can't say I have. I'm not sure I'd be that good at it. You might've noticed I have quite a limp, so I'm not the speediest hoss on the range. Besides, most folks don't cotton to Injin women, and I hate the word but, Twilly is a half-breed. No, I'm afraid we wouldn't fit in around most folks."

"Wouldn't you want to make life a little easier for Lilly and maybe have Twilly go to school one day?" Jed asked the old man.

"I never give much thought to such things. We go along, day by day, plenty of eats and a warm bed. Like I said, I kill something, Lilly tans the hide, then I sell it for shells, coffee, and such. No, we do just fine."

"Well," Jed told him, "Like I told you, this is my land and it's pretty big. I could use a little help. It wouldn't be anything real hard, just help around the place. I notice you take good care of your horse and family, that's good enough for me. I think my wife and Lilly would hit it off just fine. The pay wouldn't be much, maybe five dollars a month. Anna, that's my wife, has a small garden, I'm sure she would share it with Lilly. If you decide you want to stay, we could build you a small cabin."

"Hold up, you sure do go on. Are you offering me a job? That's a lot to swaller. I'd have to ponder some on that."

"Tell you what," Jed went on, "Why don't you and your little family come home with me and try it out?" Jed liked this old man.

"Well, it seems we gotta move anyways, I reckon we could mosey on to your place and see what's what."

Anna had been out in her garden when Tag began barking and wagging his tail. She knew Jed was retuning by Tags greeting bark and hurried into the house to freshen up.

Anna waited on the porch as Tag raced out to greet Jed and his new found friends. She was surprised to see what looked like a woman on horseback and she seemed to be dragging something behind it. She also made out a man in buckskins, strolling along beside her.

Jed rode into the yard, ahead of the couple. Alighting from his mount, he took Anna into his arms, kissed her soundly and said how much he'd missed her. Before she could recover from his greeting, Jed held her at arm's length, declaring, "I brung you some company. It's a man and his Indian wife, with their little baby girl. I'm hoping to keep them on as hired hands, that is if they decide to stay."

Anna looked shocked. Her mouth was open and her eyes wide with alarm. *What is he thinking? Don't I have enough to do without worrying about Indians?* "Indian? How do we know we'll be safe?"

"Oh Anna, don't worry, they are just like us, you wait and see. I really think you'll enjoy the company. Wait 'til you see the baby."

As Jed finished speaking, Ezra and Lilly came into the yard. Just as he'd predicted, Anna's eyes immediately went to the pretty little baby. Ezra lifted the child from Lilly, then held the horse as she dismounted. They approached Anna, each woman appraising the other. Jed introduced them. When a smiling Ezra reached out to shake her hand, Anna saw he wasn't Indian. Deciding at least this old man seems to have some manners.

CHAPTER FORTY FOUR

As Jed introduced Anna to the trio he went on to explain how Twilly's name had come about, to which Anna only smiled. She was nervous. The only things she knew about Indians were the tales told of savage attacks and murderous deeds. *What was Jed thinking?*

Jed interrupted her thoughts. "You got anything we can feed these folks?"

Anna stared at Jed, unable to believe what he was saying.

Jed didn't notice, as he motioned Lilly and Ezra to go on in the door. Lilly hesitated, the women in her village were never allowed to enter first.

The two peered about as Jed directed them to the table. Lilly looked spellbound. Anna brought some beans, coffee, bread, and butter for them to eat. When she was near Lilly or Ezra, she was repelled by the smell of grease and smoke that clung to their clothing and bodies.

Lilly watched closely, as the others buttered their bread, then copied them. A look of pleasure came over her pretty face as she asked, "What is this?"

"Why," Ezra chuckled, "I guess you never et butter before. It comes from a cow."

"How? Is it inside the cow?"

Anna was surprised to hear Lilly speak English. *Maybe it wouldn't be so bad to have another woman around even if she was Indian. She does seem to be a good mother.*

"No, no," smiled Anna, "I'll show you how to make butter, that is if you and your husband stay."

Ezra chided in, "Well, we'll see how it goes. I gotta say, the women folk do seem to hit off. I didn't figure there was so much in this old world that Lilly hadn't seen. It might be a good thing for Twilly too. Mind ye though, I could git a hankerin' to move on anytime."

∽──∾

So Ezra, Lilly, and Twilly stayed. Ezra fed the animals, carried wood, and water. He went with Jed to check on the cattle and helped work about the ranch.

Lilly and Anna soon became fast friends. Each teaching the other their way of doing things. Lilly learned to milk the cow and make butter.

After a couple of weeks, Ezra told Jed, he thought he would stay on. Lilly liked the white man's house, so the men built a small two room cabin. Anna gave Lilly a few items from her kitchen. When the cabin was complete, Lilly cooked a special dinner for all on their first night in the new home.

Spring had turned into summer. Anna was beginning to grow rather large. She'd made a couple roomier dresses that would accommodate her growing girth. Lilly had been amazed by what the sewing machine could do. Anna taught her how to make a dress for both her and Twilly. When they were done, they went out to find Ezra and show off their new clothing.

Ezra had been working near the barn, when Lilly came in view. Seeing how pretty Lilly and Twilly were, Ezra told them they looked mighty fine. He thought, *Well maybe it wouldn't hurt Lilly and his little girl to learn how other folks lived. After all the white people were moving west and the Indians were being stamped out. Yes sir, someday Twilly will probably be living just like 'em.* He spat a stream of tobacco onto the dusty ground, and giving Lilly a hug, he went back to work.

Jed rode into the yard as the two were leaving. "That's a pretty sight," he commented, nodding his head toward the retreating two.

"Yup," Ezra replied. "She was just showin' me the new dresses she made. I suppose it's a lot easier than tannin' hides, but it'll take some gittin' use to.

"It seems to me that you and your family have gotten use to a lot of things and seem pretty happy."

Ezra had been repairing a gate and he stopped. Looking thoughtfully at Jed he said, "Ya know I think you're right. This here ranch work ain't been too bad. In fact, life seems a lot easier for this ol' hoss. Yes sir, you might have something here. Why, I don't have to always be worrin' bout making sure where the next meals coming from or what the weathers gonna do. Meby this will work out fine, as long as I don't get an itch to see what's on the other side of the mountain."

Jed smiled, "I guess that means I got myself a ramrod, in case I ever get me some more hired hands."

"Ramrod. I like the sound of that. Yes sir, we can shake on that. I'm sure enough your man. Ramrod Ezra."

They shook hands and Jed suggested they take a break in the shade of a nearby tree.

"Yes sir boss!" declared a jovial Ezra.

⌒⌒

It was nearing fall. Anna was getting very large. She was grateful for Lilly, not only for the company, but for her help with the work that had to be done. Lilly was also able to tell Anna what to expect as her pregnancy progressed.

Anna noted that Jed was now less affectionate. This she didn't talk about with Lilly. She wasn't sure if the change was because the newness of marriage had worn off or if her ballooning body reminded him that she was carrying another man's child.

Anna wasn't far wrong. It did seem to Jed that the question of who had fathered the baby entered his mind more, as he observed her growing size. He found himself wondering what Anna's child would be like as he watched little Twilly.

He never thought of the coming baby as his… it was Anna's child. He was upset with this new observation for he knew it would cause Anna unhappiness if she guessed how he felt, but….

His thoughts were interrupted by Ezra's hand on his shoulder, "Say where ya been? I was wantin' to know if we were gonna cut hay or wood tomorrow. I asked ya twice."

"Oh, I'm sorry Ezra, I guess I was wool gathering."

"It didn't take no genius to figger that out. You got trouble I kin help out with?"

"No, no, it's nothing." Jed had really grown to like this older man.

CHAPTER FORTY FIVE

Much to Ezra's surprise, he'd taken to ranching like a duck takes to water. As the days went by, Ezra seemed to grow younger and stronger. Yes, he thought, this arrangement had turned out just fine.

"Well," Jed said, "I guess we better start filling the barn with hay for winter, then we'll worry about the wood. I been meaning to ask how you felt about staying here this winter, while I take Anna into town to have her baby?"

"Heck, that's no problem, but I don't see why she's gotta be in town. My Lilly had Twilly all by herself with no trouble."

"I know but I worry. You see, Ezra, I was married before and when it was time for our baby to come, both my wife and baby died."

"I'm sorry to hear that. That must've been a terrible thing. Something like that could make a fella a little gun shy. Your Anna seems good and strong to me. I don't think she'll have trouble. Well if we're gonna do hay I guess we better git to it."

The two gathered the tools needed for the work ahead, and as they started for the wagon it struck Ezra that it was odd for Jed to say he was taking Anna to town to have *her* baby. *Don't he know it takes two?*

Fall had come and it was nearing winter. The hay was in, the wood was stacked, and the cattle brought in to closer pastures. Jed and Ezra had stored corn for the animals and Anna's garden had yielded quite a lot. Potatoes, onions, and squash were stored away in the root cellar. The nights had a chill and sparkling frost trimmed everything when mornings arrived.

Anna had long since finished making baby clothes. Lilly seemed more excited about the coming child than anyone. Anna was not only getting nervous, she was beginning to grow really uncomfortable, as her size ever increased. She tired easily and found daily tasks sometimes a little difficult.

Once she'd approached Jed about naming the baby. He said he would leave that up to her, so she let it drop. She sensed his inability to feel any interest in the child growing within her. He was helpful and saw to it that she didn't have to do any heavy chores, but grew less and less attentive with each passing day.

It was the end of November and Anna decided to have a special dinner, a sort of Thanksgiving dinner that would also be a farewell meal. Jed thought it was getting close to the time to head for Meade. Ezra bagged a couple fat grouse, and Anna made pumpkin pie. Lilly was impressed and everyone enjoyed the day. Anna felt she had a good deal to be grateful for, even if she had the constant fear of losing Jed's love. Her love for him had deepened as his seemed to wane.

On an early December morning, they were leaving the ranch in the hands of Ezra and Lilly and headed to town. Anna had knitted scarves and gloves for each of them for Christmas. She handed the wrapped gifts to Lilly, giving strict orders that they were not to be opened until Christmas morning. Lilly only looked confused. Ezra promised he'd try to explain to Lilly and they would abide her wishes, if he could figger out which day was Christmas.

With many last minute instructions and fond goodbyes, the loaded wagon pulled out of the yard, with Tag happily trailing behind. Anna couldn't help feeling afraid and sad. This place had become home to her. The future was full of changes. She hoped the baby would be healthy and that Jed would come to except it.

There was a little snow, but it didn't affect their travel. They'd stopped briefly at the old resting place. It was getting cold and nearly dark as they drove into Meade.

Arriving in the yard of the town house seemed strange to Anna. Now she would have to adjust to living back in town. *Well maybe it won't be so bad, at least I won't have to milk the cow and such.* Tag had long since jumped up and ridden in the wagon, now he hopped down and began exploring his old familiar stomping grounds.

There was a light on in the barn and at the sound of the wagon, Lee and Susie came bounding out with happy greetings. Susie was amazed at Anna's size. Together, amongst happy chatter, the wagon was unloaded and fires built to warm the house. Susie brought some soup for the two travelers. It soon became apparent Anna was getting tired and so they all retired.

Jed was restless in town. He was use to spending long days working around the ranch. He spent some time at the house making sure everything was in good repair but mostly he stayed at his livery in town. There, he cleaned things up and repaired fences and such.

Anna found enough to fill her days with regular household chores. Sarah stopped by when heard saw Anna was back. She kept telling Anna to enjoy her peaceful days as they would soon be over. Doc dropped by, saying she was as healthy as a horse. She hadn't gone into town and was pleasantly surprised when Mary had come to see her. She filled Anna in on all the people at the hotel.

Susie spent a lot of time with Anna. She was amazed to hear of Lilly. It was hard for her to conceive an Indian living at the ranch and asked many questions about it. Anna hadn't confided on how Jed seemed to be growing distant from her. She didn't need to. One afternoon, all knowing Susie asked, "Mr. Jed seem unhappy in town. Does he miss his ranch or is he worry about baby?"

"I don't know," Anna had answered. "He's use to working all day, so this is hard for him." She didn't mention Jed seemed to have no interest in the baby.

"It all work out," replied Susie, a small look of concern on her usually calm face.

"I hope so," a subdued Anna replied.

As Christmas approached, Anna had found a few ways to decorate the house. She missed having a tree like her folks always had when she was a child. While spending time at the livery, Jed had made a cradle for the baby. He gave it to Anna a few days before Christmas. He told Anna it was his gift, so she could get it ready for the baby. It gave Anna hope, *Maybe he's starting to warm up to the idea that I'm having a baby.* They had been using the downstairs bedroom and she had Jed put the little cradle in there. She found great delight in preparing the small bed.

Jed came home one day with the news that Mary and Mickey wanted them to come for Christmas dinner. Anna wasn't sure how she felt about going any place, now that she was so big, but thought it would be nice to get out of the house and see her old friends.

Christmas Eve was quiet with just Anna and Jed. He had given her a pretty blue shawl and she gave him a scarf and glove she'd knitted. They went to bed early. Jed had given her a peck on the cheek and quickly went to sleep. Sleep was something that Anna was struggling with. She couldn't seem to find a comfortable position because of her large size.

The next day was clear and crisp. Frost sparkled on trees and grasses. A weak winter sun shone down on them as they rode into town in a small carriage.

Mary had decorated the dining room and it looked very festive. Anna was glad she'd decided to go to the dinner. To her delight she saw Susie and Lee were guests too. Dinner was very special, with ham and all the fixings. Cookie had outdone himself. All in all it was an extremely pleasant affair. Jed was in a better mood than he'd been for some time, even being more attentive to Anna than he had in weeks.

After many thanks and wishes for a Merry Christmas they headed out the door to find a light snow falling. Anna felt very happy and content as they made their way home. She was tired after so much excitement and they retired early.

Sometime in the middle of the night, Anna awoke with what she perceived as a backache. Thinking she had gotten over tired, she tried to go back to sleep, and when she was seized with a horrible pain, she knew what was happening. She gritted her teeth until the pain subsided. Laying perfectly still, so as not to wake Jed, she placed her hands on her stomach. After a few minutes she felt another, even stronger contraction. This pain was almost unbearable and she wondered how women survived this torture. She couldn't help but groan from the pain and Jed awoke.

"Anna, what's wrong?"

"I think the baby is coming," she replied in a strained voice.

"Oh my God," Jed cried, as he scrambled from the bed and into his clothes. "You just rest easy. I'll go get Doc, we'll be back in no time." He came to her side, a worried look on his face.

"Anna if anything happens to you I don't think I could stand it." That said he raced to the barn to get his horse.

The noise woke Susie and Lee. Lee came from their room to investigate. "Oh, Mr. Jed, it's you. Why you up so early?"

"Anna's having her baby, I'm going to get Doc."

CHAPTER FORTY SIX

"You no worry," Lee reassured him, "Susie and me take care of her."

Shouting thanks to Lee, Jed jumped on his horse and raced toward Doc's.

Susie'd been listening to Lee and Jed. She was already dressed when Lee came in to get her. The two hurried over to Jed's house. Lee started a fire to warm water and make coffee.

He'd gone through this when several of his younger brothers were born. Lee was well aware that babies seem to take their time and it would probably be a long night. Susie went into the bedroom and found Anna standing with a puddle about her bare feet.

"Oh, Susie," Anna said, "Look at this. I guess my water broke." She clenched her fists, as another wave of pain consumed her. She was no longer able to control herself and cried out in pain.

Taking Anna's hand in hers, Susie helped her back into bed. "You no worry about anything but having baby. I clean floor. Mr. Jed bring doctor."

When Jed reached Doc's place he ran up the few steps and began to pound on the door.

Doc awoke from a deep sleep but it didn't take the old doctor long to figure out what the commotion was. It seemed to him babies always waited until the middle of the night to come into this world, especially when the weather was bad.

Doc was in his nightshirt, as he shuffled to answer the incessant pounding. "Hold on!" he shouted, as he reached the door. He wasn't surprised to see Jed standing before him, "I figured it was you. I guess Anna has decided to have the baby?"

"Hurry, Doc, she seems to be in terrible pain. I just don't know what I'd do if anything happens this time."

The old doctor couldn't help but smile. "Calm down, Jed. Women folk been doing this for centuries. I doubt any of them waltzed through it without pain. As for being in a hurry, these things usually take their own sweet time, no matter how we'd like to speed them up. You can go out and hook up my buggy. Nora and I will be right out."

Nodding his head, Jed rushed towards the barn.

Doc returned to the bedroom to find a dressed Nora laying his clothes out. "I'll get your valise while you dress. Is it Anna?" she asked, smiling.

"Yes, that was Jed. He's beside himself. It's no wonder, the way things went with his first wife and baby. Anna's a strong young woman, I'm sure she'll do just fine."

In a short while they were on their way. There was still a light snow falling but Doc's old horse just trotted along.

Nora took a gloved hand from under the lap robe that protected their legs and reaching across, covering Doc's hand with hers, she said, "This never gets old to me. I'm so amazed when a new life comes into this world."

"Yes, I know what you mean. This should help Jed to get over losing his first child."

When they reached Jed's, the excited Jed came rushing to the buggy and helped Nora down, "Doc you go to Anna, I'll take care of your rig."

Doc gave Jed a patient smile. He knew, as a general rule, there wasn't much reason to hurry. Babies always came when they felt like it. Father's to be never seemed to understand that.

As Nora and Doc entered the kitchen they were pleased to see Lee had things under control.

"Good morning Lee," Doc smiled. "I'm glad to see you have some coffee made. We'll probably be needing it before this is over."

"Well," he said to Nora, "I'd better go see how things are progressing."

Just then Anna cried out in pain.

"That sounds pretty serious to me," declared Nora.

"It sure does, I better get in there."

Anna's hair hung in damp ringlets about her face. Susie was wiping her forehead with a cool cloth.

Doc entered the room as Nora followed behind. "Well, well, Anna it looks like your baby wants to see this old world. Don't you worry I'm here to see that everything goes along like it should. Now let me take a look see."

Anna had a brief thought about how it was strange she didn't care what anybody did as long as it ended the torture.

As Doc was examining her, Anna had another contraction. He stood up, "You're doing fine girl. Soon the pains will come closer together. Then we'll have a new little baby. Nora will do a few things to help you be more comfortable. I'm going out to calm Jed. You just keep up the good work."

Anna thought, *Is he crazy, this isn't work, it's torture, and it's killing me. I'll never have another baby as long as I live. Is this my punishment for committing adultery?*

Doc almost ran into Jed as he opened the door to leave the room. "How is she?" asked a frantic Jed. "She sounds so awful. Shouldn't you be in there with her?"

"Now, now," Doc answered. She's doing fine. Nora and Susie are tending to her. I could sure use a cup of that coffee. Come along and join me."

They walked to the kitchen and Jed got coffee for them. Lee was already at the table.

"Nothing like a cup of hot coffee to get a man going in the morning," Doc said as he took a sip of the fragrant brew. "Tell me Jed, have you and Anna picked out any names for your soon to be child?"

Jed looked up from his cup, "No we never got around to that. I guess Anna will figure something out."

Doc found Jed's answer a little strange, after all it was Jed's baby too. He decided maybe Jed thought something might happen at this birth and he didn't want to think ahead until it was over.

"Well, it shouldn't be too much longer before we know whether you have a boy or a girl. Anna's coming along just fine."

Lee spoke up, "My mother have five fine sons after me. It always take long time. When baby come everybody happy."

There was a bustling of skirts as Nora came into the kitchen. "I think it's time," she said, a little out of breath, "You better come on back."

Doc got up from the table to scurry off toward the bedroom where Anna's cries had grown more intense. Jed started to rise from his chair to follow. Doc placed a firm hand on his shoulder. "You just rest easy boy. It'll be over soon."

Anna was sure she could endure no more. She vowed aloud never to have another child.

Doc arrived and lifting the sheet that covered Anna's legs, a broad smile came to his old face. "I see the top of your baby's head, Anna. A couple more pushes and it will all be over."

"Oh Doc, I can't. It hurts so bad. Can't you make it go away?"

"You have to do that yourself, girl. You just strain with all your might and we'll get that baby born."

Anna gripped the bed covers. With one last strain she cried out and it was over. Her body relaxed, as Doc lifted the tiny child in his hands, announcing, "You have a fine healthy son, Anna." She gave a weak smile as tears of relief and happiness rolled down her cheeks.

Doc tied the cord off and handed the baby to Nora to be cleaned up. When she was finished she laid the small bundle in Anna's arms. Anna was amazed at how sweet and small it was. Pain was soon forgotten as Anna and her son dozed off, a smile upon her face.

Doc returned to the kitchen announcing, "You have a strong son, Jed. Anna is doing fine, they're both resting now."

"I'm glad it's over. I guess she needs rest after all that," said Jed. He didn't ask about the newborn. Doc was a little taken aback by Jed's reaction, or rather his non-reaction. To him, Jed seemed uninterested in the baby. Something wasn't right but he couldn't quite put his finger on it.

Doc said, "Nora will be staying for a while to see everything goes alright. I'll be back this evening. I'd better get on home now. I never know who might be waiting at my office. You'd better get some rest too. Morning will be here before you know it."

"I guess you're right," Jed replied. "I am tired; I'll get your rig for you. Thanks again Doc."

"It's nothing. Why there's no better way to start the day than to bring a new little one into this old world."

CHAPTER FORTY SEVEN

While Jed got his buggy ready, Doc checked on Anna and the baby one more time. He gave Nora some unnecessary instructions, then was on his way. Jed was sitting at the kitchen table when Susie came in.

"Oh, Mr. Jed!" she exclaimed, her eyes shining with wonder and excitement, "What a nice baby. Missy Anna and baby asleep. Missy Nora too. So I go home now. Can I fix you some breakfast before I go?"

"Oh no, Susie. It's still very early. I'll go upstairs and lay down for a while."

"Okay, I see you later. I see Lee already go home. That good we all rest now." With that Jed was left alone.

He went upstairs, but he found it hard to sleep. He wasn't sure how he felt about the baby, now that it was here. *Why couldn't it have been a girl? The first boy should have been Anna's and mine, not... whose?* He wondered. *No, I've got to stop thinking about that.* Jed knew that was going to be hard. Eventually he fell into a restless sleep.

Anna was awakened by cries from her new son. Nora was cooing to the baby as she changed him. Wrapping the child in a small blanket, she brought the baby to Anna. "Good morning," she said, smiling down at Anna as she handed the baby to her. "I think your son is ready for something to eat."

"Oh my, I guess so," replied Anna, as she looked down at her full and leaking breasts. "I'm not sure how to go about this."

"Don't worry about that. Hungry babies figure that out for themselves."

Anna had never felt so full of love as she cradled the small bundle to her breast. "Why, look at him," she laughed. "He's no different than a newborn calf when it comes to finding his dinner."

"No. I guess not. Nature is a wonder. Have you and Jed picked a name for him?"

A small frown crossed Anna's face as she recalled Jed's reluctance to discuss naming the baby. She had chosen the name herself. "Yes, let me introduce you to Joshua James. He's named after his grandfather in St. Louis."

"That's a mighty fine name," replied Nora. She was surprised the little boy hadn't been named after Jed. It seemed to her most men wanted the first born son to carry on their name. She also wondered about Jed's seeming disinterest. He hadn't looked in on Anna or the baby at all.

After the baby was fed, Nora tended to Joshua while Anna dressed. Placing Joshua back in Anna's arms, they went out to the kitchen.

When they entered they saw that Jed had made some fresh coffee and oatmeal. "You're out of bed? I thought I'd bring you some breakfast."

Anna walked toward him, almost shyly. "Of course I'm up. I'm a little tired but I'm hungry and I bet Nora is too. Would you like to see Joshua?"

"Joshua? Oh sure." Anna stepped closer, pushing the blanket away from the baby's head as Jed peered down at the tiny face. "He sure doesn't look like anybody, does he?"

What a strange remark, Nora thought.

Jed's remark was not lost on Anna. She felt a chill in her heart, as she realized Jed didn't feel any attachment to Joshua.

Breakfast was eaten in a rather uncomfortable quiet, with Nora trying to carry on a one- sided and sunny conversation. She tidied up the kitchen while Jed and Anna sat in silence. It seemed to her these two needed some time alone. Turning from what she was doing, she said, "You know, Anna, you seem to be doing fine. If I could give you one bit of advice it would be to rest whenever you can. I think you should take that sleeping baby and go lay down. So if you don't mind, Jed, you can take me home."

Nora was disturbed by Jed's eagerness to leave the house. It didn't seem like him to be so unconcerned about Anna and the baby. On the way to town she cautioned Jed to see Anna didn't over do it for a few days. He replied she didn't need to worry, he would take care of her. Again, Jed's remarks bothered Nora. *Shouldn't he said he would take care of Anna and Joshua?*

In a short while they arrived at Doc's. Jed helped Nora from the buggy, thanking her for all she'd done. He told her he was going down to the livery to check on things.

Nora shook her old gray head as she watched Jed drive away. When she got in the house, she found Doc sitting at the kitchen table, eating pancakes.

"Why look at you!" she exclaimed. "You don't need me at all."

"Oh yes I do," he smiled, "It gets mighty lonesome around here when you're gone. I'm surprised to see you. Anna must be doing pretty good."

"Mother and child couldn't be better," Nora answered, as she got herself a cup of coffee and sat with Doc. "So, I guess it was pretty quiet around here for you?"

"Ya, Ted Simmons stopped by for some headache powder for his wife. Poor Lorene, I'm afraid Ted gives her the headaches."

Nora sat staring off into space, twisting her cup around in its saucer, a frown on her usually pleasant face.

Doc noticed she hadn't been listening. "What's eating you Nora? I can see you have something bothering you."

"Oh, I don't know, it's just that Jed doesn't seem as excited about the baby as he should. I really can't say exactly what makes me feel that way. I can't put my finger on what it is."

"Odd," replied Doc. "I had the same feeling. Most young men act like fools when their first son is born. Maybe he is worried about the responsibility; he is a serious sort a fella."

"Maybe so, Nora replied, just the same…"

<hr>

Anna slept soundly, and as the new day dawned, she slowly became aware of movement and sounds coming from the crib. She got up smiling, as at last her child was here and she was eager to care for him. Picking Joshua up she carried him to her bed to change and feed him. When she had gone to lie down, it had been with a heavy heart. Jed's indifference to Joshua had been obvious to her. Now she sat studying her new little son. She examined his tiny feet and hands. Then she looked at his face and hair. She was upset to see his hair was dark and a little curly. It reminded her of Luke's. *Oh no!* She thought with panic, *Please God don't let him look like his father. I wonder what Luke would do if he knew he had a son?*

Anna heard Jed returning from town. She put the now sleeping child back in the crib and going to the dressing table, she looked in the mirror. After brushing her hair she went to the kitchen to greet him.

Susie had come in with Jed. She rushed to Anna, giving her a hug. "How is baby? When can I see him?"

"You can see him now," said Anna, taking Susie's small hand in hers, as she led her to the bedroom.

The two stood looking down at the sleeping baby. "He so little," whispered Susie. I think he a pretty baby."

"Yes," Anna beamed. "He's a good baby too. Of course he isn't very old yet."

They quietly left the room and found Jed was at the table. "How is the baby?" he asked.

Anna was pleased that he finally showed some interest in Joshua. "He's sleeping. Nora told me new babies sleep a lot."

"That's good, you need your rest."

Anna stated that she would make some tea for Susie. Susie guided her to a chair and said she would do it. As they sat there, Susie found it hard to congratulate Jed, knowing the truth as she did. Susie could feel the tenseness between Jed and Anna. She felt very bad for them. They talked of weather and how nice the Christmas party had been. There was a lull in the conversation.

Jed spoke up, "Since Anna and the baby are doing so good and you are close by, I might go out to the ranch to see how Ezra and Lilly are doing."

Susie tried not to show how shocked she was. She could see it hurt Anna that he would leave her and the baby so soon. Putting on a brave front, Anna asked when he planned on leaving, and wasn't he worried about the weather?

"No," he replied. "The snow isn't that bad, and I'm used to being out in the cold. I need to know if Ezra has been able to take care of everything. I probably won't be more than a few days. If you want, I can hire one of Sarah's girls to come and help out. I think I'll leave in the morning."

A hurt Anna replied, "No, no we'll be fine." Rising from her chair, and fighting back tears, she said, "Susie, if you don't mind, I think I will go lay down while Joshua's asleep."

"Yes, Missy Anna, that is what you should do. Don't worry about dinner, Mary say she is bringing you some food today. I go home now, you rest."

With that, a somewhat bewildered Jed was left sitting by himself. He felt miserable. He knew Anna shouldn't be left alone at this time but he needed to think things out. *Besides no one seemed to care about anything but the baby. I won't be missed.*

When the baby was born, all he could think of was it was another man's child. He hadn't felt a part of the whole thing. Jed recalled how Anna had voiced her concerns before they were married. He had reassured her that he'd be fine with the baby's birth. Now he just wanted to get away. When he had taken Nora back to town a couple of men saw him. They had enthusiastically thumped him on the back and shook his hand, congratulating him on *his* son. It had made him feel dishonest and resentful.

Yes, I need to get away and sort out my feelings. Jed sat at the table for a little longer, then feeling guilty and restless, he went out to carry in a big supply of wood for Anna. Tag pranced about in the inch or so of snow, following Jed about as he stacked wood on the porch.

"You're a good dog," he said, as he stopped to pet the tail wagging dog. "You take care of Anna while I'm gone."

When he went into the kitchen, he saw that Anna was up and doing something at the sink. "You're up. Did you have a good rest?"

"Oh yes, I did. I'm not use to lying down during the day, but I do get tired."

"Are you sure it's okay with you if I go out to the ranch? I don't have to go."

"It's alright," she answered, not turning to face him. She was very near tears. More than anything, she wanted him to come and put his arms around her and say... well she didn't know what, but she felt so alone. Collecting her emotions, she dried her hands and went to the table to sit with Jed. "Would you like me to fix something to take along? It's a long ride."

"Oh," a miserable Jed replied, "I don't want to put you to any bother."

Anna couldn't help herself, even though Jed had disappointed her, she reached out covering his hand with hers, "I'm your wife, Jed, I like taking care of you."

He lifted his eyes to hers and she could see the love, but also uncertainty. "You are a good wife, Anna, it's..." Just then there was a knocking at the front door, and he hurried from the table to answer it. Anna didn't need to wonder who it was. She could hear Sarah's chatter as the two came towards the kitchen. Sarah was asking how Anna and the baby were and how did he like being a daddy. Of course, Jed never had a chance to answer.

Anna started to rise as they entered the room. "Sit, sit," Sarah told her, as she placed packages on the table. "I brung ya some things."

"Oh, you shouldn't have."

Sarah stilled Anna's protest, "It ain't much, just some eggs, butter, and bread. When can I see the youngin'?"

"He's sleeping, but we can peek in at him." The two headed to the bedroom. Jed had stood there for a second, then started drifting towards the bedroom. He stood in the doorway, watching the two women.

"Oh, there's the proud daddy!" said a beaming Sarah.

Jed was trapped. He didn't want to hurt Anna, by not acting the part. He smiled at Sarah, and watched as Anna pushed the blanket away from Joshua's tiny head.

"My, he's a beauty. Why, I never saw so much hair on a newborn. It's so black, he must take after one of his grandparents."

Jed couldn't help moving in for a closer look at Joshua. The baby had awakened. Sarah was cooing and fussing over him, as she held him in her arms. Suddenly she turned to Jed, holding the child out to him. He was taken aback, as Sarah stood there with the baby in her outstretched arms. He had no choice but to take him. It was frightening to him to hold such a small thing, neither was he sure how to manage it. With Sarah's help, Joshua was soon cradled in his strong arms.

Anna could sense his discomfort, and stepping forward she took the baby from him, allowing that he should go back in the cradle.

"He sure is little," Jed said to no one in particular.

"He's little now but you won't believe how fast they grow. Why in no time at all, he'll be taggin' behind your heels, askin' all sorts of questions." She chuckled, "You got years of enjoyment and aggravation ahead. Well, I'd better git home to my brood. I just love seein' a little baby, but I'm glad mine are grown."

Walking Sarah to the door, they watched as she drove away in her little cart. They stood quiet for a bit, finally Jed said, "I'm kinda mixed up on how I feel about the baby. You know when I held him, it bothered me that everybody thinks he's mine." A frown crossed his face. "Don't worry, Anna, I promised to take care of you and the baby," he paused, "It's just that all these people pattin' me on the back over my new son, it's like I'm lying to all of 'em."

"Oh, Jed, I never should have married you. I should have gone home to my folks." Unable to hold the tears back, she started to cry and felt ashamed. It was not like her, she guessed it was just part of new motherhood.

Jed stepped to Anna, putting his arms about her. It felt good to hold her. He said softly, "Don't you worry, we'll be fine. I'm still gonna go out to the ranch, to sort things out. I know one thing, when I held that little baby, I knew I would take care of him. I don't want to lose you."

CHAPTER FORTY EIGHT

Early the next morning Jed left. He stopped in town to pick up a few things he thought Ezra might be low on. He also bought a few gifts; some tobacco for Ezra, material for Lilly, and a toy for Twilly.

The trip was as he'd told Anna it would be. The snow was dry and only a few inches deep. It could have been several feet, for all Jed noticed. The horses plodded along, the only sound was their hoof beats in the soft snow. He'd been in deep, confused thought all the way to the ranch. He was surprised when he found he was at the edge of his valley. All the thinking he'd done on the way hadn't helped clear his mind. Now, he found himself wondering again who Joshua's father was and why Anna wouldn't tell him. Jed had almost approached the question once, but lost his nerve. Now there was a real person in their lives that would be a daily reminder that someone other than Anna's dead husband was the father.

He drove down into the valley and across toward the buildings of his ranch. As he approached, things looked as if Ezra had been doing a fine job. He could see the cattle and horses in fields, close to the ranch buildings.

Lilly had been outside, and seeing Jed's wagon, she ran into the barn. Presently, Ezra appeared with his big blunder bust in his hands. Jed waved to him. Seeing who it was, Ezra called Lilly and Twilly from the barn.

"Whoa there!" Jed shouted to both the team and the little family, "Don't shoot, I bring gifts. Have you had trouble? You sure seem prepared."

"Not really," replied the old man. "I thought some jaybird was sneakin' around awhile back. I shot in his direction; we ain't had any problems since. How come you be makin' a trip out here? Is everything okay? Did Anna have the youngin'?"

Jed climbed from the wagon seat. He smiled, "Yes, Anna had a baby boy and things are fine. I just had an urge to check to see how things were going with you."

Ezra spat a stream of tobacco and clamped Jed on the shoulder. "A boy, imagine that? Is he healthy? Does he look like his daddy?"

"Oh, Doc said he is very healthy," Jed answered, ignoring the question about the baby's looks.

Ezra took Jed's hand, pumping it up and down. "Congratulations, daddy," he said with a chuckle. At the news, Lilly had a smile as wide as a canyon.

"You got anything to feed a hungry man?" Jed asked.

"Why, where's our manners Lilly? We need to take care of this travelin' man."

After taking care of the wagon and horses, they went into Ezra's cabin, where Jed could smell something that made his stomach growl. He had not realized how hungry he was.

Lilly produced some very good stew and coffee. Jed ate his fill. As he ate, he was pleasantly surprised to see how neat and clean Lilly kept the place. He was, however, uncomfortable with all the questions they were asking about the baby.

They wanted to know every little detail, things he hadn't noticed in his troubled state of mind. Jed told of the gifts he had in the wagon, to get them off the subject of the baby, and brought them in. After listening to Ezra about how things had been going with the cattle and all, he said he was ready for bed.

Lilly had gone to the ranch house and built a fire to warm things up. When Jed walked into his home, it was comfortable. He walked around the empty rooms feeling lonely. It didn't feel like a home without Anna. He missed her. He drug himself into the empty bed.

Jed slept soundly. All the confusion of how he felt about the baby had exhausted him. When a weak winter sun brightened the room he realized he'd slept late. The smell of coffee drifted into the room. He knew Lilly must have come in earlier to build up the fire and put the pot on.

After dressing and going out to answer natures' call, Jed washed up and got a cup of coffee. He was sitting at the table when, after a light tap on the door, Ezra came in with his own cup in hand.

"Well, I 'bout gave you up for dead but now I see you're doing just fine."

"Ya," replied Jed, "I guess I was more tired than I thought. What are you up to today? I need to get out and do some work. Hanging around in town is not much to my likin'. Not enough to keep me busy."

Ezra looked at Jed over the rim of his cup. A quizzical expression was on his face. After a bit, he said, "Why, I'd think you'd be busy a fetching and carrying for Anna. Having a baby keeps the little ladies mighty tied up for a while 'til things settle down. Then I 'spose Anna's got lots of help there in town." Ezra had been studying Jed's face as he spoke.

Jed hadn't missed the questioning look in the old man's eyes. Now he knew it had been a bad idea to leave Anna alone at this time. Finally he spoke, "I have something gnawing at me that's real bothersome. I'd like to tell you about it but you gotta promise to keep it to yourself."

"Well now, I reckon I can handle that. I knew something was afoot when you showed up here. Why it ain't every day a man has a son but I figured you didn't come all the way out here just to let me and Lilly know."

"There's the trouble, right there. This is what you must not tell. The baby's not mine."

"What? Did I hear right? So that's why you been actin' like you wasn't interested in the little tyke. Both Lilly and me noticed it even before you left for town. Was the father her dead husband?"

"No, and she won't tell me who is. I told her I'd take care of her and the baby and I will. The trouble is everybody's so glad I have a son and I have to smile knowing it's not mine. That galls me. It's like I'm lyin' to them."

"Hmm," said Ezra, "I kin see where that could bother a straight arrow like you. But this business about the daddy, Anna don't strike me as no loose woman. No sir, seems she has a good reason for not telling who he is."

"I know," replied Jed. "It's just hard to remember that. Every time somebody shakes my hand I want to shout out *'It ain't mine!'*" He lowered his head and stared into his cup of coffee.

"Well, there's just one cure for that," stated Ezra. Jed lifted his head, a look of doubt on his face. The old man held his hands up, "Now, hear me out. The cure is time. People are that way. By the time you get back to Meade, you'll be old news. Then you can start thinking about having a brother for little…" he smiled, "See what I mean, you never even told us the baby's name."

"Joshua," Jed told him. "Joshua James, after Anna's father and grandfather."

"Why, that's a fine name. Jed, you're a fine man and Anna's a good woman. You should be able to get over this and raise that youngin' up good and proper. If'n there was one thing I could say 'bout Injins, little children are loved by all. You have Anna - that's the main thing, so whatever comes along with her, you need to except."

For the first time since Joshua was born, Jed smiled a genuine smile, saying, "I'm thinking it wasn't very thoughtful of me to leave Anna like I did. But I'm glad I came out to see you and get some sense talked into me. I'll stay and help you today, then I'm heading back to town." Rising from his chair, Jed shook the old man's hand, thanking him. "Now let's go out and see what kind of trouble we can find."

The trip back to Meade was pleasant for Jed. He was eager to get back to what would be the starting of a family. As he drove along he recalled how he and Anna had met. He smiled and spoke aloud to no one in particular. "Yes sir maybe I'll have a dozen boys before we're done." One of the horses looked back towards Jed and shook its head.

CHAPTER FORTY NINE

Jed arrived in town late in the day. He still wasn't sure how he felt about the baby, but knew he missed Anna and would take care of them both.

He left the wagon at the livery and rode his saddle horse into the yard. Anna was outside getting wood for the kitchen stove.

His heart sank, as he recalled Ezra's words about fetching and carrying. It made him feel ashamed for having left Anna the way he did.

She looked up, an expression of delight and surprise on her tired face.

Jed dismounted, tossing the reins to the nearest post. Going to her and taking the wood from her arms, he said, "You shouldn't be out here. I'm home now. You just need to take care of the baby and yourself."

Anna's eye's started to fill with tears. She was so happy to see him. She had feared he wouldn't come back to her.

They went in to the kitchen where Jed was aware of the smells of baking bread and coffee. He realized these things and Anna were what made a home. He was glad to be back.

Putting the wood down, he turned to take her in his arms and as he went to kiss her he saw the tears. "Anna what's wrong?"

"Oh, Jed, I was so afraid you had changed your mind about being married to me."

He held her close. "I could never change my mind about that. I really missed you."

"Me too," whispered a grateful Anna.

In the morning Joshua woke them with his fussing. Anna rose to change and feed him. As she sat holding the baby to her breast, she felt Jed's gaze and looked up.

"You know," he said, "That makes a mighty fine picture. He's a fair looking boy isn't he?"

"Yes," Anna smiled. "He's a pretty good baby too."

"Of course he is. He's ours."

Anna could hardly contain the fullness in her heart.

It was nearing March. While Jed had been very helpful, Anna could sense he was growing restless.   One sunny morning, while making bread, Anna asked, "When do you think we could go home to the ranch?"

Jed was drinking coffee, stopping with his cup in midair, a big smile on his handsome face, "Why any time you say. I didn't know if you were ready for the trip."

"Oh yes, I've been thinking about it a lot. I miss Lilly and I want to start my garden."

"What about Josh, will the trip be bad for him?"

"No" laughed Anna. "I'm sure he'll like it."

"That settles it. I'll start getting things ready. You make a list of the things you might need and I'll pick them up."   Going over to where she was working, Jed put his arms about her and kissed the back of her neck, saying, "You're the best wife a man could want."

Anna turned in his arms. Holding her flour covered hands out to her sides, she smiled and kissed him soundly.

"Well now, you keep teasing me like that, how am I going to get started?"

Touching his nose with a flour-covered finger, she turned back to the bread making. "You just get busy and we'll take care of other things later."

"You can count on that," replied a happy Jed, as he went out to start preparing for their trip back to the ranch.

Two days later, all was ready. Supplies were bought and packed. The house was cleaned and closed. Susie and Lee were to care for the place. Susie was excited to plant her own garden. Goodbyes were said and they were on their way.

The trip seemed long but Anna decided it seemed that way because she was so eager to get back to the ranch. Josh slept most of the time, only waking to be changed and fed. They rested the horses once, as was Jed's habit. After, what seemed like forever, the ranch came into view.

The spring weather had everything greening up. The hills on the far side of the valley still had some patches of snow in the meadows.

As they looked across the valley, a thin line of smoke curled from the fireplace in Ezra's cabin. They drove down the road and across the fertile fields. Tag ran ahead, his tail high, barking as he bounded across the fields. Ezra heard the commotion and waved his battered old hat in a greeting. Lilly had come from their cabin, Twilly in tow.

It was a joyous few minutes, the woman hugging, the men shaking hands. Anna couldn't believe how much Twilly had grown and that she was walking. The little girl hid behind Lilly's skirt, peeking out with bright blue, saucer like eyes. Her dark, curly hair was now down to her shoulders. Looking at the dress Twilly had on, Anna could see that Lilly's sewing had improved.

Lilly took Twilly by the hand and pulled her from behind, guiding her towards Anna and the baby.

Anna proudly showed Josh to Lilly as Twilly said in a sweet little voice, "Me see."

"Oh, my heavens, she talks all ready?" exclaimed an amazed Anna.

"Yes she knows a few words." Turning to Twilly and pointing at Josh, Lilly said "baby." Anna bent down to let the little girl have a better look.

A huge smile came on Twilly's face, as she mouthed the word, "baby."

"Why I can't believe how smart she is. I can't wait for Josh to grow like that."

The women went into the ranch house while the men emptied the wagon. Lilly brought some roast from her cabin and they sat in the ranch house kitchen eating and catching up on all that had happened since they'd last seen each other. It was growing late. Ezra, Lilly, and a sleepy Twilly left.

Putting a sleeping Josh in his cradle, Anna started getting ready for bed. Jed had been watching her every move.

She recognized it for what he had on his mind. Walking to him she put her arms around his waist. "What are you smiling about?" she asked slyly.

"Well," he said. "It's been a long time. I thought if you weren't too tired...?"

Giving him a provocative smile, Anna told him, "I'm so glad to be home and no I'm not that tired."

❦

In no time at all everyone was back to their old routines. Lilly had become very good at milking the cow. Twilly delighted in helping gather the eggs. The sow had a fine litter of eight fast growing piglets.

Anna had her garden in. Jed and Ezra plowed and planted five acres of corn.

Weeks flew by. Josh was aware of everything around him and Twilly kept him constantly entertained. Anna often wondered what she would do without Lilly and Twilly.

One morning, early in June, Anna was dismayed to find she was again pregnant. Josh was only six months old. Then she realized he would be a year and a half old when the new baby came. Maybe it wouldn't be so bad. The morning sickness returned with a vengeance but only lasted a short time. To her amazement, Jed was delighted with the news.   Lilly was almost as excited as Jed.

CHAPTER FIFTY

Fall came. Jed and Ezra had built a smoke house. They'd butchered a couple of pigs and filled it with ham and bacon. They'd also built a corn crib that was now filled. The rest of the pigs were turned loose to clean the corn field up. The garden had yielded huge amounts, and most of it was stored in the root cellar. The men had killed a bear. Anna wasn't too thrilled with the taste, but Lilly taught her how to cook it and she decided it wasn't too bad.

Lilly had expressed a desire to learn how to read and write, so evenings were spent teaching her. She proved to be a quick learner.

It was getting close to the end of November. Jed asked when Anna thought they should leave for town to have the baby.

"I would like to see everyone, but it might be nice to stay here. Besides, you weren't too happy staying in town so long when Josh was born." She could see a look of relief on his face, then he started to frown. "What's wrong?" she asked.

"Well, aren't you worried about having the baby all by yourself?"

"No, I've thought about it and with Lilly here, I'm not worried. Why, lots of women have their babies without doctors. It will be just fine. Besides, there's plenty of time to think about that."

Christmas time and Josh's birthday came. They were both celebrated with much joy. Josh was walking and saying quite a few words with Twilly's help.

It snowed but the weather wasn't that bad. Anna was getting a little nervous about her decision to stay at the ranch to have the baby. Lilly assured her everything would be fine. Jed worried aloud about it. Ezra regaled him with tales of women having their babies and getting back to plowing the next day or having a baby in the morning and cooking dinner for a dozen ranch hands in the afternoon or… he had a new tale every day. Jed was still doubtful.

Then the day, or rather in the wee hours of an early March morning, Anna was aware the baby was coming. The pain became difficult to bear, causing her to moan. Jed woke, asking what was wrong.

"It's the baby," Anna replied. "You better go get Lilly."

Jed was so nervous, he could hardly dress himself. He rushed off to Ezra and Lilly's cabin. They all returned shortly, a sleepy Twilly in tow.

The men waited in the kitchen as Lilly went into the bedroom to care for Anna. This birth had not taken as long as Joshua's. Lilly proved to be very helpful. She knew Indian ways that helped relieve some of the discomfort. In the end, with a final scream of pain, came the joy of a baby brother for Joshua and a son for Jed.

After the baby and Anna were cleaned up, Lilly told Jed to come and met his new son. Joshua and Twilly had heard all the commotion and tagged along behind Jed and Ezra.

Jed was beside himself. He'd worried about Anna having the baby without a doctor's care. Now he felt great relief and happiness.

Joshua knew a baby was supposed to come one day but really didn't understand until he saw it. He wasn't too impressed by the small creature and couldn't figure what all the fuss was about. Twilly was enthralled with the tiny person. Lilly could see that Anna was growing tired and she had all of them leave. After seeing that mother and child were comfortable, she went out to cook breakfast for the others.

"Well," said Ezra. "That's a fine little son you have. I told ya everything would be hunkey dorey. What ya gonna name him?"

Jed smiled, "I want to name him after my father. His name was Cyrus Odell."

Ezra sorta blinked, then said, "I reckon that's a good moniker to give the little tyke."

The second baby was much easier for Anna. She knew what to expect and Lilly was always at hand. Anna wasn't sure why she'd kept most of Joshua's baby clothes but she was glad she did. It had saved her a lot of work.

Spring gave way to a sizzling summer. As August waned, harvest began. It had been another productive year. Jed and Ezra had added another bedroom for the boys.

By early fall, Cyrus was crawling and trying to walk. He was a beguiling little boy, with Jed's hazel eyes and brown hair. Twilly had decided to nickname Cyrus, Ode, and that was what everyone called him. There was a glaring difference in their appearance, as Josh's hair was very black, with a slight curl and his eyes were deep brown.

Anna knew it bothered Jed. Once in a while she'd seen him intently studying them. He still treated Josh with some indifference.

Early in October, Jed announced he thought it was time they all went into town. He said it would give him a chance to show off his first son.

Josh looked hurt, as he protested, "I'm first, and Ode is two."

Anna's heart clenched, at the looks on both Jed's and Josh's faces.

Jed suddenly realized how much he'd favored Ode over Josh. Looking a little sheepish, he picked Josh up. "You're right, I do have two sons and you're first." From that day on, Jed paid more attention to the child. Sometimes, Anna felt that he was a little too easy on the boy.

The trip to town was a happy occasion. The boys did just fine on the almost day long ride.

It was wonderful to see their old friends and catch up on all the news. Susie and Lee were settled in. Tag checked out his old haunts, happily running here and there with his nose to the ground.

Anna had written a letter to her folks to tell of the new baby and how they were all doing.

The day after they were settled in, Anna took the boys into town to see Mary, Mickey, and the girls and mail her letter.

While mailing her letter, the postmaster gave her a letter from her mother. It told how happy they were that she seemed to be doing so well. It also stated her father had been sick but seemed to be doing better. Of course her mother sent all their love.

Anna went on to see her friends at the hotel. They all made over the boys something awful. Mary's girls were especially taken with them. It brought to Anna's mind Spook's story of how his Aunt's girls had raised him. Anna wished all Mary's girls could find the happiness she had. Gathering up her brood, they trekked on home, Tag running ahead as usual.

Sarah had heard Jed and Anna were back. She stopped by, rattling on how good it was to see them and how much Josh had grown. She also mentioned how much Ode looked like Jed. A remark that caused Anna to cringe.

Jed had decided he wanted to have a forge on the ranch. Because his father had owned the livery and blacksmith shop, Jed spent many hours there as a child. Now he was spending a great deal of time with Buck, as they worked together planning what Jed would need.

Anna was to go into town and order any supplies she thought they might want to take back to the ranch and order shoes for the boys.

Zeke and Hester were glad to see Anna and made over the boys, giving them each a peppermint stick. Josh shyly asked if he could have one for Twilly. Anna admonished him for asking. Zeke gave her a quizzical look asking, "Don't tell me you got another one somewhere."

"No, she is Jed's hired hand's little girl."

"Twilly's a strange name. Don't recall ever hear in' that one before" remarked Hester.

Anna was hesitant to say Twilly was half Indian, knowing how some folks felt about that. "Yes it's a different name but she is a sweet little girl."

Anna was in the back of the store looking at material when she heard the bell over the door jingle, announcing another customer. She thought nothing of it until she heard that voice. Her stomach dropped to her feet. *What was he doing here this time of year? There wouldn't be any trail drives.*

She didn't look up and made out to be intently studying some fabric. Her ruse didn't work, and her heart quickened as she heard the cowboy's and Zeke's approaching footsteps.

She had to look up as Zeke addressed her. "Anna, this here is the town's new Deputy, Luke Evans. Luke, this here's Jed's Anna and on the floor are his two youngin's."

There was no choice but to acknowledge the introduction. Anna gave a weak smile to the man she always thought of as "the cowboy" and quickly turned back to the fabric. Another customer drew Zeke away and they stood there alone.

"I heard Jed was in town and had brought his family along."

Anna looked up at him and was in disbelief at how he affected her. She still felt drawn to him and found herself struggling to break away from his gaze. Feeling a little weak, she asked, "You know my husband?"

"Sure, I met Jed last time he was in town. Marshal Sam introduced us. Besides, it's a deputy's job to get to know all the citizens of the town."

"We're hardly citizens, Mr. Evans. We spend most of our time on the ranch." Anna couldn't explain why she felt so defensive towards this man. He had only done what he'd come to Mary's for. It was up-setting to think he might be around to remind her of what had taken place between them. And what if people noticed what she was seeing? *Josh was the spittin' image of Luke Evans.* She remained aloof.

Luke gave her a smile that clearly conveyed his feelings for her. When he'd returned to Meade from his last trail drive, he meant to find Anna and pursue her. He'd found out her husband had died. He didn't hear about the marriage to be, or baby, until it was too late. Having already asked for and gotten the deputy job, he decided to stay on in the pleasant little town. Now he could see Anna wanted to forget what had happened between them. Well, he couldn't.

Ode began to pull himself up on Luke's pant leg. Anna bent down to lift him but Luke reached down and took the child in his arms. Ode stuck his peppermint stick into Luke's mouth. He gently pushed it away saying, "You have two fine looking sons and motherhood seems to agree with you. You're as pretty as ever." As he handed the child over, he deliberately brushed his hand against hers.

Anna couldn't stop the feeling of pleasure she felt and her face became inflamed. Turning to take Ode from him she said, in the surliest voice she could manage, "Mr. Evans, why do you insist on acting as if we are old friends. I hardly know you."

Giving her another intense look he said, "Anna I think you know the answer to that. You're not to worry. I'm an honorable man and wouldn't say or do nothing to hurt your marriage."

Anna turned pale and felt faint.

In a much louder voice than he had been using, he tipped his hat and said, "It's been nice meeting you, Mrs. Hawkins. You take care of that fine family." He turned and went out the door, leaving a shaken Anna behind thinking, *He does remember me and the time we spent together and now he's living here in Meade.*

Later on Jed asked Anna if she would like to stay in town through winter. She quickly answered no. She couldn't get out of town fast enough.

CHAPTER FIFTY ONE

Jed finished what he'd come to town for. Much to everyone's surprise, the family left a few days later.

Anna was glad to be back to what she now considered the safety of the ranch. She worried about Jed noticing the resemblance between Josh and Luke. She cringed at the thought and it never seemed to quite leave her. Every once in a while, thoughts of the cowboy and how he affected her, crept into her thinking. Anna struggled with that, knowing it was wrong.

One of Sarah's sons brought the shoes Anna had ordered for the boys, out to the ranch. They hardly wore them, as Lilly had taught Anna to make moccasins and the boys wore those all the time.

Before they knew it, Christmas arrived. A great time was had by all. Lilly was learning to enjoy all the white man's holidays.

By spring, the children had really grown. Ode followed Josh and Twilly everywhere.

Jed and Ezra had added yet another building; the one to house the forge. They were going to take the cattle out to the new spring pasture. Tag proved to be very good with cattle, so he was going with them. The men left early one morning, leaving Anna, Lilly, and the children on their own.

Jack Black had been hiding out in the hills with his newfound friends, Slick and Bear. They had returned there after not faring so good at yet another robbery attempt.

They were sitting around discussing their bad luck when Jack said, "Say, you know that Henry fella that took one of my horses to town to bring back that wife of his, then got hiself kilt? I heard his wife married some rich dude that gots a ranch around here somewhere. I think it's down in that valley over west of here. I was gonna check it out one time, but some old geezer took a shot at me. We outta ride down there and steal a couple horses to sell. That gal owes me one anyways."

"It beats sittin' around here," said Bear. "I sure don't want to go near town. I hear they got warrants out for us. They got a new deputy to help out that old Marshal too."

"Sounds good to me," chimed in Slick. "We can ride out and check the place over. Who knows what we might come across?"

The next day, the three men rode out towards Jed's valley. As they rode along through some trees, Jack suddenly held a hand up, signaling the others to stop.

Looking up ahead, they saw Jed and Ezra herding some cattle to higher ground. They were far enough away even Tag didn't detect their presence.

"Well looky there boys, I think we hit the jackpot!" proclaimed an excited Jack. "I bet that's the rancher and that old hired hand moving those cattle. That dog with 'em looks to be the one old Henry's mouthy wife had. Seems there ain't nobody takin' care of the homestead. Let's just sit awhile and let 'em pass. Then, we'll go see what we can find."

After they figured Jed was far enough out of sight, the three rode on to check the ranch out. It was easy to find. They only had to follow the tracks from the herd, back to where they had come. Looking things over, they left their horse's tied a ways from the ranch house and sneaked up to the back of the barn.

"We'll take a look see around," said Jack. "Who knows what we might find. Maybe there's some money layin' around."

Lilly had been milking. She always wore her buck skin dress when she was doing messy chores, wanting to save her cotton dresses for cleaner work. Out of habit, she carried a skinning knife strapped to one thigh. She heard the back door squeak on its rusty hinge. Thinking it was the children planning to sneak up and scare her, she hid behind some tack that hung over one of the stall railings.

To her shock, she saw it wasn't the kids. She made out the three rough looking men entering the dim light in the barn. Lilly knew at once they were up to no good. Why else would they be creeping into the barn like that?

She wasn't sure what to do. If she tried to get to the house, she was sure they would catch her. While she debated what to do, Slick said, "Hey! Somebody was milkin' this cow. Where'd they go?" The others looked about. Lilly knew they'd find her so she made a break for the door.

Jack had almost reached her hiding place, when Lilly burst from behind the rail. He reached out, grabbing her by one arm. "Hey! Look what I got!" he said, with a salacious grin on his ugly face. "It's one of them squaws. I hear they're a lot of fun in the hay."

Unnoticed, Lilly had gotten the skinning knife from its sheath and slashed the unsuspecting Jack across the face. Still holding her with one arm, he let out a scream and automatically drawing his pistol, shot Lilly point blank in the chest. She fell to the dirt floor without a sound.

"You crazy son-of-a-bitch," snarled Bear, "You just kilt a woman!"

"So what, she's nothing but an Injin. Look what she done to me," said Jack as he held a dirty kerchief to his bleeding face.

"Well, I'm gittin' out of here. Come on Slim."

"Wait," pleaded Jack. "Let's get what we come for."

Anna had heard Jack's scream, and then the shot. She knew at once something bad was happening. She ordered the children to go into one of the bedrooms and stay there. Brave little Twilly saw to it that the boys did as they were told. Anna got a shotgun and peeked out of the front window.

She saw the three men going towards the horse coral. They seemed to be in a hurry. Noticing one had a bleeding cut across his cheek, she knew Lilly had left her mark. Anna prayed Lilly was alive.

Anna wasn't sure what to do. She knew she couldn't fight off three men. Maybe, she thought, they will just take the horses and leave. They appeared to be arguing, then the one with the cut on his face started for the house.

Anna saw without a doubt, it was Jack Black. She knew what a ruthless killer he was. She now realized Lilly was probably wounded or dead. A rage grew within her and she resolved if the approaching man set one foot on the step to the porch, his days were over.

She stood there concealed by the curtain. One of the boys cried out to her, "Momma can we come out now?"

"Stay where you are," she whispered back.

"Yes Momma."

Jack stopped short of the step. He seemed to be thinking over whether he should go into the house. Deciding there were nothing but a woman and some kids in there, he started up the step, gun in hand.

Anna waited with a calm that surprised her. With steady hands, she opened the door and shot Jack at close range. The powerful shotgun caused him to fall backwards onto the dusty yard screaming, "You bitch, you shot me." Anna stood, ready to empty the other barrel but it wasn't necessary. Jack had gone still. He was dead.

Hearing the shot and seeing Jack on the ground, the other two men turned from the corral and headed to their hidden mounts.

Tears in her eyes and shaking, Anna headed for the barn, hardly noticing the two fleeing men. Getting to the door she stopped, afraid of what she would find. Anna only needed to step inside the doorway to see what she had feared the most, the motionless body of Lilly.

She approached on wooden legs. Lilly now looked so small to her. She could see she still held the knife in her hand and knew she had tried to fight.

Feeling as if she couldn't get her breath, she knelt down, taking the still warm Lilly in her arms. Racked with sorrow, tears streaming down her face, she rocked back and forth, holding the lifeless Lilly in her arms. Anna's heart was broken.

After some time and with reluctance, she lay Lilly down, covering her with one of the horse blankets. Slowly the situation sank in. It was hard to put away the grief and think of what to do next, but Anna knew she had to go to the children. Worst of all, she had to tell Twilly her mother was dead. Remembering the cow, Anna turned her loose to her calf and slowly headed to the sad task ahead.

CHAPTER FIFTY TWO

As she headed to the house, she began to worry. *What if the others came back?* Not knowing when Jed and Ezra would be home, she thought of taking the children and going into town but it was starting to get dark. Wiping her tear stained face on the skirt of her dress, she saw the front of it was covered with Lilly's blood. Not wanting the children to see it, she would have to change. Anna hadn't wanted to leave Lilly but knew there was no other choice.

Nearly stumbling over Jack's lifeless body almost paralyzed her with panic. Somehow he would have to be removed from the sight of the children. She tried to move him by pulling on his legs, but found that impossible. Giving up, she walked into the house. A small, frightened sounding voice called, "Momma is that you?"

"Yes dear, stay there for a few more minutes."

Changing her dress, she steeled herself, then told the children they could come out.

They came into the room wide-eyed and scared. Ode ran to his mother's arms. "What were you doing? What was the shooting?"

Twilly stood apart from the boys, asking in a small voice, "Where's my mother?"

At that question, Anna couldn't stop the tears. "Is she okay?" Twilly asked.

Reaching out to take the little girl in her arms, Anna told her, "I'm afraid not dear."

Jerking away, Twilly cried out, "Why not, what happened to her? Where is she? I want my momma."

Anna reached out again taking the distraught girl back into her arms, "Twilly. I have to tell you something very bad. Some bad men were here and one of them killed your mother."

Twilly stared at Anna, then screamed, "Noooo!" as she collapsed further into Anna's embrace. Anna held the devastated child close, the boys gathered around.

Hugging Twilly, Josh said, "Don't worry we'll take care of you." Tears streamed down his small face. He didn't like to see Twilly unhappy.

After some time Anna sat the bewildered group down at the table and built up the fire.

Josh spoke up, "Mommy, I'm hungry. Could we have something to eat?"

That's when Anna realized life goes on. "Of course," she answered. Getting the chicken that had been frying when she'd heard Jack's scream, she placed it on the table. The boys ate, but Twilly and Anna each picked at theirs. Every few minutes tears would flow down their faces.

The boys were getting sleepy and Anna put them in their beds. Twilly wanted to see her mother. Not knowing what to say, Anna told her she'd made her mother comfortable and they would go see her in the morning. They finally went to bed too. Twilly slept with Anna. She held the weeping child in her arms as they fell into a fitful sleep.

At the crack of dawn, a weary Anna quietly left the sleeping children. Thinking straight was hard. Her brain seemed to be in a fog. Thoughts of Lilly's lifeless body returned again and again. She had to fight for control over her grief. First Jack's body had to be moved. Getting one of the horses to pull the dead man, she tied a rope around Jack's legs then guided the somewhat unwilling horse to some trees and brush away from the house.

The hardest part was to come. Hooking up a small wagon, Anna drove it near Lilly's now cold body. It was no small task getting her into the wagon bed, but Anna knew it had to be done. Driving to Ezra and Lilly's small cabin, she struggled to get Lilly inside. Getting the body on the bed, Anna began to clean and dress Lilly in her prettiest dress. By now Anna felt there were no more tears to be had. She was physically and mentally exhausted.

When finished, she returned to the house and was relieved to find the children were still asleep. Having built the fire up, she sat with a cup of coffee still not feeling a need for food. She needed time to think. The problem whirled around in her head; should she wait for Jed and Ezra or take the children and go into the Marshal? What about the bodies? As she pondered these questions the children began to stir.

Twilly came into the room first, her tiny face drawn with grief. She stumbled into Anna's open arms, tears streaming, "I want my momma."

Anna said in a voice choked with emotion, "I know dear, we all do." She held the weeping little girl in her arms.

The boys came into the room. Anna had to smile. They had dressed themselves, sensing it wasn't a time to bother their mother. Josh had buttoned his shirt wrong and Ode hadn't bothered dressing, wearing only underclothes. When they saw Twilly crying they became very quiet.

As with the night before, Twilly and Anna ate nothing. When the boys were finished eating she told them they would go see Lilly. She tried to explain what to expect, knowing they didn't completely understand. She hoped it would help Twilly realize her mother was no longer here.

Holding hands, the four made the solemn trek to Ezra and Lilly's small cabin. Anna could hardly breathe from controlling her grief. She felt she had to for the sake of the children.

They reached the door and Anna opened it to a silent and cold room. Lilly lay in peaceful repose. The boys held back, but Twilly raced to her mother's side. Reaching out to Lilly's unresponsive hand, Twilly quickly pulled her tiny hand away.

She cried out in a small voice, "Momma is cold."

"Yes," Anna replied. "This is just her body, she has gone to heaven."

"Why can't she come back to me?" the distraught child cried out.

Anna's throat ached from holding back tears. Taking the child in her arms she tried to explain. "This is what it means when people die sweetheart, they're gone from this earth. We can only see them in our minds and hearts. Your mother would want you to grow up into a fine young lady, and to always remember how much she loved you."

Anna knew all she'd said was of little consolation for the grief stricken child. She could only hope some of it would sink in as time went on.

The boys stood wide-eyed and silent. Twilly had returned to her mother's side, sobbing as she caressed Lilly's face and hands.

After some time, Anna told Twilly, "We need to leave your mother now. We must go to town and tell the marshal what the bad men did so he can go find them." The boys seemed eager but Twilly was reluctant to leave Lilly's side. Anna was eventually able to convince the child her mother would be fine, and the quiet group left the cabin.

Anna sent the children into the house to wait while she hitched up the wagon for the trip to town. The horses in the corral began to whinny and Anna became aware of approaching hoof beats. Terrified and her heart beating wildly, she chided herself for not keeping a gun at hand. As she raced towards the house, she glanced towards the advancing riders. Anna almost collapsed with relief. It was Jed and Ezra returning home.

They'd finished sooner than expected. Jed found Tag's actions strange as they neared the yard. The hair on his neck was up as he ran around with his nose to the ground. Jed couldn't figure what the trouble was, but he knew something wasn't right. Tag had always run ahead barking with joy to announce their return.

Anna came running towards them. As they drew close Jed saw that she seemed unsteady on her feet. He no sooner dismounted, when she fell weeping into his arms. It was as if a dam inside her had been released. Jed held her at arm's length asking in an alarmed voice, "Anna what's wrong?"

The children had tumbled from the house and Josh blurted out, "Some bad mans came and kilt Lilly."

Ezra had ridden in right behind Jed and heard what Josh had said. "What? What's that you're saying?"

Jed looked at Anna and she could only nod her head in affirmation. "Oh My Lord in Heaven! Where is she?" demanded a wild looking Ezra. Anna could only point to his cabin and he raced off.

Jed continued to hold her as they soon heard the heartbreaking cries from within Ezra's cabin.

"Anna, you must gather yourself and tell me what happened. Are the rest of you okay?"

"Yes," she said. "None of us are hurt, but it's been awful." She told Jed the whole story. He told her to go to the children, and he would tend to Ezra.

Jed found the old man on his knees, beside Lilly's body. He had never seen a man so broken.

Ezra looked up at Jed, tears streaming down his leathery old face, "This is about the end of me. I don't know what I'll do without her. What happened?" Jed told all that Anna had related to him. "Well, I'm going after those two, and they'll curse the day they had any part in this."

Jed looked at his old friend, "First we have to give Lilly a proper burial. Then we'll go get the marshal and some men to bring those two in."

Ezra rose up from his knees in anger, "I'm not waitin' for no marshal. I'm going after 'em myself. When I find 'em they're gonna git some Injin justice. They'll wish they'd never been born. I can tell you that."

"Well, I reckon that's your right and I understand, but we need to take care of Lilly first. I'll let the marshal take care of that other body. I don't want him buried on my land."

"No!" the old man said, "I'll take care of him too. That skunk don't deserve to be buried. I'll drag him out into the hills for the wolves and that's settled."

Jed felt it was a small justice for his friend and he didn't argue.

They built a coffin and prepared a grave by Ezra's cabin. Anna wanted a place for Twilly to visit her mother. The somber group stood beside the open grave and recited the Twenty-Third Psalm. Anna picked up a handful of dirt and dropped it on to the plain wooden coffin. The children copied her. Twilly had found some dandelions and wanted to place them at the head of the gravesite. Anna could barely control her grief as she watched the sad little girl place the flowers on the ground and told her mother goodbye. Anna took the children to the ranch house as Jed and Ezra finished their grim task.

It was evening when they finished. Everyone was exhausted. They decided to leave for town at daybreak. Anna was concerned about the animals. Jed assured they would be fine until he returned with the marshal. Jed was more concerned about his old friend going after the two men by hiself.

CHAPTER FIFTY THREE

Ezra had announced he was going after the two men Anna had spoke of at first light. Sure enough, there was no sign of him in the morning. The evening before he'd told Jed he'd check the trail of the fleeing men and it looked they weren't too bright. It would be an easy thing to track them. He said he'd leave sign for the posse to follow. Jed had known better than to try and talk Ezra out of it.

Ezra figured these outlaws were either pretty dumb or they planned on leaving the country. He didn't slow down for anything. The killers already had a two day start. He saw where they had stopped to camp on the first night. *I guess they think a woman and some kids are nothing to worry about,* thought Ezra. *Well they don't know the trouble they're in for.*

Late in the afternoon, Bear and Slick reached their hideout. They were tired and hungry and after eating, they drank a lot of whiskey and went to bed. They planned on taking off for new country in the morning.

Ezra stopped when it got too dark to follow the men, but was on their trail again at first light. He found the hideout with no trouble. All seemed quiet, but he approached the rundown shack with caution. Hearing snoring through the thin cabin walls, he cocked his buffalo gun and kicked in the flimsy door.

The two men jumped to their feet. Looking down the barrel of that gun made them cautious. They knew one shot at this distance could blow a man in half.

Raising his hands, Slick demanded, "Who the hell are you and what do you want?"

"Why, I'm the husband of that Indian gal you kilt."

"Wait a minute, we had nothing to do with that," Slick pleaded.

"That don't make no never mind. You was there. I tracked ya here and now you're gonna pay for what ya done."

"But we---" started Bear.

"Just shut your trap. I didn't come here to palaver with the likes of you."

Tossing a length of rope to Slick, Ezra ordered him to tie Bear's hands behind him. Slick could see Ezra meant business and did as he was told. After he finished, Ezra had him turn around, and he quickly and expertly tied Slick in the same manner. Then he checked Bears ropes to make sure Slick had done a good job, he was taking no chances on these two getting away.

Poking them with his big rifle, he told them to get outside. The outlaws hadn't even unsaddled their horses. The poor neglected animals stood in dejection. Ezra sat the men down while he watered and grained the two horses. Keeping a close eye on the men he told them, "These here horses need to be in good shape for where I'm takin' the likes of you."

When the horses were ready, Ezra led them, one by one, to a very large log. He got each man up on the log and onto their saddles, then tied their feet under the horse's bellies. After putting a rope around each of their waists, he tied them to their saddle horns, and putting a line on the two horses, he started leading them away.

"Are you taking us to the law?" asked a worried Slick.

"Nope," replied Ezra. "That'd be too good for scum like you. Nope, I figure my wife's family would like to take care of the worthless rats that kilt their daughter."

"Why, you can't do that," a nervous Bear said. "The Indians are on the reservation, they ain't the law."

"Well, ain't that the truth," chuckled Ezra. "Why don't you know those red buggers are a lot better at breakin' the law than you two ever were. They got grand ways of handling somebody that kills one of their own."

Everyone had heard tales of Indian torture. Ezra delighted at the thought of how desperate his captives must feel.

It was a full day's ride to the Indian village. Slick and Bear kept hoping Ezra would slip up so they could make some kind of break. They didn't know once Ezra made up his mind about something, he was like a dog with a bone. There would be no such slip up from him.

When at last they reached the village, Ezra took them to Lilly's father's teepee. The old chief seemed happy to see his son-in-law. They'd become great friends during Ezra's time in the village. The chief eyed the trussed up men. Speaking to him in his native tongue, Ezra told what had happened and who the men were. A circle of fierce looking warriors had gathered and as the tale was revealed, a grumbling began amongst them. The old Indian nodded solemnly replying he was saddened at the loss of his daughter and happy Ezra had brought the men to him. He went on to say before the two died they would be very sorry for what they had done.

At a slight signal from the chief, the warriors took the lead rope from Ezra and walked the now terrified men away. Women of the village threw dirt, and rocks, and spat at them.

The old chief invited Ezra to stay for a while. Just being in the village where he and Lilly had been happy was painful to him, so he declined. Ezra looked around the camp and saw how the Indians were living. He noted during the exchange between the chief and himself, Lilly's mother had shown no interest in her granddaughter's welfare and decided Twilly was better off living at the ranch. He said his goodbyes and headed for home.

꒰ ꒱

Anna and Jed arrived in town in the early afternoon. Jed unhitched the wagon while Anna tended to the children, then rode back to the marshal's office.

Soon, he was back at the house telling Anna he needed to get a few things. He was leaving with marshal and his men. He mentioned even Luke was going. Hearing Jed calling the cowboy by his first name made Anna uneasy. The last thing she wanted was for Jed to become friends with Josh's father.

Anna had a frown on her face as Jed made to kiss her goodbye. Noticing, he told her, "Don't you worry, I'll be fine. We'll catch those two. You just take care of yourself and the kids."

Anna felt ashamed. Jed thought she was worried about him and she was upset about the growing friendship between Jed and Luke. The thought of one or the other seeing the great resemblance between Luke and Josh terrified her.

꒰ ꒱

The marshal and his posse spent the night at Jed's ranch. They'd traveled hard from town and were going to give chase at first light. They started out, following the signs Ezra had left for them. By the next morning, they reached the run-down cabin.

Luke looked around, telling the Marshal it looked to him like Ezra had taken the outlaws someplace else.

"I think that's the direction of the Indian's encampment. He's probably gonna let them take care of those two."

Marshal Sam frowned. "I'm not sure what to do about that. The army is supposed to handle the law on the reservations. Well, I guess we should at least find out what Ezra's up to."

The men had traveled most of the day, when they met Ezra riding back. They all made camp for the night.

Ezra told them he felt it was only right for the Indians to take care of the men. "Besides," he declared, "I figure by the time you reached the village, it most likely would be settled. Why not just chalk it up to a shootout and forget it."

It was talked over and all agreed they might as well return to town. When they arrived back at Jed's ranch, Ezra asked Jed if it was okay if he and Twilly stayed on, now that she had no mother. Jed told him that would be fine with him but he would have to talk to Anna about it. Jed knew it could be another burden for her, now that she no longer had Lilly's help with things.

Luke and Jed had hit it off and that evening, as Jed showed him around the ranch, Luke remarked how much harder things might be for Anna. He told Jed maybe he should think about hiring an extra hand, or someone to help her out.

"Yes," Jed answered. "I've been thinking about that. She'll need help, what with Lilly gone, and now Twilly to care for. Anna seems to love that little girl, so I know she'll want her to stay with us."

Luke looked around saying, "From what I can see, you're gonna need more help anyway. You've got quite a spread going here and it looks to be a lot for one and a half men to take care of. No offence but Ezra is pretty crippled up."

"Yeah," Jed replied. "Ezra's a great worker but he is old and a little slow."

"You know, when I was trail boss, there was a young kid that really didn't belong herding cows. He was strong and a hard worker. He's a good kid. I never thought he should be on the trail, but I guess he had no other place to go. His name is Abe. He always talked about wantin' to work on a ranch. There should be a herd coming through Meade soon, if you want I can look him up and you can see what you think of him. The boys were good at teaching him how to spend what little money he made. It just struck me that a kid like that could use a better life."

"I guess it wouldn't hurt to meet him. Go ahead and bring him out if you run into him."

The two men joined the others in the ranch house and after a while they all turned in. The men were eager to return to their homes and Jed needed to bring his now larger family back from town.

CHAPTER FIFTY FOUR

The family left for the ranch the day after the posse returned to Meade. There'd been no question they would keep Twilly. Anna knew it would be hard, but she loved the little girl. It amazed Anna how quickly Twilly adjusted to her new life. She delighted in having a little girl. Twilly became very attached to Anna and in a couple weeks she was calling her mamma, like the boys.

Jed had been doing the morning milking but a day came when he told Anna he and Ezra needed to check on the cattle.

Jed mentioned the kid Luke had talked of. He was taken aback by Anna's attitude. She commented they didn't know Luke well enough to take his word on anything, and stormed off. Jed decided Luke had been right. Anna was working too hard.

The first time Anna went to the barn to milk, she couldn't help but recall the day she found Lilly dead. It was as if the grief had been like a painful wound that had been healing. Now it was torn open again. It took some time to control the sorrow she was again feeling.

It had only been three weeks since Luke had talked to Jed about the kid, as he called him. They rode into the ranch yard. Anna was extremely upset at the obvious friendship that had developed between Jed and Luke. She was politely cool to Luke as he bestowed his radiant smile upon her.

Turning to Jed and Ezra, Luke said, "This is the kid I was telling you about. His name is Abe Johansson. Like I told ya, he's a hard workin' hand."

Abe was a tall, well-built boy of about eighteen, with shaggy blond hair, and gray eyes. He stepped forward with his hand outstretched and said, "Howdy." Jed noted right off, the boy had a strong handshake, in fact he looked to be in very good shape.

Luke went on to tell Jed he'd told Abe the pay would be a little better than what he got on the trail and he could learn a lot about ranchin'. Then he smiled at Anna, saying, "I told him the food would be great too."

Anna gave Abe a smile and went into the house, taking the children with her.

"I'm not sure she's ready to cook for another hand but Ezra and me talked about it and it seems there might be a lot he could help with."

"I'd sure like to try, sir."

"Well first off, you can call me Jed, and Ezra here is my ramrod." The old man grinned from ear to ear. He hadn't had much to smile about for a while. "You and Luke can bunk with Ezra. How do you feel about milking cows Abe?"

"Oh, I've done plenty of that on my uncle's farm."

That surprised Luke, he'd never asked the boy about his past. They all walked out to the barn. When the cow was ready, Jed could see Abe knew what he was doing. He left the men, saying he was going in the house to see Anna about their dinner.

"Well, Anna," he said with a big smile. "You won't have to milk anymore, that boy's a wonder. I think this is gonna work out just fine."

"Maybe for you," snapped Anna. "You don't have to do all the cooking."

Jed was shocked. "Why, Anna, I thought you liked to cook and you'll have more time now."

Anna felt ashamed for her outburst. She knew Jed was right but she worried about Luke getting so close to her family, especially Josh. She wondered if Luke still thought he recognized her from some place, as he had put it. She was resentful and frightened.

Jed gave her waist a little squeeze. "You'll see, honey."

Anna mumbled she'd have dinner ready soon. Jed pecked her on the cheek and left her to her sour mood. He just didn't understand womenfolk.

When the men came in, the children had already been fed and sent to bed. The room was filled with the pleasant smell of steak, potatoes, and fresh peas from the garden. After they had eaten, the four men sat at the table with their coffee. Jed asked Abe if he was sure he'd like to stay on. Abe said he wanted to try. Jed found Abe to be a very agreeable young man.

Then the conversation turned to maybe building a bunkhouse and if Ezra didn't mind, adding a bedroom onto the ranch house, for Twilly, for then Anna could keep a better eye on her.

Still occupied with her worries about Luke, Anna had been only half listening to the conversation. That is, until with dismay she heard Luke say, "Why if ya want, I can take a few days off and give ya a hand. After all, I brought this extra hand out."

Jed grew excited, "That would be great, Luke. When do ya think that could be?"

"I reckon anytime ya say. Things in town will be quiet for a while. I don't think another drive will come through for at least two or three weeks."

They all left to turn in, leaving Anna alone with Jed. As they prepared for bed, Jed was so excited over the plans to build a bunkhouse, he failed to notice how upset Anna was.

Sleep eluded her as she tossed and turned. Now Luke was going to be around even more. Anna tried not to think of that smile. It seemed to her Luke meant it to have special meaning and she realized, with shame, it did.

CHAPTER FIFTY FOUR

In the days that followed, Abe dove right into his given tasks and was everything Luke had bragged about. He did all the milking, and kept the wood box full with stove wood and kindling. Jed had installed a pump in the kitchen so he didn't need to haul water unless Anna needed some larger amounts carried on wash days. He fed the hogs and cows. He did everything asked of him, with an always present smile.

Anna grew to really like the boy and Abe seemed to enjoy his new life. The children adored him and he always found time to play with them.

Ezra had made a trip to town for building supplies they felt would be needed. Jed and he had already done some work towards building the bunkhouse. Luke returned with Ezra.

In the days that followed, the four men added a small bedroom to the ranch house and made a good start on the bunkhouse. It would be large enough to sleep two or three men. There would be a wood heater and a table with benches.

All the building had kept Anna busy preparing meals for four hard working men. She stayed away from the activity as much as she could, not wanting to interact with Luke in any way. On occasion, when they were having their meals, she would find Luke watching her and it unnerved her.

Finally, to Anna's relief, Luke declared he thought he'd better get back to town. It didn't take Jed, Ezra, and Abe long to finish the bunkhouse and things were back to normal. Abe moved into the bunkhouse, and Twilly was thrilled with her new bedroom. Ezra seemed relieved to be alone in his cabin.

Summer had turned to fall and preparations were being made for the coming winter. The children were growing by leaps and bounds. Twilly was now almost six, Josh was five, and Ode was almost three.

Fall was fading when Jed told Anna that he and Ezra were going to bring the cattle in to closer pasture. He would take Tag along as he had proved to be a very good cattle dog and he felt Abe could take care of any problems.

Abe was out working in the barn and Anna was working in the kitchen when she heard the children shouting greetings to someone. When she stepped out to the porch, she was shocked to see Luke entering the yard.

He greeted the children, then walked purposely to Anna, a serious look on his handsome face.

"Jed's not here," Anna stated flatly.

"I'm not here to see Jed."

Anna's heart almost stopped. *Why did he want to see her? Was it about what had happened between them?* "What do you want?" she asked, afraid of what he had to say.

Luke reached inside his jacket, handing Anna a telegram. With shaking hands, she read it. *Anna dear, your Father has died. Mother.*

She felt weak in the knees and Luke reached out and helped her back into the house. He led her to a chair. She tried not to cry but the tears flowed of their own free will.

Luke patted her on the shoulder, saying he was sorry about her father.

Anna found his concern to be comforting. Then, recalling what had taken place between them, she felt his touch was a little too intimate.

The children had followed the two into the house. They'd become very quiet at seeing Anna's distress. Luke went to the stove and got him and Anna a cup of coffee.

Anna sat wiping tears away, shaking her head in disbelief. "I'm not sure what to do. Poor Mother."

Luke spoke up, "If you want, I'll wait and take an answer back in the morning. That will give you time to get over the shock and think about what you want to do."

"Oh yes," she said as she regained her composure. "What am I thinking, you must be tired and hungry from riding all that way. Thank you for bringing the telegram, it was very kind of you."

"Well, turns out that's part of my job. I wouldn't mind a bite to eat though."

Anna told Luke it was time to start dinner anyway, and it wouldn't be too long before it was ready. He went out to put his horse away and place his bedroll in the bunkhouse. Abe was happy to see Luke again and the two came into the house together.

After finishing the meal they all sat at the table. Ode sat on Luke's lap; Twilly and Josh hanging onto Abe.

Anna sat thinking about what she should say to her mother. She couldn't see how she could go back home, and she mused out loud, "I wonder if mother would consider coming out here. She's never seen her grandchildren. She could sell everything and if Jed didn't care she could stay at the house in town."

Luke interrupted Anna saying "That sounds like a fine idea to me. I'm sure Jed would think so too. Why, every youngin' should have a grandma. My grandma was my favorite person in the world."

"Maybe you're right. I'll write a message for you to take back to town."

"Sounds fine, and when your mother replies, I'll bring it out to you. It's always nice to come out here anyway. I don't know that I told you folks, I bought the old Miller place in town. It ain't much. After his wife died, he lived there alone. Now he lives back east, with his daughter and put the place up for sale. It was pretty run down but the price was right. It's close to the marshal's office. That makes it handy. Oh, and I got a dog with the place too. Her name is Millie. She's good company."

Abe spoke up, "What you need is a good wife, somebody like Anna, here."

"Abe," Anna admonished the boy.

"No, Anna, the boy is right as rain." Then looking straight at Anna, Luke continued, "The problem is, Abe, the only woman for me is already taken."

Anna hoped the heat rising to her face wasn't noticed. She found it hard to avoid Luke's gaze. It was if he had some power over her. She looked away saying, "I'd better clean up here."

Realizing he'd caused Anna some embarrassment, Luke nodded his head in agreement. "I'll go help Abe finish his chores, and then turn in for the night." Rising from the table he thanked Anna for the dinner. He noticed Anna had avoided looking at him as she replied that she would see them in the morning.

CHAPTER FIFTY FIVE

Anna composed what she thought was brief and to the point:

Dear Mother, I was saddened to read of Father's passing. I wish I could come home to be with you, however, it would be all but impossible. Please consider moving out here to be with your grandchildren. You would need nothing but your personal belongings. We have a place in town that you could stay in. Please let me know right away. Your loving Daughter, Anna. She folded the paper and went to bed.

Anna had trouble getting to sleep, between worrying about her mother and thinking about the way Luke had looked at her when he talked about finding a wife. She finally fell asleep only to be awakened with a start. She had been dreaming of the night she and Luke had spent together, and was horrified. *This can't happen. I'm a married woman, married to a fine man. I cannot be dreaming of another man. What if it happens again, with Jed in bed beside me?* She prayed, *Please God, turn me from my sinful ways.*

Anna was up early and had breakfast ready before the children woke. She was thankful they could pretty much dress themselves. Anna was tired from not sleeping well, and she looked it. Luke and Abe came in with the milk and she told them to eat while she took care of it.

When the men finished, Anna brought coffee to the table. Luke looked at her saying "You look like you had a bad night. I'm sorry your father died, but I'm sure everything will work out fine."

"Yes," Anna murmured, not looking directly at him. "I've written a message for you to take to the telegraph. You don't have to ride all the way out here to bring the reply. One of Sarah's boys could do that."

"Oh, I don't mind. Maybe next time Jed and Ezra will be here. Well, I guess I'd better be on my way." The children had all gotten up and tumbled out after Luke, shouting their goodbyes.

A couple days passed and Jed and Ezra returned. She had broken down in tears, as she told of her father's death. Jed was gladdened about the possibility of Anna's mother coming to Meade. He had been very gentle with Anna, holding her until the sobs of relief subsided.

She mostly had been able to push all thoughts of Luke aside, but once in a while caught herself recalling how drawn to him she was. Anna was also beginning to see that Luke was a good man. Once, she felt guilty as she realized he was being robbed of his son. He'd all but come out and said he would have married her.

After a few days, Luke returned with an answer to Anna's telegram. Her mother replied she thought moving to Meade might be just the thing for her. She went on to say when things were taken care of, she would send a wire telling them when to expect her.

The thought of seeing her mother again was wonderful to Anna. It seemed so long ago since she'd left her home. She was delighted to tell the children that their grandmother was coming to live in Meade. Anna knew they didn't quite understand, but her joy was infectious.

It was mid-November when Jed said he needed to spend some time at the livery and asked Anna if she thought they should go into Meade to get things ready for her mother's arrival.

Anna wasn't sure what to do with Twilly. She now spent all her time with Jed and her. Ezra didn't ignore her but he didn't seek her out either. Anna asked about taking Twilly to town with them, to which Ezra had answered he thought she would be a lot happier with the boys then alone with Abe and him.

So the trip was planned. Anna asked Ezra and Abe to come into town Thanksgiving, saying they would find a place for them to stay. After much preparation they were on their way. Twilly was so excited, she had never been in a town before. The trip went well. Everyone had been bundled against the cold, and part of the way the boys napped.

Friends in town were happy to see the family but there were some surprised looks at Twilly. Anna had expressed her concern to Jed that some folks might not accept a half-breed. She hated that word, for now she thought of Twilly as her daughter. However, she knew some people had strong feelings about Indians. Jed had told Anna not to worry about it, he felt the people that they were closest to would accept her. It turned out to be true. It seemed that Twilly, with her dark curly hair, and blue eyes, charmed everyone that she came in contact with.

Anna worked to prepare a place for her mother. She decided on putting the boys in one bedroom and hoped her mother wouldn't mind sleeping in the other with Twilly.

A few days after the family had arrived in town a telegram came. Anna's mother would arrive the next week - with a surprise. It was decided that they would have Thanksgiving the day after her mother arrived. Ezra and Abe had come into town and Jed arranged for them to stay with Luke.

Finally, the eagerly awaited day arrived. The stage was arriving in the late afternoon. Time seemed to drag by as Anna attempted to keep the children rested and tidy. As the hour neared, the family piled into a wagon and headed to the stage depot. Waiting was torture but at last the stage came wheeling into town and stopped at the depot.

The arrival of the stage always drew a small crowd. The town folk were gathered to meet it, including Sam and Luke. The drivers climbed down from their seats. One moved to the back to take care of luggage, while the other moved to open the door for the passengers.

Anna's mother stepped from the interior, and to Anna's surprise and amazement, the next passenger was her half-sister, Angel. There were audible murmurs as Angel came into full view.

"Now that's a handsome woman," commented Sam.

"You can say that again, she's gonna stir things up around here. I wonder who she is?"

Noticing who Luke was looking at, Sam said, "Not her, I mean the one that looks to be Anna's mother."

"Oh yeah, I guess you're right, but that blonde is a real beauty."

Anna was dumbstruck, so this was the surprise her mother had written about. Suddenly she felt very dowdy, standing there in her rather plain clothes with three children clinging to her skirts.

Angel was a vision, dressed in a light blue and tight fitting spotless travel suit. Her blonde curly hair was topped with a jaunty blue hat, the same color as her big blue eyes. She flashed a smile at Anna, showing perfect teeth.

Anna's mother came towards her and they embraced, tears flowing freely at the joy of being together again after so long. After a bit Anna introduce Jed and the children.

Jed stepped forward as Anna told him that this was her mother: Abigale.

"Oh, this is glorious. Jed if you want, please call me mother, and I'm a grandma too." She began hugging and fussing over the children.

Angel appeared beside the group saying, "It looks like you've been very busy Anna," bestowing a seductive look on Jed. "You have a handsome family."

CHAPTER FIFTY SIX

"Oh! Where are my manners?" stammered Anna.

Angel reached out her gloved hand, taking Jed's. She purred, "I'm so happy to meet the man that has taken such good care of my little sister." Jed actually blushed and seemed speechless. Sam, Ezra, Abe, and Luke had moved closer to the happy group.

Anna turned to them. "Sam, this is my mother, Mrs. Merriweather, and my sister, Angel. Mother, this is our Marshal, Sam Jefferson, and his Deputy, Luke Evans. Ezra is Jed's Ramrod, and Abe is our hired hand." They all acknowledged one another with smiles and set about helping Jed with the baggage. As they got back into the wagon, Anna was surprised to hear Jed tell Sam and Luke he would see them at dinner tomorrow, along with Abe and Ezra.

Not only did she need to figure where to put Angel, she felt like she was feeding half the town. The wagon seat would only hold three people, so Anna was seated in the back with the children and baggage. She was feeling a little rejected, and to her surprise, a little jealous, as she watched Angel brazenly flirt with Jed. Anna had already noticed that unlike her mother, Angel had no interest in the children. It seemed she only cared about being the center of attention.

On arriving home, Anna asked her mother if she minded sharing a room with Twilly. She replied that it would be great fun. Angel was given her own room and the boys would sleep in Jed and Anna's room. Jed carried in the baggage while Anna and her mother fed the children. Anna offered a tour of the place. Angel wanted to rest.

As evening grew near, Anna got out some cold beef, cheese, and apple pie. The children had been put down for the night. Jed was out working in the barn and the women sat with coffee. Anna talked about what a job she would have the next day, preparing Thanksgiving dinner. Her mother cheered her by saying not to worry, she would help with all the work.

"I'm so excited to be here and now we are going to have a real family Thanksgiving. Why, your father and I have spent the last few holidays alone. This is going to be so nice."

They sat up a little longer. She told Anna how her father had never recovered from the pneumonia and just seemed to gradually fade away. The doctor had said his heart gave out. She also told of selling everything after receiving Anna's letter. One day, Angel had shown up. Her husband had died too and she had come home to help. Angel made all the trip arrangements, and now here they were.

"Well, I'm very happy you're here, but I think we should try to get some rest. Tomorrow is going to be a very busy day."

The next morning was filed with hustle and bustle. Anna's mother was a tremendous help, as she dove right in with the food preparations while Anna tended to the children. Angel didn't come downstairs until breakfast was long over. Anna had wondered what on earth she had been doing until she appeared. Apparently Angel had spent all morning on her personal appearance. Jed had already left for the livery and Anna was glad, as she compared her looks to the perfectly put together Angel.

It didn't take long to see Angel had no interest in cooking, and reluctantly accepted some small tasks, she was asked to do. Anna thought she acted like a spoiled child and heaven forbid any of the children got near her with their "messy" hands. She was beginning to get on Anna's nerves. Anna's mother was in such a happy mood, she didn't seem to notice anything amiss.

Dinner was to be in the early afternoon. Jed had come home to clean up. Anna was a little surprised when she saw the obvious extra effort he had gone to. Angel, of course, greeted him with over sweetness and offered to get him a cup of coffee, the most work she had done all day.

Anna was really beginning to resent Angel, especially when Jed had said it looked like they had been working very hard and Angel remarked it had been fun.

Anna's mother hadn't been as unobservant as Anna had thought, remarking that she could handle things if Anna wanted to gather the children and get them ready for dinner.

Anna was so grateful, she put her arms about her saying, "I'm so glad you're here." After getting the children changed, she felt anything she had to wear would look matronly compared to Angel. Now Anna wished she'd spent more time on her appearance. *Well, I'll just have to do the best I can.* In the end, Anna picked out the newest dress she had.

Looking in the mirror she decided she still had a fair shape even after having two children. Sighing, she went out to the dining area.

She was surprised to see everyone had arrived. Her mother was arranging a few last minute things on the table that Jed had set up that morning. All the men were gathered around Angel as she carried on about the trip to Meade.

When Luke saw Anna he walked over to her. "I want to thank you for having me to dinner. I haven't been to a real Thanksgiving since I was six or seven. This is special." Anna gave him a bland smile, saying they were happy to have him and she must go help her mother.

Everyone was seated, Grace was said, and the food was served. All ate their fill of a delicious dinner. After eating, the men sat about the parlor while the women cleaned things up. Even the children were more help than Angel, who couldn't wait to get back to the seemingly enchanted men. Eventually everyone bid goodnight and a weary Anna and family went to bed.

Morning came with the usual flurry of dressing children and getting breakfast. Angel and Anna's mother weren't up yet and Jed and Anna had some time alone.

Jed sipped his coffee and looking at Anna he said, "You did a great job yesterday. It's so nice to have your mom here."

"Yes, it is wonderful. I had missed her so much and she seems so happy with the children."

"I notice Angel doesn't have much to do with them," commented Jed.

Anna was surprised by Jed's remark. She thought all the men had been to blind to any faults Angel might have. "Well, she was married to a much older man. She hasn't spent much time around small children."

"Your mom sure made an impression on Sam. I think he's smitten with her."

Anna smiled, "Really? I think that's kind of sweet. Imagine that. I wonder if she noticed?"

"Noticed what?" asked Anna's mother as she came into the kitchen.

Anna greeted her with a smile. "Jed tells me that you already have an admirer."

"Go on with you now, Sam was just being nice."

"Sam, is it? We didn't say who the admirer was," joked Jed.

Anna's mother changed the subject, asking where the children were, saying she hadn't even heard Twilly get up.

"They're outside with Tag. I'm sure they'll be in soon. It's a little cold out."

Jed was putting his jacket on saying he needed to catch Abe and Ezra before they left for the ranch. He said goodbye, and gave Anna a peck on the cheek.

"He's a good man, you are very lucky."

"I know." Anna sat with her mother as she had some breakfast. "Mother, Jed wants to get back out to the ranch. I'm not sure what to do. He told me I could stay here in town with you but I really think I need to get the children back home. The problem is, I thought you would be going back with us." Anna paused for a bit. "But now that Angel is here, I can't see how that would work. We don't have a lot of room. I don't want to leave you here alone. I don't know what to do."

Angel flounced into the kitchen. "Do about what?"

Anna was taken aback. She didn't want to repeat what she'd told her mother, but she needn't have worried, Taking the situation in her usual straight forward way, her mother said,

"Well, Angel, it appears Anna and Jed thought I would be going back to the ranch with them. Now that you are here, it could be a problem. One thing, they don't have that many bedrooms, and they don't think you would like the isolation."

Angel started to chuckle. "Don't worry about me. You're right about me living in the wilderness, I'm a city girl. Even Meade is too small for me, although some of the men are interesting. I wouldn't mind getting to know that handsome Luke a little better."

Anna stared at Angel, her mouth open. She couldn't believe how bold she was.

"What's the matter, Anna?" Angel cooed. "Do you think I couldn't take him away from you? I saw the way he watches your every move."

Anna's face flushed with guilt. "What are you talking about? I'm a married woman. And Luke isn't interested in me."

"Really? I may not have a lot of domestic talents, but I know men. Yes, I'm going to get to know Deputy Luke better. Much better."

CHAPTER FIFTY SEVEN

Anna's mother spoke up, "Does this mean you intend staying in Meade, even if I go to the ranch with Anna?"

"Mother I'm a grown woman. Yes, I'd like to stay here for a while. I'll stay in that nice hotel in town."

"If Meade is so small for you, why would you want to stay?"

"Why, Anna, I just told you. I'd like to get to know Luke better. Imagine, a real cowboy. That could be very interesting."

Anna was wondering if Luke could be taken in by Angel's charms. *Well, it's none of my business.* She knew in her heart, the last thing she wanted to see, was Luke with the scheming Angel.

"No, don't worry about me. You all go back to your ranch. I'll be just fine. Hopefully, Luke will see to that."

"Well then, that's settled. I'll tell Jed we're ready to go home. Mother do you think you're up to the trip?"

"Why of course dear. I'm not that old. I'll start packing as soon as we clean up here. When do you think we will be leaving?"

"Oh, mother, hold on. There is a lot to do, but as eager as Jed is to get back, I'd say in a day or two."

Angel spoke up, "I'd better make arrangements at the hotel. Anna, could someone drive me into town?"

"Yes, Jed should be home later, he'll see to it." Anna thought, *It's sure too bad you can't walk, or if Sarah came by, she could take you in her little cart.* Then scolded herself for having such evil thoughts, but she couldn't help but smile at the thought of Angel in Sarah's messy little cart.

Just then as if on cue, there was a ruckus in the front yard as Tag and the children greeted Sarah.

"Hello the house!" Sarah shouted, as she burst in the parlor door. Her arms were filled with the usual eggs and butter.

"Oh, Sarah someday you're going to drop those eggs."

"Na, I ain't dropped 'em yet. How's everybody doing?"

"I'm glad you stopped by. We were just talking about getting ready to go back to the ranch. Oh, I guess you haven't been introduced to my mother or sister. This is my mother, Mrs. Merriweather and my sister, Angel."

"Pleased to meet 'cha. Say what's this talk of leavin', you just got here. I'll miss you and the little ones but I know Jed wants to get back out to your place to take care of things. Do ya need any help with anything?"

Angel spoke up, "If you're going into town could you stop at the livery and ask Jed to send a buggy to take me into the hotel?"

"Better still, if mother will watch the children," said Anna, "I'll ride in with you and go see Jed myself. He doesn't know we've decided to go home."

Anna's mother beamed at the chance to watch her grandchildren. Angel announced that she had to go pack.

Anna followed Sarah out to her cart. It was nice to get away from the house and children and the two women happily chatted. Sarah commented on the stir Angel had caused among the men in town, saying what fools they were when it came to pretty women.

Anna found Jed in the livery office. He was glad to hear they could head back to the ranch. Traveling to town or back to the ranch had become routine and Jed thought they could leave in a day or two.

He told Anna to have Buck hook up one of the larger buggies for Angel's things and he would come home later to load her luggage. He also told her she should stop at the store and order anything thing she might need.

Anna spent time saying goodbye to her friends at the hotel. Then she went on to the general store. She was so intent on looking at yardage, she didn't hear the bell above the door announce a customer. It wasn't long before she was keenly aware of the deep voice that always sent her heart racing. As usual, her thinking became a mess. She tried to keep on the task at hand but her nerves were on edge and it was nearly impossible.

Without looking she knew he had seen her and was approaching. Then he was beside her. "Hello Anna. What a surprise. Where are all the kids?"

"Oh, Luke," she said as if she had just become aware of him. "Mother's watching them. We've decided to go back to the ranch, so I'm getting the supplies we need." She avoided looking at him as she spoke.

"Well, I'm gonna miss you… that is all of you. When are you leaving?"

"In a couple days I think. There's always so much to do. I have to pack things and get Angel settled in town."

"She's not going with you?"

"No, she wants to stay in Meade for a while then she will go back east." Anna wanted to tell him Angel's reason for staying just to see his reaction, but she restrained herself.

"She don't strike me as a country girl, she probably won't stay here very long."

"No, but you never know with Angel."

"That was some dinner you put on. I don't know when I had better. It had to be a heap of work."

"Oh, mother was a great help."

"I could see that. Sam ain't gonna be very happy to hear she's leaving. She made quite an impression on him."

Anna couldn't help but look up at Luke and smile, as she recalled how her mother had reacted that morning. "Yes, Jed and I noticed that too. I think it's sweet."

Gazing into her eyes, he said, "That's nice."

"Yes," Anna replied.

"I meant your smile. It seems you never want to talk to me or have me about."

"Don't be silly," she stumbled to find words, "I guess I always have my mind on other things."

"Sure you do," Luke answered. "Well anyway, it would be nice for Sam to have someone, it's no fun being alone."

Anna could tell Luke was also referring to himself and became uncomfortable. With difficulty she tore her eyes away from his. "I'm afraid I must get along with what I need to do here, I don't want to take advantage of mother. Taking care of those three can be quite a job."

"I can imagine. I noticed your sister don't seem to cotton much to kids, but I'm sure your mom is enjoying herself."

For the second time that day, Anna was surprised that not everyone had been fooled by Angel. She was a little ashamed of herself for feeling so pleased that Luke had noticed how shallow Angel was. She realized she was acting like a school girl. "She's never been around small children. She was married to a much older man."

"Oh. Well I'll let you get on with your shopping. I hope you folks come back to town soon." He smiled fondly at her, touched the brim of his hat and turned to leave.

Anna felt at odds at his leaving, realizing she actually wanted him to stay. Without thinking she called out to him, "Luke."

He turned, a questioning look on his handsome face, "Yes?"

"Well," Anna again stumbled with words, "If the weather's not too bad why don't you and Sam ride out to the ranch and spend Christmas with us? If Angel's still in town you could bring her too."

He walked back to Anna with a smile as wide as a canyon, "Why, I don't think a blizzard could keep Sam away. All he talks about is your mother. I know I would surly enjoy it. Thanks." Again he turned to leave.

Anna had trouble finishing the shopping. She knew she was flirting with danger. *What is wrong with me? I have a wonderful husband and great family, but that man stirs me up something awful.*

CHAPTER FIFTY EIGHT

Two mornings later, Angel was settled in at the hotel and the family was bundled up and on their way. All the hustle and bustle had brought Anna back to earth and thoughts of Luke slipped away.

The trip had been great fun. Anna's mother was so excited it was infectious. Even Tag and the children seemed more exuberant than usual.

She was impressed with the ranch. Ezra and Abe were glad to see them. The men unloaded things while the women got the children fed and off to bed.

Things got back to normal. Life was much easier for Anna. Her mother was such a great help. Anna hadn't realized how much she'd missed Lily's company and help. She and her mother never seemed to run out of things to talk about.

One day Anna mentioned they needed to start thinking about Christmas.

Her mother looked up from peeling potatoes, "Why, we've been so busy I didn't even notice how the days have flown by. You're right. What fun a real Christmas will be, with all my family."

"Oh, did I mention Sam and Luke might come out for Christmas? I asked them to bring Angel if she was still in Meade."

"Really?" gushed her mother. She quickly regained her composure. "That would be nice." Anna couldn't help but notice her mother's apparent giddiness as she smiled back at her.

For the next few weeks there was a lot of activity as the children made little gifts to give. Strings of popcorn were made and colorful paper decorations, for a rather scraggly Christmas tree. Excitement grew.

At last, the day of Christmas Eve arrived. In the early afternoon Luke and Sam drove a wagon into the yard. It had a large canvas covered item in the bed. The children had run into the house all talking at once. Anna could hardly make sense of what they were carrying on about.

Jed, Ezra, and Abe came from the barn and there was a lot of greeting and hand shaking.

She was secretly pleased to see Angel hadn't come with Luke and Sam. When asked about it, Luke had only answered she'd left town.

Having driven the wagon as close to the porch as they could, Jed stepped to Anna's side. Putting his arm about her waist he said, "Merry Christmas honey," as Luke and Sam removed the canvas from the mysterious object. There sat the piano from the house in town.

Anna was stunned and almost speechless. "What a perfect Christmas gift. Now we can have a special Christmas Eve."

It was special, with Christmas carols, good food, gingerbread men cookies for the children, and hot toddies for the grownups. Everyone gathered about the piano as Anna started playing Christmas Carols. Anna's mother happened to notice Luke, it was if he couldn't take his eyes from Anna. She began to wonder, maybe Angel was right about Anna and Luke.

The children were so wound up it was hard to get them to sleep. When they were finally settled down, Anna and her mother, began putting gifts under the tree. They were surprised when the men began bringing gifts also.

The morning started with an excited flurry of nightshirt clad children. Anna's mother had gotten up before anyone else and had a wonderful breakfast ready. As each wandered in, they gratefully helped themselves.

Everyone gathered about the Christmas tree, as the gifts were handed out to the excited children. Sam had brought a doll for Twilly and toy guns for the boys. Luke had brought candy for all and Jed had made hand tooled belts for the boys and a crib for Twilly's doll. Anna and her mother had knitted gloves and scarves for all. Sam gave Abby a beautiful lace shall. Abe was thrilled with his gifts, saying he had never had a Christmas before.

Everyone settled down. Jed, Luke, Ezra, and Abe went out to do chores. Sam lingered behind. When Anna's mother announced she would clean the kitchen, Sam followed her. He self-consciously and a little clumsily, offered to help. She poured them coffee and asked him to sit with her for a bit before she started. They smiled across the table at one another.

Anna's mother spoke first. "It was such a great morning, wasn't it?"

"Why, I can't remember having such a fine Christmas. You cooked all that good food. You must be tired."

"Yes, I'm a little tired but I've enjoyed every minute of it. This has been the best Christmas since Anna was tiny. There's nothing like children to make Christmas special. It's too bad Angel didn't stay long enough to join us."

Sam looked somewhat uncomfortable at the mention of Angel's name. A frown crept across his otherwise pleasant face. "Well, I don't think she would've liked the trip out here, especially since what happened between her and Luke."

"Oh? Can you tell me about it?"

"I suppose it wouldn't do no harm. Luke told me she all but chased him down. He took her out to dinner once. He said once was enough. I guess she wanted him to take a trip back east with her, anyway he said she was pretty and all that but he didn't care to spend any more time with her. Sorry to speak ill of your daughter Mrs. Merriweather but, well, she didn't seem to fit in out here in the wilderness, as Luke said she called it."

"First of all, could you just call me Abby? Mrs. Merriweather sounds so formal. Don't you worry about talking ill of Angel. She always did like the finer things in life." Anna's mother recalled the conversation that had taken place in Meade. She thought Angel probably had been upset because she didn't get her way with Luke. She also remembered Angel's remark about taking Luke away from Anna. She had to admit, after observing the behavior of Luke and Anna, there seemed to be something between the two but she couldn't put her finger on it.

Getting up from the table, she declared she'd better get busy because it wouldn't be long before she and Anna would have to start dinner.

When dinnertime rolled around Anna had thought she'd never seen men so busy with their meal. Jed's smoked ham and all the trimmings were a hit along with the pies that topped off the meal. Anna didn't see how there would be a scrap of food left.

Sam again offered to help in the kitchen. He and Abby seemed to enjoy the time together, allowing Anna to rest a bit. Anna had smiled at the two, commenting she hoped the two could handle it.

Soon there was another evening of music and laughter. Once during the evening, Jed happened to notice Luke watching Anna. There was something in the way he was looking at her that bothered him. It was almost as if he was in love with her. Then he thought he was being foolish, as everyone seemed to love Anna. Still, he couldn't get it off his mind.

The next morning goodbyes and thanks were said as Luke and Sam headed back to Meade.

They hadn't gone far when, with a big grin on his face Sam announced, "I'm gonna ask Abby to marry me the next time I come out. Do you think she will?"

Luke gave him a friendly slap on the back. "Why, of course she will, you handsome devil! I only hope you invite me to dinner sometime. Those two women can sure cook. I told Jed to send Abe into town if he wanted help with branding in the spring. You can come along. I want to be there when you pop the question." Luke was envious. He wondered if he would ever find someone. Anna was the only woman for him and she was taken.

CHAPTER FIFTY NINE

The next few months flew by. Anna and her mother spent their time sewing new clothing for the ever growing children. They talked about the years they'd been apart.

One afternoon, Anna told what really had happened to Henry. She told how she had been left alone and Jed came along and brought her into Meade that cold day in February.

That night, Abby had trouble getting to sleep. She wasn't sure what was bothering her. Then with a shock, she realized what had been nibbling at the back of her mind. Anna had led her to believe Josh was Henry's child but there was no way that could be so. The timing didn't add up. Anna had lied to her. *Why would she do that? Josh must be Jed's son. She wouldn't be the first woman to be pregnant before she got married and she won't be the last.* With that settled in her mind, Abby drifted off to sleep, a small smile on her face.

❧——☙

Spring finally began its showing. The snow was disappearing, and the cows were starting to drop their calves.

Jed thought they could begin the branding in a few weeks. Jed, Ezra, and Abe began separating the cows with calves from the rest of the herd to have them ready.

Everyone was a little excited about the upcoming event. That is everyone but Anna. She knew Luke would be coming to help and having him about unsettled her. She was always worried someone would notice how his presence affected her or how much Josh was beginning to look like Luke.

Anna wasn't the only one that was worried. Jed remembered how Luke had looked at Anna during the Christmas celebration. He'd been unable to shake the uneasy feeling it had given him. He was in his blacksmith shop wanting to make more branding irons. His mind wasn't on the job at hand. *There must be something between them,* he thought. Then it hit him, *Was Luke Josh's father?* He stood there, trying to picture any resemblance.

He was so deep in thought, he didn't hear the wood in the fire shift. A shower of sparks flew to the floor near a kindling pile. In no time at all the flames began to grow, spreading to the outer wall. Jed didn't come out of his reverie until the fire was well under way. Smoke began to burn his nostrils and eyes as he turned around to find an out of control blaze. He ran outside to yell for help and get water. As he ran back into the inferno to throw water onto the fire, the wall collapsed upon him. He was able to free himself, but not before his clothing caught fire.

The others heard his cry for help and arrived as Jed crawled from the now fully engulfed building. They raced to his side, not sure of what to do first. Ezra got a bucket of water and threw it on Jed. That did put the fire on his clothing out, but it was clear to all, that Jed was badly burned.

The building forgotten, Ezra and Abe hooked their arms under Jed's and drug him away from the flames. Jed had gone still.

Ezra told Abe to get a couple horses and ride into town to get Doc. "Ride one until it's tired then turn it loose and go as fast as you can on the other. "Hurry boy, this is bad!"

Anna was thankful for Ezra, as he worked to make a travois, so they could get Jed into the house. It took a great deal of effort.

The children had stood silently aside, sensing this was not the time to bother anyone. Anna glanced at them and saw the worried looks on their small faces. Ode looked ready to cry and Twilly had her arm about him and he was holding hands with Josh.

Once they got Jed in the house, they left him in the travois, not wanting to move him any more than they had to. Holding back tears Anna got warm water and her mother brought clean strips of material. As Jed lay unconscious, they gently tried removing as much of the burned clothing they could. Anna could see burned and bloody flesh on most of his chest, arms, and legs. Somehow the flames had not touched his face, but his hair was singed.

Every once in a while, he moaned and it tore Anna's heart out, she wanted to ease his pain, but knew they had to wait for Doc. She wished Lilly was there with some of her medical wisdom.

The hours drug by. Once Jed asked for water, and Anna worked to get some down him. Sometimes he was so quiet, Anna feared he had died. Other times he moaned or spoke to her in a stained voice.

"Oh Anna, it hurts so bad."

She reached out towards him, then realizing she couldn't touch him without causing more pain, she said, "Just lay as quiet as you can. Abe went after Doc. He should be here soon." Anna's heart gladdened. He wasn't dead but how long could he endure this pain?

Anna's mother had taken the children away from the sad scene and kept them busy. Ezra sometimes sat with Anna and sometimes stepped outside. Anna could see the old man was struggling with his emotions. He had grown very fond of Jed and the life he had been living. Jed would wake for short periods then drift off again. The moaning was painful to hear.

Around midnight, Tag jumped up from where he had been laying. Anna was half asleep, as were Ezra, the children, and her mother. Tag's movements brought them wide awake. They could hear hoof beats and raced to the door. To her relief, there stood Doc, Abe, and to her amazement, Luke.

As Doc approached Jed, Anna could see the look of shock and worry on his face. Luke had stood in the doorway with his arm around Anna's mother. Abe sat at the table with Ezra.

Anna stayed by Doc as he did what he could for Jed. He was able to get something down him to ease the pain, and when he saw Jed was unaware of things, he directed the men to help get Jed into a clean bed.

When that was done Doc turned to Anna, "I think we need to go out to the kitchen and have a talk."

Anna nodded her weary head. Luke had been standing near. "I'll stay with him, in case he wakes. You go on with Doc," Luke walked over to the bed.

Doc told him, "He might be aware of things for a bit but I gave him a strong dose of medicine that should put him out in a bit."

Luke stood by Jed and was surprised to hear him speak. He had appeared to be asleep. Jed was still covered with the sheet and Luke could see where blood was seeping through.

"Luke, is that you? I need to talk to you." His voice was weak and raspy.

"It's me old buddy. You need to rest. We can talk later."

"No, I'm afraid this is it." Luke started to protest but Jed went on, "I want you to take care of Anna. I've seen how you admire her." He stopped to take a wheezing breath then lay still.

Luke stood beside him, feeling dumbstruck. *Had his friend seen how he felt about his wife?* It made him sorry and ashamed.

Jed stirred, coughed a painful sounding cough, and spoke again. "Luke I have to know, is Josh your son? Anna never told me…" Jed then lay still, very still, he was no longer breathing.

Luke felt as if he had been hit in the stomach. He could tell Jed was gone and just stood there, not knowing what to do. Luke was so consumed with grief from losing his friend, it seemed to cloud his thinking. Jed's remarks forgotten, he stood with tears in his eyes then gently pulled the sheet over Jed's head.

CHAPTER SIXTY

Anna and Doc came into the room. Anna's eyes were rimmed in red. Doc had told her as gently as he could, he was sure Jed wasn't going to make it. They'd come to be with him. One look told them it was too late.

Anna fell on her knees beside the still body. Holding one of Jed's burned hands she kept saying his name over and over between gut wrenching sobs. "I should have been with you."

Doc said quietly to a shaken Luke, "It would have taken a miracle for anyone to live through that. He was a good man." He took out a handkerchief and wiped at his tired old eyes. "I don't think I'll ever get use to something like this."

Anna's mother stood in the doorway, silent tears streaming down her face, as it was hard for her to see Anna in such pain. She'd grown to love Jed and wondered what life without him was going to be like.

Ezra heard Anna's cries and knew his friend had passed. He got up from where he was sitting with Abe and walked out of the house toward his small cabin. He felt as if everyone he loved was gone, Lilly and now Jed. He went to Lilly's grave and fell on his knees, sobbing.

Abe was in shock. He'd seen death on the trail drives but hadn't been close to any of those men. Jed had been so kind and patient with him, he felt as if he'd found a father. Now he experienced an over-whelming loss.

Doc walked to where Anna's mother stood and placing an arm about her shoulders, he quietly said, "I'm going to see if I can get Anna to leave Jed. Here's some laudanum. I'd like you to see if you can get her to take a spoonful. It will help her rest. We all need to get some sleep. We'll have a lot to do in the morning."

Anna was still on her knees beside Jed, her head resting on his hand. Doc touched her on the shoulder. "Anna, he's in a better place now. You know, he most likely would have never been able to walk again after such terrible wounds. You made him a happy man. He wouldn't want you to grieve so. We all need to get some rest. You still have the children to care for."

All Doc's words didn't mean much to Anna, as she allowed him to lift her to standing and led her towards her mother. She didn't seem able to think clearly and gave no fuss when her mother gave her the liquid and guided her to the bedroom, she shared with Twilly. When she returned to the kitchen she saw the men had gone out to the bunk-house and so returned to her room to lay down by Anna who was now asleep but sobbed every so often, even crying Jed's name out.

⌒⌒⌒

Everyone had tried to sleep. All but Anna were up early, as she had eventually fallen into a deep sleep. Anna's mother had gotten the children dressed and also fed everyone. The men were out making a coffin for Jed and she was sitting at the table with coffee when Anna shuffled into the room.

A lost looking Anna sat with her. "Mom, I feel like I'm in a fog. I don't know what to do first." Tears began anew. "What will I do without him? He was so good to me."

"Anna dear, I know what it's like. Remember, I lost your father not long ago. It was very hard at first but God never gives us more than we can handle. You just have to go day by day. Time will help, you'll see."

They sat at the kitchen table for a while, then a somber Anna rose and went into the bedroom where Jed still lay. Getting on her knees beside him, she bowed her head. "Jed, what am I going to do without you? All the helpful words people say can't take this hurt away. If your spirit is still here, let me feel your arms about me, so that I can make it through this. I feel as if half of me is gone."

Anna didn't know if it was real or because she wished it so, but she experienced a calmness. She felt as if Jed had encircled her with his strong arms and it gave her renewed strength. Standing up, she un-covered his face and kissed his forehead in a final goodbye, and at that moment she knew Jed was gone and nothing remained but his earthly body. She would carry on and Jed's spirit would always be with her. Gently and lovingly she covered his face with the sheet and returned to where her mother still sat.

The men returned soon after. Everyone was quiet as they sat or stood around holding cups of coffee in their tired hands. Anna broke the silence. "I think Jed would have wanted to be buried beside his son, mother, and father, so if you could help, we will take him into Meade to the cemetery by the church.

Luke looked at her as Jed's words came back to him, *"Take care of Anna."* He wanted to do anything that would give her comfort, then he recalled Jed's question, *"Is Josh your son?" Why in the world would Jed ask that? He must have been out of his mind with pain.*

It was settled. They would take Jed's body into Meade. Abe would stay at the ranch for that day then come into town for the funeral. Luke drove the wagon with Anna's mother and the children. Ezra drove a wagon with Anna, Doc, and Jed's remains. The saddle horses trailed behind on leads.

The trip seemed painfully long to Anna and she didn't want to think about it being Jed's last trip to town. They had stopped to rest the horses at Jed's usual spot. It was hard for Anna to maintain her composure because of the memories that flooded back. She was determined to keep up a strong appearance for the sake of the children, knowing they didn't understand what had happened to Jed or where he was.

There wasn't much conversation in the wagon that carried Jed. On the other wagon, the children had been subdued for a while but soon were chattering away, as they watched Tag sniffing rabbit tracks in the lingering patches of snow. Anna's mother smiled to herself, *If only life was as simple to grownups.* She'd talked some with Luke, wanting to know more about him. Even with the shock of Jed's horrible death, she couldn't shake the questions that had been bothering her. Anna had led her to believe Josh was Henry's son, She'd decided Jed must be the real father of the boy that is until Josh came to her side, "Grandmother, are we almost there?" Luke answered the boy and as the two spoke. Anna's mother was suddenly aware of how much the two looked alike.

Curious, she asked, "Luke, how is it that you came to Meade? You sound like you're from Texas."

"You're right as rain. I am from Texas. Before I went to work with Sam, I was a trail boss. We drove cattle from Texas to Abilene. One of our stops was Meade. I got to likin' the town and when Sam offered me a job as deputy, I jumped at it." Of course Luke didn't mention he hoped to pursue Anna but when he got back to Meade from Abilene, he found she'd married Jed. He thought, *Sometimes when she looks at me, I can tell she feels something for me. I'm as sure of that as blue sky means sunshine. Now she was free again. This isn't the time to think about that, but I'll not let her get away again.* He sat there recalling the night they had been together.

All of the sudden he wondered, *Could Josh be my son?* Luke sat there remembering the time of year he'd been with Anna, and blurted out, "Oh my God in Heaven!!!"

CHAPTER SIXTY ONE

Anna's mother looked up, startled at Luke's outburst. "What's the matter?"

Luke stammered, trying to think of a reply to her question. "Oh, I just remembered, Jed was getting ready to brand the new calves. Mrs. Merriweather, do you think Anna would mind if I went back to the ranch with Ezra and Abe to finish the job?"

"What a thoughtful man you are. She's not thinking very straight right now. I'll mention it to her, I'm sure it would be okay. There are so many things for her to think about. That would be one less problem. Luke would you mind calling me Abby? Sam already does. All this Mrs. Stuff seems so formal."

The solemn group arrived in Meade in the afternoon. They first stopped at the undertaker's to leave Jed's body and make arrangements for his burial. After dropping Doc off, they went on to the town house.

News of Jed's untimely death traveled fast through the small, close knit town. Almost as soon as they were settled, people began bringing dishes of food and words of condolences. Anna just gave each a weak smile and a thank-you. None of what was said seemed to sink in.

The preacher showed up early the next morning. Arrangements were made and the service was to be in the afternoon of the next day. Abby had been thoughtful enough to bring some widow's weeds from her clothes at the ranch. Anna had given no thought to such things. Fortunately, with a few alterations things fit fine, not that Anna cared.

Sarah showed up right after the preacher left. Her arms were loaded as usual but there was no constant chatter from her dear friend. She was subdued and compassionate. It was one of the few times Anna broke down as she realized how much Jed had meant to everyone. Sarah told Anna the women of town were going to take care of things after the service, providing food and drink. Anna was grateful to these kind people.

The day of the service was a clear spring day. As Sarah had promised, the church was beautiful. Spring flowers were all about Jed's casket.

It looked as if everyone from miles around was there. All of the town's businesses were closed. Anna was amazed at the number of people. It was hard for her to maintain her composure. As she walked into the church to her seat, she felt as if she were walking on unfamiliar legs. The faces she passed were just a blur.

The preacher gave a perfect eulogy. Sam, Luke, Ezra, Abe, Mickey, and Gabby carried Jed out to the cemetery, to his final resting place. More words were spoken and Jed was lowered into the ground. People walked by the open grave, pausing to add a handful of dirt onto the casket. The grave diggers took over and Anna remained until the last shovelful was added. It was hard for her to tear away from the site.

Luke had stood by a tree, some distance off. His heart ached for the woman he'd grown to love and he also felt a great loss. When her mother urged Anna to leave, he followed behind.

The town women had prepared a feast on the outside grounds of the church. Anna sat in a daze, as the townsfolk gave her their condolences. She felt so lost and alone. After a couple of hours, Ezra drove her home. Sam insisted on taking Abby and the children. Luke was heartbroken to see the pain Anna was enduring. He wanted so much to take her in his arms and comfort her. *All in good time.* His dog, Maggie nuzzled his hand, as if she understood his heartache.

Early the next morning, Susie knocked at the back door. As Anna answered, she noticed Susie seemed nervous. They embraced and a few tears flowed.

"I sorry to bother you but I have a big worry."

"What's the matter? Can I help?"

"I think so. Missy, where I lived, when someone die, we give food and gifts to help them live in the afterworld. If no one care for them they will be *Equi.* That mean Hungry Ghost. Hungry Ghost will attack people left behind. Make them sick or hurt them. Is it okay if I take Mr. Jed some food and gifts? I no want to do if you say no. He was good to us."

Anna was deeply touched by her friend's concern for Jed's soul and even asked to go with her to observe the time honored ritual. When she arrived back home Luke was there. He'd come to see if Anna's mother had spoken to Anna about the branding.

In all the fuss of the funeral, she'd forgotten and as soon as she saw Luke, she turned to Anna telling her of his request to go back to the ranch with Ezra and Abe to finish the branding.

Anna was surprised and felt a new respect for him as she smiled and said of course, telling him how thoughtful it was of him and how Jed would be pleased....if he were here. She started to tear up. It was all Luke could do to keep from taking her in is arms.

CHAPTER SIXTY TWO

The days in town seemed to drag by for Anna. She did daily things out of habit. She was so grateful for her mother. Her energy was low and it seemed as if there was nothing to look forward to each morning.

The boys and Twilly adjusted to their new life, as children do, finding new adventures at every turn.

After a week or so, Anna began to think about what her financial circumstances might be. She'd never wanted for anything. Jed always took care of the money. *Did he have any money? Would she have to sell the ranch or the house in town? Did Jed owe anyone?* She began to worry about what she should do.

A few days later, there was a knock on the front door. Anna opened it to a rather stuffy looking young man, dressed in a suit and tie. He was tall and pale, and looked as if he never spent a day outside. He introduced himself as Ustes Monroe, from the town's bank. Pulling a letter from inside his jacket, he handed it to Anna, saying he was instructed to wait for a reply.

Anna's hands were unsteady as she opened the official looking envelope. The note inside stated the bank's vice president, needed to speak with her, requesting she come to the bank at her earliest convenience. It would be appreciated if she would give the young man a time and date to expect her. It was signed: Mr. Jim Thompson, Bank President. Now Anna was really worried. Was this the bad news she had expected? She sent the required information back with Ustes, closed the door, and stood with a very upset look on her pale face.

Her mother had heard the young man tell Anna he was from the bank and waited to see what he had come for. As she approached Anna, she could tell something had upset her.

"What's the matter, dear?"

"I'm not sure, mom. I'm supposed to go to the bank. I don't know why, but I'm afraid it might be bad news. What else could it be?"

⌒──⌒

Anna had made the appointment for the very next morning, not wanting to put things off. She dressed with special care, noting she hadn't bothered to even brush her hair properly for days. The night before had been a restless one. Jed had never mentioned anything about the bank. She was of the belief, women took care of the home and men handled financial affairs. In fact, he'd never talked about money. Her mother assured her there was no reason to worry. If they had to, they could open a dress shop in Meade.

Gabby had sent a buggy to the house for Anna's use and she prepared for the drive to the bank. How different this trip into town felt. She'd always enjoyed walking along the dusty tree lined road to town, Tag running alongside her. Now everything was changed. At thoughts like that, it was hard to keep control of the ever near tears.

The banker stood as Anna was shown into his office by an unsmiling Ustes. The rotund and somewhat red-faced banker held out his pudgy hand indicating a chair across from his desk saying, "Please be seated, Mrs. Hawkins. I don't believe we've met. I'm Jim Thompson. I was at Jed's service, but it was not a time for formalities. He was a good man and I offer my sincere condolences. This other gentleman is the Bank's Vice President. Adam Nichols."

Mr. Nichols smiled and nodded at Anna. He was tall and thin with dark curly hair. He was impeccably dressed. She found him pleasant enough, but grew nervous as he looked at her with intense brown eyes.

"First, let me tell you how sorry I was to hear of Jed's death. We had a long and amicable relationship. I will miss him as will everyone." The banker then sat behind his massive desk. Mr. Nichols settled himself at one end. He had a large folder in front of him.

"Well, Mrs. Hawkins, I'd like to ask if Jed ever discussed his finances with you?"

"No, I'm afraid not."

The banker frowned. "Then, I'm afraid you are in for quite a shock. However, this matter is better handled by Adam, so I'll leave you two to discuss your affairs." Smiling, he stood and left the room.

As Adam Nichols moved into the banker's chair, he thought to himself, *This is where I belong, not in that cubbyhole of an office. That old fool Thompson doesn't know anything about what goes on in this bank. He wouldn't even have this job if his banker daddy hadn't arranged it for him.*

Anna could feel her face grow pale. *So, this is it. How can that man smile, when I'm about to be told I'm destitute?* Anna felt as if she couldn't take a deep breath. She tried to steal herself for the bad news.

Adam cleared his throat, "Mrs. Hawkins, I'm afraid this is going to overwhelm you. I've been Jed's bookkeeper for several years. I'll be more than happy to assist you in any way I can. Did Jed ever mention a will?"

"Will?" Anna asked in an unsteady voice. "No, Jed never mentioned anything about a will."

"My, I'm surprised at that. Never the less, he did leave a will and as his wife everything goes to you."

"Everything?" Echoed Anna, *now here comes the part where I'm told what is owed.*

"Yes, Mrs. Hawkins, everything. The house in town, the ranch, interest in several businesses in Meade, including the Town Hotel, the Bar-Non-Saloon, and general store." Holding one hand up to stop him mid-sentence, she gasped, "Are you telling me that Jed owns all that?"

"Why yes, Mrs. Hawkins, that, the livery, and also the home behind it. All but the livery have contracts with the bank and those people aren't aware Jed carried them. That was the way he wanted things."

Anna was speechless. She'd never given any thought to how or where Jed got his money. He'd cared for the children and her and they had never lacked for anything. Tears began to spring to her eyes. Here she'd been so worried and now to find Jed had taken care of everything, even in death.

Mr. Nichols went on to tell how generous Jed had been. "When someone in the area was in financial trouble, Jed arranged with the bank to lend them money and he would carry the contract. *Incognito* of course. I can see this has all come as quite a shock to you, Mrs. Hawkins. Why don't you go on home and we'll have another meeting in a few days, however I will be out of town for several days. Let's say in about a week, if that will work for you. Just send word and let me know when you wish to come in. We can go over things in depth. There will be some decisions you need to make. Until then you get some rest."

A shaken Anna nodded her head and rose to leave.

"Don't forget, Mrs. Hawkins, I'm here to assist you in any way I can. You are not to worry. Things will be just fine." *Yes indeed, just fine. Think of it, he thought, a rich, not too bad looking young widow, and she knows nothing about finances. She doesn't even realize she's one of, if not the richest, widow in the state of Kansas.*

Anna left the bank in a daze. She didn't realize she was headed in the wrong direction until she noted the whinny of another horse. Looking about, she saw she was approaching the cemetery. *Jed must have directed me here.* Anna stopped the buggy and getting down she walked to Jed's gravesite. The flowers had all died and she gathered them up, brushing the debris away with gloved hands. On her knees and with tear filled eyes, she spoke quietly to the mound in front of her. "Oh Jed, why did you have to leave me? Nothing is the same. I feel as if half of me is gone. Now I must learn to take care of all the things you did. Please give me some guidance."

Anna stayed on her knees and prayed that Jed was happy where he was and that he would forgive her for not loving him as completely as he had her. All at once, she felt a warmth about her shoulders and she knew Jed's spirit was with her and always would be. She rose slowly and headed for the buggy.

A ways down the street, Luke had been watching Anna. His heart ached to go comfort her. *One day soon,* he told himself.

CHAPTER SIXTY THREE

At the sound of the wagon, Anna's mother went out the kitchen door to greet Anna. Anna had decided not to tell her mother everything until she knew how to handle Jed's desire to keep it all a secret.

Seeing the look of concern on Abby's face, she put an arm about her waist, kissed her forehead, and announced they didn't need to worry. Jed had left her plenty of money.

"If you don't mind, I'd like to lay down a bit. I guess I was more worried than I thought and now I feel drained. Where are the children?"

"Those scalawags have been playing in a pile of dirt all morning. I swear I never in all my life saw children so easily entertained. You just go rest a little and I'll start lunch for those hungry bears."

Abby couldn't help but notice the folder Anna had in her arms but resisted asking about it. It could wait.

Not long after Anna had retired, Abby heard the excited children and Tag greeting someone. As she opened the kitchen door, she saw that Luke had returned from the ranch. She watched smiling, as the handsome young man came towards her.

Luke mounted the stairs in a single bound, giving her a small hug. "How you all doing? How's Anna getting along?"

"Oh, we're doing the best we can. Anna's resting right now. I hope the children didn't wake her. She hasn't been sleeping well."

"I guess I can understand that. Losing Jed was an awful shock to all of us. I just got back a little while ago. I wanted to tell her we finished the branding and took the cattle to the summer pasture. Don't tell her, but we cleaned up the burned building too. She doesn't need to have that as a reminder of what happened."

"That was very thoughtful of you Luke."

"Naw, anybody would do the same. Is Anna going back to the ranch?"

"I don't think she knows what she's going to do. Well look at me, you must be tired and hungry?"

"A cup of coffee would be great, but I don't want you going to any trouble."

"Don't worry about that. I was just starting lunch for that tribe out-side so it won't be any bother. Besides it'll be nice having you."

Luke sat with the cup of coffee. He spoke up, an impish smile on his face, "Ya seen much of Sam?"

Abby turned from her work, a little color coming to her pleasant face. "Why yes, he's stopped by a time or two to see how Anna was doing."

"Sure," smiled Luke, "Just to see about Anna."

Abby went back to her work and ignored Luke's pointed remark. "I'll be done here in a bit. Would you like some pie with your sandwich?"

"That sounds like heaven," he paused for a bit, then said, "Abby, when I was out at the ranch, I could see that Abe and Ezra aren't gon-na be able to keep things up like Jed would have wanted. It seems to me Anna needs somebody that knows cattle to help out. Do you think she would want me to do it?"

Abby carried Luke's sandwich to him. She had a look of surprise on her face. "I don't know. You would need to be paid. Anna's been worried about money. She went to the bank today but I don't know what she found out. You would have to quit your job as deputy, what about that?"

"Oh, none of that would be a problem. Sam can always find some-body to take my place. Why, I practically talked him into giving me the job in the first place. Anna wouldn't need to pay me until she sold off some of the steers. Anyway, cattle is what I know best and if you don't mind my saying so, I'm pretty good at it. It's all I've ever done. I never was too fond of the deputy business."

Abby brought a plate of additional roast beef sandwiches to the table saying, "You help yourself, I'm gonna take some out to the children. They think it's great fun eating outside. Besides, I don't want them racing in and waking Anna."

Luke liked being in the pleasant kitchen. He sat daydreaming what it would be like if he and Anna were married. Jed came to mind. *Did he guess how I felt about Anna? Should I feel guilty? He did ask me to take care of her, and besides the more I see of Josh, the more I'm sure he is my son.* A scowl crossed his handsome face. *When will I be able to ask Anna about it? Well, not for a while, that's for sure.*

Luke had been so deep in thought, he didn't hear Abby return to the kitchen. She studied him for a bit then said, "You look as if something is troubling you."

Luke looked at her and shaking his head as if to clear it said, "Oh, I didn't hear you come back. I guess I was thinking about Jed."

"We all do a lot of that around here. Why, you haven't even touched your sandwich."

"I was waiting for you, it's the least I can do after you did all this work."

Abby got some coffee for herself and warmed Luke's up, then sat down to eat with him. They ate in silence for a bit, then the ever curious Abby spoke up, "Luke how come you settled in Meade? I thought you were from Texas?"

"Well, I was born in Texas, but my folks are all gone. I've seen a lot of places while driving cattle and sometimes a place seems like home. That's how Meade strikes me. I just feel at home here."

Abby controlled herself. She was sure of the real reason for Luke staying in Meade. She wanted to come right out and ask him, instead she said, "Yes, I know what you mean. I felt the same way. Of course Anna and my grandchildren are here. They are the joy of my life."

The voices from the kitchen filtered into Anna's dreams and she awakened. She slowly shuffled towards what had disturbed her. Reaching the doorway, she was surprised to see Luke. He looked up and smiled. She wanted to run into his arms, then felt guilty at such thoughts.

"Oh dear, did we wake you?"

"No mother, I just needed a little rest. Luke you're back. How are Ezra and Abe doing?"

Luke had to calm himself. He was so pleased to see Anna. "They seem to be doing okay but I was telling your mother we got the branding done and moved some of the cattle to summer pasture."

Abby jumped up to get Anna some coffee. "Sit down dear, and have a bite to eat. You must be hungry."

Anna sat across from Luke, avoiding his eyes. "It was very kind of you to help Ezra out. I'm afraid I didn't pay much attention to all the things Jed took care of. I have so many things to learn now."

There was a long silence. Abby decided to take the bull by the horns. "Anna, Luke was wondering if you would consider hiring him to run things at the ranch? He thinks it's too much for Ezra and Abe alone and cattle are what he knows. He wouldn't need pay until you sold some of the stock. What do you think?"

Anna looked from her mother to Luke. "What about your deputy job?"

"Like I told your mother, I was never real fond of the job, all I've ever done is cattle. Besides, it seems to me Jed's death took something out of Ezra. It's like he don't care about things anymore. I would really like to do the job. Jed meant a lot to me."

"Jed meant a lot to everyone. I can understand how Ezra feels. If you really want to do it, I guess it would be wise of me to accept your offer. We will have to talk about wages before you get ready to go to the ranch. I can't see that I'll be going back for some time. I just found out I have a lot of things to take care of here in town."

Luke was beside himself with joy. Now he would see more of Anna and also felt good about taking care of the ranch for his friend Jed. "I have to check in with Sam and give him time to find somebody to take my place. I don't think it will be a problem. I'll have to close up my house for now. I'll come talk to you in a few days if that's alright?"

"That'll be fine. If I'm not here mother will know where I am." Luke rose from the table and said he'd better get busy. He bid them goodbye and went out the door.

"I think you made him one happy man," smiled Abby."

"Yes I guess so." *Am I doing the right thing or am I so shameful that I'm dreaming of the day when Luke and I can be together?*

CHAPTER SIXTY FOUR

After Luke left, Abby looked at Anna and said, "Well, can you tell me what happened at the bank? I made some pie. Would you like a piece?"

"That sounds nice. Mother, I want to tell you but if I do, you must promise to keep it secret. It was Jed's wishes."

"My heavens, it all sounds so mysterious but I can promise to abide by your wishes."

"Alright then," said Anna. "It seems Jed held contracts on a lot of property. As his widow they're now mine. The trouble, is the bank was to keep his name secret. As far as the people that are paying on their properties know, they are only dealing with the bank."

Abby was flabbergasted. "Are you saying Jed was well off?"

"It appears so, Mother. He carried contracts for several businesses and some farm lands. All the information is in this folder. I'm to study them and take the folder back to Mr. Nichols in a few days. He's the Vice President of the bank. I'm afraid I don't even know where to begin. However, Mr. Nichols has handled all this for Jed and offered to do the same for me."

"You don't need to worry about that. I guess you didn't know, I did all the bookkeeping for our shop back home. You father didn't want to be bothered. I must say, I was quite good at it. Remember Mr. Bernstein who had a shop next to ours? Well, he taught me how to keep books. He had a saying: *bookkeeping is like a woman putting on a corset, you can stuff things into one place but it will always show up in some other spot.* I'd be more than happy to look over this Mr. Nichols' work, in fact bookkeeping is something I always enjoyed doing. What did you think of this Mr. Nichols?"

"Why, he seemed nice enough but there was something about him that made me uncomfortable. I can't say what."

"Well, I've always believed in woman's intuition. You know Jed seemed like a very trusting man but the world is full of dishonest bookkeepers. Maybe there's a good reason for you not caring for this Mr.

Nichols. You give me that folder and let me have a good look at those contracts."

"Mother, you don't think Mr. Nichols is one of those dishonest people do you?"

"You never know, just leave all this reading to me." Abby stayed up half the night, going over the books. She found everything seemed to be neat and in order, until the next morning.

There was an early knock at the door, then Sarah rushed in. She seemed even more cheerful than usual, and started right in with her constant chatter. "I brung us some fresh cinnamon rolls. This is a special day. Ya got any coffee? Yes sir, it's been a long time comin', but today's the day!"

"What's so special about today?" asked Anna.

"Why, today we make the last payment on the farm. Let me tell ya, sometimes it was pretty hard comin' up with fifteen dollars every month, but with what I made from the eggs, butter, and milk, we did it. Glory be girl, I guess you ain't never had such worries."

Anna's mother was still wondering if she could have missed something in the bookwork and had just taken a bite of her roll when she heard the amount Sarah had quoted. She started sputtering and coughing.

Anna became alarmed, "Mother, are you all right?"

"Yes dear, I guess something went down the wrong way. Maybe I was eating the cinnamon roll too fast. They're delicious Sarah. I'm happy to hear you will be able to pay off what you owed. It must have been difficult to pay fifteen dollars every month."

"Well, it was and sometimes we had to do without things but them days are over as soon as we git the deed."

Sarah continued on but Abby wasn't listening, she could hardly wait for her to be on her way. The second they said goodbye to her, she turned to Anna. "It seems you were right my dear. We both heard how much Sarah and her husband have been paying to the bank. Well, the paperwork you brought home said that they've been paying five dollars less a month."

Anna could hardly believe what Abby was telling her, "That's terrible, are you sure?"

"I may be getting old but there's one thing I still have, it's a good memory for numbers. I'll go get the papers and show you." She went to retrieve the paper work.

Anna dropped to the kitchen chair, stunned. *What did it all mean?*

Abby returned and put the folder on the table and turned to the page she wanted. "See here Anna, it's all in black and white. That Mr. Nichols has been cheating your friends. Of course we need more proof and we don't know if the Bank President is in on it too."

"This is terrible. Jed would have the law on them had he ever found out such a thing."

"And that's what we'll do when we get more proof."

"Mother, how on earth can we do that? Maybe we should just go tell Sam about it."

"Not yet dear. I think I have a plan, but first we must get that proof I spoke of. If Susie is at home, I'll see if she can watch the children for a while. We need to go to town. I'll go over to see about Susie and bring the children in to have a talk with them about being good. This plan might take an hour or two. You need to dress up a little. Are you sure this Mr. Nickols is out of town?"

"Yes, he was very clear on that. I was told to only discuss things with him. What's this plan you have in mind?"

"Never mind, I'll explain on the way to town. You get dressed."

The two women drove towards Meade. "You look fine dear, now the first thing we need to do is go to Mary and Mickey's hotel. I'll stay with the buggy. You go in and ask Mary how much they've been paying the bank on their loan. Tell her you need to know how land prices are in case you need to sell the house or ranch. You must find out what they've been paying. Then we'll know for sure that something's not right. If that's so I think we can prove it." As her mother pulled the buggy up to the hotel, she urged Anna, "Go get 'em girl!"

Anna went into the hotel lobby and across to the saloon. Mickey greeted her and asked what he could do for her. "I was wondering if Mary was in her office?"

"Why sure, go on in. It's good to see you."

Anna was nervous. She didn't like prying into other people's business. She hoped her mother knew what she was doing. Knocking on the office door, Anna smiled at hearing her old friend's loud call for her to come in.

"Well, Anna, it's nice to see you out and about. How are you doin' anyway?"

"I'm fine. Mother has been a great help. I don't know what I would have done without her."

"Yes, it's always nice to have someone close to you in bad times. What can I do for you?"

It was hard for Anna to ask, but she decided to come right out with it. "Well, I know this is none of my business but could you tell me how much you have to pay the bank each month? I might have to sell the house here in town or the ranch and I was just wondering what land goes for here in Meade."

"Why, that would be an awful shame. I know Jed didn't much care for the house. He really loved that ranch." Mary started to tear up, then composed herself when she saw it was affecting Anna. "Well, we bought this place a few years ago, but I guess prices aren't changed that much. We've done pretty good, but sometimes it's a little hard to come up with the payment, especially when herds aren't passing by. I do look forward to the day we don't have to pay that twenty dollars each month. I sure hate to think of you selling either place, but I guess ya gotta do what ya gotta do. I wish you luck. You keep in touch. Oh, how are all the little ones?"

"They're doing fine. We all are doing better each day, but it's hard." Anna gave her old friend a big hug, telling her that her mother was waiting for her and she needed to leave.

Anna hurried out to the buggy.

"Well, did you find out what they are paying?"

"Yes Mother, Mary told me twenty dollars a month."

Anna's mother clapped her gloved hands together. "It seems your intuition about Mr. Nichols was correct. Now all we have to do is get the proof. We need to get into his office and find a second set of books he's sure to have someplace."

"But mother, how in the world can we do that?"

Leaning close to Anna as they sat in the buggy, she replied. "I've given that some thought. Here's what we must do. First we make sure our friend is still out of town, drive on to the bank and I'll tell you what to do." Anna drove at a slow pace as her mother related the plan.

CHAPTER SIXTY FIVE

The two women entered the bank. Anna went to the cashiers counter and asked to see Mr. Nichols. Her mother sat in a chair, a gloved hand to her forehead.

"Why, Mrs. Hawkins, I thought you knew he was to be out of town all this week. If it would be of any help I can ask Mr. Thompson to see you."

Anna smiled sweetly, "Oh, would you mind, Ustes? That would be very helpful." The clerk knocked on the banker's office door, then stuck his head in to inform him that Mrs. Hawkins would like a word with him.

Mr. Thompson came from inside, adjusting his jacket saying, "Mrs. Hawkins, how nice to see you again. What can I do for you?"

"I'm not sure if you can help me. Oh dear, excuse me."

"What is it my dear?"

"I'm a little embarrassed. I should have eaten this morning. I thought perhaps you'd heard my stomach growl. Would you mind terribly escorting me across the street to get a little something to eat?"

"Of course not my dear. It would be a pleasure. I'll just get my hat and we'll be on our way."

Anna walked to where her mother was seated, "Mother I'm so nervous."

"Is he taking you to lunch?" Before leaving the buggy, she'd powdered her face to hide any natural color. In order to look pale.

"Yes, here he comes now. Mr. Thompson I'm sorry, I didn't mention that my mother was with me and now she tells me she's not feeling very well."

"You two go ahead," said Anna's mother. This is nothing serious. I get these spells from time to time. If I could wait someplace quiet. I'll be fine."

"Oh, mother I don't know. Are you sure?"

"Of course dear. Maybe Mr. Thompson wouldn't mind if I waited in Mr. Nichols' office, since he is gone."

Anna turned to the banker with pleading eyes. "Oh could she, Mr. Thompson? We'd be ever so grateful and I was so looking forward to having lunch with one of the town's leading citizens."

"Why, of course my dear. I can't see any harm and I'm a little hungry myself. I don't often get a chance to have lunch with an attractive young lady."

The banker led them towards the office. Her mother couldn't help giving Anna a wink.

"Oh yes, this will be fine, you two go ahead and enjoy yourselves. I'll rest here." As soon as the door closed, she locked it, and started searching any place she felt something might be hidden. She had no luck. Nothing of interest was in the drawers of the huge desk. The bottom drawer seemed to be stuck. She tugged at it, causing some object to fall from the desk top. She froze in place, hoping no one had heard and would come to investigate. She then looked about for whatever had fallen. Seeing nothing, she got on her knees to search under the desk. Spying a small metal dish and picking it up, she backed from under the desk. Rising up too soon, she bumped her head on the underside of the desk and when she reached up to her hair, felt something caught in it. Giving a tug she came away with a key in her hand. Some of the tape holding it had come loose. She was so excited, she almost fell, getting from under the desk. She unlocked the drawer. There was all she needed. She removed the paper work, relocked the drawer, and put all the evidence in her oversize bag. She then unlocked the door and sat back in the overstuffed chair, just in the nick of time,

Anna was exhausted. She had spent the entire time at lunch stalling for time, as she listened to and encouraged the most boring man she had ever met, tell his life history.

Returning to the bank, Anna went to the door of Mr. Nichols' office, opened it a crack, and whispered, "Mother we're back. Are you feeling better?"

"Come in dear, yes I'm much better. We'd better get on home to those children. How was your lunch?"

"Lunch was wonderful, thanks to Mr. Thompson here." Anna smiled up at the banker, not liking the part she was playing. "Why, he is such an interesting man, I've even forgotten what it was I wanted to ask Mr. Nichols. It can wait until he returns. Thank you again for such a nice lunch. Are you ready, Mother?"

The two women walked out of the bank. Nothing was said until the two women got in the buggy.

"I think we got him!" Said her exuberant mother. "Our Mr. Nichols had another set of books hidden and I have them."

"Mother! You stole them?"

"You bet! I can't wait to get home and study them, but first we need to tell Sam. When Nichols gets back, he'll fine them missing. We don't want him getting away."

Sam was at his desk when he heard the door open. He looked up in surprise, and stood, asking, "What brings you two ladies to town? No trouble I hope. Is everything okay?"

Anna's mother spoke to him. "Not really Sam. We've discovered Mr. Nichols, from the bank, has been cheating a lot of people around here." For the next few minutes, she related everything to Sam.

Sam held one hand up to still her and began to chuckle. "Abby, are you telling me you went into the bank and stole papers from there? That's pretty serious. I could arrest you but this thing you say about Nichols needs to be looked into. You say it can be proved?"

"You bet," she answered. "We're going home and I'm going to compare the books. Can you come with us?"

"Why sure, Abby. You two go on home. I need to see if Luke can come take over while I'm gone. It shouldn't take too long, then I'll be right along." Sam was more than happy to spend time with Abby, no matter what the reason.

Sam rode his horse down the street to Luke's small house. Millie, Luke's dog, gave a small bark as he dismounted and headed for the front gate. Luke was on the porch working on the door lock. He stood, saying, "Sam what are you up to?"

"Well, I know you worked late last night but something's come up. I have to leave the office, so I came to see if you'd cover it for me?"

"I take it you haven't found a deputy to take my place yet?"

"No, you're gonna be hard to replace. You might want to hold off a while on leaving for the ranch anyway. I'm going to Anna's to check on something that's come up."

"Is something wrong with Anna?" asked a visibly upset Luke.

"Nothing's wrong with Anna, but she and Abby have dug up quite a pickle." Sam explained what he was talking about. "I need to get up to Anna's so Abby can show me the proof. If this is true, we don't know what this fella might do. My bet is, when he finds he's been discovered, he'll hightail it out of town. We can't let that happen."

An alarmed Luke replied, "No, we can't, why, those two women might be in some danger. I'll be in the office in a couple minutes. You go on and take care of our girls."

"Our girls?" Sam smiled, he hadn't missed the longing looks Luke always gave Anna. "While I'm gone I'd like you to mosey over to the bank and see when this Nichols is supposed to be back in town. Don't let on about any of this, we don't know who might be involved. I don't know Nichols. I might have seen him at the bank. Do you know him?"

"No, can't say as I do. I'll ask around. You go on now."

CHAPTER SIXTY SIX

Sam knocked on the kitchen door and Anna answered, "Sam, you didn't take very long to get here. Come in. Mother's very excited. She's been pouring over those books and says Mr. Nichols is guilty as sin."

Abby looked up from the table, a huge smile on her face. "Oh Sam, it's just as we thought. Either the banker let Nichols handle all the contracts for the last eight years or he's in on the scheme. No one knew it, but Jed owned a great deal of property around here. His father most likely had accumulated it, and after he died, Jed sold some. Jed let the bank handle everything. For some reason, he didn't want anyone to know he held the titles. Maybe he wanted to be thought of as just one of the regular town folk. His problem seems to have been he thought everyone was as honest as he was."

Sam had seated himself at the table, "So how did this scheme work?"

"Well our Mr. Nichols had one set of books for Jed and another for the people buying property. Nichols handled all the contracts and charged the buyers a few dollars more than Jed had asked for. He pocketed the extra cash. I can tell you it has amounted to quite a large sum over the years. Here's a list of the people he cheated. It tells what they were paying Nichols and what Jed thought they were paying. You can check it out. Sarah Covington mentioned what she had been paying and Anna asked Mary. That's when we smelled a rat in the woodpile. So what do we do now?"

Sam gave Abby a look of admiration. "You don't do anything, this is a matter for the law. Luke is nosing around town now to see what he can find out about this Nichols. I'm going to check out a few of these names. If this all checks out Mr. Nichols will be greeted with a warrant for his arrest when he returns to Meade. You two stay home and out of trouble. I'll keep you informed."

Luke had first stopped to talk to Mickey. Town bartenders usually knew just about everything that went on in a small town like Meade. The bar wasn't crowded when he walked in.

"Hello Luke, what'll it be?"

" I don't want a drink Mickey. I came in to ask about that fellow, Nichols that works at the bank. You know him?"

"Not really. I seen him once in a while. He don't seem too friendly. He only goes over to the restaurant side to eat. He strikes me as a kinda strange duck. Always keeps to himself, and dresses like a dandy. I hear he stays over at the Royal. Pretty fancy for a dude that works in a bank. Why ya asking? Is he stealing from the bank?"

Luke wasn't sure how to answer. "Not that I know of. He's helping Anna take care of some of Jed's business stuff. I was just wondering about him."

"Well it's nice that you're looking out for Anna. It was a terrible thing that happened."

"It sure was Mickey. Anna seems to be doing okay. Her mother's been a lot of help for her. Well, I better get going. You take care now."

Luke went on to the bank. He tried not to arouse any suspicion. He found Nichols had a habit of going to Dodge every few months and was expected back in four more days on the evening stage. He returned to the office to wait for Sam.

"Well," Sam said as he locked the books away in a drawer. "Our girls have really opened up a bag of worms." Sam went on to explain everything to Luke.

"Do you think they're in any danger? What happens when this Nichols finds his books gone? The banker said he'll be back on the late afternoon stage on Friday."

"No, I don't think they're in any danger. We'll probably have a warrant for the guy and we can meet the stage and take him to jail. I'm going over to the bank now to talk to Thompson. I want to know how long this Nichols has been working there and where he came from."

Sam found Mr. Nichols had been at the bank for about eight years. The banker, Mr. Thompson, didn't know much about Nichols, in fact he didn't seem to know much about anything at the bank. Sam wondered what the man even did there. It appeared he let others handle everything. Sam decided to ask for a warrant for Nichols only. He went to the telegraph office and sent the information to his headquarters and asked the clerk to bring the answer as soon as it arrived.

CHAPTER SIXTY SEVEN

Both Sam and Luke seized opportunities to check on Abby and Anna often. Abby found she didn't mind at all, in fact she looked forward to Sam's visits. She realized she cared a great deal for him. Neither had the way Luke felt about Anna escaped her.

One evening, after Luke had left from yet another visit, Abby asked Anna about Luke's obvious attraction to her. "Dear, it seems we each have an admirer."

Anna kept busy, picking up coffee cups. She avoided looking at Abby. "What do you mean, Mother?"

"Anna, no one with eyes could miss how Luke feels about you."

She was ashamed to face the truth. Jed had been gone such a short time, yet she felt more drawn to Luke each day. She knew if he declared his love for her she wouldn't be able to resist him, and what about Josh? How could she tell Luke he had a son? *What will he think of me?*

Abby drew Anna back from her thoughts, "Anna look at me. Was there something between you and Luke, before you married Jed?"

Unbidden tears filled Anna's eyes. She'd felt guilty for so long. She turned to face Abby, "Oh Mother, yes. I have a terrible secret."

Abby held her arms out to enfold Anna. "I think I know your secret, it's pretty obvious."

Anna cried uncontrollably as her mother held her. After some time she seemed to be cried out. It was if all the years of shame and guilt had flowed with the tears and she felt relieved, and wanted to confess all.

They sat at the kitchen table, as Abby asked, "Josh is Luke's son, isn't he?"

Anna had sat with her eyes lowered. She looked up at her mother. "Yes mother, he is," as she told how it had come about. "I still can't explain how I could have done such a thing. I guess I was lonely. Luke made me feel loved. I reasoned it had been because I was so alone and afraid. Luke was a stranger to me and left town the next day. When I found I was pregnant, I resented him. He had gotten what he wanted, then left, but I was unable to forget him. It was as if a bond had

formed between us in that short time. He came back, but by that time
I was married to Jed. I did learn to love Jed, but never in the way I'd
felt about Luke. I never did tell him Luke was Josh's father." A new
round of tears filled Anna's eyes. She dried them and went on, "Now
Jed's gone. I feel so guilty for not loving him the way he loved me. Oh,
Mother how in the world does a woman tell what real love is?"

"That's easy, at least it was for me. You've told me your secret, now
I'll tell mine.

When I was about fifteen, I felt the same way you did with Luke, and
gave myself to a young man. Fortunately I didn't become pregnant.
A few months later, his folks moved away and I never saw that boy
again, but I couldn't forget him. Years later, I learned he was happily
married and had several children. When I met your father, I had love
for him but it was never as strong as what I'd felt for that first young
boy. I really think true love only comes to a person once in their life,
if they're lucky. If the feeling is mutual, it's a beautiful thing. All the
years I was married to your father, I would find myself thinking of
Mathew; that was his name. When you feel that kind of love it seems
to control your body and soul. You are never able to forget, never."

Abby stopped talking and stared off into space. "Mother, are you
saying you would have left father if your Mathew had returned?"

"Well, I doubt it. No, I had you, and your father was such a good
man. No, such a thing would have been too scandalous. Let me ask
you: would you've gone back to Henry if he had lived?"

Anna didn't have to think about that. "Of course not. I've decided I never did really love Henry. I was young and foolish. It all had
seemed so exciting."

Abby smiled at Anna and patted her hand. "Well I don't think you
need to worry about Jed. It seemed to me, he was very happy with you
and the children. I don't know what your plans might be, but I for one,
am going to say yes to Sam when he asks me to marry him."

"Mother I think that's wonderful. Maybe, sometime in the future
Luke and I will be together but it's too soon for that. Besides I know I
have to tell him Josh is his son. I don't know how he'll feel about that."

"Anna, I don't think you need to worry about that either. If Jed had
accepted Josh why wouldn't Luke? It has always been clear to me that
they both loved you very much."

CHAPTER SIXTY EIGHT

The afternoon for Nichols to return to Meade arrived. Sam and Luke waited with a warrant for his arrest. Time seemed to drag by as the two stood on the boardwalk in front of the stage depot. As the arrival time for the stage neared, a small crowd of townsfolk began to gather. Some there to meet someone, others just for something to do.

Luke shifted from one foot to the other. "Do you think this Nichols will give us any trouble?"

Sam looked about. "Well, ya never know. We'll just have to be ready for anything. I'm hoping he'll come along peaceful like."

A ripple of excitement ran through the waiting crowd, as the distant sound of hoof beats and the rattling of harnesses reached their ears. As the sounds grew closer, Sam and Luke stepped to the front of the crowd, as one. Amid a cloud of dust and shouting from the driver, the stage came to a halt. Handlers came forward and took control of the team. The driver and the man riding shotgun climbed down from their seats. The driver went toward the passenger's door and the other went to unleash the luggage on the back of the stage.

When the door opened, the first person to alight was a heavy set middle age woman. She smiled and waved at a small group in the crowd. Then came a young man helping a pretty girl from the stage. Sam knew they were newlyweds. He was growing nervous. *Was Nichols on the stage?* At last their man stepped down to the ground. He mounted the step to the boardwalk. Sam and Luke stepped to either side of him taking a firm hold of his arms.

"What the...!" Nichols gave a tug at his captive arms.

"Just stand still, Mr. Nichols," Sam spoke in a quiet voice. "We don't want to make a scene here. You know I'm the Marshal and this is my Deputy. I have a warrant for your arrest. It would be better if you just come along with us to the jail."

"What are you talking about? Do you know who I am? There must be some mistake."

"Well sir, we can settle that in my office. So if you'll come along with us, peaceful like, we can straighten this out."

Nichols relaxed the small struggle he'd put up. "You're making a big mistake Marshal, but I'll be happy to accommodate you. Can your deputy get my bag for me?"

"I guess that'd be alright. Luke, you wanna grab his bag? We'll wait here."

Nichols mind was racing. *What in hell have they found out about me? Was it that scheme in St Louis? I've got to get away... so here goes nothing.*

The heavy set woman was directly behind Sam. She was surrounded by excited grandchildren. Nichols turned to face Sam and gave him a shove, causing him to lose his balance. Sam fell backwards, amid screaming children and an angry woman. Before Sam could recover, Nichols was around the corner and down an alley.

Luke looked up to see Sam sputtering and working desperately to untangle himself from the woman's skirts. He saw Nichols running and raced towards where he had last seen him. Sam came up behind Luke and they both surveyed the empty street behind the stage depot.

"Where do you think he went?" asked Luke. Sam looked thoughtful.

"Well he sure won't go to the hotel. He hasn't got a horse, if he did we'd see him ride out. I'll go down to the livery and warn Zeke to watch for him. I'll get a few men to help us find him. You go to the other end of town and keep your eyes peeled. I sure never expected this. He can't get far, but it's gonna be dark pretty soon."

⌒‿⌒

Nichols had been quick and ran to the back door of the bank. Taking a key from his vest pocket, he fumbled to unlock it and relock the door behind him. Going into his office he sat down, his breath coming in large gulps. He wasn't use to any physical exertion. His mind was in a whirl. *It's a good thing I had that key made. They won't look here for a while. What have they found out? I've got to get out of this backwater town. It's a good thing I put all my money in the safe at the bank in Dodge. All I've got to do is get there and leave this territory. I'll stay here until its dark enough to sneak away.*

He sat for a bit to catch his breath, then reached under the desk to retrieve the drawer key. Looking for the gun he'd hidden under some papers, he realized the set of books were gone. *So that's it. How did that stupid banker figure things out? Well, I can't think about that now. Could that sweet widow, Anna Hawkins, have something to do with it? Maybe I'll just give her a call. She must have a horse I can take and that other set of books too. Yes, as soon as it's dark enough that's where I'm headed.*

Sam had felt sure they would find their escapee, but as everyone looked for Nichols, and finding no sign, he became worried. It had grown quite dark when he looked Luke up. "I can't figure where he could be. Everybody's on the lookout and he just seems to have disappeared into thin air." Suddenly Sam recalled something Abby had mentioned, when she'd brought the books to his office. "You know, Abby told me when she got into that locked drawer of his there was a pistol there. I think we'd better talk to the banker. I'm feeling uneasy about this. Maybe Nichols got in there somehow." The two men left for the banker's home.

Having waited until full darkness, Nichols cautiously opened the back door of the bank. Peering about and seeing no one, he ran across the street, hiding in the overgrown brush along it. He remained quiet for some time to make sure no one had seen him. Threading his way through the bushes lining the roadway was not easy. It was quite dark. Some of the brush snagged at his clothing and at times he would stumble and fall to his knees. Every few feet he would stop and listen for the sound of horses. He needed to travel the half mile to Anna's place with this method. After a good hour, he made out the light, coming from the back door of the house.

As he approached, Tag began barking. Anna looked up from some needle work she'd been working on and spoke. "I wonder what has Tag going. I hope he doesn't wake the children. Maybe Sam is coming to tell us they have Mr. Nichols in jail."

"I hope so, it's been hard waiting to hear what happened at the stage station, but Tag has never barked like that at Sam. Well, he's quiet now, maybe it was someone passing by, although I don't recall hearing a horse. Maybe you should call to him."

Anna stepped to the kitchen door and unlocked it. Sam had told the two women to stay home and lock things up.

Nichols had called to the leery Tag and as he approached the house he petted and talked quietly to him. He reached the door just as Anna opened it.

Nichols entered the room. "What are you doing here?" burst out a frightened Anna.

He lifted the gun and pointing at her replying with unmistakable anger in his tone, "I think you and I have something to discuss. It seems someone has told the marshal some things that have caused me a great deal of trouble. Now I find I must leave Meade, but not before you give me those books back and I'll need to borrow a horse. So if you don't mind, the books first." At this point Nichols waved his pistol about, then held it on Anna.

Abby had been standing by the stove, her face a mask of fear, as she took in the sight of the tattered and dusty man. Tag had come in the still open door and stood emitting a low warning growl. The hair on his back was straight up and at the sight of the gun being pointed at his beloved Anna he jumped at Nichols arm.

All hell broke loose. Anna screamed as the gun went off, harmlessly striking a picture on the kitchen wall. Nichols was yelling in pain and cussing the dog, trying to shake Tag loose. Abby suddenly grabbed the nearest thing she could lay her hands on, a big cast iron skillet from the back of the stove top and let the suffering Nichols have one alongside his head. You could have heard a pin drop as Nichols collapsed in a heap on the floor. The two women stood looking at each other then at their victim. Tag stood still, except his wagging tail. He still held onto Nichols arm.

"Mother do you think you killed him?"

"No! Of course not. Quick! We need to tie him up before he comes to. Grab some dish towels. That should do the trick." Anna called the triumphant dog off and they tied Nichols up.

When Nichols began groaning and coming aware of what had happened, he started out with a stream of cuss words, while trying to wiggle from his bonds. That caused Tag to straddle the man again, staring down into his face with bared teeth.

"Call off this damn dog!" Nichols shouted.

"Now Mr. Nichols," Abby cooed, ignoring Tag. "That's no way to talk in front of ladies."

"Ladies?" Snarled a defeated Nichols, "You two need to be committed."

"What should we do now?" asked a now calm Anna. "We need to get Sam or Luke to take him to jail."

"One of them should show up here pretty soon, but isn't it about time for Lee and Susie to come home from work?" inquired Abby.

"Of course," Anna replied. "So we can just wait. My, that was wonderful of Tag, wasn't it and you? I can't wait to see what Sam will have to say about this." Nichols didn't have too much to say, other than to complain about his bleeding arm. Abby wiped his wounds with some alcohol that caused him even more pain. Seeing her look of satisfaction at his suffering, he lay still, trying to figure a way out of his predicament, while cursing the two women under his breath.

Abby and Anna were having a cup of tea when Tag left his post on Nichols chest. He ran to the still open door at the sound of Lee and Susie coming home. Anna went to the porch and called to them. The couple was shocked at what they saw. Anna explained and asked Lee to take a horse and go get Sam or Luke.

It wasn't too long before both men showed up at a full gallop. Running up to the kitchen door, Sam and Luke all but got themselves stuck as they tried to race in together. They were coming to the rescue of their damsels in distress.

As quickly as they had entered, guns drawn, they stopped, dumbstruck by what lay before them. As a sense of relief came over them, they both began to smile. Sam spook up first, "Maybe I should just turn my marshaling over to you two. How in the world did you manage this? It seems the bad guys don't stand a chance with you women around." Glancing at the bandage on Abby's hand he asked her, "What happened to your hand?"

Abby gave Sam a smile, "Well, the skillet I hit him with was warmer than I thought."

"I guess that explains the grease spots on his pretty suit." Sam just shook his head in disbelief. Maybe we'd better get a few skillets for our arsenal Luke." Nichols glared up at the group as Anna explained all that had happened.

Luke put handcuffs on the resigned Nichols and untied the towels, handing them to Anna. "I'm guessin' you'll want to wash these."

Abby spoke up, smiling, "No, maybe Sam could use them for catching crooks."

"You know Abby," Sam said, "A woman like you needs to be corralled to keep out of trouble. I think I'd like that job."

"Why, Sam are you courting me?"

At that, Sam began to sputter, his face now red. "Courtin'? Hells fire woman, I'm askin' you to marry me... how about it?"

Abby waited a bit, looking the uncomfortable Sam over. "I suppose I could do worse. You do seem to be a steady sort." Smiling at him she walked over and put an arm about his waist. "Why don't you take care of this suffering man, then come back and we'll talk about it."

A happy Sam and Luke left, putting Nichols on one of the horses from the barn. As they rode along, Luke spoke up. "I wish I could ask Anna to marry me, but it's too soon and I don't know how she feels about me."

"I don't think you have to worry about that, you'll see." Luke thought Sam was too wrapped up in his own happiness to understand. By now he was sure Josh was his son. *Had Jed known? Did Anna resent him for leaving town? How could she. She never told him she was pregnant. Now she's pretty well set and I got nothing to offer her. Well, in time maybe I'll get enough nerve to ask her. Until then...*

CHAPTER SIXTY NINE

A whole month went by before Nichols had his trial and was sent to prison. A bank book had been found in the inside breast pocket of his suit. Abby had determined what amounts were owed the cheated people. Another person might have kept the money, but Anna knew it wasn't what Jed would have wanted. So it was that all the people on the list Abby had made, were told to come to Mary's hotel dining room on a certain date and they were presented with the monies owed them. It was a day of great jubilation.

Luke had returned to the ranch to keep things in order. Ezra became more morose each day. Some days he begged off chores, claiming his "Rumitize was actin' up." Luke knew Jed's death had been hard on the old man. One evening he spied Ezra kneeling beside Lilly's grave, his now thin shoulders heaving from the tears he was shedding. Shortly after, Ezra announced he decided to "Go see the other side of the mountain."

Luke knew the old man wanted to spend what time he had left in the wilderness and away from all the sorrow he'd faced on the ranch, but he was also sad to see him go. He told Ezra he understood and would be welcome back anytime he felt like it, also saying he could just retire there. Telling him it would be what Jed would have wanted. The old man solemnly shook his head and replied, "Well then I think I'll be leavin' in the mornin'. It looks to be good weather for travelin'. I never did cottin' to stayin' in one place fer long. It's been good knowin' ya. You're a good man, I'll be sayin' goodbye." The two men shook hands and in the early morning hours Luke heard the old man leaving. He felt it was another great loss.

Abe had become a very dependable and steady worker, but now with Ezra gone and the ranch needing more done every day, Luke decided he needed to tell Anna about Ezra's leaving and maybe see about more help. He left Abe to take care of things for a couple days and headed into Meade.

His heart beat a little faster as he rode into the yard of Anna's house. He knocked on the kitchen door. It opened.

There stood Anna, drying her hands on a towel. "Why Luke, come in." Anna felt her face flush with the excitement of seeing him. She worked to control the affect he always had on her. Their eyes met for a moment and each felt an overwhelming urge to rush into the other's arms.

Luke stammered, his usually strong voice cracking a little with the emotion of seeing Anna again. "Hello Anna. I hope you're not busy. I have a few things I need to tell you."

"Why Luke, I'm never too busy for you, besides, I've been wondering how things were going on the ranch. I miss it something awful, and so do the children. Sit down. I'll get us some coffee." As she got cups and coffee, Anna's hands were shaking. Another affect Luke had on her.

Luke had removed his hat and sat at the small kitchen table. His eyes not able to drink in enough of the woman he loved. "Well, that's why I'm here," he started as Anna sat across from him. "First, tell me how all of you are. Where's your mom and the kids? I didn't see 'em when I rode in."

"Oh, they're all out in the barn. One of the barn cats had a batch of kittens, they play with them all the time. Mother's there to make sure the kittens don't suffer from too much love. Mother and Sam have set a wedding date, sometime this fall. I'm so happy for them. If I go back to the ranch, they will live here. Anyway, now we have these plans for the wedding to take care of. Of course, Sam just wants to get it over with but mother loves celebrations, she's had so few of them. All the paperwork from what Nichols did is straightened out too."

Luke's heart quickened and he interrupted her, "You mean you might come back to the ranch after their wedding?"

Anna didn't miss Luke's look of joy. "Well, like I said, I miss it, my garden and everything about the place." She stopped and took a sip of coffee. "I know it will be hard at first, because of what happened to Jed, but it's something I need to face and I can't do it here in town." She looked down at her cup, reflecting on the loss of Jed, and yet across the table from her, sat the man she'd been unable to forget for all these years.

"I know what you mean, it was hard for me to go back, but Jed was my friend and he was so proud of what he'd done out there. I just wanted to do what I could." Luke thought. *And I wanted to stay close to you. This is downright torture sitting so close to you. I don't know how much longer I can wait to make you mine.*

Luke had stopped talking and was now staring at the table. Anna spoke to him twice. "Luke?" He looked up. "My goodness where were you?"

If only you knew. "I'm sorry, I didn't hear you. Well, I came to tell you that Ezra's gone off to be by himself for a while. I hope he comes back, but I doubt he will. After Jed was gone he didn't much care about anything anymore. It's something these old codgers seem to do when life is too much for them. Anyways, the way things are going out at the ranch, Abe and me could use another hand. I was wonderin' if maybe you'd let me hire someone?"

Anna loved listening to Luke's voice, and found herself staring into his handsome face, unable to look away. The look of undeniable love was in his eyes as he spoke to her. Luke's voice trailed off as the two sat staring into one another's hearts, through their eyes. Then he spoke. His voice now quieter.

"Anna I need to ask you a couple things."

Anna sensed what he was about to ask and became very nervous, yet excited. She looked down at her coffee, not wanting to reveal her feelings. *Maybe I'm wrong about what he's going to ask.*

"Anna, look at me. I'm sure you know how I feel about you, but ever since that night in the hotel..." At this, Anna again looked away. Her hands rested on the table and Luke took one in his, running his rough thumb over the back of it. The sensation of that act, was almost more than Anna could take. She knew she wanted this man more than anything in the world. Luke continued, "There was something so special about that night. I couldn't forget you. I came back to Meade to find you but you and Jed were already married. I wanted to stick around just to be near you." Tears began to fill Anna's eyes.

"Why are you crying?"

Anna couldn't help herself, it was time to confess her love to Luke. "I'm not sure why I'm crying. Maybe because I've felt the same way about you and deceived Jed all these years. He was such a good man and deserved a wife who didn't constantly have another man on her mind."

Luke started to rise from the table to take Anna in his arms, then thought better of it. "Anna, that night Jed died and you were in the other room with Doc, Jed came to a little. He knew I was with him. He asked me to take care of you." A new round of tears dripped from

Anna's eyes. "I don't know if he knew how I felt about you, I never let on to him. I do know you made him a happy man. There is something else Jed asked me." At this point Luke looked deep into Anna's eyes. "He wanted to know if Josh was my son?"

Anna drew in a sharp breath. "Oh no! I never wanted him to know it was you. I was going to tell him someday, but then when you two became such good friends, I couldn't"

Luke was happy that he finally knew the truth but felt bad for all the time that Anna had carried this secret alone. "Anna I'm so sorry I didn't stay in Meade. You should have told me you were going to have a baby. I want to make it up to you now. I don't have anything to offer you. I'm just a ranch hand, but will you marry me, when the time is proper?"

Being a typical female, Anna couldn't stop the water works now. She only happily nodded her head yes.

EPILOGUE

Of course this being a figment of the imagination, everything turns out hunky dory. Luke and Anna marry the next spring. He turns the ranch into an even more successful endeavor. A couple of Sarah's boys worked for him, until some of Anna's and his eight sons, were old enough to help out. Sam and Abby married and stayed in the town house, happy beyond words. Twilly became a school teacher, married and had three girls. Nothing was ever heard of Ezra. Mary and Mickey chose to take the money they received from the Nichols incident, sell the hotel, and move to sunny California. The new owner, Anna, turned the hotel into a proper establishment. Spook ran the bar. His new wife, Ruby, took care of the restaurant. The employees stayed in the rooms upstairs. Josh became an attorney. Ode took over the ranch after Luke and Anna were gone. The rest of Anna and Luke's sons all prospered, some settling in Kansas others in Texas. Tag and Luke's dog, Millie, had a few litters of pups, all of which became valued herders for cattlemen and sheep men as well. Life went on in the sleepy town of Meade. Many things changed but Luke and Anna's love remained the same until the end. The little grave yard has a few more residents now. Among them, one tombstone tells the story:

Luke J. Evans	Anna L. Evans
Born April 1843	Born May 1846
Died May 1936	Died June 1936
Texan	Wife
Husband	Mother
Together Forever	

So you see, Anna finally learned how to throw that lariat around love.